The Strangler Fig

It was ridiculous to make so much—out of what? A few shreds of brown matter, an ill-natured scene or two, a young man's excitement, and a native superstition. That was it. This silly story of the strangler fig had got under his skin. But in his heart he knew that this fear had nothing to do with the strangler fig. It was something more concrete than a legend, much stronger. Legends do not lean down out of trees and strangle men. It takes something more tangible than a legendary vine to do that.

Books by John Stephen Strange:

The Strangler Fig

John Stephen Strange

Original Copyright 1930 by Dorothy Stockbridge Tillett,
Copyright renewal 1957

Also published under the title: *Murder at World's End*

ISBN 978-1-304-43500-2

Editing, Typesetting and Annotation by Kymberly MacAgy

Cover Design © 2014 by Rachel MacAgy, www.DarkCityDesign.com
Cover photo © Can Stock Photo Inc./hankmann

For more information about J.S. Strange and her books, or to
purchase more books, go to: www.JSStrangeMysteryNovels.info

To
Hannah C. Denton
In grateful remembrance
of her story of the strangler fig
upon which this tale
is founded

Chapter I

The cracker village of Summerville lies on the east coast of Florida near the southern tip. It is a desolate little place: shanties grouped around a general store, and a tiny station into which a one-car train puffs daily, and departs again, back along its single track, to Patona, forty miles away. In the station is a telegraph office with a sleepy clerk intermittently in attendance, and in the general store is a post office. When you have viewed these points of interest you have seen the best that Summerville can boast.

At first sight one wonders why a village exists at all in such a place, but the reason is not far to seek. Harbors are scarce on this coast, and Summerville possesses a harbor of sorts, sufficient, at any rate, for the small fishing vessels that come and go across its shifting sand bars.

But Summerville is only mildly interested in fishing—is, as a matter of fact, only mildly interested in anything. Like Alice's dormouse, it spends most of its time in a profound and slumberous inertia, rousing only occasionally to shout, "Twinkle, twinkle," and relapsing into somnolence again.

The arrival of the eleven o'clock train is the high spot of the day and calls forth the town's whole strength of fifty-odd souls. The women stand in the doorways of their unpainted shacks, with their hands rolled in their aprons, and watch silently the train's wheezing approach, while the male population, clad mostly in ragged overalls, lines up on the little platform, jaws working in admirable unison. And the children, pale, silver-haired little creatures, run along beside the engine, shouting.

Lem Hawks is the big man at these gatherings. Lem Hawks is the sheriff, and he is tall and fat and wears a limp palm-beach suit and a soiled white vest. In his somewhat pompous person he combines the offices of sheriff, stationmaster, local doctor, and leading politician of the township.

On the Saturday morning of the last week in January 1929, at the first bleat of the approaching train, Lem Hawks came, as usual, out of the little ticket office and proceeded through the waiting room onto the platform. He nodded with tolerant condescension to the group already gathered there, spoke more warmly to Andy Grover, who had just crossed the road from the general store, carrying a limp sack of mail, and approached a young man standing alone and nervously smoking a cigarette.

"Morning, Mr. Myron," he said cordially. "Expecting somebody on the train, hey?"

The young man turned. He bore no resemblance whatever to the group leaning against the station house. He was about twenty-five, with lean, well-cut features and dark hair. His face was burned a warm brown, and his eyes had a pleasant, steady light. He wore a neat, dark-blue uniform vaguely suggestive of the sea.

"Morning, sheriff," he replied, smiling. "Yes, I've come to meet a man from Baltimore—lawyer—more your line than mine."

"I should think," drawled Lem, "you'da got aplenty over to the island already. What with motor cars and special trains, a man can't rest. That Grass feller, now. They tell me he's a pretty big fish back in the puddle he come from."

"Lord, yes!" The young man grinned. "Mr. Grass is pretty near all there is to politics in New York."

"You don't say!" Mr. Hawks spat with great nicety onto the tracks. "This feller that's coming now—he in politics, too?"

Myron shook his head.

"Nope. I guess not. Queer card, from what I hear; but smart—awful smart."

But Myron had no opportunity to descant further on the smartness of the expected arrival, for at this moment the train slid around a concealing sand dune and drew into the station.

A curious vehicle it was, relic of the barbarous ages of thirty years ago: a small engine with an abnormally long smokestack, and a single car, half baggage and half passenger coach. But the vehicle itself was hardly more curious than the single passenger who alighted from it and stood waiting, while the conductor lifted his bags onto the platform.

He was the sort of man for whom cartoonists are grateful. It took so little to push him over the edge into absurdity. He was more than six feet tall, and very thin, with wide shoulders that seemed to turn up at the outer corners, where his knotted arm joints stood up like peaks above the slope of his shoulder bones. His trick of posture accentuated this peculiarity: hands hitched forward in the pockets of his gray tweed jacket, shoulders up about his ears, his head bent between them, his foot poking at the rough boarding while he waited.

Myron cast an amused glance at the sheriff and went forward.

"Mr. Bolivar Brown, sir?"

But he experienced an abrupt reversal of feeling as Bolivar Brown looked swiftly up at him and smiled. He saw then that the eyes under the odd brows were curiously penetrating, and that the wry smile, at once humorous and pathetic, had a disarming quality of friendliness, like a child's.

"Yes," said Bolivar Brown. "I expect you're Myron. Mrs. Huntington wrote that you would meet me."

"Yes, sir." Myron appropriated two heavy bags from the conductor. "Have you a trunk, sir?"

"No," said Mr. Brown. "I began to wish I didn't have these by the time I got to Patona. I was always leaving one of them behind. Is it far to walk?"

"Just a step, sir. The wharf's over there by the baggage room."

They moved off. As they passed the little telegraph office the operator stuck his head through the window.

"Just had word they's hurricane signals out all along the coast," he said to Myron, looking sidewise at Brown. "Blowing up from the West Indies, 'tis. You a stranger in these parts?"

"Yes," said Brown, amused.

"Don't let that feller drowned you on the way across," the telegraph operator warned with a cackle of amusement. "Ef you don't hurry you're like to hev a rough passage."

They crossed the track and went down onto the wharf, where a smart-looking speedboat was moored. Myron put the bags aboard and stood a moment looking up at the sky.

"May have trouble, at that," he said then. "But we've time to spare to make World's End. If you'll get aboard, sir, I'll just get the mail, and then we're off."

Five minutes later they were headed down channel.

"Far to go?" asked Brown presently above the growing hum of the engine.

"Ten miles, about," said Myron and lapsed into silence. He gave his attention to the difficult passage, and the lawyer looked about him with interest.

They were moving cautiously through what seemed to be a landlocked lake, whose shores were rolling sand dunes fringed with beach grass. But presently they approached a narrow channel through the dunes and, twisting cautiously, emerged into the open sea. Looking back, Brown saw a magnificent silver-white beach that extended unbroken, except for the gap through which they had come, as far as he could see in each direction.

Brown turned to Myron, opened his mouth to speak, and closed it again, for there was a look on the boatman's face that caused the lawyer to follow his intent gaze with startled interest. He became aware for the first time that the sunlight in which he had arrived had changed to a strange, coppery twilight. At this moment Myron threw in the switch, and the boat leaped forward, hurling great fanlike bastions of water behind their furious progress.

They were headed, apparently, for the open sea. Ahead of them, to the south, saffron clouds were banking up, and the sea, as they watched, changed from its habitual brilliant blue to a strange, oily black, touched along the crests of the waves with a sickly yellow light. Myron glanced sideways at Brown.

"It's got a bad look," he shouted above the roar of the engine, "but we'll make it."

Brown smiled faintly and nodded. He looked back and was surprised to see how far the land had dropped behind. The sea held them like a burnished copper plate; the sky pressed close and hard above them like an inverted copper bowl. Brown was moved to sudden enthusiasm.

"I've never seen anything like it before."

Myron looked at him absently. He was thinking of his boats and of whether he could get them safely moored before the storm broke.

Presently a sharp black line appeared before them on the sea.

"That's World's End," shouted Myron. "We'll be there in no time now."

Brown, looking with interest at the distant island swimming in that molten light, thought that it looked indeed like the end and the edge of the world.

"It's bigger than I'd imagined," he said.

"About a mile long," Myron told him. "But narrow—very narrow. Not more than five hundred feet across."

They drove toward it at breath-taking speed, and presently Brown could begin to see it in greater detail. It was flat, except for a slight rise in the middle, on the crest of which stood a huge white house. To the left, at the end of the island, was a little group of buildings—servants' quarters, probably. To the right lay what appeared to be a stretch of gardens, and beyond that an acre or two of heavy growth: trees surprisingly tall for such an exposed place. And beyond that again, at the right-hand tip, a little summerhouse on the sand. The whole island, as far as he could see, was ringed with a wide, beautiful beach.

Brown had heard the strange story of World's End Island and the tragedy in which it had culminated. As the scene of that tragedy grew more distinct before him, he studied the island thoughtfully. What a backdrop it made for that bizarre and terrible tale!

Senator Stephen Huntington had discovered the island when he went to Florida just after the war to recuperate from his arduous labors on the Shipping Board. He had been on a fishing trip along the coast, and his guide had put into World's End to shelter from a sudden squall.

At that time the island was a wilderness, covered with jungle growth. At one end were a few deserted fishing shanties, from which the inhabitants had fled. There was a curious legend about a vine that grew in that jungle—a vine that ate men.

The guide had told Stephen Huntington the story as they sat over their coffee and fried fish, cooked on a driftwood fire on the beach, and the tale had caught the senator's imagination. While they waited for the wind to die down, he had explored the island, and had come upon that low hill in the middle from which one could look out as far as the eye could reach, over jungle and beach, over sand bars across which the water glowed in incredible shades of pink and lavender and aquamarine, to the aching, purple blue of the Gulf Stream, and the far horizon.

One can only guess at what Stephen Huntington thought while he stood on that hill and looked out to sea. No doubt he was already picturing this place as a fitting background for Madeleine Bingham's dark, gorgeous beauty.

Huntington had been a widower some five years at this time. Until recently he had not thought of remarrying. Absorbed in his political career and in his two children—Justin almost ready for college, and Adele, the darling of his heart—he had been tolerably content. But just before he left Washington he had met Madeleine Bingham and had fallen in love with her. No doubt, as he stood on World's End, he dreamed of taking her there. At any rate, he bought the island when they were married that spring, and built on it. In 1922 they went there to spend the winter. And on a calm, lovely evening, Senator Stephen Huntington walked out on the terrace for an after-dinner cigar—and was never seen again. Local superstition had it that he had been devoured by the strangler fig.

Bolivar Brown promised himself a close inspection of this interesting plant.

He was roused from his absorbed speculations by a shout from Myron.

"That's the boathouse—there," cried the young man, pointing. "There's a lagoon just below the house, and it's been made into a little harbor. We turn in there."

Brown looked up toward the house. He could see it quite clearly now. There were figures on the terrace. As he watched, two of these figures ran quickly down a path toward the boathouse. Brown followed them with his eyes. The girl, he was sure, was Adele Huntington. And suddenly the feeling of strangeness, which had been settling over him for the last few minutes, was dissipated in a warm glow of pleasure.

Brown was vaguely aware that the roar of the motor had subsided to a gentle humming and that Myron was nosing the boat carefully along a curving channel into still water. The next minute they slid expertly into a slip under a boathouse roof and came to a stop, and a young man in white flannels was shaking him enthusiastically by the hand.

It was Justin Huntington, of course. Brown had met him two or three times at the Huntington home in Washington. The lawyer shook hands with him warmly. And then he looked for Adele. She came forward eagerly, her little face pale, her eyes big in the shadow.

"I'm so glad to see you," she cried cordially. "We began to be afraid you'd get caught by the storm. Isn't it the most gorgeous sight you ever saw?"

Brown looked down at her with his crooked smile. What a little thing she was! And how extraordinarily glad he was to see her! A sense of elation took possession of him; a certainty such as he had never felt before. For he knew now what he had come to World's End to seek.

Chapter II

Bolivar Brown was thirty-five, and he had been practicing law for ten years. Before that he had been an office boy, and then a clerk in the firm of Tompkins & Tompkins in Baltimore and had read law at night in a little hall bedroom in a rickety old house at the wrong end of Broadway. In the intervals of his other occupations he had poked his nose into affairs that did not concern him, for, like the Elephant's Child, he was inflamed by a "'satiable curiosity."[1]

As nature abhors a vacuum, so Bolivar Brown's mind abhorred the unknown. The unsolved riddle, the unsounded personality, the unexplained situation, inflamed his imagination and he could not rest until he had probed it to the bottom. He worried it as a dog worries a bone. His mind hovered over a problem with relentless pertinacity. He would attack it from this angle and from that; he would turn away and look back on it over his shoulder, so to speak, but leave it he could not until the answer was his.

This peculiarity had made him a marked success in his profession, but it was a success that must be reckoned in its own terms. The strange, the bizarre, the baffling case gravitated to him as naturally as steel to a magnet, but cases of this type did not, as a rule, bring nice fat fees in their wake. Nevertheless, Mr. Brown was extraordinarily content.

When, after a brief and unexciting sojourn at various army camps, he was admitted to the bar in the year following the war, he was advised to attach himself to some established firm, but six months' experience of routine law practice exhausted its possibilities as far as he was concerned. He hired himself an unobtrusive and somewhat shabby office in an old building near the courthouse and sat down to wait.

Contrary to all dark predictions, business came to him. His first case was productive of results that are worth recording. It happened this way:

When he unlocked his office door at nine o'clock one hot July morning, Bolivar Brown found a single envelope lying on the sill. The envelope contained a letter from an acquaintance, a gentleman by the name of Simpkins, who requested Mr. Brown to look into the matter of some rent, long overdue, of a building in Charles Street, and to take such steps as seemed necessary for its collection.

---

1   "The Elephant's Child" is a Rubyard Kipling tale published in *Just So Stories*, 1902.

Mr. Brown, who had opened the envelope with some excitement, grunted disgustedly.

"I agree," said a voice behind him. "Life is like that, isn't it?"

Mr. Brown swung round. In the open doorway stood a cheerful little man in a light tweed suit, with a felt hat on the back of his head. He was short and quite fat and largely bald, although he could not have been more than twenty-four or five. And he radiated an amiable confidence and cheerful effrontery that interested Mr. Brown.

"My card, sir," said this apparition, extending an oblong of pasteboard in a square, ungloved hand. "You, I perceive, are Mr. Brown. And you are finding the world, at the moment, not entirely to your liking."

Brown chuckled as he took the card, and he regarded his visitor with his characteristic crooked smile.

"If you have had any experience with the law," he said, "you already know that much of it is dull and flat, even if profitable."

"Experience," stated the young man unexpectedly, "is what I am looking for. I've just graduated from law school, and I'm looking for a job."

Inspiration sprang full-fledged into the mind of Bolivar Brown. He looked at the card in his hand. It read: "E. Kenyon Jones."

"What does the 'E' stand for?" he asked, glancing up at Mr. Jones under his brows.

The visitor flushed and, removing his hat, rubbed an embarrassed hand over his bald head.

"Well," he said apologetically, "I was named for my grandfather, who's supposed to leave his money to me, if he ever dies, but I think it's dear at the price. I'll tell you what," he finished in a rush of confidence, "I don't usually admit it, but since I'm going to work for you I'll tell you. The 'E' stands for Eliphalet."

Mr. Brown looked at him severely.

"Do you love the law, Eliphalet?" he asked. "Do you like collecting money and drawing wills and—er—all that sort of thing?"

Mr. Jones's face, which had quivered painfully at the use of his first name, glowed again.

"I'll tell the world!" he cried fervently. "That's what I like about the law—making wills and contracts and drawing up nice neat papers about things."

Mr. Brown turned the card over and looked at the back of it, as though for enlightenment.

"Of course," he said coldly, "I'll have to have all kinds of references and things."

Mr. Jones chortled reassuringly.

"Lord, sir, you can have a bushel, if you want 'em. I know everybody in town. We've lived here for ages."

Bolivar Brown threw the card on the desk.

"Oh," he said, "you're one of those Joneses. Well, I'm sorry, Mr. Jones, but I can't offer you employment, for the simple reason that I can't pay you a salary. Would you be interested in a partnership?"

For the first time Mr. Brown threw back his head and looked his visitor in the eye. E. Kenyon Jones stared at him for a moment as though he fancied that the lawyer had lost his mind. Then he looked about him, discovered an unoccupied hook, and hung up his hat.

"Give me that letter you were groaning over," he said. "We can talk terms later."

Brown picked up the letter and handed it over with a laugh.

"It's my first case," he admitted ruefully.

"It won't be our last," predicted E. Kenyon Jones.

And he turned out to be a good prophet.

As has been indicated, with the passage of years the firm of Brown & Jones grew both prosperous and famous, in a modest fashion. Mr. Jones, as he was fond of explaining, took care of the prosperity, while Mr. Brown attended to the fame. And the instinctive liking that had drawn the ill-assorted pair together at their first meeting ripened into a warm devotion. Wherefore Jones observed with some anxiety the restlessness that became apparent in Mr. Brown's behavior in the fall of 1928. He even spoke about it to his wife.

"The poor old chap's worn out," he said. "Doesn't sleep. Smokes too much. He needs a vacation."

Mrs. Jones tossed her pretty red head and laughed.

"I should think," she said tartly, "you'd had experience enough to know what that means. Bet you it's a girl."

"What's the use of betting with you?" grumbled Mr. Jones. "You never pay up. And Bolivar's never looked at a girl in his life."

"Mark my words," said Mrs. Jones darkly.

But E. Kenyon was unconvinced. He began to urge his partner to take a holiday. His efforts, however, met with no success until one day in the middle of January.

For several weeks Bolivar Brown had shown marked signs of depression and fatigue. Jones had fallen into the way of watching him anxiously. On this particular morning he chanced to look across from his desk just as Brown was going through his morning mail. He saw him open a small gray envelope and read the enclosure. And he saw the change that came over Mr. Brown's face. As Mr. Jones described it to Mrs. Jones afterward, "he looked as though he'd suddenly had a month's rest and a cocktail." That afternoon Brown remarked casually that he guessed his partner was right and a week or so in Florida wouldn't do him any harm.

"Didn't I tell you so?" asked Mrs. Jones of Mr. Jones.

And that is how it happened that, on this Saturday afternoon, in the last week of January, 1929, Bolivar Brown stood in the window of a guest room on World's End Island, a silent and deeply moved spectator of the prologue to the drama in which he was destined to play a leading part.

He was thinking of Adele Huntington as he stood there. Or, perhaps, thinking is not the right word. He was deeply conscious of her. Conscious of the fact that she was in the same house with him, that he had recently seen her and would see her again. He took his pipe out of his pocket and filled it carefully, tamping down the tobacco.

From his window he could see the length of the island: the boathouse on the right, the gardens below, the jungle-like coppice behind them, and beyond that again the sea. In all that stretch not a leaf moved. Only in the sea he sensed a deep, troubled stirring. The air was hot and motionless. The coppery light had deepened and darkened to a sullen, warning note as sharp as a tocsin bell.[2] As he watched it grew still darker, and the air began to beat against his face in little hot puffs, as though someone were blowing it out of a bellows.

He heard sharp, reverberating sounds on the terrace below him and leaned out. Men were fastening up shutters against the ground-floor windows. They were rolling up and taking away the striped awning over the end of the terrace. He looked along the wall of the house and saw hands reaching out and closing the shutters outside the second-story windows. He examined his own windows and found they were provided with shutters. He closed two of them, but the third he left open and stood in it, watching the superb approach of the storm.

A hurricane! What was that? He had read about them, of course, but nevertheless the word sounded strange and meaningless to his Northern ears. What would it do? He had read of the roofs of houses being ripped off by hurricanes. Did that really happen? Were they, perhaps, in serious danger?

The sounds below had ceased. The house, it appeared, was ready for whatever might come. It waited, silent, vaguely expectant, bracing itself against it knew not what. And Bolivar Brown waited in his window, curious, fascinated.

The little hot puffs came more frequently now, quick panting, like an animal breathing. He could hear an uneasy sound in the distant

---

2 Tocsin bell: a warning or signal bell.

coppice, like the sigh of someone who has held his breath for terror and can hold it no longer. The blooming orange trees in the garden below were swaying, and suddenly a branch snapped with a sharp crack and sagged pathetically, and was presently torn off and hurled against the house.

From the boathouse came a sudden roaring sound, and Brown realized that Myron must be shutting the huge doors over the water. After a moment he saw the boatman come out and close the landward door after him. He paused to lock it and test its fastenings, and then he came running up toward the house, the coat which he held in his hand blown out before him by the wind at his back.

Brown was suddenly aware that his room was full of the storm—things blowing about. A chair blew over with a bang. He leaned out to close the shutters.

Suddenly, sweeping with incredible speed from horizon to horizon, a beam of sunlight came through a rift in the clouds, like the shaft of a searchlight. It showed the waters black and angry, whipping to fury; it picked out for a breath-taking instant the white sails of a schooner beating down toward World's End like a terrified creature driven before the storm. In that breathless instant, before he slammed and barred the shutters, Brown saw it coming. And he saw, too, the wall of water reaching from edge to edge of the sea, threatening to engulf the world. Then the light went out—all light went out—as though the wind had blown out the sun.

Through a house that was wrenched and shaken until it seemed as though it would be torn up and hurled into the sea, a house filled with the hissing of waters and the creak of timbers unmercifully strained; through halls black as midnight, loud with hurrying feet and voices sharp with terror, Brown felt his way.

The stairs were over here to the left, of course. He moved toward them and saw them suddenly illuminated by a light from below. He was surprised to find, as he descended, that the light came from a candle that stood on the hall table and that the flame burned quite steadily, unblown.

Servants were hurrying about with lamps and candles, lighting one room after another. The drawing room on his left was already alight. He turned into it. There was no one there, but in the little room beyond he heard voices. One of the voices was Adele's. He went toward the open door and paused there for a moment, looking in.

At first he did not see Adele. He saw only a young man of twenty-six or so, a young man of medium height and very thin, with a narrow face newly sunburned. Brown remembered vaguely that he had met him on his arrival. Stuart was the name. That was it. He was standing half turned away from the door, looking at someone just beyond Brown's line of vision.

Brown had suddenly a sense of being an intruder. For some inexplicable reason he felt cold, shaken. And then he knew why it was, for Adele came forward and stood looking at Stuart with a look her face had never worn for Bolivar Brown. She did not see the man in the doorway; she saw nothing in the world but young Stuart. And then, before Brown could move or speak, she walked forward into Stuart's arms.

Brown turned away and went back into the drawing room. When Mrs. Huntington, Adele's stepmother, came in a minute later, she was surprised to find him standing in front of a shuttered window, staring at it as though he could see through it into the storm.

He turned with a start as she spoke to him, and she mistook the gray look in his face for fear.

"There's nothing to worry about now," she said reassuringly. "It's a very well built house. The only danger was the roof, but if that had been going it would have gone in the first gust."

"Oh—that!" he said vaguely. And then he pulled himself together. "You'll be amused," he said with a half smile, "but I wasn't even thinking of the storm. I'd forgotten about it."

Mrs. Huntington looked at him with some curiosity, but she only said:

"You're clever if you can do that—or perhaps a little deaf?"

He listened. Outside the wind howled and shrieked and the blown sand hissed against the walls. Inside there was no sound—except those voices in the next room. Madeleine Huntington seemed to hear them, too. She was in the act of opening a silver cigarette box on the table when she heard them. For an instant her hand remained extended toward the box, her head jerked back, eyes fixed on that open doorway, a swift frown on her suddenly darkened face.

Brown studied her with reawakened curiosity. Since he had first met her in Washington, and had heard the dramatic story of her life, Adele's stepmother had exercised a great fascination on him. Not that he found her attractive: rather the reverse; but he was intensely curious to know what lay behind the smooth, polished surface of her manner.

Undoubtedly she had once been a strikingly handsome woman, but the glow had gone out of her, leaving her face burnt out, her black eyes hard and flat, her nose too sharp, her clever mouth faintly ill-natured. As a young woman, though, she must have been lovely. There was still a warmth that came sometimes.

Brown wondered about her. What had she thought, what had she felt on that night seven years ago when Stephen Huntington had walked out of this house, never to be seen again? For seven years she had not known whether he was alive or dead. What did she think about it now? What did she feel? The mask she held before her face concealed her thoughts and feelings. As far as he knew that mask never slipped.

And yet, perhaps, the mask slipped for an instant just now as she leaned over the cigarette box, her gaze fixed on that open doorway through which came the voices of her stepdaughter and young Stuart, her black brows drawn in a sudden frown. But the revelation was only momentary. Then her fingers completed their journey to the box, opened it, took out a cigarette, and lighted it.

The atmosphere of the room was tense with sudden drama, as though the curtain had gone up on the first act of a play.

Chapter III

Through two long days, while the storm buffeted World's End Island, this sense of impending drama grew more acute. Brown became aware—just how he could not have said—of cross currents battling under the apparently placid surface of affairs; of sides being taken and animosities entertained.

The outlines of the struggle were nebulous at first. Take Daniel Lane, for instance. How was one to fit him into the picture? And Jacob Grass? And Dr. Simpson? Brown noted at the time, and recalled many times afterward, a curious little scene.

It was late Sunday evening, and the four men were together in the library, lingering over a nightcap and a final smoke. Brown, through a blue haze of pipe smoke, had been thoughtfully studying his fellow guests. They were such a curious collection. He had been vainly seeking the common thread that drew them together.

Take Lane and Grass, for instance: It was hard to imagine two men more sharply contrasted. Lane was president of a company that operated coastwise passenger and freight ships to South America; a quiet man of medium height, with a shrewd, forceful face, and hair going a little gray at the temples; a distinguished-looking man. Grass, politician, prizefight promoter, real-estate speculator, was a big, heavy man with an offensively hearty manner and a passion for jewelry. What on earth had brought these two together at World's End? And as for Simpson—

Brown looked with disfavor at the man's insignificant face, pale in spite of days on the beach; its pale eyes with their slightly reddened lids. A fussy man, always afraid of getting his feet wet, inordinately vain, with an objectionable way of talking to a woman. Brown knew little about Simpson, except that someone had told him that the doctor was connected with the Port of New York; a political job of some sort.

It was Dr. Simpson who started the conversation.

"What, after all, *is* the Enoch Arden law?"

For a moment no one spoke. Then Grass removed a fat cigar from his mouth and squinted thoughtfully at the glowing tip.

"It's pretty indefinite, unfortunately," he said. "Largely up to the judgment of the courts. And they hate like the devil to act at all in cases of disappearance."

"I thought," persisted Simpson, and his voice held a querulous note, as though he felt personally aggrieved, "I thought that there was a certain limitation of time—that, for instance, after seven years a man was presumed to be dead."

Lane spoke now for the first time, almost sharply.

"That's a popular superstition," he said. "There's no such thing as a set limit of time in such matters."

"But suppose," urged Simpson aggrievedly, "a man stayed away for twenty years."

"When he came back," Lane insisted, "he could still claim his property."

"That's so," said Grass, and he looked heavily across at Brown. "That's so, isn't it?" he repeated.

They all looked at Brown. He nodded.

"It's a difficult problem at law," he said. "Sometimes the courts have decided one way and sometimes another."

"But surely," persisted Simpson with a trace of eagerness, "a woman could get a divorce on grounds of desertion—after seven years?"

"Certainly," agreed the lawyer. "In considerably less than seven years."

"But," objected Grass heavily, "there would remain the question of the property."

"Probably," suggested Lane, "after seven years the courts would make some temporary disposition."

"As to the management of the property and the handling of the income, yes," agreed Brown.

"But they wouldn't admit a will to probate?" persisted Simpson.

"Hardly," said Bolivar Brown.

"But Mrs. Huntington's lawyers—" Simpson broke off suddenly as though he had said more than he meant to say.

Grass laughed rumblingly.

"There's no secret about it," he said to Brown. "Mrs. Huntington has appealed to the courts to declare her husband officially dead and to admit his will to probate."

Brown nodded thoughtfully. Another lifting of the mask, perhaps? He wondered.

Simpson laughed—an unexpected, high-pitched giggle.

"It's an interesting will," Grass went on. "Leaves everything to the lovely Madeleine, so I've heard—at least during her lifetime. With the exception of a bequest to Justin when he reaches the age of twenty-five and to Adele when she marries."

"And you say," reiterated Simpson, "that it can't be probated?"

"Absolutely not," said Daniel Lane.

And then they all looked at Brown, who shook his head.

"Mr. Lane is quite right," he said.

That was all. A moment later they said goodnight and went upstairs.

But Brown sat for an hour over his pipe in that empty room, revolving the matter in his mind.

Did this account for the unquestionable hatred that existed between Mrs. Huntington and her stepdaughter? Was hatred, perhaps, too strong a word for the antagonism between them? Brown thought not. Careful as they were to conceal it, there could be no doubt that the feeling existed. It smoldered constantly under the amenities of casual intercourse, as a cigarette butt may smolder for hours under a pile of dry leaves, waiting only the sudden gust to blow it into flames.

Brown rose at last and knocked the ashes out of his pipe. He was suddenly intensely sleepy. Contrary to all precedent, his eminently reasonable mind entertained no faintest premonition that in a few hours this smoldering fire was destined to burst into an uncontrollable conflagration.

The Tuesday following Brown's arrival at World's End dawned still and clear, so gentle and mild, so innocently disarming that, but for the mute witness of wrecked trees and shrubbery, piled sand and debris, one could not have believed that a storm had ever visited the place.

In the afternoon Myron went over to Summerville for the mail and came back with a tale of disrupted communications—telegraph wires torn down and tracks demolished. He brought only one telegram, which had been received on Saturday, before the storm broke. It was for Mrs. Huntington. She tore it open, glanced at the long message it contained, and dropped it in her lap with an impatient exclamation.

Most of the house party were gathered on the terrace for tea, at the time, and it seemed to Brown that they were all watching her with covert curiosity. And then suddenly Adele Huntington spoke. It seemed to Brown afterward that with those words, the tragedy of World's End Island took coherent form and began to move to its inevitable end.

"Is it from Faulkner & Hayden?" asked Adele.

Brown recognized the name of a well-known firm of lawyers in New York.

Mrs. Huntington nodded.

"May I see it?"

For an instant the older woman seemed to hesitate. Then, with a curious laugh, she tossed the telegram across to her stepdaughter. Adele bent her sleek brown head over it for a moment. Then, without looking up, she said:

"It would be so convenient, wouldn't it, if you could just prove that father is—dead?"

The sentence was like a flick of a whip lash. A half-audible gasp ran round the group among the teacups. And then young Stuart, sitting beside Adele, added an astonishing remark:

"I can imagine a point of view," he said quietly, "which would not find it at all convenient to have the fact of Mr. Huntington's death established."

No one spoke. Brown stared at him, astounded. Such things simply weren't said. And yet Stuart had said them. One after the other, coolly, quietly, they had been spoken. And no one had protested them. Mrs. Huntington had turned as though about to speak, but she had, after all, said nothing.

And then a maid came out of the house with a tray of cocktails, and the conversation became general.

Down near the far tip of the island a group of workmen were engaged clearing up the debris left by the storm, trimming out the torn and mangled underbrush, and cutting down the trees that the wind had twisted and broken. Brown, walking on the beach after tea, could hear the sound of their axes. Moved by a sudden impulse he turned and walked toward them.

The disagreeable impression of the scene he had just witnessed was still strong on him, and as he walked his mind was full of curious speculation. What had Stuart meant when he inferred that there might be someone who would find proof of Huntington's death inconvenient? Had there been any suspicion of foul play in connection with the disappearance? Brown could not remember any rumors of the sort—nothing definite, anyway.

He looked ahead at what remained of the jungle coppice. Adele had told him that at one time, years ago, a path, now completely overgrown, had run through this jungle. But her father had been obliged to bring men down from the North to cut that path, for none of the natives would go near the place for fear of the strangler fig which grew there. They said that years before, when there was only a fishing village on the island, men had been caught by this vine and devoured and were never seen again. Brown looked out over the deceptively quiet surface of the sea. Sharks, probably.

But was it a shark that had got Stephen Huntington seven years before? With that unquiet house behind him and jungle before, that strange story of disappearance took on a sinister aspect. To walk out of one's house one fine evening, hatless, in dinner clothes, to leave a delightful party of friends and a charming wife, hardly more than a bride, and disappear as completely as though one had stepped out of the front door into space ... Brown regarded the coppice ahead of him with a curious eye. He remembered hearing someone say that the path through the jungle had been a favorite walk of Senator Huntington's.

Suppose, for sake of argument...

But the argument reduced itself immediately to absurdity and left him struggling with the notion of the strangler fig. He'd read about it somewhere—a book of travel—some such thing. Haiti, or perhaps the Virgin Islands. No, Haiti. He had it now. A vine that was called the *figue maudit*, the accursed fig. It destroyed and devoured whatever its tendrils touched. Or so the natives claimed for it. Curious how identical superstitions cropped up, here and there, all over the world. Folklore, springing direct from the imaginations and the fears of primitive peoples.

He smiled. Well, the jungle and its *figue maudit* would do no harm to anyone now—for a time, at least. The storm had ripped it to pieces, strewn the underbrush far and wide. As he approached Brown saw heavy black vines, thick as a man's arm, torn from their holds, coiled across the beach like huge snakes, strangely still. He paused at the edge of the thicket to watch Platt, the English gardener, and his helpers at their work. A group of Negroes, nervous to go near the vine, yet drawn by a strange curiosity, stood at a little distance, looking on.

"Terrific mess, isn't it?" said a voice at his elbow. Brown turned with a start to find young Stuart beside him. He had come across the turf that ran down to the low embankment of rock along the beach.

Brown was a little startled at this sudden apparition. He nodded slowly, looking up at the young man above him; noting that the new sunburn only partly hid the black lines of fatigue under the eyes; observing the thin body upon which the light gray tweed suit seemed to hang too loosely, the thin, nervous hands. Badly overworked, Brown would have said by the look of him. But the job of secretary to a man like Jacob Grass would certainly be no sinecure.

"Thought I'd join you for a breather," Stuart explained. "Been cooped up so long. The storm made a clean sweep, didn't it?"

"Look here," said Brown suddenly, "you're working yourself to death, you know. You are, positively. I was restless last night and chanced to look out of my window at four o'clock. There was a light in your room still, and I could see you at the table inside the window, hard at it. And you've been at it all day, too. You'll do yourself in, you know."

Stuart laughed sharply.

"Oh," he said carelessly, "a man can stand anything—temporarily. I don't mean to stick it indefinitely." The saturnine lips curved into a curious smile. "I've never meant to stick it indefinitely."

He did not look at Brown as he spoke, but off to sea. There was a look in his eyes as though he were amused by some secret thought. Brown was baffled. There was something about this young man that defied analysis. Clever—clever as the devil; and there was ruthlessness there, too. And some secret, unexplained motive power... The lawyer surrendered the problem for the moment with a shrug.

"Let's go have a look at what they're doing in there," he suggested.

As they approached a tall man in a blue shirt was hewing away at what looked like a gnarled tree trunk, which lay half upon the ground and half coiled, in some curious fashion, about a dead palm that lay uprooted near by. As they watched, the trunk parted under the blows of the ax, and the five men working in the wood came up and looked at it with more interest than the occasion seemed to merit. For a moment they spoke in low tone, and then Platt straightened up and saw Brown and Stuart. He stepped at once onto the beach to meet them. Brown noticed as he came up, that the man's face was full of suppressed excitement, and that the hands with which he held his ax were trembling slightly.

"Would you step this way a moment, please?" he began. "I'm sure it's a new thing in my experience, sir, and I don't hardly know what to do about it."

"Found something, have you?" asked Stuart eagerly.

"Found something, sir!" the man exclaimed. "But come quietly, if you please. We don't want them to know." And he jerked his head toward the silent group on the beach.

Together they proceeded into the wood, clambering over the piles of rubbish. About fifty feet into the jungle, near the point where one might imagine the path to have penetrated, they came to the place where the felled tree lay. And then Brown saw that it was not a tree at all, but a vine, coiled round and round some inner core, so close that the folds appeared at a little distance to be the rough coat of bark on a tree trunk.

"What is it?" asked Stuart, in some surprise.

The man in the blue shirt enlightened him.

"It's a strangler fig, sir," he said in a lugubrious voice. "At least, that's what they call it in these parts, sir. First it winds itself round everything in sight—look how it strangled that palm tree there—and then it turns round, with an unnatural perversity, sir, and up and strangles itself. This here one's dead, sir, as you will have noticed from the sound of the ax. It killed itself, sir."

Brown looked with a smile at this suicidal tree, or vine, or whatever it might be. But he fancied that Platt had not brought them there to inspect this arboreal perversion. He looked inquiringly at the head gardener. The man answered his look with a gesture.

"Come round here, sir," he said, "where you can see into the end of the thing."

Brown bent and looked, and he saw what it was that had so upset the imperturbable Briton. A tingle of suppressed excitement ran up his spine. For protruding from the opening left by the felling of the vine was the foot of a skeleton, with the remnant of a leather shoe dangling from the bleached bones.

Chapter IV

For a moment Brown had the dizzy, delirious feeling of a man confronted suddenly with a portent. For an instant the normal perspectives of the world around him shifted, and he had a swift glimpse into a world where the supposition that vines devoured men would cause no disturbance of the natural—or rather supernatural— laws, where rabbits' feet had an acknowledged potency, and the evil eye must be averted by crossed fingers. The voice of Platt, the gardener, brought him to himself with a start.

"Strikes you all of a heap, don't it?" he murmured. "And what's to be done about it, sir? There'll be a riot yonder if this gets about."

The lugubrious man in the blue shirt spoke again.

"It don't pay to laugh at things in this world," he said. "We all laughed when those chaps said the trees in this wood eat men." And he looked somberly into the wood.

Brown glanced at the fellow and smiled involuntarily. It seemed improbable that the blue-shirted man was much given to the improvidence of laughter. He had a long, solemn, churchly countenance, with slightly arched brows and drooping lids that conferred on him, without effort on his part, the air of an undertaker welcoming the relatives of the deceased. But the lawyer's observations were suddenly cut short by a new voice that spoke directly behind him —a voice pitched high and quivering with excitement.

"Aren't you going to see who it is?"

Brown turned and looked at the speaker. It was Stuart, right enough, but a new Stuart. His face was drawn and quivering, and his eyes black with some inexplicable emotion. Bolivar's glance returned to the dangling foot.

"I don't suppose there'll be much chance of identifying the fellow," he said thoughtfully. "But of course we must try. There may be something. Let's rip the vine off, anyway, and see. The tree will hardly have digested any bits of metal he may have had about him." And he grinned at the blue-shirted one.

The men fell to with a will, and the rotten wood gave readily to their efforts. Following Brown's directions, they cut through the wood lengthwise, turning it back and leaving the skeleton as nearly as possible in position. For a moment Stuart stood watching them. Then he turned to Brown, seized him by the arm, and drew him a little aside.

"It's Huntington, of course," he said, his voice tense with excitement. "There can't be any doubt of it, do you think?"

He smoothed his twitching face with his hand, and Brown saw with some astonishment that he was trembling all over.

"I should think it must be Huntington—certainly," assented the lawyer.

"Must be!" repeated Stuart impatiently. "My God! It is! Of course it's Huntington." He laughed sharply. "What a situation! You can't convict a vine of—murder, can you?"

"Look here," said Brown abruptly, "what do you know about this?"

Stuart looked at him coolly.

"Nothing," he said calmly. "Or rather, I should say, a whale of a lot, but nothing that could be proved—yet. But I mean to find out."

At this moment, before Brown could speak, Platt said behind him: "There you are, sir."

They turned and found that the wooden shell had been completely split and the skeleton lay uncovered in the hollow. Brown knelt beside it, examining it with close attention.

The clothing had, for the most part, disintegrated in the damp, semi-tropical climate, but bits still clung to the gaunt frame—pieces that identified themselves unmistakably as black broadcloth. Lying under the skeleton, in the curve of the shell, was an oblong, glittering object that Brown picked up and turned over curiously. It was a gold cigarette case, and on the side were engraved the initials S. H. Curiously enough, that cigarette case completely restored Brown's natural equilibrium. It eliminated the disturbing element of black magic in the situation and transformed the case into a routine matter of identification, with which the lawyer was entirely familiar. He looked up at the ring of faces above him, most of them curious and a little awed. Stuart's was still drawn with that surprising excitement.

"Any of you here in Stephen Huntington's time—before he disappeared?" he asked.

The men glanced at each other. Then the man in the blue shirt nodded solemnly.

"Yes, sir," he said. "I was here. I came with him when he bought the island—ten years ago. I was here when he disappeared—seven years ago."

"Can you identify this?" Brown held out the cigarette case.

"Yes, sir, I can. I was valet to Mr. Huntington in those days, sir. I put that case into the pocket of his dress coat when he went down to dinner the night he disappeared."

"My God!" whispered Stuart. "I knew it!" He seized the case eagerly and turned it over in shaking hands. "I knew it," he repeated. Then he thrust it into Brown's hand and turned away, staring out to sea, apparently oblivious of what was going on around him.

The lawyer looked at him curiously. Then he turned his attention again to the case. He opened it. It was full of dust—the dust of the cigarettes that had been in it on that mysterious night. He snapped the case shut and, sitting back on his heels, stared at the bleached bones of the man who had been master of this island, master of the millions that had bought it and built on it, that had maintained the house and its retinue—that still maintained it—Adele's father. A phrase echoed in his head. "It would be so convenient, wouldn't it, if you could just prove that father is—dead!"

His mind was full of fantastic ideas. How had this man met the strange fate that had fallen on him? How had he lain for so many years undiscovered? To be devoured by a vine—even the strangler fig—was a bit fantastic. But then the whole incident was too fantastic for credence. The lawyer had a sudden wild vision of Stephen Huntington walking along the path through the jungle, and a long, snakelike tentacle of vine reaching out, twisting itself around him, drawing him into the thicket, entwining him in its coils, stifling his cries . . . And then his practical mind asserted itself, for his eyes, searching the content of the hollow shell with interest, picked out one detail among the many minutiæ that presented themselves to his attention, and his mind reverted to Stuart, and his mysterious knowledge.

After an instant's consideration he took an envelope from his pocket and, leaning over, transferred to this receptacle several bits of some brownish substance that he found lying over and under the skeleton. Then he stood up.

"Suppose you cover this over and leave someone here to look after it," he suggested to Platt. "Mrs. Huntington should be told at once." He hesitated. "I suppose I'd better tell her." He glanced at the head gardener. "I'll let you know later what to do about this."

Platt drew a long breath. It was clear he did not relish having any responsibility in the matter.

"Very good, sir. I'm obliged to you, I'm sure."

"That's right, don't you think—" Brown turned toward Stuart, but broke off suddenly, for Stuart was no longer there. He was already halfway up the island, striding toward the house with long, purposeful strides.

Thoroughly perplexed and intensely curious, Brown followed in the young man's wake. After climbing over several piles of debris, however, he gave up that route and turned aside toward the beach, intending to return the way he had come. At a little distance he passed again the group of Negroes squatting on the sand. They had been talking excitedly, but fell silent as he approached. One of them—a huge, very dark fellow—rose and came toward him.

"What did you find in the woods?" he asked, his grin a little wan.

Brown laughed.

"Just been looking at the strangler fig," he said. "You'll be glad to know it's dead—dead and rotted."

"Is that right?" cried the big man. "Is that vine dead?" He turned and looked into the wood. "Then there'll be no more vultures circling, and wheeling, and screaming. I reckon they'll take their shadows away from World's End."

An undeniable cold chill chased itself up Brown's spine.

"Vultures?" he repeated. "Do you have many vultures here?"

"Those birds will take the food off anybody's table," the big man said earnestly, and this time he forgot to grin, "even the strangler fig's. You couldn't find anybody in ten hundred miles ain't heard of the vultures of World's End."

Brown revolved the little incident in his mind as he walked back to the house. It had made a most unpleasant impression on him. He could not have said why, but since Stuart's unexplained departure a weight had begun to fall upon his spirits, which for lack of a better word he called a premonition. There was not the faintest trace of superstition in his eminently reasonable mind, but he felt that there was something in this situation that he did not understand, something disquieting, something stranger, even, than the finding of Huntington's skeleton wrapped in the folds of a vine. Something that connected itself with those brownish fragments even now in the envelope in his pocket. If they meant what they seemed to mean, they spelled trouble, pain, and anguish of mind for someone—perhaps someone very dear to him. For a moment he thought of dropping those brown fragments into the sea. And then he recalled Stuart's curious excitement, and he changed his mind. After all, he knew nothing yet—nothing at all. He must wait until he knew what he was doing.

He tried to push from him the sense of impending disaster, tried to laugh himself out of his depression. How E. Kenyon Jones would have roared with amusement at the notion of Brown struggling with the strangler fig! Bolivar Brown conjured up a comforting vision of their pleasant, dusty office and its rows of law books in worn, solid calfskin; the glimpse through the window of red-brick houses across the street and their polished white stone steps; of E. Kenyon himself, stout and bald, aggressively commonplace and matter-of-fact. But the vision was hard to hold, absurdly transparent. Through it, as on a double negative, showed palm trees, and blue sea, and pounding surf; the blood red of poinsettias, the crushed fragrant whiteness of orange blossoms.

But Brown clung to that vanishing illusion. It was ridiculous to make so much—out of what? A few shreds of brown matter, an ill-natured scene or two, a young man's excitement, and a native superstition. That was it. This silly story of the strangler fig had got under his skin. But in his heart he knew that this fear had nothing to do with the strangler fig. It was something more concrete than a legend, much stronger. Legends do not lean down out of trees and strangle men. It takes something more tangible than a legendary vine to do that.

The terrace under the striped awning was silent and empty. It seemed to him suddenly that there wasn't a sound or a human being in the world. He knew perfectly well that this was because the house party had gone upstairs to dress for dinner, but somehow it added to his depression. Perhaps it was just as well that his feeling went no farther than a premonition, that he could not see with greater clarity what awaited him—what awaited them all—at the turn of the next corner.

Chapter V

It was almost half-past six when Brown at last made his way into the house, went upstairs, and knocked on Justin Huntington's door. He intended to tell him at once about the finding of his father's body, but when no one answered the lawyer felt a queer sense of relief, which he would have been hard put to it to explain. He turned back and went along the corridor to Stuart's room.

But here, with his hand raised to knock, he paused. There were voices inside—or, rather, there was a voice. Stuart was talking rapidly, softly, with an extraordinarily quiet emphasis. Brown heard no distinct words, but only the insistent note in his voice going on and on, uninterrupted.

The lawyer glanced at his watch. Just half-past six. Mrs. Huntington would be dressing now. Better wait until after dinner, when he could see Justin alone, and let Justin break the news to his stepmother. If he had another reason for his delay he did not admit it, but the truth is that the little brownish fragments in his pocket worried him. If he could only be sure!

Once in his own room he took them out and examined them closely. But he knew nothing of such things. He'd have to have the opinion of an expert. With a sigh he replaced them in the envelope, put the envelope in his billfold, threw off his clothes, and proceeded to indulge himself in a prolonged cold shower.

He emerged from it, however, without that sense of well-being that was customary with him. He was fretted and nervous—"like an hysterical woman," he told himself severely. Everything went wrong. He dropped a glass of water on his bathroom floor, and most of the contents splashed into his patent-leather evening shoes. He spent ten minutes looking for his cuff links and dress studs, only to find them at last attached to the shirt he had worn the evening before. Finally he dropped his collar button, and no amount of crawling about on the floor revealed its whereabouts. He got to his feet at last, impotently furious, dusted the knees of his dinner trousers, and expressed himself softly and concisely.

He had notable gifts in this direction, but in the middle of a sounding period he caught a glimpse of his face in the mirror over the dressing table and stopped, so to speak, in mid-flight.

"Look here!" he told himself severely. "You're up against it. It's no good telling yourself it isn't true. Something's wrong. Something's horribly wrong, and you know it. Pull yourself together and see what you're going to do about it."

He felt better, somehow, after that, and smoothed his hair with a steady hand. There remained the problem of the collar button. Dr. Simpson's room was next door. No doubt the doctor came supplied with whole boxes of collar buttons. Brown slipped on his dressing gown and went out into the hall.

The long corridor was dark. Clearly the servants had forgotten to turn up the lights. But the darkness was cut by a shaft of light coming through an open door about midway of its length; Stuart's door. Brown had only a momentary impression of that light, and of a shadow cast by it against the opposite wall. And he had a momentary impression of something else—the sound of water running into a basin. Then the door was shut. Clearly Stuart's visitor, whoever he was, had taken his departure. Brown moved a step or two down the corridor, as though to go to Stuart's room, and then he stopped. It must be nearly seven. He'd hardly have time now for the sort of talk he meant to have with Stuart. Better wait till later.

He knocked instead on Dr. Simpson's door. No one answered. For an instant he hesitated. Then he turned the knob and entered. Simpson had evidently dressed and gone. His flannels were neatly laid across a chair. On the bureau was an open box of tooled leather, and in it was a collar button. But as Brown investigated he was not thinking of Simpson or his collar button. His mind still dwelt perplexedly on the little incident of the closing door. There had been something odd about it. And then he realized what it was. He had expected someone to come out—and nobody had come out.

When he went downstairs fifteen minutes later he almost collided with a butler who came swiftly through the drawing room door carrying an empty tray. The man drew back with a murmured apology, and something in the funereal timbre of his voice caused Brown's eyes to swing swiftly to his face. It was none other than the man in the blue shirt.

"Well!" cried the lawyer in lively surprise. "Damned if you aren't the butler!"

"Yes, sir," said that official sadly.

"I didn't recognize you."

The man sighed.

"Why should you, sir?" he asked with the air of one magnanimously determined to pardon the frailties of mankind. "Nobody ever looks at a butler, sir."

Brown grinned.

"What's your name?"

"Franklin, sir."

"I suppose," said the lawyer diffidently, "it's too much to hope that your first name is Benjamin?"

"No, sir," said Franklin regretfully. "Given name—Richard."

"Alas, poor Richard," murmured Brown. "That's almost better. And they say that this is an imperfect world. You've said nothing to Mrs. Huntington, I suppose?"

"Oh, no, sir." Franklin glanced over his shoulder at the open drawing room door and sank his voice to a whisper. "It's a strange thing, sir, this happening to-night, just when they're all here again."

"All here again?" repeated the lawyer. "What do you mean? All what?"

"All the people that were here the night Senator Huntington disappeared, sir. Every last one of them."

In the instant that followed, the sound of talk and laughter could be distinctly heard in the drawing room beyond the arch, but no sound at all in the still, cool hall. Then Brown spoke again in a very different voice. All trace of banter had gone out of it.

"Do you mean to say that this same group of people were staying here seven years ago on the night—"

Franklin so far forgot himself as to interrupt. He was flushed with excitement and delighted at making an impression.

"Yes, sir. It's the same identical house party, with the exception, of course, of Miss Lane, who was too young to be going to house parties then, and the young chap who's secretary to Mr. Grass—Mr. Stuart, sir."

For a moment Brown stood quite still, his shoulders hunched about his ears, his hands hitched forward in the pockets of his dinner jacket, his foot poking at the pattern of the parquet flooring.

"An interesting coincidence," he murmured. And then he glanced up under his brows and grinned at Franklin. "The world is full of interesting coincidences—fate playing havoc with our affairs."

"Ah, indeed, sir," assented Franklin, and he shook his head solemnly.

Brown went on into the drawing room. A moment later he was standing in the window embrasure, drinking a pinkish cocktail and surveying his fellow guests with a keen but unobtrusive interest. As though Franklin's suggestion had been the integrating force he had unconsciously been awaiting, the disordered activities of his mind had fallen into place. He was conscious of a sweet and luminous clarity of thought, a smoothness of functioning, such as visited him occasionally in moments of inspiration.

For the arresting thought had occurred to him that there might be one among the lot to whom the news that Huntington's skeleton lay in the jungle coppice would be no news at all. He was aware that there must be a hundred subtle threads connecting these people with each other and with the dead man in the jungle. It seemed to him suddenly that every gesture they made, every word they exchanged, was full of portent.

Solomon Jura, for instance, sitting across the room on the divan beside pretty, empty-headed Mrs. Drew: who was he? Brown studied his tall, stooped, emaciated figure, his distinguished, narrow face with deep-set eyes and bushy gray brows, and his singularly sweet smile. Jura's face was tanned and weather-beaten with much exposure and looked even browner than it was, by contrast with his gray-white hair. A charming looking fellow, probably between fifty and sixty, an Hungarian, an old friend of Mrs. Huntington, a naturalist who had traveled in out-of-the-way corners of the world and had written books about fish and birds. So far so good. But what did that really tell about him? How was one to know what his relations had been to that dead man in the jungle?

And his companion? Brown had known Stella Drew in Washington: a harmless, silly little creature with red hair and baby-blue eyes. Her husband was employed in one of the government departments—a colorless fellow. One never saw him. She amused herself rather indiscreetly with the floating population of senators. Brown was fairly certain that she was, at the moment, amusing herself rather indiscreetly with Mr. Grass. But there was, as far as he knew, no great harm in her. What possible concern could she have in this? He gave up the enigma with a sigh. He was not getting very far.

Adele was sitting near the door, as he had been instantly aware when he entered the room. But while her eyes had followed him absently he knew that she had hardly been aware of his entrance. She was crouched back in a huge, linen-covered chair, her little white face strained and intent. What a little thing she was—the quietest, palest, dearest little thing, rather pitifully over-shadowed by her more showy stepmother. And she was unhappy. He couldn't define what was the matter. Was Stuart making her miserable? Or Mrs. Huntington? Certainly there was something very wrong.

His eyes lingered on her with sudden penetration. He realized now that there had been something wrong that day he first arrived at World's End—long before that, when he had seen her in Washington. She hadn't the air of a young girl secure in her own home. She wore her clothes with an apologetic awkwardness—she who need not apologize to anyone in the world. There was an uncertainty about everything she did. He fancied her stepmother bullied her in private as she snubbed her in public. He'd like to wring the neck of anyone who snubbed or bullied her! His gaze lingered on her gray eyes and soft brown hair. His look betrayed him, but there was no one to see. For whom was she waiting? Whom was she seeking with those covert glances toward the stairs? He did not need to ask, but he glanced about the room, nevertheless. Stuart was not there.

Brown withdrew his eyes from her with some effort of will and took further stock of the company. Over by the piano Mrs. Huntington was talking to Dr. Simpson. Brown wondered what she would say, what she would do, if he were suddenly to announce to her, across the room, that discovery in the jungle. More than ever he felt the secret power in her dark-browed face, her undeniable fascination.

Across the room Justin was talking to a pretty girl in an orange frock, cut daringly low in the back. This was Isabel Lane, Justin's fiancée, and niece of Daniel Lane. An attractive little piece, certainly, and entertaining in a pert and cocky fashion, but at the moment Brown's glance passed her rather cavalierly. She so obviously did not fall within the scope of his inquiry.

But at this point his thought was interrupted by a voice speaking directly behind him.

"On the contrary, I think it would be the easiest thing in the world to commit a murder in such a way that one would never be found out."

Brown turned toward the voice. Just behind him the three remaining members of the house party were grouped in animated discussion: Lydia Vaughan, Jacob Grass, and Daniel Lane. It was Miss Vaughan who had just spoken. Brown had known her for years: a delightful soul! About forty-five, he fancied; a thorough sportswoman, radiating energy and possessed of a superb aplomb that enabled her to get away with anything, even the atrocious scarlet gown in which she was at the moment attired. He had met her for years at dinner parties in Baltimore and Washington. They got on admirably.

As he turned she caught his eye and beckoned to him.

"Look here," she said to Daniel Lane, as though she had been arguing a point with him. "Here's a lawyer: let's get his opinion about it." She turned toward Brown with a smile. "Mr. Lane says that all murderers are caught sooner or later. There's always a slip somewhere that gives them away. Do you believe that?"

"Oh, come now," protested Daniel Lane, smiling. "Not quite that, you know. I said almost all. Let's say all but two per cent. Do you agree, Mr. Brown?"

Brown wondered which of the three had started the discussion, but he only said with a smile:

"I hadn't thought about it. I dare say you're right."

"Traitor!" cried Lydia Vaughan.

Grass broke heatedly into the dispute.

"Two per cent?" he repeated scornfully. "Nearer fifty, if you ask me. Look at Chicago! Look at those gang murders along the Bowery. Say! Everybody knows who did them, all right, but do they get pulled in? Not on your life. They know a man who knows a man—or else the police think it's healthy to let them alone. Or maybe they're smart and fix it so the 'tecs can't get anything on them. But everybody knows who did it all the same."

"How nice," gurgled Miss Vaughan, "to have that on such good authority!" Clearly Lydia, with her taste for eccentricities, derived innocent merriment from the egregious Mr. Grass. "But that isn't exactly what I mean. I'll bet there are hundreds of murders every year where the murderer is never suspected—where even a murder is never suspected. Deaths that are laid to other causes—natural causes, accident, suicide, or—or disappearance because somebody's done a really intelligent job and left no loose ends."

Grass laughed heavily.

"Intelligent job, eh? Come now, Miss Vaughan—" with elephantine playfulness—"that's naughty. You talk as though murder was a game or a business."

"Apparently it is—sometimes," she answered dryly.

"Or a fine art," interjected Lane, smiling.

"You get my point," she said briskly. "It's an art I've wanted to practice more than once. Perhaps I may, someday. I have my little list."

"It has one disadvantage," Daniel Lane pointed out. "One would have to do without applause from the gallery."

Lydia Vaughan burst out laughing at the preposterous edifice they had erected.

"Nice man!" she commented approvingly, and took a cigarette from Lane's proffered case.

But she did not smoke the cigarette, for at this moment Franklin appeared in the doorway, and Mrs. Huntington rose.

"Shall we go in to dinner?" she said.

A voice broke clearly through the soft chatter of conversation.

"Mr. Stuart hasn't come down yet," said Adele.

"Oh," cried Jacob Grass with a laugh, "we needn't wait for that young feller, if he don't know enough to come down to his dinner, eh, Miss Huntington?"

Brown noticed that she held her eyes away from him as though from something offensive. But she said nothing further. As they moved toward the dining room the lawyer saw her glance wistfully at the empty doorway into the hall before she followed the others.

It was difficult for him to sit beside her at table. His thoughts ran all together into an incoherent mass from which he could pick nothing to say. But to sit there beside her, acutely aware of every move she made, and say nothing, was even more painful.

"What have you been doing with yourself all day?" he asked inanely.

The gray eyes she turned to him held a spark of resentment.

"Don't bother to be nice to me," she said sharply. "It's nothing to me whether you open your mouth during dinner or not."

This brought him to himself, like a dose of cold water in the face.

"Isn't it really?" he murmured. "Do you mind telling me why?"

"Not at all," she retorted equably. "It's just that there seems to be something about me that turns people into half-witted imbeciles the instant they start talking to me. There's quite enough silly chatter going on round this table without your adding to it."

"Oh," murmured Brown with reviving relish. "So you think I'm a half-witted imbecile?"

"Well, don't you? 'What have I been doing all day!'" she quoted scornfully.

He did not reply, but studied her covertly, for it suddenly occurred to him that this was not ill temper, but nerves strained to the breaking point. Something was wrong. Something was very wrong. He probed delicately.

"This Mr. John Stuart," he said craftily. "He's hardly a half-witted imbecile, should you say?"

Glancing at her sidewise, he saw a dull red creep up her throat and tint the ear nearest him. But she said nothing. She seemed determined to say nothing further.

Brown took occasion to look round the long table and the eleven people who sat at it. Jacob Grass sat at his left, and beyond him, at the end of the table, Mrs. Huntington. Looking at their faces, it startled him to see how much they had changed since they had all sat together at lunch. Rather, of course, they had not changed, but his view of them had altered. He was really looking at them, this evening, for the first time. He was seeing the lines their characters had put in their faces, and the revelation was a little startling.

At Mrs. Huntington's left sat Daniel Lane, and then Mrs. Drew. On her left, across the table, was John Stuart's empty chair and beyond that again Dr. Simpson. Next to Simpson was Lydia Vaughan, and beside her, Justin Huntington, upholding the honors of the table's foot. Isabel Lane sat at Justin's other hand, and between her and Adele, completing the circle, was Solomon Jura. And that was the lot. Not a promising group in which to hunt for a murderer. He brought himself up with a jerk. Murderer? After seven years, how was one to be sure?

The general clatter of conversation was suddenly caught and focused by Miss Vaughan, who leaned forward and spoke down the length of the table to her hostess.

"I wonder what can have happened to Mr. Stuart," she said in her pleasant, cordial voice. "I saw him going upstairs to dress—oh, surely an hour and a half ago."

"Perhaps he's fallen asleep," suggested Isabel Lane.

"Don't bother about him," boomed Jacob Grass. "It'll teach him a lesson to miss his dinner."

Adele Huntington's smoldering eyes burned scornfully on Mr. Grass.

"He was very tired, I know," she said clearly. "He'd been up most of the night over his work."

Grass grew faintly purple about the ears. He drove his secretary like a galley slave, but he heartily disliked any mention of the fact. Mrs. Huntington intervened hastily:

"Franklin," she directed the butler, "please go upstairs and see what detains Mr. Stuart."

There was a moment of uncomfortable silence after Franklin's departure, and then they all plunged into conversation. Brown's eyes lingered on John Stuart's empty chair, and his ears strained for the sound of Franklin's returning step. Not that there was any reason for alarm, but something of the tenseness of the girl beside him communicated itself to his own mood. Consequently he heard, as she did, the hurried step descending the stairs and crossing the wide hallway. He smiled to himself. What a fuss to make because a young man fell asleep and slept through the dinner hour!

But it was not Stuart who appeared. It was Franklin, and his face was as white as paper. The man hesitated in the doorway, swaying a little, as though uncertain what to do next. Before anyone else had collected himself enough to move, Brown crossed the room and drew the butler out into the hall.

"What's the matter? Speak up, man!" he commanded brusquely.

The butler wet his dry lips with his tongue.

"It's Mr. Stuart, sir. He—he's hanged himself. I knocked on the door and when he didn't answer I went in. I found him hanging by the cord of his dressing gown—against the closet door, sir."

Chapter VI

The words, spoken in a gasping whisper, could not have reached the group in the dining room, but some sense of perturbation had evidently fallen on them, for as Brown turned he saw their faces wearing one common look of strained attention. His glance turned instinctively to Adele. The girl's face was bloodless, and her hands were clasped together in a gesture that seemed to entreat mercy from the fates. Brown, with a pang of pity, tempered his words to that look.

"I'm sorry," he said. "There has been an—an accident."

She made no sound beyond a little gasp between her parted lips. Brown could not look at her. He turned to Dr. Simpson.

"Stuart has been hurt," he said. "Perhaps you'll come."

Simpson rose at once and Justin followed them into the hall and shut the door after him. Franklin led the way upstairs, almost at a run, and an instant later they were in the little bedroom at the head of the stairs that had been allotted to Mr. Grass's secretary.

It was a small room, with one window looking out to sea. Before the window was a table desk, on which lay neat piles of correspondence, carefully weighted. The only untidy thing in the room was the sprawled, half-dressed figure on the floor beside the open closet door.

"I—I cut it down, sir," said Franklin uncertainly. "I thought perhaps..."

Dr. Simpson bent over the body.

"My God!" he muttered, and straightening up, he looked at Brown with a white face.

"Get at it, man!" cried Brown. "There might be a chance."

"There's no chance," said Simpson in a shaky voice. "He's dead. He's been dead some time!"

"Any way of telling how long?"

Simpson flushed at the obvious impatience in the lawyer's voice.

"Certainly," he said with offended dignity. "Anyone who understands such things can tell with a reasonable certainty."

"Do you understand such things?" inquired Bolivar politely.

Simpson said nothing. He knelt down, took up the dead man's hand and laid it slowly down again, examined the eyelids and drew them down over the horribly staring eyes. For a moment more he knelt there, studying the dead face thoughtfully. Then he got to his feet.

"He's been dead about an hour," he said at last.

Brown looked at his watch.

"It's just eight now. That would make it seven o'clock?"

"Just about then," assented Simpson.

"Suicide!" muttered Justin in the bewildered manner of a man trying to convince himself of an impossibility. And he looked at the overturned chair on which young Stuart had stood against the closet door, and which he had kicked out from under him when the rope was adjusted.

Brown, with his hands in his pockets, was staring down at the dead man.

"He's got the trousers of his dinner clothes on," he said in a surprised voice. He glanced at the bed where lay the discarded gray suit that Stuart had worn when he met him on the beach. He looked inquiringly at Dr. Simpson and at Justin Huntington. "Is there anything about a pair of dinner trousers that makes them more suitable attire for a suicide than—well, say, than gray tweeds?"

Justin shrugged impatiently.

"What are you getting at?" he demanded. "Probably he was already partly dressed for dinner before the idea of doing away with himself occurred to him."

"Ah," murmured Brown admiringly, "you've hit it the first time. Now what was it that caused him, in the very act of dressing for dinner, to decide suddenly that life was no longer bearable to him? Why didn't he think of it ten minutes earlier—or several hours later?"

Justin looked perplexed. Then he shrugged again.

"Well," he said, "I don't see how you're going to find that out now."

"Neither do I," agreed the lawyer amiably. After an instant of hesitation he stepped round Stuart's body and examined the piece of cord that still hung from the hook. Then he glanced at the discarded dressing gown, thrown over a chair near the door. Undoubtedly, as Franklin had said, the cord belonged to the dressing gown. Thoughtfully he considered the relations of the various objects in the room: the dressing gown on the chair near the hall door; the bed against the right wall as one entered the room; the closet just beyond; and beyond that a folding screen. Brown crossed the room and looked behind the screen. He discovered a basin with running water, a shelf and a mirror over it. Stuart's shaving things, still damp from recent use, were on the shelf, and a damp towel was dropped over the edge of the basin. He looked round at the body, clad in dress trousers and undershirt. Apparently Stuart had even gone to the length of shaving.

For a moment the commonplace articles—the razor and the damp towel on the edge of the basin—conjured up such a vivid picture of young Stuart moving about this room that Brown felt an involuntary shudder, as though at the passing of a ghost. He turned back and found Justin conferring with Dr. Simpson.

"I suppose we must notify the police?" he was saying hesitantly.

Simpson looked very uncomfortable.

"I suppose so," he said slowly. "Although there's really nothing for them to do. It's an absolutely clear case. However—"

"I fancy we have no choice in the matter," said the lawyer politely.

"Quite so," agreed Simpson stiffly. He had not forgiven Brown's implied criticism.

"I'll just lock the door," said Brown, "so we can be sure nothing is disturbed before the sheriff gets here."

Simpson swung on him, splotches of angry red showing on his pale face. He opened his mouth to speak, but after all, said nothing. He marched out of the room and waited with the others while Brown locked the door. Then together, yet a little apart, as though a strangeness had entered into their relationship, they went downstairs.

On the way down Brown thought rapidly, and before he had crossed the hall he had made up his mind what he would do. But as he laid his hand on the knob of the dining room door it was wrenched away. The door flew open, and Adele confronted him.

"What's the matter?" she demanded. "Is he badly hurt?"

For an instant Brown's heart failed him, but only for an instant.

"Yes," he said, and his voice was stern. "Mr. Stuart is dead. It looks as though he had hanged himself."

Surely that instant of shocked, gasping silence must mean that the news had come upon them all unprepared? Brown hoped that there would be some telltale sign, but there was not. Or, rather, there were too many. Mrs. Huntington half started up from her chair. Grass ejaculated a startled oath under his breath. Lane's hand jerked and upset the glass at his elbow. Natural enough, surely. Or was it? Could any or all of these things be deliberate, an act planned during those moments of suspense while they waited? But his meditations were interrupted by Adele. He would hardly have known her voice, so harsh and twisted was it. She leaned over the table and spoke almost in Jacob Grass's face.

"You did it," said this strange voice. "You killed him."

Grass grew purple; he pushed his chair back, away from that little face frozen into a mask of hate and grief. Dr. Simpson spoke up then.

"My dear Miss Huntington," he said, "nobody killed him. Or, rather, I should say, he killed himself."

For an instant she seemed not to take in what he had said. Then she swung on him.

"I don't believe it." Her frantic eyes turned from the doctor's to her brother's averted face, and at long last, to Brown. Meeting his eyes, her lips quivered painfully. "Is it true?"

Brown steeled himself to meet that look. At last he said:

"It seems so."

If his words had been a bullet going to her breast she could have acted no differently. She jerked and stiffened like a wounded animal, but she did not fall. Instead, after an instant, she turned back to Jacob Grass.

"You did it, all the same," she cried. "You drove him and drove him; you wore him out until he didn't know what he was doing. Just as much as though you killed him with your own hands, you're his murderer." Her control had snapped utterly. She was shrieking hysterically. Her stepmother came round the end of the table, but Adele turned on her. "Leave me alone," she cried. "Leave me alone."

Suddenly Isabel Lane ran to her and put her arms around the poor little figure, shuddering with sobs now.

"Poor darling," said Isabel gently. "Poor little thing! Come with me." And with an unexpected tenderness that was very moving she led Adele out of the room.

As the door closed behind them Brown took out his handkerchief and wiped his wet forehead.

"Mrs. Huntington," he said, turning to his hostess, "as I understand it, you have had no sort of communication from Mr. Huntington during the last seven years?"

The face she turned to him was full of startled wonder.

"No," she said.

"From the moment he walked out of this house on the night he disappeared you have no knowledge of where he went, or what he did, or what became of him?"

Her hands knotted themselves together, and she drew a long, shivering breath.

"None whatever."

He put his hand in his pocket and took out the gold cigarette case. For an instant he balanced it thoughtfully. Then he laid it before her on the table.

"Can you identify this?"

She stared at it as though it had been a ghost, shrinking from it. Then she looked from it to Brown and back again, and she wet her dry lips with her tongue.

"Yes," she said at last. "It's Stephen's." And then she did a surprising thing. She started to her feet, staring over her shoulder as though she expected to see an apparition standing behind her. Then she turned back to the lawyer. "Where is he? What has happened?"

Brown took up the case and put it back in his pocket.

"Huntington is dead," he said. "The workmen found his body this afternoon when they were clearing out the jungle."

For an instant no one spoke or moved. Then Mrs. Huntington said breathlessly:

"Dead! How did he—die?"

Brown looked round the circle of white faces.

"I'm not quite sure," he said. "When he was found, his body was entwined in the folds of the strangler fig."

A shivering breath, as though a cold wind had suddenly blown upon them. In the stillness the distant chant of voices drifted in through the open windows from the shanties on the point. Then Grass laughed uncertainly.

"By God!" he said. "Are you trying to tell us you believe that nonsense?"

"No," said Bolivar Brown. "I am trying to tell you that I believe Huntington was strangled."

Suddenly Justin spoke up from his end of the table. The boy's face was white, his lips bloodless.

"When was this discovery made?" he asked.

"Just before dinner," Brown told him. "I went to your room to tell you about it at six-thirty, but I couldn't find you."

No one else said anything. Brown took the key of Stuart's room out of his pocket and laid it on the table.

"The police have got to be notified about this," he said, "and they'll want to see Huntington, of course, and Stuart's body, and the room where he died. I've locked the door. Here's the key. I suggest we give it into the custody of—well, say Miss Vaughan, and make her responsible for it until the sheriff comes."

Simpson pulled himself out of the lethargy of horror that engulfed them all.

"I must say," he said, spluttering, "there's something very odd about your manner, Brown. The thing is manifestly suicide, and why you should want to stir up a police investigation..."

Madeleine Huntington had pulled herself together.

"I agree with Dr. Simpson, Mr. Brown. I can't think of permitting the police to be called in. It's—it's preposterous."

Brown smiled grimly.

"I don't think," he said, "that you quite understand the situation. We're in a bad mess—all of us. And it's quite impossible to bury either Mr. Huntington or Stuart without a doctor's certificate. Dr. Simpson knows as well as I do that neither he nor any other physician can give a certificate in cases of violent death without notifying the authorities. If he attempts to tell you otherwise he is misleading you."

"Naturally I am aware of the law relating to such matters," said Simpson angrily. "What I object to is this matter of locking up the room as though there were some doubt that the affair is suicide."

Brown looked at him with a curious smile.

"Is there any doubt?" he asked politely. "Locking the room is merely a matter of routine formality, as I see it, so that none of us may subsequently be open to criticism."

"Well—er—of course—from that point of view," conceded Simpson hesitantly.

"If no one has any objections, then—" Brown paused, but no one spoke. Their faces, as he looked from one to the other, were pallid and strained. He turned at last to Lydia Vaughan and held out the key to her.

She took it without a word and dropped it into the vanity case that was lying in her lap. As she closed the case the snap was distinctly audible.

Ten minutes later, when Franklin, armed with a note from Justin to the sheriff in Summerville, stepped onto the pier to board the launch that was to take him to the mainland, a dim figure detached itself from the shadows of the boathouse and came forward.

"I say," said Brown, thrusting an envelope into Franklin's hands. "Give this to the sheriff along with the other one and say nothing about it, eh? It's a little private matter between us." Something clinked and changed hands in the darkness. "Just our little secret, eh?"

"Oh, my Gawd, sir," whispered Franklin, his voice electric with excitement, "do you really think there's something in it?"

"Something in it? Something in what?"

"You know, sir. They're all here—every last one of them—that was here when Mr. Huntington—"

A sound. The crack of a twig under an incautious foot, the rustle of leaves bent by a passing figure—Brown could not have said; but something stirred in the darkness beyond the boathouse. His hand clamped tight on Franklin's arm.

"That's all right," he said. "Better not to talk about it."

When the butler had gone, Bolivar Brown stood for a long time while the throb of the engine died down in the distance, waiting for a repetition of that sound. Such a little sound it was, coming from somewhere in the shrubbery that bordered the path, or perhaps from the shadow beyond the boathouse. And standing so he was for the first time fully aware of the danger of the game he was playing, and his blood leaped. Some spirit of adventure, long dormant, came to life within him. For a long time he stood, hardly breathing. Some little animal prowling, no doubt. But he was grateful to it for putting him on his guard.

With a last look at the lights of the launch, now almost lost in the distant darkness, he turned back to the house. What a night it was! Heavily sweet with jasmine flowers, full of silence and the silver radiance of moonlight. A night for lovers, not for murder; a night for poets, not for a man skulking under a bush, making little furtive sounds. He stood quite still in the path and listened again. Nothing! While he waited Justin Huntington and Isabel Lane came out through the long drawing room window. As they left the light behind them, Justin's arm went round the girl, and Brown heard the tone of her voice as she spoke to him. A night for lovers! He sighed and went on. As he passed the wing of the house where the family bedrooms were located he heard from an open window above him the sound of irrepressible, heart-broken weeping. A night for murder! Brown set his teeth and went back into the house.

Chapter VII

Sheriff Hawks, dragged from his bed by Franklin, arrived soon after eleven, made his examination, and was gone again by midnight, having washed his hands of the whole affair. He asked to see and question each member of the household separately, and did so with such dispatch that the whole proceeding took hardly more than half an hour. He saw Brown last.

As the lawyer, summoned by Franklin, crossed the hall toward the library, the door opened, and Hawks came out with Jacob Grass. The sheriff was smoking one of Grass's fat cigars and was plainly full of a delicious, reverential excitement.

"Well, now, Mr. Grass," he was saying, "that sure is good of you. The right word in the right quarter, eh? Makes a lot o' difference. It's mighty good of you, and I thank you hearty, sir."

Grass murmured something that Brown did not catch, and Hawks said:

"Lord, no, sir. Not a mite of trouble. Glad to oblige you, sir. I won't forget it."

At this moment he caught sight of Brown and broke off.

"Be with you in a moment, Mr. Brown." He turned back to Grass and held out a large and flabby hand. "Happy to meet you, sir. Hope you're planning to stay with us a while. Anything I can do for you..."

Brown fancied that Grass was not too pleased by these expressions of esteem. He muttered something, shook the extended hand, and turned away. The sheriff motioned grandly to Brown to precede him into the library.

"Fine man, Mr. Grass, sir," opined Hawks, puffing appreciatively at the cigar. "Fine type of old-school politician. It's a pity, sir, that we have not more such men in the public service." Mr. Hawks's soiled white vest, already bulging with importance, bulged still further, and Mr. Brown had an uneasy feeling that he was about to deliver a political speech. "It takes," stated the sheriff importantly, "a great man to appreciate talent in others. I have often observed it."

Brown looked at him shrewdly.

"Ah," he nodded. "As I understand it, you're quite a politician yourself."

Hawks waved the cigar with a deprecating gesture.

"In a small way—in a small way, Mr. Brown. I think I may say that I have some weight in the affairs of this county, sir."

"Ever thought of running for state office?" murmured Brown, and he looked up at Hawks under his brows.

The sheriff flushed faintly.

"I have—er—been urged to do so," he admitted modestly.

"Mr. Grass been urging you?"

Hawks's importance fell from him. He looked at Brown with sudden attention. Then he turned abruptly away to the table, on which lay two or three sheets of paper covered with scrawls, and an open letter. It was the note that Brown had sent by Franklin. He picked it up and turned back to Brown.

"See here," he drawled, and he poked with a stubby finger at the letter. "What's all this about—" he held the paper up before his short-sighted eyes—"about abrasions on the wrists and around the mouth of Stuart's body? This is as plain a case of suicide as ever I see in my life. What do you mean—abrasions?"

"I mean," said the lawyer patiently, "scratches—cuts—wounds."

"Uh-huh," nodded the sheriff. "I suspicioned that was what you meant. But what do you mean *by* it? Why should there be scratches—or cuts or wounds, for the matter of that?"

"I'm sure I don't know," murmured Brown, watching him. "I thought you might be interested, so I just asked you to take a look—as a matter of curiosity."

"Well, then," said the sheriff, "as a matter of curiosity I'll tell you there ain't any—nary scratch nor cut nor wound."

"Ah," said Brown. "That's interesting. I thought I'd noticed a mark on the face—but of course I had no real opportunity to examine the body."

"Well," conceded the sheriff, "there was a little mark on the lower lip—jest such a mark as he might have made biting his lip in his death agony."

Brown's eyes glowed suddenly under his bent brows.

"Interesting!" he murmured. "Have you ever been hanged, sheriff? No? One doesn't bite one's lip, even in one's death agony, when one is being hanged, sheriff." The tone was politely informative, but the sheriff flushed angrily.

"Look here!" he said, more briskly now. "I don't know what your game is, sir, but I'm giving you some advice for your own good. You keep out of this. This is a plain case of suicide, like I said, and that goes. You amatoor sleuths love to go poking your noses into what don't concern you. You take a tip from me and stay outa this."

Brown looked thoughtfully at the floor.

"I suppose," he said diffidently, "there's no doubt that Mr. Huntington's death was—accidental?"

The sheriff laughed with more amiability.

"Hard to say," he admitted. "Probably had an attack of heart failure and fell among the bushes. But that, I fear, sir, is one of the things we'll never really be sure of."

"Do you think so?" murmured Brown. "Do you know, sheriff, I don't share your fear. I fancy that before very long we'll be entirely sure how Huntington died. I think I could make a pretty good guess—right now."

There was a moment of silence, and then Hawks said uneasily:

"If you're thinking of snakes, sir, you're wrong. There isn't a snake on the island."

"As a matter of fact," said Brown slowly, "I wasn't. I was thinking of murder. Huntington was murdered, and so was Stuart. Think that over. If your political career is too important to let you think—well, I'll go over your head to Patona. As sure as God made little apples, sheriff, I will."

For a moment the sheriff's bloodshot eyes peered closely at the lawyer's face.

"I've done all the thinking I need to," he said. He tore the note into small pieces and dropped them into a convenient waste-paper basket. "That's the end of it, as far as I'm concerned."

"Better think it over a bit," urged Brown. "Maybe, on second thought, you'd find it worthwhile to take some further action."

"I've given 'em permission to bury the bodies. I reckon they don't need me to help 'em do that. It's a plain case of suicide and a plain case of accidental death, like I said before. There ain't nothing more for me to do—'cept go home and get me a little sleep. Take my advice, brother, and turn in. You'll have slept it off by mawnin'!"

When the sheriff had gone Brown went out into the hall, and there he met Lydia Vaughan on her way upstairs. Dr. Simpson was with her, and they were evidently in the midst of an argument of some sort, for as Brown approached he heard her say with faintly irritated emphasis:

"My dear man, I don't care why you want it. As I told you before, I gave it to the sheriff, and I haven't the faintest idea what happened to it after that."

Then Simpson saw Brown, and muttering something to the effect that it was all right and didn't matter anyway he went upstairs. Lydia turned to the lawyer with a faint smile.

"What a day!" she said. "Thank heaven we can say that it's over now."

"What's Simpson been pestering you about—if it's not impertinent to ask?"

She shrugged and glanced uncertainly toward the turn of the stairs, where he had disappeared.

"It's queer. He's been after me all evening to let him have the key to Stuart's room. Said he'd left something there—his watch, I believe. Said he'd taken it out to feel Stuart's pulse and laid it down."

"Well, he didn't take it out to feel Stuart's pulse," said Brown, "because he didn't feel Stuart's pulse."

"And he didn't leave it in Stuart's room because I saw him looking at it when Franklin started off to get the sheriff."

For a moment they stared at each other speculatively. Then Brown reverted to her first remark.

"Does it really strike you that this is over?" he asked softly. "I'll confess it seemed to me to be just beginning."

"Just beginning!" she repeated, and he saw suddenly that her face looked worn and tired. "Do you really think—"

"Come into the library and I'll tell you."

"It's after midnight," she demurred.

"When graveyards yawn," he added, smiling. "Come to think of it, they yawn at other times too."

"And I'm past the age when I can do without my beauty sleep."

"You're far too handsome for a single lady, as it is."

She looked at him suspiciously.

"You're not going to pour tender confidences in my ear, are you?" she demanded. "I've just been listening to Justin for an hour, and I can't stand any more."

Instead of answering her he cast a swift glance around the shadowy hall. Then he said in a low voice:

"I'm going to preach a sermon on your own text—something you said before dinner: that many murders are committed that are never discovered. That deaths by murder are often laid to other causes— accident or suicide."

Again that look of insupportable weariness in the fine eyes.

"The sheriff says accident and suicide," she urged.

"You know as well as I do," he said softly, "that the sheriff is wrong."

For an instant she put her hand to her face as though to rub this horror from her mind. Then she looked at him with her habitual poised composure.

"What do you want me to do about it?" she asked.

"I want you to help me."

Without another word she turned toward the library, and he led her to a chair at the other end of the long room, well away from window or door or any possible place of concealment, a fact which did not escape her shrewd notice.

In that short passage across the room she had quite recovered herself. Now she crossed her shapely legs, took a cigarette from a tortoise-shell case in her bag, and lighted it.

"I've carried my own," she said, "ever since a rude young man complained to me about the cadging women do. But I never offer to supply the sterner sex. It undermines their sense of superiority."

Brown chuckled as he took out his pipe.

"You're so logical," he complained. "I hate logical women. They lack charm."

Lydia Vaughan leaned over, surprisingly, and patted his hand.

"You're quite a darling, you know," she said, with an odd softness in her clear voice. For a moment she studied him speculatively. Then she said: "Have you any good reason for thinking that Stuart's death may not be—suicide? Or are you just guessing?"

For an instant Brown paused, collecting his ideas. Then he shrugged.

"I'll admit my reasons sound foolish, taken each by itself. They're all little things. But taken all together they add up to quite a total. Item one: Stuart's door wasn't locked when Franklin went up to call him to dinner. If you were going to hang yourself to a hook in your closet, wouldn't you lock your bedroom door first?"

Lydia Vaughan shivered slightly.

"I wish you wouldn't be so personal," she complained. "Nothing would induce me to pick that means of exit from the world. Well?"

"Item two: this silly business of the dress trousers. No one applauds more heartily than I the good old British custom of dressing for dinner, but when it comes to dressing for one's own hanging—I protest. If he'd been going to shoot himself, I could understand it, but hanging is, at best, an undress affair. One can't, for instance, go in for collars—"

Lydia paled, and the hand that held her cigarette shook.

"I think," she said, "you'll have to be a little less hard-boiled about this."

"I beg your pardon," said Brown contritely. "I don't see how one is to face such a situation at all if one isn't hard-boiled."

"But motive? Motive?" cried Miss Vaughan. "You can't have a murder without a motive."

"You can't have a suicide without a motive, either," Brown reminded her. "And I happen to know one reason, and I can guess at another, that Stuart had for living. This talk about Grass working him to death is all fiddle-me-eye. Stuart was no fool. If he worked hard for Grass it was because he had a reason for it. He could have got another job if he'd wanted to. He was young, and sound in wind and limb; he was shrewd as the devil. Unless all signs fail"—Brown said the words with a rush as though bound to get through with them—"he was conducting a highly successful wooing."

"Of a highly eligible heiress," nodded Miss Vaughan.

"You've noticed it too?" he asked, and Lydia, for all her astuteness, failed to observe the tightness in his voice.

"Who could help it? Even if one could have overlooked the very obvious fact of Adele's obsession, Madeleine's attitude would have made it plain."

"So it's true that Mrs. Huntington opposed the match?"

"Opposed? Well," said Lydia thoughtfully, "that's certainly not exaggerating. She was quite violent about it."

Brown applied his fifth match to his pipe before he went on.

"Is Mrs. Huntington the sort of woman who would be influenced in her attitude by Huntington's will?"

"So you know about that, too," murmured Lydia. "You have certainly not wasted your time." She smoothed the scarlet taffeta on her knee with a thoughtful gesture. At last she looked up at him shrewdly. "I don't know. Long as I have known Madeleine, well as I know her—in some ways—there are things about her I have never understood. What you suggest might be true—and it might not. She is as hard as flint in some ways—and amazingly tender in others. She's a very strange creature. I advise you not to jump to conclusions concerning her."

Brown nodded.

"You're absolutely priceless," he said. "So priceless that I'm going to tell you something I'd no intention of confiding to a soul. I'm going to tell you why Stuart was killed." He described to her briefly the scene in the jungle when Huntington's skeleton was identified and Stuart's obvious excitement about it.

"You mean," she said when he had finished, "that Stuart may have had some knowledge of Mr. Huntington's death and that someone did away with him to silence him?"

"No," said Brown sternly. "I don't mean that. I mean that Stuart *did* have some knowledge of Huntington's murder; that when he came back to the house he taxed the murderer with his guilt— No, on second thoughts, that's a bit strong. He probably confronted the person he suspected with such evidence as he had and asked him—or her—to explain it. It's entirely conceivable that explanations would be —a little difficult. It's quite conceivable that the only argument that would silence Stuart—"

Brown broke off suddenly in mid-sentence. His startled eyes tensed and focused upon something behind Lydia Vaughan. She glanced nervously over her shoulder before she realized that it was at nothing corporeal that he was staring but at some vision of his mind's eye. The truth was that Brown was suddenly seeing a dark corridor, cut by a beam of light through Stuart's open door—a beam that cast a distorted shadow on the opposite wall. And he knew why it was that the closing of that door had struck him as odd. No one had come out, because the murderer had gone in!

Desperately he tried to recapture the elusive shape of that shadow on the wall, but it escaped him. He could not even be sure if it had been the shadow of a man or of a woman. Long, grotesque, menacing, it had stretched across the floor and up the wall for a fleeting instant and had been blotted out.

Chapter VIII

Brown flung out of his chair impatiently and took a long turn up and down the room. Presently he came back and stood in front of Miss Vaughan, pipe clenched in his teeth, head thrust forward between his hunched shoulders. He looked like a strange, uncouth bird of prey foiled of his supper.

"Do you know," he growled, "that I practically had this whole thing in my hand—if I'd asked a question or made a move—almost any move—good Lord! What an ass! What an imbecile!" He ran an aggrieved hand through his hair, but succeeded only in making himself look startled as well as indignant. "If I'd so much as put out my hand I could hardly have failed to touch the murderer's coat tales—or petticoat! And instead," he finished scornfully, "I went hunting for a collar button!" Again he paused, so to speak, in the middle of a breath, remembering Simpson's empty room. Where had the doctor been half an hour before dinnertime, with his rabbit's face and pinkish eyes? Abruptly Brown sat down again, took the pipe out of his mouth, and leaned forward, elbows on his knees.

"Now," he said, "since we're playing question and answer, you tell me something. How did it happen that it was Stuart who had this information concerning Huntington's death?"

She shrank wearily back in her chair. In his excitement it escaped him that she looked gray and old.

"I don't understand," she said.

"I mean," he went on, as though this made everything clear, "why wasn't it Grass, or Lane, or Jura—or even Mrs. Huntington?"

She managed to summon a wan smile.

"This isn't question and answer," she complained. "It's a conundrum, and I can't guess it."

"Probably," he said patiently, "you haven't realized that the same crowd is here that was here at the time of Huntington's disappearance."

He noticed it then. He could not help but notice it. Her lips were blue.

"I'm sorry!" he cried contritely. "I'd forgotten, for the moment, that this is something more than an academic question to you."

She drew a long, quivering breath.

"It's all right," she said. "I had realized it, of course, but I hadn't quite realized its—significance. I'm afraid I'm very slow, but I don't yet understand your question."

"It struck me as odd," said Brown more gently, "that Stuart—who was not here when Huntington disappeared—should happen to be the one that was possessed of evidence which would convict Huntington's murderer. Where did he get it? How did he get it? If he'd been here— but he wasn't. He—"

And then Brown saw to his consternation that Lydia Vaughan was crying—strange, unaccustomed tears that streaked unnoticed across the faint rouge on her cheeks. He stopped, appalled. She took a handkerchief out of her bag and wiped the tears away.

"It must be all of ten years since I've done that," she said calmly. "You said before that Stephen Huntington was murdered, but I think I didn't quite take it in. Is it true?"

"Yes," said Brown. "I haven't proved it yet, but I can. It's capable of proof. He was murdered, and Stuart, by some curious means, found out something that indicated who did it. He confronted the person he suspected with this evidence—and he was killed. It was," said Brown, and there was a note of surprise in his voice, "a singularly stupid act— for a man as intelligent as Stuart."

Lydia opened her mouth to say something, but Brown stopped her with a gesture.

"Wait a minute," he said softly. "Wait a minute. I've got hold of something. What sort of evidence could it have been that would have been valid after seven years? What must it have been? Not hearsay, surely—not a rumor—something definite, concrete—something that would be telling and conclusive after a long passage of time. Something—written?"

Lydia Vaughan stared at him, fascinated. There was a flush on his sharp cheekbones; his eyes shone with an extraordinary brilliance. Suddenly he brought his hand down on his knee with a light gesture of triumph.

"My God!" he said softly. "Why wasn't there a bathroom attached to Stuart's room?"

Lydia gasped. She had a horrible sensation of the logical world falling out from under her. Had he lost his wits? But before she could make up her mind what to say Brown went on:

"Who would furnish a bedroom with office furniture? Who would paper a bedroom with grass paper?"

Miss Vaughan had only a frantic impulse to humor him.

"Why, no one, I should think," she said soothingly.

"Right the first time," cried Bolivar Brown, and he grinned broadly. "Consequently it isn't a bedroom."

"But—" Lydia's brain was completely reeling now—"but there's a bed in it."

"Certainly there's a bed in it," agreed the lawyer patiently. "That's what misled me. It's so easy to be misled by superficial observation. If one sees a bed in a room one jumps at once to the conclusion that that room was meant to sleep in, but Stuart's room wasn't meant to sleep in. It was meant to work in. It has a big, flat office desk under the window, with a swivel office chair in front of it. It has one of those extension office bookcases against the left wall, and a file case. And it's papered with brown grass paper. And it hasn't a bathroom. Whoever heard of a guest room in a house of this pretension that didn't have a communicating bath?"

"You mean—" Lydia leaned toward him, and her face was almost as excited as his.

"I mean," said Brown, "that, ten to one, that room used to be Huntington's study. It certainly was some man's study, and Huntington's the only man who would have had a study in this house."

"Yes," breathed Miss Vaughan. "It was his study. Of course it was his study."

"And they put Stuart in there because the house was full and because he, being Grass's secretary, would need a desk to work at—Huntington's desk."

"I can't bear it," whispered Lydia Vaughan. "You mean that, in Stephen's desk—"

"In Stephen Huntington's desk," said Brown, "he found something —a paper—a letter—something that had been overlooked when the desk was cleaned out—something that had slipped behind a drawer, or under the shelf you pull out to write on—"

He broke off. He did not need to finish the sentence. They stared at each other.

"Suppose," said the lawyer, "you tell me everything you can—every last detail you can remember—about the night Stephen Huntington disappeared and the people who were here."

Lydia Vaughan took another cigarette out of her tortoise-shell case and lit it with steady hands. Her eyes were suddenly thoughtful. Brown waited patiently. All around them was stillness, acute, aching, punctuated only by the slow beat of surf on the seaward beach.

"All right," said Lydia at last. "I can tell you a good deal about that night because, I may as well confess, I've had some thoughts of my own about that business, and I've speculated about it, on and off, a good deal.

"You see, I've known Stephen Huntington all my life. We used to meet at Bar Harbor in the summer, when we were youngsters. He was several years older than I, but for several summers we were great pals

—swimming, sailing, playing together. Then he graduated from college and went to work, and I didn't see him for a long time. Next thing I knew, I got the announcement of his marriage.

"I never knew the first Mrs. Huntington. I met her, of course, but hardly more than that. Indeed, I hardly saw Stephen during her lifetime. He was busy doubling the fortune his father left him. But after her death I began to see something of him again. He went into politics about that time. He ran on some fusion reform ticket and was elected Senator from New York. And when he came to live in Washington he came to see me. From then on until his disappearance I saw a good deal of him. In fact, I introduced him to the present Mrs. Huntington. She was Madeleine Bingham then, widow of Waldo Bingham, the naturalist.

"She's a handsome woman now, but ten years ago she was stunning. She looked like a dark-haired Diana, a little worn, to be sure, but fascinating. And there was a sort of glamour about her. She'd traveled with Bingham all over the world, to the most outlandish places, and some of the color and thrill of her adventures had clung to her. Stephen fell for her like a shot. They were married within four months.

"About this time he bought World's End and began to build here. Three years later—that is seven years ago—I was invited to visit them. It was during that visit that Stephen disappeared."

"You make it singularly clear," said Brown. "Now, about the other people who were here."

"Yes. Well, you must remember that Stephen was in politics at that time, and the social life of a senator is usually semi-political. Most of these people were connected with him in one or other of his political enterprises. Jacob Grass with one of the powers behind the throne at Albany and had been instrumental in getting Stephen elected. Mr. Lane was then Senator from Pennsylvania, and one of Stephen's fellow workers on the Shipping Board. Dr. Simpson's connection is not so clear. He was one of the Port of New York doctors, and he may have been angling for something better. I gathered that he and Stephen had had dealings before, but just what it was all about I don't know."

Miss Vaughan paused to tamp out her cigarette, and Brown asked:

"How about Mrs. Drew?"

Lydia shrugged and laughed.

"I've never gone in much for ladies of Mrs. Drew's type. I never could see how Madeleine stands her. She rather fancies herself as a lady lobbyist, I think. Anyway, she's always cultivating one senator or another."

Brown smiled.

"I gathered as much. I've run across her in Washington."

"I might have known *you'd* know about her," said Lydia tartly. "She's a great friend of Mr. Grass." After a moment she added: "The lady has a husband, you know. She's buried him somewhere in the civil service. There was some gossip last fall that he'd plucked up courage enough to have some words with Mr. Grass, but I can't vouch for the truth of the tale."

"And Jura?"

Miss Vaughan knit her handsome brows.

"I've never been able to fit Jura into the picture," she admitted, "or, indeed, any picture. He arrived just after I did, in a ridiculous little launch, towing a glass-bottomed boat. He'd been making a voyage along the coast, studying fish, so he said. I gathered that he'd been making World's End his headquarters all winter, coming and going when it pleased him. I think his presence at that particular moment was an accident. I don't believe he had any connection with the people here—except, of course, Madeleine."

"And what connection," murmured Brown, "had he with her?"

"He was an old friend. I'd never seen him before, but I'd often heard her speak of him. She'd met him on one of the trips she made with Waldo Bingham."

"And that's the lot, isn't it?" asked Brown. "Except, of course, Adele and Justin."

Lydia nodded.

"Adele was a little girl—thirteen or fourteen. And Justin was in college. He was here at the time, though. It must have been his mid-year holiday."

"I've got it straight, I think," the lawyer told her. "Now for the night of Huntington's disappearance."

"The funny thing about that night," said Lydia slowly, "was that it was all so perfectly natural. It was very warm, and we dined with all the windows open on the terrace—a lovely starlit night, as I remember. We were all very gay, and for the life of me I can't recall a sense of strain or any feeling that anything was wrong."

"Huntington quite as usual?"

"Oh, in his best vein. He was a charming man—really charming. And he had wit. I remember that he seemed overflowing with satisfaction and good nature. He was perfectly crazy about Madeleine, and she played up to him—I'll say that for her."

"Do I seem to detect," murmured Bolivar Brown, "that you lose no love in that direction?"

Lydia made a face.

"Don't ask too much of a mere human woman," she said. She took out another cigarette and lighted it. "I'm fond of Madeleine, of course. But she's the sort of woman that other women will always be catty about."

Brown laughed.

"Well?" he prodded.

"Well," Miss Vaughn went on, "as I said before, everything was quite smooth and balmy at dinner. Afterward we had coffee on the terrace and then someone suggested bridge. I was tired from my journey and begged off. Jura didn't play bridge. He sat and talked to me for a while, and then he went off. I don't know, of my own knowledge, anything more about him that night. He said, afterward, that he had been in his room all evening, working on a paper for the Geographic. Justin went off right after dinner, with Adele.

"That left five. No, wait a minute: six. I'd almost forgotten Dr. Simpson. He hadn't come down to dinner at all, by the way. He'd burned his shoulders raw on the beach the day before and was laid up in his room.

"So that leaves Madeleine, Stephen, Mr. Grass, Mr. Lane, and Mrs. Drew to be accounted for. I could see them in the drawing room through the long windows. Franklin brought in a card table, and they had some sort of polite argument about who should play. At last Stephen said he'd smoke a cigar on the terrace and join them later. So Madeleine, Mr. Lane, Mrs. Drew, and Mr. Grass sat down to play.

"From my chair on the terrace I could see them at their game. Stephen strolled up and down for a while. I could see the tip of his cigar glowing in the darkness. When Jura left me and went upstairs Stephen came over to me. We chatted for about fifteen minutes, and then he got up and said he guessed he'd take a stroll down the island. 'Want to come?' he asked. But I told him I was too tired. So he went off by himself. It was so still I could hear his footsteps far down the island. And the voices of the people at their game. And even the slap of the cards as they shuffled and dealt." Lydia Vaughan's eyes were suddenly bright with unaccustomed moisture. "I wish I had gone with him," she said softly. "How many times since I've wished that I had gone with him. Perhaps, if I had—" She blinked rapidly for a moment. Then she gave a shamefaced little laugh.

"There's no fool like an old fool," she said ruefully, "That, I believe, was the last that was seen of Stephen Huntington—alive."

"You say you talked with Senator Huntington for fifteen minutes or so. What about?"

"Nothing particular. This and that. As a matter of fact, I did most of the talking. And then I noticed that he was unusually silent and taxed him with it."

"Silent?" interrupted Brown. "Do you mean that he seemed disturbed about anything?"

"No. He seemed thoughtful, abstracted. For a moment he didn't answer. Then he said, apropos of nothing we had been talking about, 'Remember that time we got caught in a storm off Bar Harbor—in your sailboat, wasn't it, Lydia—the *Catbird?*'

"I said I remembered. And then he said something I've puzzled over a good deal since. He said: 'Just before the storm came up it was very quiet, if you recall; and there was a curious effect on the water that seemed to make the land look nearer than it was and the horizon much farther away. It altered all the natural perspectives. My perspectives have changed a lot since then. Sometimes it's not very easy to keep them straight.'

"I expected him to go on, but he didn't. He got up then and said he'd take a stroll down the island, and I knew that whatever confidence had lurked in the back of his mind he had decided to leave it there."

"And that was all?"

"Every last word."

"What happened to the others—the bridge players?"

"They played a rubber, and then Lane said they should give Huntington a chance, so he came out to look for him. He called, and I told him that Stephen had walked on down the island. Lane strolled down the path a little way, and then after a few minutes, he came back."

"Could you see him all the time?"

"No; but he couldn't have gone far, for I could hear his steps, except for a minute or two when he stood, I suppose, and looked down the island. Presently he came back and said he could see no sign of Stephen. He went indoors, and they began to play again. Soon after that I went upstairs."

"What time was that?"

"Oh, about eleven, I suppose. I can't be sure exactly, but it certainly wasn't much later than that."

"And do you know what time they began to look for Huntington?"

"I heard voices under my window about one o'clock, and gathering that something was wrong, I went out to inquire. I met Madeleine and Solomon Jura coming upstairs. She told me that they had just been down to the point to look for Stephen but had not found him, so they had roused the servants to make a search. They supposed he must have fallen asleep somewhere. Just then Mr. Grass and Mr. Lane and Dr. Simpson came out of their rooms, and when they heard what was wrong they offered to join the search party. Nobody had any more sleep that night.

"They searched for an hour, and then Franklin served up a sort of breakfast-supper, and they waited for daylight. Then they were at it again. They searched the island from end to end, but they couldn't find a trace of him. Nor could they find any indication that a boat had touched at the island that night. And every boat belonging to the island was at its moorings—except a rowboat, moored to a stake at the far end, beyond the jungle, where there is a little summerhouse on the rocks."

Brown nodded.

"I know the place."

"Yes. Well, that boat was gone."

For a moment neither spoke. They were oppressed with their own thoughts. Then Brown asked:

"And no one—except Huntington—was gone from the island?"

"No one." She looked thoughtfully at Brown. "The boat could have drifted away," she said.

"It could have been untied and turned loose," said Brown. "Naturally, a way had to be provided for Huntington to leave the island."

Again that odd little silence. Then Lydia resumed her story.

"When they were quite sure they couldn't find Stephen, they called in the police. Not that they did any good. They looked for the boat, and when they couldn't find it they decided that one of two things must have happened: either Mr. Huntington must have made land in his rowboat and gone off—or he had capsized and been drowned. And neither supposition," she finished dryly, "was particularly helpful."

"Did you believe that Huntington had gone off in this manner?" the lawyer asked.

She answered him dully, not looking at him.

"No."

"What did you believe?"

"I? What did it matter what I believed?" Suddenly something flared up in Miss Vaughan's handsome face that Brown had never seen there before—an emotion so deep and powerful that it swept all thought of concealment before it. "Do you know what I have thought—all these years? I've thought that perhaps—perhaps, mind you!—Madeleine and her dear old friend disposed of Stephen and threw him into the sea!"

"Oh, come now!" remonstrated Bolivar Brown. "You don't really think that, you know. If you did, you'd hardly be here, would you?"

Lydia Vaughan was ghastly white. She put her hands up to her head in a distraught gesture.

"What on earth made me say that?" she asked. "No, of course, I don't think it. Things like that aren't—aren't done. It's just that the thought has run through my mind at moments—what if they had, you know. No one really knew where Mr. Jura had been that evening—and they had gone down the island together, in the middle of the night— and Madeleine never had loved Stephen—never! You see," said Lydia wearily, "you see, I'd have married Stephen Huntington—if he'd ever asked me. But he never did. And so I've cultivated a sense of humor instead. But it isn't always—so very funny."

She rose and looked down at him for a moment.

"You see, I was right," she said with something approaching her usual manner. "I do need my beauty sleep."

And with a little nod she left him, staring, in amazed conjecture, at the spot she had vacated.

Chapter IX

After Miss Vaughan had left him, Brown went upstairs and tried the handle of Stuart's door. The handle turned, but the door would not open. For a moment he stared at it thoughtfully, debating the importance of an immediate search. Was it possible that the murderer would have left behind him the incriminating document—letter or paper—supposing that it had actually existed? Brown, recalling his impression of Stuart, tried to reconstruct the scene that must have taken place in that locked room.

He realized now, with a start, that he must himself have overheard part of that interview. He recalled that when he first came upstairs he had stood outside this door and heard Stuart's voice running on and on to some unseen listener. Yet could that, after all, have been the murderer to whom Stuart was talking? It was almost half an hour later that Brown had seen Stuart's door standing open, and then closing softly upon someone who went in and shut it after him.

The lawyer hesitated, perplexed. Surely, after the closing of that door, there would not have been time for the interview that must have taken place between young Stuart and the person who killed him. There would not have been time for this person to make up his—or her—mind to the murder, to commit it, and to get downstairs before Brown himself had descended. It had been only a matter of half an hour at the outside. And every other member of the house party had been in the drawing room when he went down.

And then, once again, the mixed, kaleidoscopic colors fell into a clear pattern. He remembered suddenly the sound of water running into a basin, which he had heard through that open door, and the memory, oddly enough, threw the whole, confused situation into focus. Stuart had been shaving behind the screen when the murderer entered that last time! Brown went back to the beginning and started again.

Stuart had rushed back to the house after the identification of Huntington's skeleton, eager to confront some person unknown with the fact of the discovery and the proof of the unknown's guilt in connection with it. He had at once taken this person to his room and had accused him of guilty knowledge of Huntington's death. Had he actually produced his evidence, or had he merely stated that he held it? Brown debated the point in his mind. After all, Stuart was an exceedingly shrewd young man, and he must have been aware that he was dealing with a man who would not stick at trifles. The odds were all against his betraying to this unseen visitor where he kept his proof.

In which case the letter—or other paper—would still be in that locked room unless the murderer had found it and taken it away! Could he have done that in the time at his disposal? Brown returned to his reconstruction of events.

Whether the interview included a threat of blackmail, or whether Stuart's interest in the matter was a pure desire to further the ends of justice, might never be known. Either way, it must have left the guilty party—man or woman—with the information that his secret was known. No doubt he agreed to think the matter over and returned to his room. That must be it, of course. To strangle a wiry, athletic young man would be no easy matter to anyone but a master of *jiu-jitsu*. Certainly it could not be done by direct frontal attack, with no element of surprise thrown in. There had been no sound—and no signs—of violent struggle. So the murderer must have gone away—that was it, of course!

He had gone away, decided on his line of action, gone back, heard the sound of running water in Stuart's room, guessed that he would be behind the screen, and let himself quietly into the room. Perhaps he had gone provided with a cord, but, seeing the dressing gown lying over the chair within reach of his hand, had used that cord instead, as less likely to attract attention to any possible outside agent. Perhaps he had substituted the dressing gown cord after his work was done. Anyway, he must have crept up to the screen, caught Stuart unawares, jerked the cord before he could cry out—

Brown came to himself with a start, and found himself still standing in the dim hallway, staring at Stuart's locked door. He shivered faintly. It was all an elaborate tissue of guesses, but somehow the guesses had the ring of fact about them. He looked at his watch: after one o'clock. He'd have a go at Jura first and then see about getting into this room, when everyone would be sure to have turned in. Thrusting his watch back into his pocket, he went along the corridor to Jura's room.

He found the older man in an ancient dressing gown, reading by the open window.

Brown had never been in this room before, and as they chatted he looked about him with interest. It was evidently a sitting room, with a bedroom beyond. Around three walls were glass cases filled with specimens of exotic-looking birds, carefully stuffed and mounted. And above the cases the walls were covered with watercolor sketches of strange-looking fish, some extraordinarily beautiful, and others monstrosities, whose natural habitat, one would have said, must be the disturbed waters of a nightmare.

"Your work?" Brown asked.

The naturalist nodded.

"Watercolor painting is a hobby of mine, and it's so useful to me that I cultivate it. Mrs. Huntington is kind enough to let me use this room as a sort of museum," he went on, as though feeling that the collection needed an explanation. "For years now I've been exploring this coast, and I don't know how I'd manage if she didn't let me keep a sort of *pied à terre* here."[3]

"Fascinating work, I should think," commented Brown, his eyes including the whole collection.

The older man's fine, intelligent face flamed suddenly with a glow of enthusiasm.

"A sort of glorified amusement," he said, smiling. "It's a fortunate man who can make a profession of his hobby."

His gaze went lovingly from one specimen to another, and Brown studied him, unobserved.

It seemed to the lawyer that he had seldom seen a more open, frank, and charming countenance. Jura's eyes had a clear, candid look and his manner the unassuming, open honesty of a man who has spent his life in careful observation of the truth. Brown's long experience as a lawyer had taught him to weigh and judge the honesty of the men upon whose testimony he had to depend, and the bland innocence of the expert swindler was well known to him. Here, unless he was sadly mistaken, was virtue of a different brand.

Jura's eyes, completing the circuit of the room, came back to his visitor in time to glimpse, so to speak, the vanishing coat tails of his speculation. A curious look replaced, for an instant, the candor in the naturalist's face: a strange, furtive, almost terrified look. It was gone instantly, but it had been there; unmistakably it had been there. And suddenly Brown realized that he had seen that look before.

What could it mean? He had done nothing whatever to indicate suspicion of any sort. As a matter of fact, he had no suspicion. He liked Jura. His look could have betrayed nothing more than a certain speculation, a wonder. Was there something that Jura did not want anyone to "wonder" about? That speculation, for some reason, frightened him? Brown listened to the older man's easy talk of his experience and marveled. His imagination was playing tricks with him; that was it. But secretly he knew that his imagination had nothing to do with it. There was something—however innocent—that Jura did not want him to know. Something so imminent and terrible to the naturalist that it instantly leaped to his mind when anyone looked at him with more than ordinary interest. What was it? Brown set the query aside for future consideration.

---

3 *Pied-à-terre*: French literal: "foot to the ground"; a temporary lodging.

"Speaking of marvels," he said suddenly, "do you know anything about this vine they call the strangler fig?"

Jura nodded, quite himself again.

"Certainly I know it." He spoke English with the utmost freedom, but his voice had a faint trace of foreign intonation that was more a pleasant eccentricity than an accent. "Certainly I know it. A most curious growth. A parasite. In Haiti they call it the *figue maudit*. It germinates on the branch, let us say, of a tree, puts down strong, reaching tentacles that twine themselves about any object they encounter. I've known it to go painstakingly through a wood, killing every tree within reach, and wind up by strangling itself. The local name, of course, is derived from its peculiar characteristics. The fig part of it comes from the fruit of the vine, which looks a little like a ripe fig."

"Curious," commented Brown. "Do you think that this vine could actually strangle a human being? One hears such tales," he excused himself.

Jura laughed, a pleasant, ringing laugh that sounded reassuringly normal.

"Oh, dear, no! That's local superstition, pure and simple."

"You don't believe then," said the lawyer with his crooked smile, "that local superstitions have their foundation in a certain amount of fact?"

"No doubt, no doubt," Jura nodded. "But one must be careful not to interpret them too literally. This vine grows rapidly, it is true—very rapidly. About some unmoving object—a tree, for example—it could place its stranglehold in—well, say a month, two months. More than that it could not do. It is, after all, not a boa constrictor. It is alive only in the sense that plants live—not with the life of a man."

"Not with the life of a man," repeated Brown thoughtfully. "Thanks very much. That is just what I was getting at."

Jura looked at him with some shrewdness in his candid eyes.

"Of course," he said, "I cannot help knowing of what you are thinking."

Brown nodded, but he said nothing. He was seeing a path through a jungle, and a coil, a coil of something, he could not be sure what, reaching out, twining about the figure of a man walking in that path, jerking him sideways into the heavy growth, into oblivion. And against this mental image another image formed, like a double exposure on a single negative, blurring and mingling with the original picture: a small, tidy room, with neatly weighted piles of correspondence on the desk; a young man in black trousers and undershirt coming round a screen, and a coil of something—in this case a twisted cord belonging to a bath robe—twisting about his neck, stifling his cries, lifting him against a swinging closet door. Brown took from his pocket the envelope containing the brown matter he had taken from Huntington's skeleton. He turned it over and over in his hands for a moment. Then he looked across at the naturalist.

"Have you a microscope with you?" he asked.

Jura's brows went up in surprise.

"A small one," he admitted. "I occasionally use it on my travels and always carry it with me."

He pulled open a drawer under his table and brought out a neat leather case. From it he took the instrument and set it up on the table. Then he turned to the lawyer.

"You want me to examine something for you?"

Brown took one of the little brown scraps from the envelope.

"Look at this, will you?" he begged. "Do you think you can tell me what it is?"

He waited patiently while Jura adjusted the lenses of the microscope and bent over it. For what seemed an interminable time the naturalist studied the tiny brown strip. At length he straightened up and looked across at Brown.

"This is—interesting," he said, "in view of what we have been saying. This is a very much rotted strand of hempen rope."

"You have no doubt of that?" demanded the younger man eagerly.

"There can be no possible doubt of it."

Brown replaced the strands in the envelope with hands that were suddenly a little unsteady with excitement.

"Thank you very much," he said. "I was almost sure of it, but I had to be positive."

For a moment Jura stood staring down at the microscope between his hands. At last he said slowly:

"We give over too easily our belief in the mysterious—in the unseen workings of fate—destiny—what you will. Who could have believed that this crime would ever come to light?"

Brown nodded. As he went back to his room along the silent corridor he was very thoughtful.

With his door locked behind him, Brown did something he had never done in his life before. He looked into the closets and under the bed for a possible intruder. For there could no longer be any doubt of it. He had stumbled upon the trail of an intrigue the end of which he could not see, but the path to that end was fraught with no uncertain danger—danger not less acute because he could not see from what point it might come. When he was quite sure he was alone he again took out the envelope and weighed it thoughtfully in his hand. Those little strips might, for all he knew, serve again as a noose to jerk the life out of a man, even as they had once served. For when he found them they had been twisted over and under the neck of Stephen Huntington's skeleton, where it lay entwined in the core of the strangler fig.

Suddenly, as he stood there with the envelope in his hands, something happened. There was a step in the hall outside, and a faint knock on the door. He put the envelope back in his pocket and went to the door.

"Who is it?" he asked through the panels.

"It is I—Adele Huntington."

For an instant he was too amazed to move. Then he turned the key and opened the door. To his astonishment she brushed past him, closed the door behind her and leaned against it, breathing quickly as though she had been running. His face must have betrayed him, for she answered his unspoken question.

"Yes," she said, "I know it's two o'clock in the morning. But I've got to talk to you now. There's something I've got to know."

She swayed, her face deathly white, her hands clutching the folds of her blue dressing gown across her breast. Brown was almost as white. He put her into a chair and stood helplessly watching her. He would have given joyfully anything he possessed to have been able to take that look of suffering from her eyes. What did she know—what did she suspect? What was it that was tormenting her? She had changed pitifully in the last few hours. She looked so frail, so broken.

"Let me call somebody," he urged. "Mrs. Huntington—"

But the look in her face stopped him.

"I won't have that woman come near me," she said through bloodless lips. "You're like all the rest—blind." She put her hands before her eyes. "I'm sorry. I'm not myself. It's been pretty bad—all evening. I won't keep you long. But there's something I must know. They gave me a sleeping powder to take, but I didn't take it. There was something I had to think out before I could sleep. Something I had to remember. So I waited until they thought I was asleep and went away. Then I got up and walked up and down."

Brown drew a chair in front of her and sat down. He took her fluttering, helpless hands and held them gently. The touch seemed to steady her. Something of the wildness in her eyes died down. After a moment he prompted her gently:

"You walked up and down trying to remember?"

"Yes. All evening I've known there was something—something I didn't understand about John. It crossed my mind just at first, and then I suffered so, I forgot again. Something I couldn't understand."

Again she paused. It seemed to the lawyer that he had never seen such exhaustion. It was as though the girl were holding herself upright by sheer force of will, all strength being gone from her frail body. Again he prompted her.

"And after a while you remembered what it was?"

"Yes," she said. "I remembered I wanted to ask you something. When Franklin came up to—to call Mr. Stuart, he came down again to the dining room almost at once. Almost at once. How did he find out so quickly—what had happened?"

Brown hesitated.

"I don't understand what you mean," he said gently.

"He didn't have time to break the lock of Mr. Stuart's door. Did he have a pass key?"

"Oh, that!" said the lawyer, enlightened. "He didn't need a key. Mr. Stuart's door wasn't locked."

"It wasn't locked?" repeated Adele Huntington. Suddenly she was on her feet, clutching at his arm, staring into his face. "Did you say the door wasn't locked?"

"I'll confess it seemed strange to me, too," admitted Brown. "But Franklin himself told me it was unlocked. He knocked, and when no one answered, he opened he door."

"But, Mr. Brown," said Adele quietly, "that door was locked. I myself know that it was locked."

A sudden chill quivered along the lawyer's spine—some premonition, perhaps, of what the girl was about to say.

"How do you know that?" he demanded.

"On my way down to dinner," she told him, "I knocked on Mr. Stuart's door. There was—there was something I had to say to him. He didn't answer, yet I knew there was someone in the room, for I could hear a noise inside. So I spoke. I told him it was I. Still there was no answer, although the noise went on. I could hear someone coming along the hall, beyond the turn, and I didn't want to be found standing there, so I turned the knob. Mr. Brown, I turned it hard and firmly, and the door wouldn't open. It was locked. That must have been—according to what Dr. Simpson said—only a very few minutes before he—before he—" She broke off, but went on after a moment: "Do you mean to tell me that he unlocked that door before he—killed himself?"

"My dear, he didn't kill himself; there's not a chance in the world that he killed himself." Brown broke off. His mind was turning over this new aspect of the situation. There were several points in this story that were not clear to him.

"You say you heard a sound in Stuart's room," he said at last. "What sort of sound? Someone moving about? Voices? What?"

The girl's brow knit in perplexity.

"A funny sound—a sort of irregular knocking, as though someone were knocking on another door. But I knew of course, that there wasn't any other door to that room."

"Except," said Brown, "the closet door."

Realization of the full import of what had been said seemed to come to them both at the same instant. They stared at each other, and it would have been hard to say which face was the most bloodless.

"Oh, my God!" whispered the girl.

For they both knew as clearly as though they had looked through the locked door and seen it, that the sound Adele had heard had been the convulsive kicking of heels against that closet door.

Chapter X

When Adele had left him, Brown waited until her light step had died away down the corridor. Then he took off his patent-leather shoes, put on his bedroom slippers, snapped off his light, and slipped out into the dark hallway. There was no sound. Apparently the weary household had at last gone to sleep. He felt his way along to Stuart's room and tried the door. It was still locked. This was no more than he expected. He stood for a minute debating whether he should go out and try to make his way through the window, or whether it would be feasible to find Franklin in the servant's wing. And then a thought came to him. He went back to his own room, took the key from his door, and tried it in Stuart's lock. With a little persuasion, it turned. He grinned crookedly. He might have remembered that all bedroom door keys fit all bedroom locks. He wondered, as he felt for the switch and shut the door after him, whether any other member of the house party had thought of that interesting fact.

As the lights from the wall brackets flooded the little room he saw that somebody had. Unmistakably the place had been searched. Papers were taken from the desk drawers and strewn over the tabletop; the pockets of Stuart's tweed suit had been turned out. Brown frowned and abused himself for his carelessness. Then, with characteristic thoroughness, he went about the business of repairing, as far as possible, his mistake. He moved the key to the inside of the lock, turned it, and proceeded to go over the room inch by inch.

Stuart's body had been laid decently on the bed and a sheet drawn over it. He turned the sheet back and made swift and careful examination of the face and wrists. If there were signs that Stuart had been gagged and bound his theory of the way the murder had been done went by the board. But there were no signs. No bruises on the wrists, and the mark he had noticed near the lip was obviously a razor cut. When he had finished, he drew the sheet back in place with considerable relief and turned to the closet.

The hook on the inside of the door, from which Stuart had hung, was a small, strong metal hook attached to the wood by two strong, firm screws. Below it, near the bottom of the door, showing clearly on the paint, were the marks of his battering heels. The closet, Brown saw at once, was empty, except for the vest and dinner jacket suspended on one hanger, a winter overcoat on another, a gray fedora on the shelf above, and two pieces of hand luggage on the floor. One was a small black suitcase which proved to be empty, and the other was a battered brown extension bag, packed to its fullest capacity, and very heavy. The lawyer studied them curiously. Why had that brown bag been packed? And why—more important still—had it not been searched? His heart sank as the answer to the second question leaped into his mind. Because the searcher had already found what he was looking for.

Brown closed the closet door gently and turned to survey the rifled desk and the papers strewn on the easy chair where Stuart's discarded gray tweed had been thrown. Was there any conceivable way of guessing what sort of paper it was that the unknown had been seeking? He turned over the contents of Stuart's pockets thoughtfully. Three business letters, worn by being carried round in his pocket; an old-fashioned gold watch with no chain; a fountain pen; a key ring; a handkerchief. Nothing else. Brown laid them in a little pile on the bureau and turned to the desk. He drew up the desk chair in front of it and sat down.

Before tackling the confusion of letters and papers on top, he went methodically through drawer after drawer, all empty now. He took them out and turned them upside down on the floor and searched the cavities they left for any paper that might have fallen in behind. When he came to the bottom drawer it stuck, and no juggling would open it. Brown looked at it thoughtfully. There was no lock. Clearly it was a typical office desk of the sort that is so arranged that the closing of the shallow top drawer locks all the rest. He slipped the top drawer back into place and tried again. Still the big drawer would not open. He returned the other drawers to their places and pushed them all firmly in; then pulled them out a little and tried the bottom drawer. Still it stuck. Perhaps the leaf intended for letter writing had jammed the mechanism in some way. It was warped and stuck a little, but Brown jerked it out and bent again to reach the handle of that bottom drawer. And then suddenly, in mid-action, so to speak, he paused and sat staring.

The leaf, apparently, had been little used—probably owing to the difficulty in drawing it out—and was thickly covered with dust, rubbed along the right angle where a coat sleeve had rested on it. But in the middle of the dust coating was an oblong patch where no dust was. Brown rubbed his finger on the wood and looked at the tip. It was perfectly clean—as clean as though whatever had protected that place had only just been removed from it.

The lawyer pursed his lips in a silent whistle and, sitting back, stared at that rectangle of polished wood. His eyes traveled from it to the papers on top of the desk and back again. Presently he leaned forward and picked up a sheet of unused business-letter paper with "World's End Island" engraved in the upper right-hand corner. With infinite care, lest it should blur the sharp edge of the dust line, he laid it down on the clean space. It fitted to a hair's breadth.

Bolivar Brown slept only fitfully, and his sleep was haunted by disturbing dreams. He woke finally and irrevocably at seven o'clock and lay for a moment staring at the high, white ceiling of his room, dim with bluish shadow. Then he sat up.

Beyond the striped awning that shaded his window the sun had risen a hand's breadth above the sea and was slanting across the gardens, which in this extraordinary climate, had already begun to recover from the effects of the storm. The light caught and shivered on the crests of the waves rolling in along the beach. It shone on the wreck of the jungle coppice. Brown got up and began to put on his clothes.

When he went downstairs a few minutes later he encountered a pretty Irish girl, with an apron not much larger than a postage stamp, dusting the drawing room. She paused as he came in, flushing a little, and looking as though she were uncertain whether or not to go on with her task. He nodded pleasantly.

"Don't let me disturb you," he said.

She smiled as she resumed her interrupted work.

"You're down early, sir," she said.

He watched her thoughtfully while she dusted a mahogany tabletop. His uninstructed masculine eye could see little difference in the mahogany where her cloth had polished it and the surface as yet untouched.

"I shouldn't think," he said diffidently, "that there'd be much of that to do here. Where does the dust come from?"

She giggled a little consciously.

"It's gritty enough now, sir, Lord knows, after the storm. The sand seemed to blow fair through the walls and all. But ordinary times, to be sure, there's little enough. Sure, you could dust no more than once a month and nobody'd know the difference."

Once a month, thought Bolivar Brown. That meant, surely, that many months—years—had gone to the making of that dust coating on the leaf of the desk upstairs. Years ago a letter had been written on that little sliding shelf. But why had it been left there? And who had found it? And was it still in existence? If the murderer had taken it, it would certainly have been destroyed by now. But if somebody else had found it...

Brown pigeonholed the questions for future consideration and strolled out through the long window onto the terrace. His quick ear had caught the sound of footsteps, and as he emerged he saw Justin hurrying down the flagged walk into the garden. He called, and the boy turned as though he had been shot, lifting a white, haggard face. Brown joined him in the garden.

"You're going down to the jungle, of course," he said kindly. "Let me go with you, if you don't mind."

"I thought," said Justin, "I'd just like to—to look around before everybody is up and about."

"Of course," assented Brown and fell into step beside him.

It was a perfect morning, still and cool. The encircling blue of sea was streaked with color: aquamarine and strange, shifting purples, and a pearly light over the sandbars. In the stillness the beat of the surf on the outer beach came distinctly to their ears. The air was sweet with the smell of the sea and the faint scent of jasmine.

"It doesn't seem possible," said Justin, and there was a break in his voice.

Brown understood and said nothing. It did not seem possible that, in such a world, fresh and lovely as on the first morning such sinister things could happen.

The path through the gardens had been cleared, and they walked quickly, approaching the edge of the jungle. Beyond, in the underbrush, they could see someone moving. It was only when the turn of the path brought them within sight of the place where Stephen Huntington's body lay under its covering of sailcloth that they saw who this person was. And then Brown recognized with a start of surprise the tall, gaunt figure. It was Solomon Jura.

Clearly Platt had considered his duty done when he had covered the skeleton, for there was no one on guard. Jura had turned back the sailcloth and was standing beside it, looking down at what lay beneath. He raised his head as they came up, almost with a start as though he had been too absorbed to notice their approach.

"You'll forgive me," he said to Brown. "I haven't touched anything."

"Good God!" whispered Justin Huntington.

With a pitying glance at the boy, Jura joined Brown, and they waited at a little distance, leaving the youngster alone with his first realization of what had happened.

Brown studied Jura curiously. What was the man doing here? He wondered. Was it only curiosity that had brought him out so early, or was it some other motive? And, if so, what was it? The lawyer's speculative gaze turned to Justin, standing with bent head by the skeleton.

"I suppose," he murmured, "after seven years it would be quite impossible to tell just where the original path ran and how far this tree stood from it? I mean, of course, the tree that supported Huntington's body?"

Jura's gaze turned from the lawyer's face to the skeleton and back again. There was a curious look of perplexity in his eyes.

"Yes," he said slowly. "I can tell you where the path ran, but I can't understand— However, you see that huge stump there—the live oak stump? The path ran round the base of that tree, to the left. It went in just about here, circled that tree, and went on in a fairly straight line to the summerhouse at the tip of the island."

Brown considered the lay of the land.

"But," he objected, "that makes Huntington's tree eight or ten feet from the path, back in the heavy growth."

"Yes," admitted Jura. He ran his hand through his gray hair and frowned dubiously at the tree.

"Strikes you as odd, doesn't it?" suggested Brown. "Why?"

"I don't see," said Jura slowly, "how the murderer got Huntington's body back there—into the growth, I mean. It was very heavy—almost impenetrable. And Huntington was a big man."

"No doubt," suggested Brown, "he killed Huntington first and then, by means of a rope passed over a branch of that tree, jerked the body sideways and up out of sight." He glanced at Jura as he finished and was surprised at the greenish pallor of the man's face.

The Hungarian nodded but said nothing. He seemed unable to speak.

"That would explain," pursued Brown, "why the body was never found, even if, as I take to be the case, this patch of jungle was searched?"

Jura seemed to recover himself.

"It was searched from end to end," he said. "I myself took part in the search, and it was very thorough."

"And all the time," said Brown with some incredulity, "the thing you were looking for was hanging directly over your heads?"

"It's a horrible idea," admitted Jura, "but you must be right. Of course, after that first frantic search, the wood was abandoned. I don't suppose anybody ever used the path again, and it quickly grew over."

"And the strangler fig," said Brown softly, his eyes on the older man's face, "was left to devour its prey."

The tenseness of the naturalist's face yielded suddenly to a half smile.

"As you were suggesting last night," he said, "it is strange how often one finds some curious basis of fact for the most outlandish legends. Men love to embellish cold fact with the accoutrements of poetry. Cold murder," he finished softly, "with the graceful legend of a vine that eats men."

"Murder?" repeated a voice beside them, and they started from their absorption to find that Justin Huntington had come up while they were talking. "You used that word last night," the boy went on to Brown. "My father hadn't an enemy in the world—nobody who could wish to harm him. I don't believe it was murder."

The boy's eyes were full. Jura turned away with a muttered excuse. After a step or two he turned back to Brown.

"If there's anything I can do—" he said. And then he turned abruptly away, and they could, after a moment, hear his steps on the hard sand of the beach.

Justin blew his nose.

"Sorry," he muttered. "But—murder? I mean to say—" He was stark white under his tan. He sat down suddenly on the felled trunk of a tree beside him. "I'd be glad if you'd tell me just why you think it was —murder." He halted on the word as though he found it very hard to say. Brown told him briefly his reasons for using it. When he had finished, Justin looked down at his hands as though he had never seen them before, examining them carefully, and turning them over in the sun. Then he got to his feet.

"The sheriff," he said, "claims it was an accidental death, and Madeleine is sure it must have been an accident. You're just guessing. You can't prove any of this. You didn't know my father. You don't know how impossible it is that anybody could have wanted to harm him."

"It wasn't an accident," persisted Brown stubbornly. "Do you think it could have been suicide?"

Justin stared at him, flushing to the tips of his ears.

"Are you crazy?" he demanded. "I don't know what's the matter with the whole lot of you. Mad's a perfectly lovely person and she was crazy about Father. The whole mess makes me sick. I—"

He broke off suddenly, as if realizing that he had said more than he meant to say. Brown looked at him with surprised attention. This was emphatically not what he had expected.

"Just which mess are you referring to?" he asked.

Justin looked sullenly at the path.

"Oh, nothing," he muttered. "Sis doesn't like Madeleine, that's all, and she's always saying things that make me sore. I thought you'd swallowed some of them, that's all. I'll get on now. But if you think I'll stand for Mad's being bothered about this—well, I won't, that's all. You may as well understand that first as last. She's suffered enough through father's—disappearance. I won't have her made to suffer now he's dead."

With which extraordinary remark he turned on his heel and swung off up the island, leaving Brown to gape at his departing back.

Chapter XI

As Brown strolled back to the house he revolved a new thought in his mind. Had there been friction between Huntington and his wife—friction not generally known but of which both Justin and his sister were aware? Did this account for Adele's dislike of her stepmother—something deeper and more bitter than their antagonism over his will? He wondered. Lydia Vaughan had suggested nothing of the kind. Or had she? Did her veiled suggestion that Madeleine had never loved her husband hint at domestic complications? Once again he was obliged to table the question temporarily. He had nothing to go on.

At the tennis courts he came on Isabel Lane. She was sitting on a stone bench leaning back on her supporting hands, her little feet in heavy, rubber-soled shoes stretched across the path. She wore a white tennis frock with no particular back, and her racket lay on the grass beside her.

"I suppose," she said, cocking her pretty brown head at Bolivar, "that you're not in the mood for a game?"

Brown looked down at her with his crooked smile.

"Have you a good imagination?" he asked. "Imagine what a figure of fun I would be on the tennis court."

"That's just what I was thinking," she said saucily. "I need a good laugh. I've just had a quarrel with my boyfriend."

Brown glanced toward the house where Justin could be seen vanishing indoors.

"Uh-huh," assented Miss Lane. "I just invited him to play with me, and he turned me down cold. Whereupon," she finished sweetly, "we had words."

"You're an unfeeling little brute," said Brown, smiling.

"That's what Justin said—or words to that general effect," she retorted. "Hey-ho! I'm having quite a time keeping two quarrels going at once. It's remarkably stimulating. I won't need any coffee this morning."

"I suppose," said Brown, grinning, "it's my cue to ask who is the other victim of your displeasure."

The girl giggled delightedly.

"You *are* nice. I've quarreled with the head of the family, the source of all good and perfect things, including the quarterly allowance—Uncle Daniel himself, in person. And, in case you should ask what it is all about, I will now tell you, because it's rather amusing."

"You know," said Brown, sitting down beside her, "if you were my child I should spank you every morning."

"If I were your child," corrected Isabel, "you would instantly double my allowance and give me a shiny red roadster. Well, when I came downstairs this morning Uncle Daniel was up—believe it or not. He was up—UP, up—and down, by which I mean downstairs, and he had been out, strolling in the fresh morning ozone. And if you wish me to tell you with whom he was up and down and out I will confide to your startled ear that I do not know. And his shoes were full of sand, which hurt him, and his temper was a little mite—what shall I say? Let's take a big plunge—exacerbated! Which is to say he was sore as a blister. And I should have known better than to ask him at that moment for the speed boat, but you see—"

"Just a minute," pleaded Brown. "One thing at a time! Did you by chance inquire of Uncle Daniel where he had been and what he had been doing?"

"Ah!" nodded Isabel darkly. "That was when we got into the heart of the argument, as you might say. And I says to him: 'With which lady friend have you been walking in the cool of the morning?' And would you believe it, he looked so mad I really thought I'd hit on something that might be useful to me later on, but I couldn't get any further in that direction."

"You little devil," commented Brown sincerely.

The girl gurgled with impish delight.

"We're full of compliments this morning. But don't quarrel with me, or I shall have no one left to talk to."

He left her swinging her feet and looking up at him crosswise under her mop of short, curly hair.

As he approached the house he saw that breakfast was being served on the shady terrace outside the dining room windows. The sound of voices came to him across the garden. He glanced at his watch; eight-thirty. He had been longer than he realized.

On the front steps he met Lane, resplendent in white flannels and discreet tie. Brown conceded instant appreciation of the other man's well turned out appearance and the distinction of his clear-cut, deeply lined face. He looked entirely fresh and composed, no signs remaining on the scene so vividly described by his scapegrace niece.

"I suppose," said Lane abruptly, "you've been down to the jungle."

Brown nodded.

"Yes," he said. "It's the most curious affair that has ever come to my attention."

Lane looked at him curiously.

"Do you still think Huntington was murdered?" he asked.

"Yes," said Bolivar Brown, and he said nothing more. He stood quite still, hands hitched forward in the pockets of his coat, staring up at the man on the steps above him. Lane was gazing out over the lagoon, across the sea to the thin line of mainland ten miles away. Suddenly he gave a short, mirthless laugh.

"So that's that! Funny! I always thought he'd gone off in a boat— not the boat that drifted off from the summerhouse moorings, but another one."

"Why not the boat from the summerhouse?" murmured Brown.

Lane looked at him sharply.

"There was something fishy about that. As the police pointed out at the time, there weren't any footsteps leading across the sand to the boat. Whoever cast it loose took care to lay a board first."

"Huntington might have done that," suggested Brown helpfully.

"He might," conceded Lane dryly, "but why should he? He could not have hoped to disguise the fact that he'd disappeared from the island."

Brown pondered the point for a moment.

"You spoke of another boat," he said slowly. "What other boat? I thought it had been established that no other boat had been at the island that night—and left it again."

"Well," objected Lane, "you see I knew there had been a boat here. I never said anything. It was no business of mine, if Huntington wanted to sneak off. And now you say he didn't go after all." Lane brought his gaze back from the horizon to Brown's face. "I suppose," he said slowly, "there's no doubt that it actually is Huntington?"

"None whatever," the lawyer assured him. "At least, no reasonable doubt." He looked shrewdly at the older man. "To come back to the point, however—I thought the beaches had been carefully searched and that there was no sign of any landing made the night of Huntington's disappearance."

"There wasn't any landing made," said Lane. "But there was a boat here—and it was gone before the police arrived."

"Perhaps you like riddles," murmured Brown.

Lane smiled faintly.

"This wasn't a riddle—or, if it was, it was a transparent one. It was a boat with a glass bottom. And the reason it wasn't noticed was that it was so awfully obvious, and everybody was so familiar with it and thought nothing of its going and coming at odd hours. But the boat was in the lagoon yonder the night Huntington disappeared, and the next day at noon when the police got here, it was gone—and Solomon Jura with it. And—so I have always thought—Stephen Huntington with it, too."

"And you mean to say that you never spoke of it to a soul—your suspicion?"

"My dear young man," said Lane patiently. "I never bother people. If Huntington had gone that way it was because he chose to go so. It was not my business."

Brown looked at him shrewdly.

"I fancy you had a better reason than that," he murmured.

"Ah?" Lane grinned frankly now. "I hoped you would find that sufficient. However, whatever my reason, I said nothing to anyone. But this—well, this is something else. But I suppose, after all these years, it will be difficult to establish the fact that Huntington was murdered."

Brown looked at him curiously. What was the man driving at? What game was he playing?

"I shouldn't think," he said slowly, "that it would be very difficult."

Lane glanced swiftly at him, and as swiftly away again, out over the lagoon, to the sea.

"Well," he said, "I've always made rather a point of keeping out of affairs that don't concern me. But there are several curious things about that night—" He broke off, frowning thoughtfully. "We were playing bridge just inside the library windows yonder: Mrs. Huntington, Mrs. Drew, Grass, and myself. Huntington, as we thought, was out here, smoking on the terrace. I came out after a while to persuade him to take my place, but he wasn't here, and Miss Vaughan called to me that he'd gone down the island. I walked down the path, looking for him, but I didn't see him, so I turned back. Just then I saw Jura coming along the beach. He was walking quickly—almost running—down toward the lagoon where his boat was moored, so I didn't speak to him. I don't think he saw me, although he passed within fifteen feet. I was standing right down there—" Lane pointed to a place where the path ran near the landward beach—"in the shadow of that poinsettia bush. I wondered where he was going in such a hurry, so I turned to watch him. He didn't turn off toward his boat, as I expected, but hurried on. It was a perfectly still night, and I could hear his footsteps long after I couldn't see him any more. I could hear him distinctly, almost to the end of the island."

"And the next day," Brown finished the thought for him, "Jura went off in his boat before the police arrived."

Was he mistaken, or did Lane release a breath, held in suspense for his answer? Why had Lane told him all this? What was behind the older man's candid glance?

"Curious, isn't it?" murmured Lane. "Well, I shan't say anything about it. No use raking up that old affair now. In spite of what you say, I should think there wasn't much hope of proving anything now."

Again his eyes dropped swiftly to Brown's. The lawyer smiled.

"You share the police view of the affair?" he asked.

Lane laughed.

"He's a card, isn't he—the sheriff, I mean? Well, I won't keep you." He went down the steps. At the bottom, however, he turned and came back. "By the way," he said, "where was Jura last evening after dinner?"

"Where was he?" repeated Brown, mystified. "In his room, I suppose. I talked to him there after the sheriff had gone."

"There's something queer about that fellow," insisted Lane. "The sheriff wanted to talk to him after he'd seen me last night, and I went myself to look for him. He wasn't in his room then—or in the house, as far as I could discover. The butler and I searched the place over for him, and he wasn't there."

Brown was very thoughtful as he at length made his way up the wide steps and into the cool, shady hall. His mind was racing; full of kaleidoscopic speculation, suspicions, and theories. But as he crossed the hall the thread of his thoughts was rudely broken. Franklin came out through the dining room door, and, with a mysterious jerk of the head most unbecoming in a butler, beckoned him into the library.

"I say, sir," whispered Franklin with lugubrious excitement. "Here's a queer thing. At breakfast in the servants' hall this morning I was talking to Myron, sir—but if you'll step through here, sir, you can just hear for yourself."

He led the way across the library to a door on the far side that opened into a little back hall. Here he showed Brown into a small room that was evidently a sort of butler's office. As they entered, Myron rose from a chair by the window. Brown recognized him as the man who had met him in Summerville on the day of his arrival.

"It seems, sir," said Franklin impressively, endeavoring to cover with his magisterial dignity the faint quiver of excitement of his voice, "that Myron had a conversation with Mr. Stuart yesterday afternoon which I thought, sir, might be of some slight interest to you. Just tell Mr. Brown what you told me this morning."

Brown smothered a smile and turned to Myron.

"I don't think it's anything, sir," the boatman stammered awkwardly. "I wouldn't have troubled you with it myself, sir, but Franklin seemed to think you might be interested, and it is a bit queer, I suppose."

"What's a bit queer?" asked Brown. "Suppose you begin at the beginning."

"Well, sir," said Myron, trying to collect his thoughts. "It's a bit queer Mr. Stuart arranging with me to motor him over to Summerville last night."

"What?" cried Brown in lively astonishment. "Mr. Stuart asked you to run him over to Summerville—when?"

"Last night, after dinner. It was this way, sir. Yesterday afternoon Mr. Stuart came down to the boathouse and asked me would I do a favor for him. We'd been quite friendly off and on. I'd taken him fishing, odd times, and we'd chinned together more than once. So I said, sure, I'd be glad to help him out. Well, he said that he had to go to New York right away on private business, but that Mr. Grass, his boss, wouldn't let him go. But he was going anyway. He had to. He acted real excited over it, and sorta nervous, I thought. He asked me would I run him over to Summerville as soon after dinner as he could get away. He figured he could get a car there and motor to some place where he could get a train North sometime in the night. I said I'd be glad to. And then he made me promise I wouldn't tell, and I wouldn't have, sir, except that his death seems to have changed all that. At first I thought I wouldn't say anything, but it didn't seem right, somehow. And I thought, you being a lawyer, sir..."

Brown studied the anxious countenance for a minute. Plainly the man was telling the truth. He nodded briefly.

"You've done just right," he said. "Where were you to meet Mr. Stuart to take him ashore?"

"He was to come to the boathouse as soon after ten as he could make it."

"Do you know if he planned to take any luggage with him—a handbag, perhaps?"

"Yes, sir, a handbag. I was to go to his room and get it while everybody was at dinner."

Brown considered the point rapidly. That accounted, of course, for the packed bag in Stuart's closet. What, in the name of all that was wonderful, was it all about?

"I take it," he said, "that you didn't go up for the bag."

"Yes, sir," said Myron. "I went to get it, all right, but the room was locked, and I heard from Franklin that Mr. Stuart was dead, sir, and you had locked the door until the police could get here."

Brown thrust his hands into his jacket pockets and considered the pattern of the carpet. He was deeply excited. Here was a lead indeed! Where it would take him he could not tell, but sooner or later, he was confident, all these strands would twist together to lead him to the heart of the maze. He turned to the boatman.

"Just say nothing about this for the moment, will you? What you've told me is very suggestive. I'm obliged to you."

Myron drew a long breath of relief.

"I'll be thankful to leave it in your hands, sir," he said. "I'm sure I didn't know what I ought to do about it."

At this instant a knock fell on the door, and the pretty Irish parlor maid stepped in. She looked brightly at Brown, with a half smile that showed her pretty teeth.

"Mrs. Huntington is asking for you, sir. I thought I saw you come this way, so I took the liberty of following. She would be glad if you would step up to her sitting room, sir."

Chapter XII

Brown had never been in Madeleine Huntington's sitting room before, and he looked about him with interest while he waited for her maid to announce him. It was a big corner room on the landward side of the house. From its windows, one could see on one side the length of the island with the jungle coppice in the distance, and the roof of the white summerhouse beyond. And on the other side one looked down toward the boathouse, and far away, a thread on the horizon, the Florida coast. On this latter side the long French windows opened on a little balcony.

It was a charming room, furnished in admirable taste. Most of the house succeeded in being entirely impersonal, as though it were designed to be a luxurious hotel to accommodate fastidious house parties, but in this room Madeleine Huntington's personality thrust itself out, found definite expression. One wall was lined with books, chiefly, as Brown saw at a glance, books of travel. Here and there about the room were curious objects, evidently brought back from her wanderings: weapons of one sort and another, an exquisite little Chinese Kuan Yin, a row of crude but fascinating ivory statuettes. He was examining the latter when a voice spoke behind him. He swung round to find that Mrs. Huntington had entered quietly.

"Those are from the Congo," she informed him, nodding at the statuette in his hand. "They're native work, but they almost look as though they might be some of this modern stuff, don't they—with their curious planes and surfaces?"

"The Congo!" he repeated. "You've been there?"

"With my first husband, Waldo Bingham." She took the little statue from him and turned it over in her hands. "That was the time I met Mr. Jura, by the way; at a tiny settlement of three or four huts on the Congo River. We were on our way into the interior and were obliged to wait over for a boat to carry us farther up. We three were the only white people in the place, and we became quite friendly."

"When was that?" asked Brown. And wondered, even as he asked it, why she had thrust this information on him.

She put the statuette back in place on the shelf.

"Oh, several years before the war—before 1914, that is. It must have been about 1909."

Brown looked about the room.

"You've so many lovely things," he said. "Do you know, I envy you your travels, and your knowledge of—of all this"—with a wave of his hand and speaking a trifle wistfully. "There are so many fields of knowledge I've never had time to look into. Someday, perhaps—"

He glanced down at the table on which lay a paper-bound French book with a delicate handkerchief thrust into it to keep a place.

"You read French, too," he sighed.

And then she surprised him. She thrust out her hand as though to snatch the book away from him. Then as suddenly withdrew it.

"Yes, I speak French quite easily. I had a French governess when I was a child."

In the funny little pause that followed Brown wondered what it was that had disturbed her. Certainly the little book was innocent enough. It was only an inexpensive copy of *Lettres de mon Moulin.*

But the question remained for the moment unanswered. She took the book from him, pulled out the handkerchief, and thrust the volume into a gap in the row of books on the top shelf. Then she turned back to him.

"It was good of you to come up," she said hurriedly. "You must have wondered at my sending for you."

He smiled faintly.

"Not at all."

"Sit down, won't you?" she rushed on. "I want so much to talk to you. Justin has just been here—" She broke off, staring for a moment blindly through the open window. Then she sat down and motioned him to a chair beside her. "I don't know just how to begin," she confessed candidly: "how to make my position clear to you."

Brown looked at her then, keen and smiling.

"Let me help you," he said at last gently. "Justin has told you that I believe that Mr. Huntington was murdered and that he does not agree with me. And you are inclined to think he is right."

"I know he is right!" The face she turned to him was flushed with eagerness. "Mr. Brown, I beg you to believe me! You never knew my husband, and so of course you can't judge, but he hadn't any enemy in the world. It isn't possible that anyone could have wished to harm him."

"Yet someone did harm him," said Brown sternly. "Someone slipped a noose around his neck and hanged him to a tree!"

She grew so pale that he thought she would faint.

"But—but the sheriff said it was an—an accident," she murmured through white lips.

"The sheriff was told to say it was an accident," said Brown. "Mr. Grass told him to say it."

For some reason this brought an unexpected look of speculation into her eyes.

"Mr. Grass?" she repeated. Brown said nothing. After a moment she went on: "I don't believe it. I don't believe any of it, Mr. Brown. You're guessing. You can't prove that Mr. Huntington was—hanged."

Silence invaded the room—a silence acute and pulsating with the tension of their eyes. His look was a silent question: "Why are you lying to me?" and hers was a defiant retort: "You will never find out!"

At last she said quietly:

"In any case, it doesn't matter, does it? We have done all the proper things—notified the police and got permission for burial—all the official things. So we really have no further responsibility in the matter and can drop the whole thing." She turned the rings on her firm square fingers thoughtfully. Then she added: "No doubt you think it strange, Mr. Brown, that I should wish to make no effort to—revenge Mr. Huntington's death—granting for the moment that he was murdered, as you say. Perhaps, if I believed it possible, after seven years, to arrive at the truth, I should—" She broke off with a shrug. "Who can say? One never knows. In any case, as it is, I am content to leave the matter where the police have dropped it and to agree that it was an accident." She lifted her eyes to the lawyer's. "From what Justin said, I fancied that you were making some sort of inquiry into the circumstances. So I thought I had better tell you at once what my attitude is and that I do not care to have any investigation made."

Brown's steady look never left her face. She rushed on:

"Of course I realize that we must establish legal proof that the—the skeleton found in the jungle is really—is really—" She found it impossible to say the words. "I have been wondering if, in the absence of my lawyers, you would undertake this for me, Mr. Brown?"

Her voice hung poised on the question. Clever, thought Bolivar Brown, to put him into the position of acting as her agent and so stopping his mouth and blinding him. And for the first time an unwilling admiration crept into his feeling for her.

"You see," she said with a pretty air of helplessness that was not too convincing, "Justin is so young and inexperienced—and you would know just what evidence the law would require in a matter of that sort."

Brown leaned forward, elbows on knees, and studied the pattern of the rug at his feet. After a moment he looked up at her under his brows.

"I think I should warn you," he said, "that you would be wise to wire your lawyers and to have their advice in this matter without delay."

"But I thought," she objected, "that as you are here, on the spot—"

He rose, thrusting his chair back impatiently. He towered over her like a strange bird of prey, his head thrust forward between his shoulders.

"Don't delude yourself, Mrs. Huntington. You're a clever woman and you have some knowledge of the world. I can't make up my mind what game you are playing, but we both know it is a game. You can't shut my mouth about this—and if you could, it would only stave off an investigation for a few days. Perhaps, if it were only young Stuart, the affair could be passed off as suicide, but men like Huntington aren't discovered with the rotted remains of a piece of hempen rope around their necks without questions being asked—particularly when they leave behind them wills involving millions of dollars. Questions will be asked."

She was white enough now. Her face, in the unforgiving morning light, was haggard. She wet her dry lips with her tongue.

"Questions?" she whispered. "What—sort of questions?"

"One of the questions will be," Brown told her, "'Who benefits by Huntington's will?' And another will be: 'Why has his wife done everything in her power to put obstacles in the way of any inquiry into the causes of his death?'"

And now Brown suddenly discovered the stuff she was made of. She threw her head back and laughed.

"Really, Mr. Brown! You are ingenious! I take it, then, that you refuse the case?"

"Oh, quite!" murmured the lawyer.

"How public spirited of you!" she mocked. "Well, then I've no choice but to write to my lawyers and have them send someone down. That will take two days at least, I suppose. How annoying! I can't persuade you to change your mind?"

He shook his head.

"No."

And now she took one final thrust.

"I suppose," she said, "that Adele has put you up to this? You'll regret it, Mr. Bolivar Brown. If you put your hand into that fire you will be burned."

Black rage rose in him, but he choked it back. She laughed again.

"I see," she said dryly, "that my warning comes too late."

He looked her in the eye then, and her look was a thrown gage.[4] It said: "This is war to the death." He smiled faintly.

"If I were you," he said gently, "in communicating with your lawyers I should adopt the slogan of the Western Union: 'Don't wire: telegraph!' And I should do it," he finished softly, "without an

---

4 Gage: a token of defiance, a glove or cap thrown down in challenge.

instant's delay."

He left her standing silent, her eyes flashing defiance at his retreating back.

By this time Bolivar Brown had completely forgotten the minor fact that he had had no breakfast. His mind was straining at the leash. His spiritual nose, so to speak, was sniffling at the scent. It filled the air around him, but he could make no guess at its source.

"Sherlock Holmes," he told himself severely, "with half the clues I've got, would already have leaped to a solution."

There was, of course, one thing that needed doing at once. He went along the corridor to Stuart's room and tried the handle. Still locked. He could, at least, find out to whom the key had been given when the sheriff left. It might be a blind alley, but it might, on the other hand, lead him to the person who had searched the room the night before. He went in search of Franklin. He found that worthy still in the butler's office, engaged in the business of the day. Brown installed himself luxuriously in a rocking chair by the window and surveyed Franklin's earnest countenance with gentle gravity.

"Luxurious quarters you have here," he remarked, shaking his head reprovingly. "I'm afraid, Franklin, that, unlike your famous namesake, you are something of a sybarite."[5]

"Oh, no, sir," protested Franklin, "there's not a drop of Hebrew blood in my veins, sir. You're wrong indeed."

For a moment perplexity ruffled Bolivar's smooth brow. Then he smiled.

"Not Semite," he explained, "sybarite. There is a distinction, Franklin, which is recognized in the best dictionaries."

"Ah," assented Franklin imperturbably. "No doubt you're right, sir."

"When I was young," Brown went on gravely, "we used to play a game called 'Twenty Questions.' It was a nice game. You began by asking whether the object in question was animal, vegetable, or mineral; and when you came to the end of twenty questions you had the answer. But the trouble with that is that someone has to know the answer."

"I should think so indeed, sir," said Franklin sympathetically.

"Now, I've asked about a hundred and fifty questions, and I'm no nearer the answer than when I started. And yet someone does know the answer, but I can't get him to play with me. He isn't in a playful mood, Franklin."

The butler looked at him dubiously. He had a vague idea that

---

5   Sybarite: from the notorious luxury of the Sybarite people.

Brown was trying to be funny, and he suspected humor in any form.

"Indeed, sir!" he murmured respectfully, and was relieved to find that the answer sufficed admirably.

"Alas, indeed, Franklin," assented Brown. "Now, here's another question. I'll ask it, and perhaps you'll be able to answer it, but I'll lay you ten to one it won't help any. Why is the door of Mr. Stuart's room locked?"

Franklin laid down the stack of household bills which he had been turning over in his hand since Brown entered, and came a step nearer.

"Now, it's a funny thing you should ask that, sir," he confided, after a swift glance over his shoulder. "There's things going on in this house I do not understand, sir."

"You don't say!" cried Brown in a surprised voice.

"Yes, sir," reiterated Franklin firmly: "things going on I don't understand. Why, for instance, would the undertaker come over before it was hardly light this morning and take young Mr. Stuart's body away, sir?"

Brown sprang out of his chair as though he had suddenly discovered that it was sizzling hot.

"What?" he cried in lively astonishment. "Do you mean to say they've already removed Stuart's body?"

"About dawn this morning," assented Franklin. "Routed me out of my bed to let them in, too."

"Who arranged that?" demanded the lawyer.

"Well, sir, Mr. Grass has sort of been arranging things for the family. He said to me last night, sir, as he was going upstairs, that the undertaker would be over from Summerville at five o'clock, and I was to let him in. The sheriff was to get in touch with him when he went back last night. 'I don't want Mrs. Huntington to be worried about this,' he said to me. 'I feel personally responsible,' he said."

"So Grass did it, did he?" murmured Brown thoughtfully. "And did he lock the door, too?"

"He locked it last night, sir, and gave me the key."

"No, no; I mean this morning, after Stuart's body had been removed."

"Oh, no, sir; I locked the door."

"You did, eh? What did you do that for, and where's the key?"

"I did it, sir," said Franklin with dignity, "because Mr. Grass asked me to, and I gave him the key when he came downstairs for breakfast."

Brown groaned.

"And you never told me a word about all this?"

A gleam of excitement pierced the somber gravity of the Franklin visage.

"Do you mean to say, sir," he asked with what amounted almost to eagerness, "that you think this may have something to do with—you know what, sir?"

"Do I mean to say— Oh, Franklin, you will never equal your distinguished namesake in astuteness—not if your name is ten times Richard!"

"No, sir," assented Franklin, but his assent put the bar of a butler's perfect civility between them. It was clear that his self-esteem was affronted. He would no longer permit the free interchange of man and man.

Brown made haste to retrieve his error.

"Not that I can brag," he said ruefully. "I've pulled one bone after another. I am wandering in what is known as the morass of imbecility, Franklin."

"Oh, no, sir," demurred Franklin politely. "Certainly not, sir."

Brown cast about for a graceful exit.

"So you think Mr. Grass has the key to Stuart's room?" he asked.

"I wouldn't undertake to say, sir," said Franklin firmly, "not being sufficiently astute, sir. It is a fact, however, that I gave it to him this morning at eight-thirty when he came down to breakfast."

"Ah—er—thanks very much," murmured the lawyer, and betook himself humbly out of the presence.

Chapter XIII

Returning to the main house through the library, Brown encountered Adele Huntington and Grass in the hall. So absorbed were they that they did not hear him, and Brown, sensing instantly that a scene was in progress, stepped back through the doorway. Their voices came to him distinctly. Adele was half crying, storming at Grass.

"What right had you—what right?" she demanded over and over. "I should have been consulted."

"My dear Miss Huntington," protested Grass suavely, "why on earth should I think you would be interested? Stuart was my secretary; I brought him here assuming I could rely on him to behave himself. I made myself responsible for his actions. When he ran off the rails and pulled this suicide stuff, the least I could do was to get him out of the way as soon as I could and relieve Mrs. Huntington of any unnecessary unpleasantness."

"Unpleasantness!" cried the poor girl bitterly. "You drive a man to kill himself and then talk of—unpleasantness!"

Grass's tone took on an edge.

"My dear Miss Huntington, last night, when you said that, I made allowance for the shock—and you being upset and everything. But let me remind you that if you go around repeating that accusation it may amount to criminal libel. And I warn you right now I won't stand for it. You think it over, young lady."

"I've been thinking it over," said Adele in a lower voice. "All night long I've been thinking it over. I want to know why you had Mr. Stuart's body removed from this house without any examination, before I—before anyone had been consulted."

"Both Dr. Simpson and the sheriff examined the body last night. And the sheriff gave permission for burial."

"Dr. Simpson!" cried Adele scornfully.

"I'm sorry," said Grass coldly. "That's all I've got to say about it. You have no cause for complaint—no legal cause. Everything is absolutely in order."

Brown barely heard Adele's whispered reply.

"I haven't much use for—for legal cause. I've found out that the only justice you get in this world is the justice you take for yourself."

Grass laughed gratingly.

"Are you threatening me, Miss Huntington?"

"No." The girl's voice had a note of exhaustion that struck Brown to the heart. "What would be the use of threatening you?"

Brown heard heavy footsteps as Grass crossed the hall and went away. Then suddenly Adele brushed through the doorway almost into his arms. For a moment she clung to him as if for actual physical support. Then suddenly her head swung against his shoulder and she began to cry as he had never heard anyone cry in his life before. For a moment he could only pat her shoulder awkwardly, and then suddenly his arms went round her and he held her close with a strange, rapturous anguish, such as he had never felt before. The full tide of his love for this girl swept over his head, leaving him blind and gasping. And she was crying her heart out for another man. Bolivar Brown appreciated the full irony of the situation, and it hurt rather cruelly. At last the violence of her sobs subsided; she drew back a little, wiping her eyes awkwardly on an inadequate handkerchief. There was nothing graceful about her grief. For that very reason, perhaps, it was the more heart stirring. Brown thrust a clean handkerchief into her hands and turned away to the window. His face was as white as paper. After a moment she spoke in a choked little voice:

"They've taken him away."

Brown did not pretend not to understand her.

"I know, my dear," he said gently.

"What—what are we going to do about it?"

"I've been thinking. I'm not just sure what we can do. Do you know if he had any relatives who might have some claim? That would be the simplest way."

"He—he hadn't a relative in the world. He told me so. No one—except me—who would care whether he lived or died."

"By the way," said Brown, "did you know that he was planning to leave World's End last night and go to New York?"

"Yes," said Adele, surprisingly. "That's why I knocked on his door on my way downstairs, because I—I had something to say to him, and I knew I probably wouldn't see him again—alone."

Brown had a sudden clear vision of her, knocking forlornly on that closed door, turning the knob—and suddenly his mind turned about, as a ship jibs when the hand leaves the helm. Why had she turned the knob? Surely it was not usual for girls to turn the knobs of young men's doors? Just casual young men? Not girls like Adele. He asked the question almost before it was completely in his mind, almost as one might throw out an unwelcome intruder.

"Adele, for heaven's sake, trust me. Why was Stuart going to New York? What was it you had to say to him? And why did you try to turn the handle of his door when he didn't answer your knock?"

She threw her head back and stared at him, her pinched little face pathetically blotched with tears. For the moment she met his anxious gaze. Then she capitulated.

"I knew he was going to leave Mr. Grass's employ. He'd been offered a job in New York—a very good job—and he was going to take it. I had to speak to him to find out if he'd been able to make arrangements to get away, because, you see, I'd made up my mind to go with him. There didn't seem to be any reason for me to stay here when he went."

Brown had already a premonition of the truth, but he said gently:

"I don't quite understand."

"Why should you?" asked the girl, with a weary smile, sadder than the sobs that had so shaken her. "How could you know that we were married last Friday—the day before the storm?"

The spoken words fulfilled some dim expectation that had been hovering in the back of his mind since the night before, but they cut him to the heart no less sharply on that account. He winced and stiffened as from a blow. But after a moment he put his personal feelings from him and considered this new development in the light of the general situation.

From one point of view it explained a good deal, and from another it complicated things still further. He said gently:

"Perhaps you wouldn't mind telling me just how it happened and why it was kept secret."

Adele looked down at her twisted hands.

"It was simple enough," she said softly. "We met in Washington in the fall—and—and liked each other so much. But he hadn't anything, and Madeleine had complete control of my affairs, of course, until just last month, when I was twenty-one. But before I left Washington we were engaged. And then, when he came down here with Mr. Grass, and there was a lot of talk of Madeleine getting a divorce from father and trying to have his will probated and everything, then John said we'd better get married right away, because I needed someone to look out for my interests. I didn't care about that, but—" She broke off again, her lips trembling.

Brown watched her with an aching pity. Poor little lonely thing—easy dupe of any easy kindness! He remembered Stuart's clever, cold face.

"Friday," she went on, "we got Myron to run us over to Miami. He didn't know what we were doing, of course. He thought we were shopping. We were married in the parsonage of a little church there."

"You have the marriage certificate, of course?" Brown asked gently.

She nodded dully.

"It's upstairs. I'll show it to you presently. It has everything in it."

Brown could not trust himself to look at her. He looked down at the floor, poking at it with his foot.

"This may simplify a lot of things, you know," he said.

"That's why I told you," she answered quietly. "When you said that about his family having a claim, it occurred to me that, after all, I had a claim—the best claim in the world. I don't know why I didn't think of it at once, except that, since Father's disappearance, I've been made to feel that I hadn't any sort of claim on anyone at all."

The bitterness that Brown was accustomed to throbbed and trembled in her voice. He had a fleeting vision of the woman in the room upstairs.

"Does Mrs. Huntington know of your marriage?" he asked.

"No!" The girl flung back her head. "Why should I tell her? She was bitterly opposed to my marrying at all. Why wouldn't she be? If Father's will was ever probated she stood to lose a good deal by it. And she's not the sort that likes to lose—anything."

"Adele," cried Bolivar Brown, "why do you hate her so?"

"Hate her? I don't hate her," said the girl. "I despise her. She's the one that does the hating. Ever since that night when I came on her—" She broke off and then went on steadily: "Ever since the night of Father's death she's hated and feared me. She's hated me because I know and she's feared me because I might tell."

"Because you might tell—what?"

Adele stared down at the floor.

"It's got nothing to do with this," she said at last in a tired voice. "I can't see that any good can come of telling now."

"My dear Adele—" Brown hesitated and then went on resolutely —"has anybody told you that your father's body has been found?"

She nodded dully.

"Justin told me."

"And did he tell you that there can be no doubt that he was murdered?"

She turned her face to him with a jerk. She might have been dead, so lifeless was it, with only her great eyes burning on him through the blue-white mask. Her lips moved faintly. She seemed to be saying: "Oh, no! Oh, no!" over and over. He dashed into the dining room and brought back a glass of wine from the decanter on the sideboard, cursing himself for a fool. Slowly her extreme pallor lessened. A tinge of color returned to her white lips.

"Tell me about it," she said.

"Are you sure—" he began anxiously. He felt as though he had stuck a knife into her side. How white she was, poor fragile little thing! But she would not let him off.

"Tell me about it," she reiterated peremptorily. "Tell me about it—every word. All you know. If you can show me that this is true, perhaps—perhaps I do know something that ought to be told—something the police ought to know."

"You're not well enough."

She stretched out her hands to him in a gesture of entreaty.

"I'm well enough to be told the truth. It's the uncertainty that's killing me. I'll be quite calm about it, I promise you."

And so perforce he told her of the finding of Huntington's body and his reasons for believing that the millionaire had been murdered. When he had finished, Adele drew a long breath. Every sign of her recent agitation had left her. She was more composed, to outward seeming, than Brown himself. She looked at him appealingly, yet with a look that seemed to read his thought, so shrewd and piercing was it.

"Tell me one thing more," she begged. "Why are you taking all this trouble in a matter which, on the surface—does not seem to concern you at all?"

For a moment his heart stood in his eyes. He wanted to tell her that anything that concerned her was of the deepest concern to him. That any trouble or difficulty of hers could command him, body and soul. But he knew that he must not say that now, so he temporized.

"I have no choice but to concern myself in the matter," he told her gravely. "I stumbled across the information—quite by accident—that two murders have been committed. To fail to act upon that information would be, in a sense, to put myself in the position of accessory to the crime." But here, for an instant his courage deserted him, and he added stumbling: "You are in trouble. Trust me if you can. I would so gladly help you. I would be so happy—if you could let me be your friend."

For a moment her eyes brimmed full. Impulsively she put her hand in his.

"I do trust you. I've felt from the beginning that you were my friend. And there's no one else I can go to for help. She's completely hoodwinked Justin."

Brown reflected again, as he had done before, on her odd unwillingness to use her stepmother's name.

"I think the best thing I can do," Adele went on, "is to tell you everything I know or suspect, everything I've noticed, and let you weed out what you think is irrelevant. I'm too near it, I've brooded over it too much, to be able to hold fast to the central thread any more.

"When my father disappeared I was fourteen years old. Up to that time I don't think it had ever occurred to me that the world was anything but a safe and beautiful place. If anything queer was going on, I didn't know it. He was so sane, so clever and wise, he would have made everything seem right, anyway.

"When I went upstairs with Justin that night after dinner, I don't suppose any child ever felt more secure, more unthinkingly happy and content. That was Justin's freshman year in college, and he was down here for a little vacation after his mid-year examinations. I remember we sat on the balcony outside his room, and he told me stories of his adventures. It was a perfect evening, like—like last evening, except that there was no moon. The stars were very brilliant, however, and we could smell the flowers in the garden below us. I can remember how ecstatically content I was.

"I saw Father come out on the terrace after a while and walk up and down, smoking. I said to Justin: 'I'm going to call to him.' But Justin wouldn't let me. He said, why shouldn't I behave myself when there was a house party? So we hid behind the vines and snickered and whispered nonsense, and presently he walked away down the path.

"'Let's follow and play spies,' I suggested, and Justin agreed, for he was only a kid, really, for all his grown-up airs and graces. So we ran down the back stairs, round the edge of the garden, and caught Father up just as he was crossing the open place between the garden and the jungle path. And then we saw that he wasn't alone. There was a man with him, but we couldn't tell who it was, for we daren't go near. There wasn't any cover just there. And it was too dark to tell at a distance. We wouldn't have been sure the second man was Father if we hadn't heard him laugh. But he laughed right out loud while we stood in the shadow of the big poinsettia bush by the far side of the garden and waited.

"Then he and the man went into the wood. We waited what seemed a long time, but they didn't come back. Justin dared me to go after them into the wood, but that was just because he knew I wouldn't dare. He didn't like it any too well himself at night, it was so spooky. But he wouldn't admit being afraid of anything himself. Well, we got tired of waiting after a while, and sleepy, too, so we went back to the house—round by the beach this time. We almost ran into Mr. Jura, but we heard him coming in time and dodged out of sight."

"Heard him coming?" repeated Brown. "Where?"

"Along the beach. Walking very fast—almost running. I wanted to jump out at him, but Justin wouldn't let me. He was afraid of being laughed at, I guess." The girl's face was suddenly convulsed. "If I only had jumped out at him! Perhaps he wouldn't have dared, if he'd known that someone saw him."

After a moment she collected herself and went on:

"We were sort of between the devil and the deep sea, for Mr. Lane had come out on the terrace while we'd been gone and was standing not ten feet from us when Mr. Jura passed. We hadn't seen him at first, but we spotted him then. I don't think he'd seen us, for he stood for a while looking after Mr. Jura, and then he turned round and went back into the house.

"We waited till he'd gone, and then we ran round by the back door again and hustled upstairs, giggling and carrying on. Justin wouldn't let me in his room again, because he said he had to write a letter. He looked so silly and mysterious about it that I wanted to hang round and bother him, but he shoved me in my room and locked the door, and then he shouted through the keyhole for me to be a good girl and go to bed. I kicked the door for a while, and then I did go to bed.

"It must have been sometime after midnight that I was wakened by voices in the hall; the sound of people talking excitedly. I didn't think anything of it at first, and then—well, I suppose I must have caught some note of anxiety in the voices. I called out, but nobody heard me, and the people—whoever they were—went off down the hall. I tried to go to sleep again, but I kept getting wider and wider awake and more and more frightened. I thought I'd have to go and find out what was wrong. I put on my wrapper and tried the door—and it wouldn't open.

"It was a full minute before I remembered that Justin had locked it, and in that minute I became frantic with terror. Something was wrong —I was sure of it. I must get out of that room and find out what it was. I couldn't budge the door, and nobody heard me call. The only occupied room near mine was Justin's, and I learned afterward that he had gone out with the others to search the island. So I went to the window and leaned out.

"The roof of the pergola over the dining terrace is just under my window. Of course, it's open, but the timbers are strong, and I thought I could make it if I was careful. So I got out and began to feel my way along, leaning against the house to steady myself.

"There was the window of the empty guest room just beyond, but the shutters were closed, and I could not open them from the outside, so I went on to the next room—her room—just beyond. I could see the light streaming through the open window, and it helped me to find my footing on the pergola. At last, by leaning forward, I could reach the sill of the window. I pulled myself along and stood looking into the room.

"She was so near that I could almost have touched her. She was lying on the sofa just inside the window, and he—he was kneeling beside her."

"He?" repeated Brown, mystified.

The girl's haunted eyes turned to him, but she hardly looked at him.

She seemed to be standing again at that lighted window, looking in, seeing—what?"

"Solomon Jura was kneeling beside her," she said, "and holding her in his arms."

Adele had succeeded in astonishing her hearer. Bolivar Brown gasped, as if she had flung a glass of ice water in his face. Was this the explanation of that look in Jura's eyes, of Mrs. Huntington's solicitude? It turned him faintly sick for a moment. And then he recovered himself. It was preposterous. Impossible to link Mrs. Huntington with a backstairs affair, and still more impossible to think of Jura in such a connection. He spoke gently to Adele.

"Surely you don't mean to imply—what your words suggest?"

"I don't mean to imply—anything," cried Adele wretchedly. "I'm not suggesting anything. I'm telling you what I saw."

"There are several possible explanations," Brown went on. "For instance—"

"Don't talk to me as if I were a child," the girl rushed on. "I've thought about it and thought about it till I'm half crazy. And I can explain everything—everything but the look on their faces when they saw me. Terror, Mr. Brown—blank, stark terror. Two rats caught in a trap—that's what they looked like."

"'Where's Father?' I remember asking. 'What time is it?'

"They told me Father hadn't come in yet—that they were worried —he could not be found. I said I would go and help look for him. And then they took me between them and told me I must never—never, as long as I lived—tell anybody that I had seen Mr. Jura there. I wasn't at all clear, then, what it was all about, but I was frightened and confused. I remember I kept saying: 'I must tell Father; I must tell Father.' And at last she said: 'Yes, tell your father, but no one else—promise me, Adele, nobody else—as long as you live.'"

"Well, I promised. I would have promised anything, I think, to get out of that room. I suppose their fear was contagious. I was horribly afraid. When they let me go at last, I ran away and hid myself in my father's closet. I remember clinging to his dressing gown and shivering with cold, although it was a hot night. Justin found me, after a while, and took me back to my room. He wanted to get *her* to look after me, but I cried, so he got one of the maids instead. In the morning they told me that Father could not be found."

She stopped suddenly and put her hands to her face as though rubbing away some vision. Then she looked at Brown more collectedly.

"Do I make it clear to you?" she asked.

He pulled himself with a start out of the atmosphere of horror her tale had evoked.

"Quite clear," he assured her. "But see here a minute. You have yourself proved that there's nothing in your suspicion concerning your stepmother and Mr. Jura. When you told her you were going to tell your father about finding Jura in her room she said to do so, but to tell no one else. If the affair had been what you suppose, she would never have agreed to allow you to tell your father—"

But he did not finish the sentence, for Adele interrupted him.

"Unless," she said, and her voice shook uncontrollably, "unless she already knew that I would never have another opportunity to tell my father—anything."

Chapter XIV

There was a long pause in the quiet library, a pause during which the beating of the surf on the windward beach, the distant blows of workmen's axes, and the voices of people talking in the garden could be distinctly heard. But neither of the two people in that long, shady room was conscious of these sounds. Bolivar Brown was seeing in his mind's eye Jura running along the beach, Jura leaving World's End in his boat, Jura absenting himself the night before, when the sheriff arrived. He shut his eyes against these sights only to be confronted with a more terrible one: Jura moving through a dark wood at night, setting his trap, springing it—and coming back to conduct, next morning, a search for the man he—

Brown brushed his hand across his eyes and looked at Adele. She was staring up at him intently, questioningly, as though begging him to refute the argument she had brought forward. He took himself firmly in hand.

"Look here," he said suddenly. "You should have someone to act for you. What lawyer handles your affairs?"

"Nobody. Justin and I haven't any affairs. She takes charge of everything."

Brown hesitated.

"If you'd let me take the matter on—it would make me very happy to do anything in the world that can be done."

Perhaps more feeling crept into his quiet voice than he was aware of. At any rate, the girl looked at him with sudden intentness, and her face softened and brightened. She rose impulsively and held out her hand to him.

"You've done so much already. And I've been quite a beast to you." Her lips trembled suddenly and her eyes filled. She steadied herself with an effort and grasped his hand quite firmly. "I shall be very glad indeed to place the whole matter entirely in your hands."

Brown looked down at the little hand held in his. For the moment he dared not meet her eyes. He only said in a matter-of-fact tone:

"Thank you. That will simplify things very much."

Twenty minutes later Bolivar Brown went upstairs. He was on his way to find Jacob Grass and suggest that they should make a careful search of Stuart's papers with a view to finding some possible clue to his death. But he found that he had been forestalled. Someone was ahead of him. As he reached the top of the stairs he saw that Stuart's door was unlocked. It had been closed, but the latch had not quite caught, and through the crack voices came plainly: Grass's rumbling tones and Dr. Simpson's shrill and agitated treble. As Brown came up Simpson was saying excitedly:

"I tell you it's an outrage. The letters are mine, and you've no earthly right to seize them. I don't care if Stuart was your secretary, my private correspondence with him is no business of yours."

A rumble of laughter succeeded this remonstrance, and then Grass said:

"But they're so poetic—they're marvelous—greatest things I ever read! You should sell them to the *Graphic News*. Gosh! Just listen to this: 'Surely she can have no suspicion on my motives. Madeleine must know that I have loved her—adored her—for years, since I first met her, before Mr. Huntington's disappearance. To see her was to love her—'"

There was a sharp sound, as of a chair overturning. Then Simpson's stifled voice:

"Give me those letters!"

"Give them to you?" cried Grass incredulously. "Give them to you? And have you destroy them in a fit of temper? Don't be a fool! These are masterpieces. Mrs. Huntington must see them. By the way—have you ever called her Madeleine to her face?"

"If you ever dare," screamed Simpson, "if you ever dare to show those to Mrs. Huntington—"

Grass abruptly stopped laughing. His voice when he answered was venomous.

"If I ever dare? Why, you little fool, I could crush you with one hand. And I will, if you don't stop this nonsense. You leave Mrs. Huntington alone, or I will show her these letters, and then she'll have her butler throw you out of the house."

Simpson laughed in his turn, gratingly.

"You're afraid of me, Grass; that's the truth of the matter. You want her yourself, and you're afraid she may prefer me. You know how solid I am with her."

There was a long pause, broken at last by Grass's contemptuous voice:

"You little insect! Have you ever looked at yourself in the glass? There's a mirror over the washstand."

The only answer was a gasping sound, as though Simpson choked for breath, and then the crisp rattle of paper.

"I will show them to her," said Grass. "It will at least serve the excellent end of getting rid of you. And it's getting to be a nuisance to have you round."

The end of the scene came suddenly and sharply. There was a crash, a gasping cry from Grass, and Simpson's snarling voice:

"By God!—I'll get you for this, Grass."

Brown pushed open the door and went in. Grass, his face purple, lay back against the desk across which he had fallen, and Simpson, livid with rage, clutched with his clawing fingers at the politician's heavy bull neck. It was all over in a moment, even before Brown could interfere. Grass, with a tremendous heave of his powerful bulk, righted himself, seized Simpson by his shoulders, and threw him across the room. He brought up against the bed, and crouched there, snarling. At this moment he caught sight of Brown, and a look of cunning replaced the animal rage in his face. He pointed at Grass with a shaking finger.

"Think you're smart, don't you?" he gasped. He looked up crosswise at Brown.

"He thinks he can ride roughshod over all the world. Well, nobody can get away with that stuff with me. Ask him what he knows about the *Neptune* disaster. See what he says—and if he don't say enough, come to me, and I'll tell you a story that will keep you going to the last installment. Ask him!"

Brown looked at Grass. The big man's florid face had gone livid. He said nothing. His very breathing seemed to be suspended. For a moment there was no sound at all in the room.

Brown knew very well to what Simpson referred: the particularly horrible wreck, in an almost calm sea, of a passenger ship bound from New York to Panama, in which almost half the souls on board had been drowned. A wreck due solely to the avarice of shipbuilders who had scrimped their building specifications, and corrupt harbor officials who had passed an unseaworthy ship. It was an old story, but not one that could easily be forgotten. The papers had been full of it for weeks, screaming charges and countercharges while the official investigations were going on. As Brown remembered, all that had happened was that a port inspector had been sent to jail for accepting a bribe to keep his eyes shut. And after that the hullabaloo had died down. It must have been all of seven or eight years ago. Brown's mind skipped a cog and then caught again with a jolt. It had been during the early winter of nineteen twenty-one–twenty-two, the winter when Huntington had disappeared! For a breathless moment the world reeled round Bolivar Brown. Then Grass's voice brought him to himself.

"Don't be a fool, Simpson!"

But Simpson was beyond hearing the note of warning in the voice.

"There are fools and fools," he cried, "and you're a bigger one than I ever was. You wait a minute!"

He was gone through the door with the rapidity of the rabbit he so much resembled. Brown and Grass stared at each other. The politician rubbed his hands together as though gently dusting them.

"Funny, isn't it?" he said with a shrug. "Find the way to a man's vanity, and you've hit his weakest spot. Fancies himself a gay Lothario! Him!" It is impossible to convey in print the contempt in the big man's voice. "He'll tell the greatest string of lies just to get even with me for laughing at him. Hard to believe, isn't it?" Grass's tone was virtue itself. He shook his head over human frailty, one eye on Brown.

At this moment Simpson came back, and behind him was Daniel Lane. The little man pulled Lane in, shut the door after him, and leaned against it, breathing heavily. Lane looked slightly bewildered. He glanced from Brown to Grass and back again.

"What is this?" he asked, smiling faintly. "A conference or a conspiracy? From your faces it's a little difficult to tell."

"Just a moment," said Brown gently. "Suppose I just take charge of this. Dr. Simpson suggested a moment ago that I should ask Mr. Grass a question. Evidently he wanted a witness to Mr. Grass's answer. Now that we're all here, with your permission, I'll carry on. Mr. Grass, just what do you know about the *Neptune* disaster?"

For a moment no one spoke or moved. Then Grass bent down, righted the fallen chair, and sat down. He took from his pocket a fat cigar and glanced at Brown.

"Smoke? Anybody?" No one answered him. He stuck the cigar in his mouth and lighted it thoughtfully. Then he settled back and looked up at Brown. "Of course," he said smoothly, "I don't concede that you have any right to question me, but—" he waved his hand deprecatingly as the lawyer opened his mouth to interrupt—"but, on the other hand, I've nothing to conceal, and if you're interested, I've no objection to answering your question. I know a good deal about that miserable affair. I was one of the witnesses at the prosecution of O'Fallon, the inspector who was convicted of negligence and sent to jail."

Brown's mind was working rapidly. He was recalling incidents of that investigation—incidents long forgotten.

"By George!" he murmured with dawning enlightenment. "Huntington was on the board appointed by Congress to look into that business, wasn't he?"

Grass smiled grimly.

"Sure he was. He was the guy that made the motion to investigate, too. He'd been elected on a reform ticket, you know, and he was breathing fire and brimstone for reform."

Lane spoke for the first time.

"I served on that board, too," he said surprisingly. "I was on the Shipping Board at the time. As a matter of fact, that's why we three were here all together. We'd come down to consult with Huntington about the whole matter."

Brown sat down on the edge of the bed and took out his pipe.

"I'll be damned," he said softly. No one spoke. They watched him while he took out his pouch and filled and lighted his pipe. Then he looked up at Simpson through the smoke. "Where do you come in?" he asked.

Grass answered.

"He corroborated my testimony that O'Fallon had accepted a bribe to clear the *Neptune*."

Brown did not take his eyes from Simpson's face.

"Is that so?" he asked.

Simpson wet his dry lips with his tongue and smiled horribly, as a man will whistle to keep his courage up. What a little rat he was, thought Brown, with hardly courage enough to fight when cornered.

"Yes," said Simpson at last. "O'Fallon got the bribe all right—five thousand, it was, too. And he got a jail term. I got it for him. I told Mr. Huntington I could and I would, the day he asked me about it here in this very room, not six hours before he disappeared. 'Can you prove your story and can you stick to it?' he asked me, and I said I could—and I did, at the trial afterward. But there was something else I could have told him—and I didn't."

"One of Dr. Simpson's most attractive characteristics," broke in Grass, "is his discretion. It has got him far in the past—and will, no doubt, carry him farther—in the future."

The politician's eyes bored into Simpson's. The little man squirmed, and then suddenly he sprang forward, whipping himself again into a white fury.

"Think you can silence me, do you? Well, you can't. You did once, but that's over now. You can't do it again." He swung round to the lawyer. "When we were all here that afternoon, Senator Huntington asked me to tell what I knew about O'Fallon. I told him I'd been in Mike's speakeasy in Mott Street around ten o'clock in the morning two weeks before the *Neptune* sailed. The back room had those dinky tables round the wall with high settled backs to the seats, so you couldn't see who was sitting in 'em except you got out in the middle of the room. Two guys came in and sat down in the place next me. They thought the room was empty, I guess, because I was in the corner, and it was kind of dark. I heard enough to show that one of them was a port inspector and the other was representing some shipbuilding firm that was mighty anxious to get the *Neptune* passed without any questions asked. They dickered about price for a while and then the inspector said he'd take five thousand. I was curious to know who they were, so I stuck my head up over the back of the seat, very quiet. I could see the inspector, all right, and I knew who he was. I'd thought so all along, from his voice, but then I was sure, for I knew O'Fallon well by sight."

He stopped, and Brown prompted him.

"So you told Huntington this? I don't see, however, how your story corroborated Mr. Grass. What did Mr. Grass know about all this?"

"Mr. Grass," said Simpson with a venomous glance at the politician, "was there too."

"But I thought," objected Brown, "that you said the room was empty."

"So it was," said Simpson. "There wasn't a soul in it but me and O'Fallon and the fellow representing the shipbuilding company."

Brown looked at Jacob Grass. The man was certainly a cool hand. He was leaning back in his chair, studying the glowing tip of his cigar with interest, his thick lips curved in a half smile.

"And did you," Brown pursued, "tell Mr. Huntington how it was that Mr. Grass was a witness of this scene?"

"No," said Simpson.

"You see," explained Grass without looking up, "I gave him the other five thou' I'd brought with me in case O'Fallon held me up for a cool ten."

"My God!" ejaculated Daniel Lane.

"It was funny—kind of," admitted Grass, "when you got asking me all those questions at the inquiry. But there was something funnier about the situation than that. Something"—and he looked sharply at Lane—"that I've always thought you had a suspicion of yourself."

Lane looked at him with sudden attention.

"I'd be careful, if I were you," he warned, "about talking too much."

Grass grinned.

"I've got my reasons," he said. "The funniest part of the whole business," he told Brown, "was that it wouldn't have made a bit of difference if Simpson had spilled the whole works to Mr. Huntington. You see, Huntington was the fellow that gave me the money to bribe O'Fallon. It was Huntington that owned about fifty-five per cent of the stock of the company that built the *Neptune*. Not openly, of course, because he was a member of the Shipping Board, but under cover of an alias."

Brown looked at Grass as though suspecting that he had suddenly taken leave of his wits. Grass grinned and nodded at Lane.

"Ask him," he said. "Ask him if he hasn't always known Huntington was mixed up in it."

Lane looked at him with disgust.

"It's true," he admitted, "that I had begun to suspect something of the sort, but it was no more than a suspicion. I was never able to prove anything. When Huntington disappeared it seemed to me fairly conclusive, but there was, after all, the chance that he was dead—and I could not bring myself to make unsubstantiated charges against a man who was—or might be—unable to answer them. I'd known Huntington for a long time, and I knew and admired his wife and his children. I thought of them."

"So that," said Brown softly, "was what you meant when you told me that you'd always thought Huntington had gone off in Jura's boat?" He spoke very quietly, betraying no hint of his excitement.

"That," said Lane, "was what I meant."

"And was that your reason for keeping silent—for saying nothing of your suspicion?"

"That," said Lane again, "was my reason."

Ten minutes later Brown, setting out in search of Myron, paused briefly to wonder whether he was the only sane man turned loose in Bedlam, or whether every other inhabitant of World's End was extraordinarily sane and he alone had lost his mind. As he sped across the quiet sea toward Summerville, with Myron silent and absorbed at the wheel, he continued to ponder the question.

Chapter XV

At twelve noon on this same Wednesday of the last week in January, E. Kenyon Jones sat in the dusty law offices of Brown & Jones in Baltimore and conversed with Thomas, the office boy. Beyond the frosty window a fine snow was falling, driven by a gusty wind. It was that particularly discouraging sort of snow that finds its way inside the most closely fitting collar and stings the face with tiny, icy particles.

But E. Kenyon regarded the weather with complacency. He was tilted back at a perilous angle in his swivel chair, his feet comfortably elevated to his blotter, and a large and fragrant cigar in his mouth. The room was blazing hot, and cheerfully garish in the light that flooded from a hideous, old-fashioned chandelier that hung from the middle of the ceiling. On the desk, beside E. Kenyon's shining shoes, a paper package lay open, disclosing half a dozen thick sandwiches, half liverwurst and half Swiss cheese, and the atmosphere was pleasantly permeated by the smell of coffee percolating on the washstand behind a burlap screen. Consequently, the lawyer bestowed upon the weather the final stamp of his approval.

"Tell you what, Thomas," he rumbled, over and round the cigar, as it were: "people complain about the winter climate here in Baltimore, but I like it. I like winter weather that is winter weather. Think it's healthy. None of your palm trees and summer breezes for me."

Thomas, who had just been round the corner to the store for the sandwiches and coffee, and who was now surreptitiously drying his wet feet against the radiator in the corner, agreed half-heartedly. He had an inordinate respect for both of his eccentric employers, and it grieved him to suspect them of being in the wrong about anything. He was a gawky youth of sixteen or seventeen, with a long, saturnine countenance, and experience had taught him to take life seriously. He was frequently afflicted by the levity of the firm.

Hannibal, the cat, lying in the warm glow of Thomas's desk lamp, regarded the pair through half-open eyes with lazy feline amusement. Hannibal was Thomas's cat, and could hardly be said to be a credit to the firm, who tolerated her for Thomas's sake. Her rusty black coat was moth-eaten and battle-scarred. She had lost half her tail in some forgotten scrimmage, and her temper was of the most uncertain. But Thomas had picked her up on an ash heap, a mewling, howling, abandoned kitten, and some subtle bond of common experience had established itself between the two waifs. Thomas's landlady had looked with disfavor on this addition to her household, so Brown &

Jones had bowed to the inevitable, and Hannibal—the name was Mr. Brown's invention—took up her abode in the office closet.

"Well, I suppose she'll act as a sort of watch dog," E. Kenyon had remarked doubtfully, rubbing his bald head. "I know I'd hate to tackle her on a dark night."

"She would if she ever stayed home," commented Bolivar acidly, regarding the little creature's mangled left ear, for even at a tender age Hannibal had displayed a roving and belligerent disposition. Hannibal had waved her tail at him noncommittally. The tragic loss of half this member had been of later date.

Now the cat lay on Thomas's desk and looked from Thomas to Mr. Jones, which would have proved to anyone familiar with cats that her attention was fixed on the liverwurst sandwiches. Convinced that she was unobserved, she gathered herself quietly, muscles rippling and tightening under her disgraceful fur. Then she leaped.

With a howl of rage, Mr. Jones withdrew his feet from the desktop and made a grab at the cat. She rewarded him with a vicious stroke of her paw that drew blood with every claw. He dropped her with a profane ejaculation, and at this moment the telephone rang.

"Why don't you feed your cat?" he demanded of Thomas, while with his uninjured hand he reached for the instrument.

"Yes, sir," stuttered Thomas. "I—I'm awfully sorry, sir."

Mr. Jones took the receiver from the hook and held it automatically to his ear, but he paid no attention to the voice that came over the wire, being full of his grievance.

"If you don't put that cat in the closet and keep it there I'll wring its neck," he informed his unseen caller.

"Yes—yes, sir," stammered Thomas, thrusting Hannibal into the closet and shutting the door on her howling remonstrances.

"For heaven's sake feed her!" shouted E. Kenyon into the receiver. "You've got some milk, haven't you? Give it to her and shut her up."

"I'm damned if I will," said a voice distinctly in Mr. Jones's ear.

"I'm s-sorry, sir," stammered Thomas, "but the milk's frozen, and I'm afraid it won't agree with her."

But Mr. Jones's attention had been caught by that distant voice.

"Eh? What? What did you say? Here, wait a minute." He turned back to Thomas. "Then give her the liverwurst and be damned to her!" he shouted. "Bolivar, is that you?"

A chuckle came over the wire.

"Your advice, while interesting, is not precisely to the point," murmured Bolivar Brown. "Although, when you come to that, there are moments when I'd like to wring her neck. But I can't put her in the closet, you see. And I doubt if she'd eat liverwurst."

"Idiot!" murmured E. Kenyon whole-heartedly. "Where are you?"

"I'm on a god-forsaken sand heap on the Florida coast, fifty miles from anywhere, using the only telephone that's still in operation after the recent unpleasantness. And I've engaged it for the next half-hour. I'm going to dictate a story to you, and you'd better have Thomas listen in on the other phone and take it down in shorthand, because after I've finished you're not going to believe it without written evidence that your ears have not deceived you. For it is the most staggering tale your credulous ears have ever listened to—and the biggest thing that has ever come our way."

"I thought," objected Jones mildly, "that you were on a vacation."

"You will leap to conclusions," complained Bolivar. "Are you all set?"

He talked for a full half-hour and more, while Hannibal gave up howling and slept philosophically in her closet. Thomas's astonished fingers trailed excited rows of dots and quirks and dashes across page after page of his notebook, and Jones, his fat face suddenly shrewd and concentrated, took notes on the pad in front of him. It was so still in the office that the soft tap of the snow on the windows could be heard, mingling with the sound of the coffee percolating hopefully and disastrously behind the screen, forgotten.

When Brown had finished, his partner sat for a moment staring down at the cryptic jottings on the pad in front of him.

"How about alibis?" he inquired at last.

"Not an alibi in the whole damn crowd," Brown told him. "Stuart was killed just before seven o'clock in the evening, and every soul in the house party, guests and family, claims to have been in his or her respective rooms dressing for dinner. Wait a minute, I take it all back. Franklin—the butler, you know—has an alibi. He was mixing cocktails in the butler's pantry, and several of the other servants saw him there."

"Speaking of the other servants," said Jones, again consulting his notes, "I suppose you've eliminated them?"

"Franklin was the only one of the lot that was there when Huntington disappeared," Brown told him. "Unless my whole theory goes by the board, he's the only one of the servants who could have had any conceivable motive in killing Stuart, because he's the only one who could have been involved in Huntington's disappearance."

"There is always—forgive me for mentioning it—the possibility that your theory may be wrong," Jones reminded him dryly.

"It isn't wrong. I've tried to console myself with that possibility, and to imagine that Stuart was killed by some mysterious unknown, dropped in from Mars. But it just isn't so. One of that neat little, sweet little party of twelve souls—of which I am one—put a cord round his neck and hung him up like an old coat on his closet door. That's as sure as sunset."

"So they were all in their rooms, were they?" murmured Jones.

"Dr. Simpson wasn't in his room," Brown corrected him softly. "He says he was, and gets very hot and bothered when questioned, but he wasn't. I went to his room to borrow a collar button at about ten minutes of seven, and he had already dressed and gone."

"I'll put him on my list," murmured Jones.

"There's another thing!" Brown's voice suddenly took on a new timbre—a brittle hardness not heard in it before. "It's a small thing— but a bit awkward—for me. Solomon Jura says he got back late that afternoon from a trip along the coast, and came up the back stairs because his shoes were wet and sandy. And he says that he got to the top of those stairs just in time to see me going back into my own door from the general direction of Stuart's room."

This time the quiet in the office was the quiet of a held breath, a suspended heartbeat.

"My God!" muttered Jones at last.

"And of course he did see me," pursued Brown. "I was going back from Dr. Simpson's room with a collar button grasped in my silly hand. But collar buttons seem so inconsequential, somehow, as an alibi for murder."

"You'd better come home," sputtered Jones. It was his first, and last indiscretion.

"Oh, no, I hadn't," retorted his partner. "Mrs. Huntington is saying that I killed Stuart because I was jealous of his attentions to my girl— and so I was jealous. She's right—right as hell about that part of it, although how she guessed I can't imagine. If I run away they'll say she's right about the other half of her statement, too. So I think, on the whole—" He chuckled suddenly. "You've no idea how nice it is down here, on these quiet isles of summer along the Florida coast. Sunshine and sea breezes; blooming orange trees; bathing all the year round—"

"Oh, go to hell!" cried his partner with exasperation.

"Don't need to go there," objected Brown sweetly. "I'll stay here— and let you work for a change. I shall bask upon the sands in a bathing suit and acquire a beautiful tan, while you slave away in the snow and cold."

"Ah," murmured Jones. "Now we come to the point. Where do I come in?"

For another five minutes Brown talked, and Jones made notes, and Thomas's pencil raced across the blank pages of his notebook. Then Bolivar Brown said good-bye and rang off. He got the long distance operator in Patona and inquired the toll. Then he got up and strolled to the window of the bare little room in which he had been talking and looked out.

It was the ticket agent's office in the way station on the branch line to Patona, and its telephone had, by some miracle, escaped demolition in the storm. Through the window Brown could see the single line of tracks, and on the other side rolling sand dues, scraggling grass, and stunted palm trees. Desolate enough. For a moment he stared at it silently, buried in thought. Then he went out, found the stationmaster held in conversation by Myron, put into his hand a bill of interesting dimensions, and thanked him warmly. A moment later he and Myron were on their way back to Summerville in one of the Huntington automobiles which they had borrowed for the occasion.

Meanwhile E. Kenyon Jones got Mrs. Jones on the telephone and broke it to her that he was catching a train for New York in an hour's time.

"If you'll just throw a few things in a suitcase," he said, "I'll send Thomas out for it. Can't get out myself. Got a million things to do. Oh, by the way—"

Mrs. Jones waited, expectant.

"Yes?"

"Remember that argument we had a while back?" asked her spouse.

"Which one?" asked the lady tactlessly.

"You know—the one about Bolivar? And you bet me—"

"Oh, that one! Yes, I remember."

"Well, you were right, for once. There is a girl."

"H'm!" grunted Mrs. Jones. "You silly old dear, of course there is.... No, I won't forget your shaving cream."

"Better put in the fur-lined mitts and a radiator," grumbled her husband. "It's the worst day you ever saw in your life. Baltimore has the damnedest, all-firedest, unmentionable climate..."

Thomas, struggling into his overcoat, grinned behind Mr. Jones's back.

It seemed to Bolivar Brown, looking back after it was all over, almost incredible that he should not have foreseen the next check in the game he was playing with his unseen antagonist. The moves, shrewd as they were, became in the light of the whole scheme so awfully obvious. Like a well-planned chess strategy, or an admirably played football offensive, weeding out all interference. Presenting pawn after pawn to his assault, leading him on, in a mood of false confidence, bringing him up suddenly, baffled and furious, to the realization that he was blocked in all directions.

"We give over too easily our belief in the mysterious." Who had said that? Jura. Jura, of course. When it was too late Brown recalled and pondered bitterly on the words. He should never for a moment have allowed himself to forget that legend of the strangler fig that killed again and again, slaying relentlessly and without compunction anything that stood in the path of its growth!

Yet actually, from a more unbiased viewpoint, his obtuseness is understandable. So many things combined to throw him off the scent. So many conflicting passions warring and jangling together, seeking their little satisfactions; so may threads of love and hatred woven and intermingling.

It began when Adele found him on the terrace about nine o'clock that evening. He had not seen her at dinner, and the keenness of his disappointment had confused him a little. He was thinking of her as he walked up and down, wondering if he might ask to see her.

Moonlight flooded the island and the quiet sea. The beaches were a ribbon of silver. The air was drenched with the scent of yellow jasmine. From the servants' quarters behind the house came the faint beat of singing—a strange, melancholy chant that was more a rhythm than a song. Strange people! Strange instinct for going directly to the heart of rhythm and beauty and drama. What a story—that tale of the strangler fig! Somehow that song recalled it to him, presented it with a new force, a new sense of its grotesque beauty. He heard again the voice of the Negro who had spoken to him on the sands: Perhaps the buzzards would "take their shadows away from World's End!"—"Take their shadows away!" A nice phrase.

And then Adele, looking herself like a little black shadow, came out of the house. She looked around and then came quickly to him. As she came into the moonlight her face looked white and lifeless above her dark gown. Only her eyes glowed and burned.

"I just wanted to ask—you were able to make all arrangements?"

Her hands were clasped nervously together. He looked down at her with eyes that must have betrayed him, had she had any eyes for what they had to say.

"Yes," he told her. "I saw—I saw the undertaker and made arrangements for the funeral on Friday—in the church. There is a little church there. It's not much, but I thought you'd rather—"

"Oh, yes!"

She stood for a minute, looking at him as though she did not know what to say next.

"I think," said Brown gently, "that, after all, Grass's motive was much what he claimed it to be—what he conceived to be consideration for the family. I was able to discover no reason why he should have wanted to—to hide Mr. Stuart's body from us."

"I'm glad," she breathed. "I'm thankful for that. I'm very thankful to you."

She turned and hurried back into the house, almost as if she were running away. Brown started to follow her. So much—so painfully much unsaid! But a voice stopped him, reminding him that the house was full of people. He stopped, took his pipe out, and slowly, carefully began to fill and light it.

Just beside him was the drawing room window, long and open. The voice that stopped him came through that open window. It was Stella Drew, singing. From where he stood he could see her sitting at the piano, touching it lightly with her pretty hands. She wore a sapphire-blue gown that molded itself to every line of her graceful figure, and the lamplight blazed on her red-gold hair. Decidedly an attractive picture!

Yet Grass, lounging heavily in a deep chair nearby, seemed not to find the prospect particularly pleasing. He scowled at the floor, altering his position occasionally to scowl at the lady. Unpleasant brute, thought Brown, noting that he looked even heavier and more bull-like than usual in his dinner coat. He was smoking savagely at his eternal black cigar.

Stella Drew's voice was pretty, and admirably suited to the silly French song she was singing, with a great deal in it about "*L'amour, tra-la-la!*" But her voice, as she finished the song and spoke to Grass, was of another timbre.

"Jacob, if you do it I'll kill myself. I swear I will." The words were softly spoken but so vibrant that they carried easily to Brown, standing by that open window.

"You!" Grass's laugh was an insult. "My dear Stella, you haven't the nerve to prick your little finger—deliberately. You'd no more think of doing yourself an injury—than I would."

She leaned toward him. Her pose was graceful, delicate, but Brown could see her face, and it was venomous.

"Then I shall kill—you!" she breathed.

An instant later he could hardly be sure he had seen that look, for steps sounded in the hall, and Mrs. Drew was back at the piano, white fingers wandering idly over the keys. The step went on, and she looked across the corner of the piano at Grass.

"L'ete reveille les fleures,"

she sang softly. "Jacob Grass," she muttered, while her hands still dwelt lightly on the running melody, "I've been useful to you in a thousand ways. I've done your errands and pulled your chestnuts out of the fire. If you throw me down to marry that woman you'll live to regret it."

"It isn't possible," murmured Grass ironically, "that you had any notion that I might marry *you?*"

She flushed to the roots of her pretty hair.

"My dear soul," she murmured with a twisted smile, "I have a husband—such as he is—already."

"Exactly," nodded Grass. "I can't see, after all, why this should make such a difference."

"Can't you?" inquired Mrs. Drew sweetly. The little tune had run its course. She began again:

> *"Le mois de Mai se reveille,*
> *Mon coeur s'ouvre a ses merveilles."*

"I'll tell you why, Jacob Grass. Because I don't choose to have you marry, and because I say that I do not agree to your bargain. I do not agree to it, my dear Mr. Grass."

He seemed to rouse himself then, and leaned toward her, capturing one of her drifting hands. The music stopped abruptly.

"My dearest girl," he murmured, "you've misunderstood me entirely. Entirely." His change of posture turned his face away, so that his voice became a confused murmur. Stella Drew sat listening to him, a strange look on her little vapid face—a look Brown could not read.

Chapter XVI

And that was all, for the moment. But an hour later Fate, or chance, or what you like, played into his hands again. He was still pacing the terrace, smoking and thinking, trying to piece together the tangle of events that confronted him, when Jacob Grass came out of the house and strolled down the path through the garden. At least, he strolled for perhaps a hundred yards, and then suddenly his pace picked up speed, and he strode off as quickly as his bulk permitted.

Brown, watching idly, wondered where he was going and whether it would be instructive to follow him, but before he could make up his mind another figure slipped out through the long drawing room window, crossed the terrace swiftly, and ran silently down the path. Brown hesitated no longer. He knocked the coals out of his pipe, thrust it into his pocket, and followed. For the second figure was Mrs. Drew—Mrs. Drew with a dark wrap drawn over her bare white shoulders, and the light, furtive step of a woman who does not wish to be observed.

Brown followed swiftly and silently, walking on the grass beside the path. But he lost her beyond the big poinsettia bush. Whether she had heard his coming and hidden herself in the shrubbery, or whether she had turned off onto the beach and lost herself in the heavy shadows cast by the moon, he was not sure. He hesitated. In the distance he heard a small branch snap under the heavy tread of Mr. Grass and decided to take a chance. He turned off to the beach himself and hurried on, keeping as much as possible in the shadow and walking lightly on the soft sand.

He saw and heard nothing more of his quarry, but surely, if he had guessed right, he would come on them presently in the summerhouse at the island's tip. And so it proved. For as he passed the wrecked jungle and turned the end of the island he heard low voices ahead of him and discerned two dim shapes etched against the moonlit waters. He stopped in his tracks and watched. Slowly, talking earnestly as they went, they crossed the beach and entered the little summerhouse.

Brown stood and debated within himself. What business of his was it if Jacob Grass and Stella Drew chose to hold clandestine meetings in the summerhouse? Now that he had satisfied himself that that was all it was, hadn't he better go back to the house and avoid the possibility of finding himself in the humiliating position of an eavesdropper? And yet there was something about the whole affair that did not explain itself on this basis. The scene he had witnessed earlier in the evening returned to him and Mrs. Drew's voice when she said: "If you do it I'll kill myself." And again: "Then I shall kill you."

And then suddenly something happened that completely shifted the values of the situation. Until now the voices of the two in the summerhouse had been deadened by the sound of the water on the beach to an indeterminate murmur, but now the woman raised her voice in what seemed like anguished protest.

"Oh, no, no! I can't!"

And the voice was not the voice of Stella Drew but of Madeleine Huntington! And suddenly Bolivar Brown knew that he must know what was going on down there on the point.

He looked about him for a possible means of approaching the summerhouse unobserved. The beach was brilliantly illuminated by the moon. If he crossed it, however silently, he would instantly be detected. But a little to the right of the summerhouse, the low fin of the reef on which it stood curved inland to the edge of the wood, a low ridge of rock in the interstices of which grew a few scraggly bushes and a little ragged beach grass. There was just a chance that by crawling along in the shadow of this flimsy barrier he might gain the shelter of the summerhouse itself and conceal himself against its low railing.

It was only when he was halfway across that he realized the probability that Mrs. Drew might be standing in the shadow of the jungle, watching him.

Well, it was too late to consider that now. He wriggled forward, acutely conscious of the general ridiculousness of his position and expecting momentarily to be challenged. But the murmur of voices ahead of him continued unbroken, and in another moment he found himself almost at the water's edge, crouching against the summerhouse wall.

He lay perfectly still. He could hear distinctly now. And what he heard made him curse himself for not arriving sooner. For Madeleine Huntington was saying frantically:

"You couldn't be so cruel—you couldn't! It's not your secret. What concern is it of yours?"

Grass answered her, his voice flat and unctuous.

"It has become my concern, all right," he told her. "It became my concern the day I fell in love with you, Madeleine. All's fair in love and war, you know."

Little love as Brown wasted on Mrs. Huntington, he longed to rise up and dip Grass in the sea for the covert insolence in his tones, the fatuous assurance. There was a little pause, and then Madeleine said in a lower voice:

"How long have you—known?"

"Oh, a year or two."

"And all that time—" There was despair in her voice.

"And all that time, my dear," said Grass smoothly, "out of consideration for you, I haven't said a word. That ought to set your mind at rest. I haven't said a word—and I won't, if you'll just—think it over a little."

"Out of consideration for me!" she cried bitterly. "You mean you were waiting until Mr. Huntington's will could be probated."

"Well, naturally," deprecated Grass with a grunt of laughter, "I couldn't hope to marry you while Huntington was still presumed to be alive."

Mrs. Huntington seemed suddenly to lose control of herself.

"What a perfectly vile creature you are!" she cried in a low, venomous voice. "Have you no conception of what an appearance you must cut to me—to any decent person?"

But Grass only laughed.

"I didn't expect," he said coolly, "that you would take it quietly."

For a moment there was no sound but the swish of the breaking waves. They swirled along the edge of the low rock on which Brown crouched. Then Grass went on:

"And I'm not going to hurry you or worry you. It's not a question of a hold-up, you know. I'm not that kind of a fool. I just thought I'd let you know that I knew all about it, don't you see, and—er—ask you to sort of think it over. And I'm not a bad sort after all, you know. We'd get along fine. With you to help along—you knowing how things ought to be done, and everything—we could cut a swath. I'd run for Senator myself—and maybe something more before I'm through."

She laughed then, and her laughter was as cutting as a knife. When Grass spoke again it was in answer to that laugh, and the conciliation was gone from his voice.

"That's one thing I wouldn't do, if I were you," he said. "It's too risky. You're a pretty woman, and a rich one, Madeleine Huntington, but I've got the whip hand, and I could make you pay dearly for a thing like that—and I might, if I lost my temper."

"I'm not afraid of you."

"Oh, yes, you are! You're so afraid of me that you're cold all over, and shaking. You're so afraid of me that you won't sleep a wink all night for worrying what I'll do next. And you've a right to be afraid. Not but what I'll be reasonable if *you* are. You think it over, my dear, that's all I ask: think it over."

The voice that answered shook uncontrollably.

"Yes—yes, I will. But you must give me—a little time."

"Sure I will. I won't rush you. This is Wednesday. I'll give you—say, till Friday. Will that do? Make it Friday."

"Yes—yes: Friday. I'll go back now. I'd better go alone."

"Sure," said Grass again, heavily unctuous. "I'll smoke a cigar here and follow you after a bit. Now, don't you fret, little woman. You just be sensible, and everything will be all right."

There followed an inarticulate gasping sound, and then the tap of swift, light steps on the sand. Madeleine Huntington passed like a hunted bird, the long ends of her light wrap flying behind her in the moonlight.

For what seemed an interminable time, Brown crouched on his rock, stiff and numbed, waiting. The smoke of Grass's cigar drifted out above him, and now and then a low chuckle of laughter. It seemed like hours, but actually it was not more than ten minutes before the big man got up and strolled back along the beach. Clearly he had no suspicion of having been followed, for he looked neither to right nor left, but strolled slowly and unconcernedly, smoking and admiring the night. When the curve of the beach took him out of sight, Brown rose, easing his cramped muscles, took out his pipe and filled and lighted it.

He was waiting for something, but nothing happened. After a moment he said softly:

"Oh—er—Mrs. Drew!"

There was a little gasp and a stir in the shadow of the wood. Then, after a minute, she came forward, hesitantly, and stood where he could barely discern her shadow on the edge of the sand. But still she said nothing. For a moment he drew carefully at his pipe, watching her through the smoke.

"Could you spare me a moment?" he said at last, courteously. "Come down into the summerhouse, won't you? I want to talk to you."

She came then, slowly, and as the light fell on her face he was shocked by the ravages of the last hour. She looked suddenly old and pinched, and her eyes burned with a strange, unnamable look. He put out his hand involuntarily to help her, for she looked as though she could hardly put one foot before the other, and was suddenly aware of something hard and cold under the black lace of her wrap. His hand closed on it, and he drew it out. She made no effort to resist him, but stared at him with defiance as he held it up and looked at it in the moonlight. It was a small, pearl-handled revolver. He looked from it to her, inquiringly.

"If you hadn't been here," she told him, "I would have killed them both. I meant to do it when I followed them here."

He slipped it into his pocket.

"I don't think you mean that," he said gently.

For a moment she stared blankly out to sea. Then suddenly her lips quivered, and she turned to him in a gust of passion.

"He kissed her—did you see? I would have killed him—I would have. I almost did as he passed me on his way back. I almost said: 'Jacob Grass, here's my good-bye to you, and good luck.' I should have liked to see his face when the bullet struck him! He said I wouldn't dare." Again she paused, and again she went on: "But I knew you were there, watching. I could see you dimly from where I stood. And he's not worth hanging for—he's not worth it!" She laughed suddenly, terribly. "Particularly when there's—another way."

Brown stared at her, a curious chill upon him.

"I think," he said at last, "you'll change your mind—when you've thought it over more calmly."

She looked at him and laughed again.

"You don't understand me," she said. "I mean there's another way—of getting even. For instance—I could tell you something I know. I could tell you," she finished softly, "something you want to know—very much."

Brown started uncontrollably and snatched the pipe from between his clenched teeth. She laughed for the third time, but her laughter bore no resemblance to mirth.

"That gets you, doesn't it?" she said. "You want to know who killed John Stuart, don't you? Well, Jacob Grass killed him—that's who. Jacob Grass killed him as sure as I stand here now."

He caught her by the shoulders, staring closely into her face.

"What do you mean?" he demanded almost roughly. "What makes you think so?"

"Because he had a terrible row with Stuart the day before he was killed. He accused Stuart of tampering with some of his private correspondence and selling political secrets to the newspapers."

"What secrets?" demanded Brown.

"I don't know. I only heard part of the row. But I gathered that Stuart was planning to leave him and go back to New York to some job he'd had offered to him on some newspaper, and Jacob flew into a terrible rage and said that no one double-crossed him and lived to get away with it. And the next night Stuart was killed."

Brown thought of that packed suitcase and Myron's story. He looked at the passion-racked woman before him.

"And you think Grass did it?" he repeated slowly.

"Don't you?" countered Mrs. Drew.

Brown said nothing. The waves beat their slow rhythm at their feet and spread their silver lace across the sand.

Chapter XVII

Bolivar Brown, ministered to by the silent Franklin, sat on the terrace sipping an early cup of coffee. No one else was down. Even the workmen were not yet about. Franklin's manner was slightly reproving but tolerant.

It was going to be another hot day. Already into the freshness of early morning, was beginning to coil an insidious oppression of heat that seemed to bind itself around the temples and make thinking difficult. In the length and breadth of the island not a leaf stirred. Brown, looking wearily out from the blue shade under the awning, marveled at the rapidity with which the island was recovering from the effects of the storm. Except for the splintered and uprooted trees, one would never have imagined that three days before the place had been a scene of desolation. What a Garden of Eden it was, ringed by its sapphire ring of sea and haunted by the fragrance of flowers!

He sighed impatiently. The peaceful beauty of the scene seemed to mock him with his impotence. He felt as though he were caught in a Circean enchantment, unable to move to penetrate the stark reality that lay beneath this loveliness.[6] He returned, as he had returned a hundred times during the night, to those scenes of the evening before, vignettes, as clear-cut as cameos, revealing—what? He saw again Mrs. Drew's face as she looked up from the piano at Jacob Grass; heard again Mrs. Huntington's voice: "You couldn't be so cruel! . . . It's not your secret." What cruelty? What secret? He felt again the sharp, cold outline of Mrs. Drew's revolver. Would she really have used it, given the opportunity? And what of her accusation of Grass? And Grass's quarrel with Stuart?

He could not doubt that Stella Drew was telling the truth as far as she knew it. There had been an unmistakable ring of verity in her passionate sentences. So Grass had quarreled with Stuart, who had learned too much about his private affairs. Had that quarrel some connection with a later quarrel, a quarrel that took place at half-past six in Stuart's room on Tuesday evening—a quarrel after which Stuart was never seen—alive?

He sighed abruptly. Questions easy to ask but hard to answer. And his head ached from his sleepless night and the oppression of the heat. He gave over the argument for the moment and returned to the

---

6   Circean: resembling Circe, the fatally attractive sorceress encountered by
    Odysseus's men.

headlines of the three-day-old paper, which he had already read three times. His eyes traversed the lines of type methodically, but they blurred and ran together and made no sense at all.

A discreet cough at his elbow roused him from his abstraction. It was Franklin, with a letter on a salver.

"For me?" asked Brown, surprised. "Surely the mail hasn't come yet?" But even as he spoke he saw that the envelope bore no stamp.

"No, sir," Franklin informed him. "This letter was in the house mail basket, sir. I found it when I was sorting out the mail for Myron to take over to Summerville. If you'll notice, sir, it's a bit queer. The address is printed like."

Franklin, burning with curiosity, got no satisfaction for it. Brown took the letter from the salver as casually as if it were his every morning custom to receive mail in this manner. But the butler's disappointment would have been assuaged if he could have seen the tumultuous excitement behind the lawyer's calm exterior. Gone were the mists of discouragement that a moment before had blotted out the sun. His headache had vanished into the limbo of forgotten things. For, unless he was sadly mistaken, the scent of the quarry at last was in his nostrils and the hunt was up.

He pushed back his plate impatiently and spread the letter before him on the table. And when he had read it he swore softly and jubilantly.

My Dear Mr. Brown:

Within reason, you can have any sum you want if you will drop out of the game and arrange to receive an urgent telegram recalling you to your own concerns. If you accept this offer, which will not be repeated, when everyone is seated at dinner to-night, introduce the subject of old paintings and mention the amount you will accept—in the course of the general conversation on that subject.

If your terms are agreeable to me, you will receive part of the sum you ask to-morrow morning. If you fulfill your bargain and leave within twenty-four hours after that, the rest of the money will be waiting for you on your return to Baltimore. And you will have satisfied your curiosity at least to the extent of being assured that you were right in believing it to be

One of Us.

Brown stared at the message in astonishment. It was printed on World's End stationery, such as was supplied in every guestroom in the house, and was, he supposed, used by the family as well. And dropped into the common mail basket. No possible way of telling from which room it had come, or whose hand had deposited it in that much used receptacle. No possible way of telling whose ear, of the many round the dinner table, might be listening intently for his reply. Shrewd! Devilish shrewd. But, at any rate, he had unearthed an antagonist. It might, to be sure, be shadow boxing, but behind the shadow there was a reality, flesh and bone that could be grappled with and overthrown, wits that could be met and outwitted. Relief flooded through him, and a sense of adequacy such as he had not felt since the beginning of this enterprise. His hand clenched itself on the empty envelope, and then he looked up to find Franklin's eyes upon him.

The butler's solemn pallor was positively flushed with excitement, and his oppressive dignity had melted like snow before the sun. He leaned toward Brown confidentially.

"Oh, sir!" he asked in a thrilling whisper. "Is it a clue?"

Brown chuckled as he folded the letter, slipped it into the rumpled envelope, and placed it carefully in his billfold.

"It is possible," he admitted. "It is entirely possible. Have you ever noticed, Franklin, that anything is possible in this best of all possible worlds? And now," he added, "if you can make it all right with the cook, I would like another cup of coffee."

That afternoon Brown had a long and private conversation with Myron, the boatman, sitting on the end of the wharf, well out of the way of possible eavesdroppers. By way of excuse they held fishing rods in their hands, and if the sport was not particularly good, that was surely not their fault.

"No one has left the island since I brought the mail back this morning. I'll take my oath to that, sir," Myron asserted at one point in the conversation.

"No one is to leave the island to-night, either," said Brown gently. He hooked the end of the pole under his knee, took out his pipe, and filled it.

Myron spoke under his breath.

"I know the telegraph man in Summerville, sir," he said. "I can fix up everything you want, I guess."

"Then you're on?" inquired Brown.

The young man's smile was singularly brilliant, white teeth gleaming in his sunburned face.

"I'll tell the world!" he remarked quietly.

Jura's footsteps sounded on the planked wharf before they could see him. He came round the corner of the boathouse, clad in blue shirt and corduroys, with long rubber boots flapping and a row of glass specimen jars clutched between arm and side. He stopped abruptly when he saw them, but came on again almost instantly, climbing into a small launch tied to the wharf. He set his jars carefully down on the floor. Then he looked up with a smile.

"Any luck?"

Brown nodded pleasantly.

"Not much." He laid his rod aside and, rising, strolled over and helped Jura cast the launch loose. "Don't want a deck hand, do you?" he asked. "You know," he confessed, smiling, "ever since I heard about this I've been trying to get my courage up to ask you to take me along. Are you going far?"

"No," said Jura abruptly. "Haven't time. Just down to the reef at the end of the island. It's rarely still enough there to use my glass-bottomed boat, and I want to take some pictures. Glad to have you come if it won't bore you."

But Brown, as he swung himself aboard and pushed the launch away from the wharf, had distinctly the impression that Jura was not glad; that he would willingly have dispensed with his new "deck hand."

Jura untied the glass-bottomed boat from its moorings on the far side of the lagoon and fastening it astern, negotiated the narrow, shallow passage with great skill, and made his way to the open sea. They chugged along the island, passed the white summerhouse at the end, and cast anchor about a hundred yards beyond. Here Jura drew the glass-bottomed boat alongside, transferred to it a camera, which he took from a locker in the launch, and invited Brown to climb aboard. But when they were established over the reef and everything was adjusted, Jura showed no eagerness to get to work. He sat idly, turning the camera in his long, slender hands, and staring out across the sea. At last he looked at Brown with an uncertain, anxious smile.

"It would be futile, wouldn't it," he began, "for me to pretend that I do not know that you suspect me of having some connection with these murders? I cannot guess just what you imagine that I know about them, but it is so obvious that you suspect something."

Brown stared down at the wavering green at his feet. There was a branch of coral, graceful as a budding maple tree in spring.

"My dear sir," he said gently, "at the present moment it is my business to suspect everybody. For that matter, with one exception, each one of us is suspecting every other one. No doubt you suspect me."

"I suspect no one," said Jura, with a sudden vein of passionate emphasis running through and through his quiet voice. "It is not my business to suspect anyone. In the course of my long life I have learned that it is not wise to pry into the secrets of human hearts. My concern is with my studies. I wish nothing but to conduct them in peace. Surely this can harm nobody?"

Brown mistook him entirely.

"I did rather force myself on you, didn't I?" he murmured.

The older man turned on him suddenly with an irradiating smile.

"I do not make myself clear," he said. "I suppose you said to yourself, 'He is an old fellow who thinks only of his fish and his sea gardens. He will not notice.' But I should be stupid indeed if I did not know that you came with me, not for interest in my pictures, but because you thought I was trying to run away."

Brown laughed ruefully.

"*Touché!*" he murmured.

Jura sighed and stirred restlessly.

"Well, I cannot blame you," he said. "When a man moves in the dark he will bark his shins on the chairs. If he breaks things, it is not his fault."

The lawyer leaned forward with sudden earnestness.

"It is quite true that I am moving in the dark," he said. "Believe me, I do not for an instant really think that you have anything to do with these murders; but I do think—if you would—you could turn on the light. I think," he said, smiling crookedly, "you could put your hand on that switch that I cannot find."

Jura's face seemed to age before his eyes. The muscles contracted, and the lines deepened. But he only said wearily:

"No."

Brown, however, ignored the refusal.

"For instance, on the night Stephen Huntington disappeared he walked down the island after dinner—and, so far as we know—was never seen again. I think, Mr. Jura, you could explain, if you would, why you followed him down the island, and where you went, and whether you saw him there."

For a long moment there was no sound in the little boat but the slap of water against the side; no movement except the slow rise and fall of the smooth ocean swell on which they rested. Hung in this little world between sea and sky, the events of the last few days seemed suddenly to Bolivar Brown strange and unreal, more dreamlike than this dreamlike moment. When Jura began to speak at last, the lawyer listened to him as to a man speaking in a dream.

"As I grow older," said Solomon Jura slowly, "it becomes increasingly strange to me to watch the forces by which human beings are manipulated—the rigidity of the forms that mold us. Consider for a moment you—and me. Actually you do not wish to drive me as you are doing, to force me to indiscreet confession. You would gladly take my word when I say that I know nothing of all this; that Huntington was my friend and I loved him and would have harmed no hair of his head;

that little Adele is sacred to me, and I would not for the world have injured one who was dear to her. You would gladly take my word for that. Actually you believe it fully. Yet you are no less obliged to force me, if you can, to answer these questions of yours. Why, I do not know. If I were to run away you would be forced to believe that I was driven by guilt. You would be obliged to have me hunted down. Yet you would know that I was not guilty."

"That is all true," agreed Bolivar thoughtfully.

"And, on the other hand, I, for my part, would gladly open my heart to you. I feel in some strange way your friendship for me. I would gladly trust you. But I too am bound. No doubt you have full proof of what you say when you state that I followed my friend Huntington down the island the night he disappeared. If you were to tell that—as you must—to the police, they will arrest me. They must arrest me. They have no choice. But you will know as well as I that it is the rigidity of the mold that holds them. That truth and fact and the organic probability of events will have nothing to do with it."

Brown shook himself free of the spell that was being woven around him.

"Come," he said, "let us compromise, then, since we must. I will not ask you what you were doing when you went down the island that night. I will ask you only if you saw anyone in the wood near where Huntington was killed."

Jura looked out over the sea and Brown noticed suddenly that the veins in his forehead were swollen and blue.

"No. I did not see anyone."

"You did not even see Huntington?"

"I saw Huntington, but no one else."

"You had gone there to meet him?"

"I had not gone there to meet him, but I saw him. I had gone down to the summerhouse on the point by way of the beach. I started to come back by the path through the jungle. But when I had come halfway I turned and went back, and walked home along the shore where the waves washed over my footsteps."

Again that sense of unreality, of lightness, of floating through and upon space.

"Why did you do that?" asked Bolivar Brown.

"Because," Jura explained, and his mouth twisted into what might have been a ghastly smile, "because I met Huntington in the wood, and he was hanging by the neck from a rope that dangled in the middle of the pathway."

Chapter XVIII

The evening that followed had a dreamlike quality to Brown. For all his practical common sense, he could not shake off the sense of unreality that engulfed him. He felt as though it had all happened before, as though he could foretell, before it was uttered, every word that would be spoken, and the name of the person who would speak it. As though he already knew, with a crushing finality, what the end of all this would be.

Adele sat beside him again, as she had sat on the evening Stuart was killed. Adele in a little black dress that made her pale face look sallow and emphasized the black hollows in which her eyes, as it seemed, lay dead. Across the table was the place where Stuart's empty chair had stood, but the chair had been removed and stood against the wall, and the two chairs on either side had been pushed together to cover that horrible emptiness. Yet Brown felt that everyone at the table was aware of the place where that chair had stood; that every time Mrs. Drew and Dr. Simpson turned toward each other, they were conscious of that invisible thing between them.

So oppressive was the sense of repetition that Brown had a sudden impulse to say to the girl beside him, as he had said that night: "What have you been doing with yourself all day?" and was momentarily horrified lest he should actually say it. He wondered what her answer would be, and dared not wonder about it, and began hastily to talk about the poor fishing he and Myron had had that afternoon. There was a rattle of conversation around the table, the nervous chatter of people who are afraid to be still. Stella Drew's syrupy voice trickled through it as she leaned forward and spoke to her hostess.

"*Dear* Madeleine," she purred, "I'm so glad to see you looking better. Positively," she informed the others, "this afternoon I was *afraid* for her, she looked so white and strained." And then the pansy-blue eyes swung to Solomon Jura. "You know, Mr. Jura, you ought not to go out in that glass-bottomed boat of yours. Of course, it's thrilling and all that, and so useful to science, but it does worry dear Madeleine so. She was positively *sick* about it this afternoon, I can assure you."

Impossible to believe that this woman had stood in the shadow of the jungle the night before, with a revolver in her hand and murder in her heart, prevented only by the merest accident from shooting down her rival in cold blood. Or was all this a subtler sort of murder? The lawyer, watching covertly, saw Mrs. Huntington catch her dry lip in her teeth before she answered coolly:

"Don't be a goose, Stella. I hate the beastly thing, to be sure, but Mr. Jura wouldn't be happy without it."

"Did you get any pictures?" asked Dr. Simpson dryly, turning to Jura. "I happened to be strolling down by the summerhouse while you were over the reef with Mr. Brown, and I imagined you must be taking pictures."

"I intended to, certainly," said Solomon Jura, "but the light was bad."

"We all wondered," continued Simpson, turning to Brown, "how you could find time for such relaxation in the midst of your other activities." The man's rabbit face was pinched and pale, and his pinkish eyes looked as though he had not slept.

Before Brown could answer Grass cut in.

"We haven't heard," he grunted, "how the investigation is getting on. Have you found a candidate for the electric chair yet?"

Stella Drew dropped the glass in her hand. It fell sideways, the water spreading in a wide semicircle across the shining damask.

"I—I can't—" She broke off, holding her hand against her trembling lips.

Lydia Vaughan broke in from her end of the table.

"How can you joke about it?" she demanded, the sane, normal indignation in her voice somehow tempering the incipient madness that seemed to hover over them all.

"Does it strike you as a joke?" inquired Grass ominously. "I must say it doesn't seem very funny to me. I've never found Mr. Brown's activities amusing."

"You don't think," said Justin suddenly, "that we'd better get some expert investigator—detective—a fellow of that sort." He looked deprecatingly at Brown. "I know, of course, that I did everything I could to head you off at first," he apologized, "but I can see now I was wrong. If you think we ought—"

"Justin!" It was Madeleine Huntington's voice, dry and harsh. She leaned toward him, her eyes black in her white face.

"I know, but, Madeleine," protested the boy wretchedly, "this is getting beyond a matter of taste and preference. We can't go on looking at each other as though each one of us believed all the rest were murderers. We've got to clear the thing up. I think—"

"You think!" The tone was full of bitter scorn. But, even as she spoke, Mrs. Huntington seemed to realize that she had gone too far. "My dear boy, surely you want to do what your father would have wished. Do you think he would have subjected his friends to a police investigation?"

"The only difficulty with that argument is," said Adele in a low voice, "that it seems that one of us—was not his friend."

Suddenly Justin seemed to grow up. The apologetic indecision vanished from his voice. He spoke with a quiet force that had not been heard from him before.

"We've got to face the fact that one of us—one of the eleven people sitting round this table, you or I or Adele or one of our guests— followed my father into the jungle coppice and killed him. And that one of us killed my sister's husband under our roof two nights ago. I think you're insane, Madeleine, to suggest that we can go on living under such an intolerable suspicion."

Brown saw Mrs. Huntington look swiftly at Jacob Grass; he saw the hunted despair in her eyes. It was only when Lane had spoken to her twice that she turned to him.

"Mrs. Huntington." And then he spoke again gently: "Mrs. Huntington!" She looked at him then, with a desperate attempt at her natural manner. "I think you don't quite realize what your hesitation implies. It leads one to think that there might be something that Huntington himself would not care to have investigated." They started at that as at a sudden galvanic shock. "Of course," Lane hastened to add, "we know that that is not your motive, but only an excessive delicacy of feeling. But if you were trying to shield anyone it would be most ill advised, believe me. No one of us will ever be safe from this implication until the whole matter has been sifted to the bottom."

But Madeleine Huntington had regained control of herself.

"My dear man!" she retorted calmly, "I haven't the faintest notion of shielding anyone. If Mr. Brown can find out anything that will definitely establish the guilt of any one of us I will act vigorously upon it, I assure you. But I simply don't believe that either my husband or Mr. Stuart was murdered. And if I did, I should find it impossible to believe that any one of those present were guilty of so horrible a crime. Why, I've known you all for years. You're my friends. Well, how any of you can believe it, and act on that assumption, I cannot understand."

"I don't believe it," said Brown.

There was a moment of stupefied silence, and then they all began talking at once.

"But you said—" cried Justin.

"You—you were so sure," stammered Stella Drew.

"I thought you'd come around," grinned Jacob Grass.

Lydia Vaughan drew a long breath.

"I hope you're right," she said.

Brown waited until the tumult of voices died down. He looked at no one. He stared down at a fork, which he was turning over and over in his long, knotted fingers. But he was intently conscious of the tense rigidity of the girl beside him. Before his mind's eye was that little white face with the black lines marking and emphasizing those exhausted eyes. And he could spare her nothing—nothing in the world. He would have given his right hand for her, but he must join the rest in making her suffer. He thought of what Jura had said that afternoon about the forces by which our wills are driven. She must live through this hell of hers. There was no other way, no way round, no shield that his love could offer.

Then, as suddenly as they had started to speak, they all fell silent. The little click of china on wood, as Franklin set a dish on the sideboard, was distinctly audible. Into this silence, as a man drops a stone into a pool, Brown dropped the most casual of all casual remarks. He turned to Mrs. Huntington and said politely:

"That's a fine portrait against the far wall of the drawing room. It's Mr. Huntington, of course?"

She caught her cue as deftly as though this had been a play which they had rehearsed together.

"I like it very much. It's an excellent likeness and a most effective picture as well."

"There's a very dramatic quality to it," agreed Brown. "Almost Rembrandtesque. The face seems to start out at you from the surrounding shadows."

It seemed to him that they stared at him as though he had suddenly gone mad. He looked from one face to another, immobilized with a curious suspense.

"Of course," he said deprecatingly, "I know so little about portraits —or pictures of any kind. But since my first and only trip abroad, years ago, I've had a great admiration for Rembrandt and the extraordinary meaning he can put into a few strokes of the brush."

Lydia Vaughan came to the rescue of what appeared to be a moribund conversation.

"As though he caught the man's whole life and circumstances and character—everything that had gone to make him what he was—into that moment of time."

"Exactly," nodded Brown.

"But—dramatic?" fluttered Mrs. Drew. "Of course I don't know much about terms used in art—" she smiled flatteringly at Brown —"but that seems a funny word to me."

Brown laid down the fork he had been handling, as though suddenly aware of it for the first time.

"Well, suppose that an artist could put any one of us on canvas, just as we are at this moment: our characters, our past, what we are thinking about..."

The last word hung suspended in silence. It was as though each one around that table repeated it, echoing it again and again against some distant mountain of understanding. Stella Drew breathed shiveringly between her heavily scarlet lips.

"I think it would be very uncomfortable to be painted that way," she pouted, "I don't think it's anybody's business what I look like inside, as long as I'm presentable outside."

"You should have been painted by Gainsborough," said Daniel Lane with a smile that implied a compliment. "All pretty women should have lived in that era. Prettiness has gone out of fashion now, more's the pity."

"Isn't he a lamb?" cried Mrs. Drew, appealing to the company at large.

"One has to be smart and clever now—or appear to be," he went on with a smile. "But that's just a conspiracy of the ugly women to get the better of the good-looking ones. It's been the same since Venus and Athene tried to wangle the apple from Paris!"

"Speaking of Gainsboroughs," said Brown. Again it seemed to him that they all leaned toward him, hanging on his words, but this he knew to be an illusion. There could only be one among them to whom what he was about to say could have any possible significance. Perhaps it was that he could not fully keep from his voice the rising excitement that filled him. "Astonishing what those pictures sell for. That last one they brought over—I forget the amount, but it was appalling. You know, it's always interested me—what sets the value on a picture. You can pay anywhere from, say, five dollars to a half a million. What makes the difference?"

"A matter of taste," ventured Lydia Vaughan.

"Ah, but whose taste? Yours or mine?"

"Supply and demand," contributed Daniel Lane.

"How much the fellow that owned the picture wanted money," suggested Jacob Grass.

"But suppose—here's a case I have in mind," said Brown softly —"suppose you owned a masterpiece—something more valuable to the person who wanted it than anything else in the world—and this person offered you any price you cared to name for it. Well, how would you go about setting that price?" He glanced around the table like one inviting an argument.

Isabel Lane took up the challenge with a laugh.

"I'd swap it for a speed boat," she declared, "and maybe a shiny red roadster thrown in."

"Listen to the girl!" said Daniel Lane in an obvious aside to Mrs.

Huntington. "I've had no peace, night or day, since we got here. A speed boat, indeed!"

"I'd take a winter on the Riviera," said Mrs. Drew. "Wouldn't I, though? A winter on the Riviera—with all the trimmings."

Lydia Vaughan laughed, but her eyes lingered speculatively on Brown.

"I'd take a trip around the world and a year in London. That is, if I didn't like the picture too much. If I did, I might sit at home and look at that."

Brown's eyes met hers across the table with one of his sudden, lifted looks, but what the meaning in them was she could not read.

Grass laughed suddenly, boisterously.

"If it was after a losing election I'd probably sell it for a meal ticket," he offered.

"And if the election had gone your way," supplemented Lane, "you'd find out the market price, double it, and add on a commission."

"Naturally," said Grass. "That's good business."

"You're all starting at the wrong end," said Simpson with a leer. "I'd find out how much the fellow had, and then I'd figure how much of that it was safe to stick him for. If a man wants a thing more than anything in the world he'll pay for it."

"Come on, Madeleine," urged Stella Drew. "You've got to get in on this, too. What would you take?"

The eyes of the two women fenced like the eyes of duelists, rapiers in hand.

"I'm very stupid about such things," murmured Mrs. Huntington. "I should take the market price, I'm afraid."

"And I," said Jura with a smile, "would never have a masterpiece to sell, because, if I ever chanced to possess one, I should lose it and never be able to find it again."

Lydia Vaughan had not taken her eyes from Brown. Now she leaned toward him across the table.

"You haven't told us your view yet. What would you take for your picture?"

"I should not sell it," said Brown quietly.

Again that pulsing silence. Was it his own fault, he wondered? Was it the timbre of his voice from which, try as he would, he could not quite keep the touch of feeling?

"Ah," murmured Grass then, with ill-concealed disdain, "you're one of these connoisseurs, are you?"

"And I think," went on Brown, "that you all misunderstood me a few moments ago. I'll correct the error before I forget it. I said, if you remember, that I did not believe that anyone present in this room had committed the two horrible murders with which we are involved. By that I meant simply that my conviction in the matter was no longer a question of simple belief. It has become a question of absolute knowledge. I now know that one of the twelve people in this room murdered Stephen Huntington seven years ago, and that the same person murdered John Stuart night before last."

Stella Drew's eyes flew from face to face, and her lips moved as though she were counting. Suddenly she sprang to her feet with a wild scream, overturning her chair behind her. Her eyes, above the horrified hands that clasped her mouth, sought the place where Stuart's chair had stood, and then shrank away from it as though fearful of touching something she saw there.

"Twelve?" she whispered. "Twelve? There aren't but eleven of us."

Grass interrupted roughly.

"Don't be a fool, Stella. He means Franklin, of course. Franklin makes twelve."

Mrs. Drew began to laugh, the wild, shrieking laughter of hysterics. Deliberately Grass picked up the glass of ice water before him and threw it into her face. She stopped as abruptly as she had begun, and burying her drenched face in her napkin, began to cry quietly.

Brown sat totally unmoved in the tumult. He glanced once at Adele, but the girl seemed to have lost completely the power of speech or movement. She sat like an icy statue, her great eyes fixed on the table before her.

After a moment Justin spoke.

"What do you mean when you say that you know one of us did it? Do you mean that you know—which one of us?"

"Not yet," said Brown quietly. "But I hold the thread in my hand. It's only a question of time. I'm waiting for something."

Chapter XIX

The little traveling clock on the bedside table in Bolivar Brown's room ticked its way slowly and methodically to midnight before the lawyer came in and switched on the light. He was no longer in dinner clothes. He had changed to a dark tweed and rubber-soled sport shoes. He glanced at the clock, ran his hands wearily through his hair, resting his head on them for a moment as though he were pretty well done in. Then, with a determined gesture, he closed the door behind him, locked it, laid his coat across a chair, kicked off his shoes, and threw himself down on the bed. But the light in his eyes bothered him. He got up again, found his pipe, filled and lighted it, and rambled restlessly to the window.

Outside the night was still and clear and silent. The round moon, almost directly overhead, bathed the shadowy island in a soft, indescribable radiance. Brown drew wearily at his pipe, his mind too tired to relax its reiterated speculations and surmises.

If only he could get in touch with Jones! He wondered how long he would have to wait for his partner's report, and whether, when it came, it would throw light on this bizarre situation. Would he actually be able to find out anything about the *Neptune* disaster—anything more, at any rate, than Brown knew in a general way already? It seemed improbable. Anyone clever enough to cover his tracks at the time of the active investigation, would surely have overlooked nothing that could give him away now, after seven years. And, in any case, had that affair anything to do with this one?

The time tallied closely, of course. The *Neptune* had gone down in late December, and the ill-fated meeting of Huntington, Lane, Grass, and Dr. Simpson had taken place just before the beginning of the official hearings in the latter part of January. But all that might be coincidence. And, again, it might not. For the hundredth time Brown ran over in his mind the connection between these four men.

Simpson, the witness who had sent O'Fallon to jail on bribery charges; Grass, who had acted as intermediary between O'Fallon and the shipbuilding company who had built the *Neptune*; Grass, who had bribed Simpson to say nothing of his—Grass's—part in the transaction; Lane, Huntington's confrere on the Shipping Board, and on the Congressional committee to investigate the disaster. He paused a moment, sticking at this point as he had stuck before. Why had Lane been one of the party? If Huntington had really been, as Grass averred, the financial power behind the shipbuilding company involved, and the three of them—Simpson, Grass, and Huntington—had met to consider their procedure during the forthcoming investigation, why had Lane been included? To furnish a respectable coloring to the gathering? Was that all? Or was there, perhaps, something fishy about the respectable Daniel Lane? If he had really suspected Huntington of being involved in the scandal, if he had believed, as he said he had believed, that Huntington had absconded, was it credible that he would have remained silent all these years? Could his silence have been adequately explained on the ground of friendship?

Brown, staring blindly out at the beauty of the night, could not answer these questions. He could only hope that Jones's investigations might answer some or all of them.

He brushed his hand over his eyes. He was tired—tired to the bone —tired with a spiritual weariness more keen than physical pain. The case had got under his skin. He was unable to treat it objectively. He cared too much. For a moment he stood so, head bowed wearily on his hand, and that other pain rose keen and bitter in him—that purely personal pain for which, so far as he could see, there was no help. He took himself in hand. There was still so much to be done. He must get some rest if he were to do it. He turned back, knocked the ashes out of his pipe, switched off the light, and again threw himself down on the bed.

Suddenly, unexpectedly, sleep fell upon him. The hands of the little clock traveled on into the early hours of the morning, and there was no other movement in the room and no other sound except the lawyer's quiet breathing. In other parts of the house there was the stir of quiet motion; lights flicked restlessly on and off, and there were faint creakings in the long hallways. Now and then, from one room or another, came faint sounds as someone, tired of tossing on a sleepless bed, rose and walked softly up and down to ease taut nerves and cramped muscles.

But toward two o'clock the house seemed to quiet down, the lights went out for the last time and the uneasy stirrings ceased. Slowly the moon crept downward toward the sea, plunged at last into that swift, final decline, hung poised for an instant on the rim of the world, and slid majestically out of sight. In the blackness left by her going the island lay like an exhausted thing, and the creatures on it lay exhausted, in heavy slumber, at last.

Then at last the star-sprinkled patch of sky that showed beyond Brown's window changed; the stars began to fade, and the blackness became gray. Light filtered up over the eastern horizon, slowly flooding the sky before it touched the monotone sea beneath, conjuring color from island gardens and the colorless ocean.

The hands of the little clock had traveled half the distance between five and six when a new sound broke suddenly into the quiet of the shadowy room. Brown, struggling up from depths of sleep, heard it and lay taut, trying to put a name to it. He had been dreaming heavily, and for a moment he could not remember where he was, what room this was in which he lay, or what sound it might be that had roused him. He was conscious only that something was wrong—vitally wrong. And then it came back to him with a rush, and he flung himself out of bed and to the open window.

The sun was not yet up, but it was light enough for him to see. He knew already that the sound he had heard was the sharp put-put of a launch, and now, leaning out of his window, he saw the launch itself and its solitary occupant. He could not see the man's face, but there was no mistaking that long, angular, stooped figure, nor the thatch of gray hair that crowned it. Jura! Jura making off into that limpid world of half-light and shadow, making for some unknown port. Brown swore under his breath. He had arranged with Myron to keep watch until midnight, and then, like the stupid fool he was, had overslept. No doubt the boatman had dropped asleep.

But as the thought crossed his mind, as he drew in from the window to make a futile dash for that vanishing boat, a shot rang out, and he looked again to see the launch wavering in an uncertain course and coming to a helpless standstill not a hundred yards from the wharf. Myron, it seemed, had not been asleep after all.

Brown slipped on his shoes in frantic haste, dashed downstairs and out of the house.

The light had changed even in that brief interval. In a few minutes the sun would be up. As he hurried along the terrace in front of the house he could distinctly see every detail of the scene before him: Jura standing in the launch, looking back toward the boathouse; Myron putting off in the rowboat. The creak of the oarlocks came to him distinctly, and, as he rounded the corner of the house, another sound.

It came from the house above him, to his right—from the balcony, as he instantly realized, that opened from Mrs. Huntington's sitting room. He looked up and saw her, leaning out between the vines, clutching a filmy wrap about her throat and staring with distended eyes at the scene below. Almost in the same instant she seemed to become aware of some presence near her, and looked down. Their eyes met and, with a startled exclamation, she drew back, out of sight. Tucking the incident away in the back of his mind for further reference, he went on to the boathouse.

Myron had already reached the launch when Brown came out on the wharf, and was fastening the rowboat's painter to her bows. An instant later he began rowing back, towing the launch after him. A strange little procession they made, coming up through the pearly light in which water and air seemed to meet together into a fused translucence. Neither, as it appeared, had said a word. As they drew in at the wharf, however, Myron said briefly:

"I'm sorry, Mr. Brown. I dropped asleep for a minute, and the first thing I knew I heard the launch drawing out from the slip. I had to break her propeller."

Brown nodded briefly.

"It was my fault," he said. "I overslept. I should have relieved you hours ago."

Jura stepped out of the boat and looked at Brown with a half smile in his tired eyes.

"So that," he said, "is that. Perhaps, after all, it simplifies things." But he looked out over the magic beauty of sky and sea with the eyes of a man who is saying farewell to everything that is dear to him in the world.

Brown left him, for the moment, to his thoughts. He drew Myron on one side and spoke briefly to him in a low voice. Then he turned back.

"Shall we go up to the house?" he said.

Jura nodded. All the way back he said not a word, and Brown made no effort to get him to talk, for he felt that the explanation of these events was to be had in that upstairs sitting room with the balcony overlooking the sea.

Brown had left the wide front door open behind him when he dashed out, and now, as they went in, he could hear in the hall above sounds of excited movement and voices exclaiming and questioning. Apparently the shot had roused the household. As they started up the stairs Brown noticed that Jura caught at the rail to steady himself for an instant, as though he found the exertion of climbing too much for him. But only for an instant. Then he went on with his usual quiet composure.

In the shadowy hall above Brown could at first see no one, but looking down the corridor toward Madeleine Huntington's room, which ended, so to speak, in the sun room, he could see against the light a silhouetted group of figures, and he turned in that direction. As he came up he took rapid inventory of those present.

Isabel Lane, in a freakish little negligee, all ruffles and marabou trimming, looking like a rumpled child with her short, tousled hair and sleep not far from her eyes; Justin in bathrobe and slippers; Daniel Lane, looking unexpectedly elderly, with his graying hair uncombed and his chin unshaven; Simpson, shivering in an ugly purple brocaded dressing gown; and Lydia Vaughan, amazingly attired in a lavender wrapper and a boudoir cap. And as they came along the hall Stella Drew came out of her room and joined the others; Stella Drew in a bewitching old-blue peignoir, with her gorgeous hair in picturesque and neatly brushed confusion down her back, and her pretty nose hastily powdered in a bad light, so that a great streak of white powder slanted up under one eye.

"Oh," she cried with a pretty shiver, "what was that awful noise? Has anyone been hurt?"

Brown counted rapidly. Six—eight, including himself and Jura; three unaccounted for. And then he felt a light touch on his arm and turned to find Adele looking up at him. He had not heard her coming. It would hardly have surprised him to know that she had floated down the hallway, so like a little white ghost she looked.

"What is the matter? Something awful has happened. I know it. Don't keep it from me."

"My dear," he said gently, taking her cold little hand in his, "nothing very dreadful has happened. Nothing to worry you. Go back to bed."

"But—the shot? It was a shot, wasn't it?"

"Mr. Jura tried to leave the island, and Myron broke the propeller on his boat—that's all. No one was hurt."

"No, not that. I don't mean that. There's something else that—" She put her hand up vaguely and rubbed it across her forehead. "I don't know," she muttered. "I was dreaming."

"You had a nightmare, that's all," said Bolivar reassuringly. "I know how it is. It gives you such a confused feeling. It will be all right once you really wake up."

"Oh, I wish it would! I wish it would!" whispered the girl suddenly, clinging to his hand with fierce intensity. "I wish I could wake up and find that I had only dreamed—all of this."

Brown was very near taking her in his arms and bidding her cry out her heartbreak on his shoulder, but now a sudden diversion occurred that brought him back to the matter in hand. The door of Mrs. Huntington's sitting room opened, and Madeleine appeared on the threshold.

Apparently in these few minutes the sun had come up over the edge of the sea, for the room behind her was a glory of golden light against which she stood darkly silhouetted. And with the sun a breeze had come up and blew freshly in their faces through her open door. Ten, counted Brown. All but Grass. Where was Grass? His room, the lawyer remembered, was directly opposite this open door, and the windows overlooked the boathouse. Surely he could not have slept through all this disturbance? He was about to cross the hall and knock on the politician's door when Madeleine spoke:

"What is the meaning of this? Is this more of your doing, Mr. Brown?"

Their faces all swung to Bolivar Brown as though, for the first time, aware of his presence among them. And in their eyes was a common question. The lawyer looked at Madeleine Huntington, and from her to Solomon Jura and back again.

"I think," he said quietly, "you know better than I what the meaning is."

Suddenly Stella Drew spoke up querulously:

"Where's Jacob? Where's Mr. Grass?"

As if in answer to her question the door of Mr. Grass's room opened. But it opened only an inch or two, and then it stopped. And Brown knew suddenly that it was no human hand that had opened that door, but the breeze from the sitting-room windows. They had all turned at the creak of that first opening; now they stood breathless, their eyes on the crack. It seemed as though their nerves, taut to breaking point, would snap if that door delayed its opening. Yet no one moved to push it open. They simply waited, their eyes hanging on it. And then a fresh gust, laden with sunlight and the cool, sweet scent of the sea, seemed to lean lightly against the swinging door and push it farther.

They could see into the room a little now: dim shadows of drawn shades, faint gleam of blue sky through an open window. Grass was asleep, of course. Why not open the door and wake him? Yet no one opened the door. And then the breeze came and opened it wide— flung it joyfully open. And there, to be sure, was Grass, asleep in a big chair. Apparently he had fallen asleep there, half undressed, for he still wore the trousers of his dinner suit and his stiff shirt. He sat there facing them, with his huge body sprawling and his head dropped forward on his chest.

"Why, Jacob!" gurgled Stella Drew, and then the gurgle turned to a stifled scream.

What had been hidden from them by the dim light and Grass's position had become suddenly clear to their more accustomed eyes. Grass's collar was off and his shirt gaping, and round the neck where the collar had been was a thin cord, drawn tight, the end of which disappeared over the back of the high chair in which he lay.

Chapter XX

The paralyzed group in the hall said nothing. It seemed as though this shock, coming on top of all that had happened in the last two days, had stricken them permanently dumb and immobile. And then Stella Drew broke from the group and rushed into the room. She stood for a moment in front of Grass, not touching him, bending over and peering into his face. Then she turned back to the others.

"Why—he's dead," she said in a strange, matter-of-fact voice. Then suddenly she began to scream, over and over. The scream came from her throat impersonally, as though it had no connection with her. It was an extraordinary performance, theatrical in the extreme. Brown caught her by the shoulder and shook her.

"Stop it!" he said roughly. "Stop it at once."

She stopped obediently, as though she were a mechanical doll that could be wound up or stopped at will. Brown looked at her for a moment curiously before he turned to the slouched figure in the big chair.

Grass was dead, there was no doubt about that. It could be seen at a glance that he was dead. Brown, lifting his hand and finding it stiff under his fingers, looked at Simpson.

"He's been dead some time, shouldn't you think?"

Simpson, his face yellow and blue above the collar of his purple robe, shuffled forward and inspected the dead man.

"Several hours," he grudgingly assented. "Probably killed soon after he came upstairs."

Brown lifted the end of the cord that dangled loosely over the chair back.

"He could hardly have strangled himself, I suppose," he said slowly, glancing at Simpson. "Not much chance of suicide here, eh?"

"Certainly not," said the doctor, flushing angrily.

Brown looked at the paralyzed group in the doorway.

"At last we come to it," he said sternly. "Murder. Not a question of opinion, but a matter of fact. This man was killed—strangled with a cord around his neck—after we all came upstairs last night."

Deliberately he held his eyes away from Stella Drew. He would make no accusations, insinuate nothing, until he had something more tangible than a threat and an hysterical outburst to go on.

"I think," said Daniel Lane quietly, "that we are entitled to know why Mr. Jura attempted to leave the island this morning."

"On my business," Mrs. Huntington cut in before Jura could speak.

"I asked him to run down to Miami to attend to a private matter for me."

"Which was?" inquired Lane.

"I have just said," retorted Madeleine Huntington coldly, "that it was my private affair."

Brown was rapidly revising his opinion of Mrs. Huntington. It seemed almost incredible that anybody could be such a fool. Did she really think her stubbornness would suffice to protect Jura? Did she really believe she could any longer delay an explanation of her conduct and his?

"You see," went on Daniel Lane to Brown, "we know that Mr. Jura followed Stephen Huntington down the island the night he was killed, and that he avoided giving any account of his behavior to the police on that occasion and on the night of John Stuart's death. I have hesitated until now to make any direct accusation, but I'm sure you'll agree, Mr. Brown, that we have a right now to ask Mr. Jura to explain himself."

"I should say," said Simpson in an ugly tone, "that we've a right to do more than that. If Mr. Brown doesn't want to hand him over to the police, I'll say we've got a right to do it ourselves. I for one don't propose to stand under any suspicion of this thing for a minute longer than I can help. And we all know Jura's guilty as hell."

"I will not resist you," said Jura suddenly.

"Do you mean—" cried Simpson, but Mrs. Huntington interrupted him. She swung on Jura, every vestige of her usual cool, self-possessed personality vanished in a rush of passion.

"You fool!" she blazed. "You poor, blind fool. Do you want to destroy us both? Have you forgotten—everything?"

"It is no longer any use," said Jura wearily.

"Do you mean," cried Simpson eagerly, "that you confess these murders?"

"No," said Jura proudly, and as he turned his face toward Simpson, Brown was again impressed by the strange, luminous nobility in that lined countenance. "No," said Jura again. "I give you my word that I know nothing about any of these deaths. The matter that Mrs. Huntington refers to is something that goes very far back—even before the death of Mr. Huntington. It goes back many years into our almost forgotten lives."

The tears were running down Madeleine's face, quite unheeded.

"You gave me your word," she cried brokenly.

Jura went to her and took her hand and patted it.

"Yes, my dear, I did. And I will keep it until you release me. But you will see very soon that it is impossible to keep it any longer."

Suddenly Adele cried out in a strange, broken little voice:

"Why do you bait him so? Can't you see he didn't do it? How can you bear to keep silent—whoever did this thing—and let the innocent suffer so? One of you did this! Be merciful and end this horror!"

And now another voice cut through the murmur of voices, a strange, tortured, passionate voice. It came from Mrs. Drew's drawn lips, but it did not sound like Mrs. Drew's voice.

"Do you hear that, Madeleine Huntington?" she cried. "Do you hear that? Stop hiding behind Mr. Jura! Come out in the open for once in your life and say that you did this. That you did it because Jacob Grass threatened to give away your wretched secret—that he wanted you to buy him off by marrying him to the Huntington millions!"

Mrs. Huntington stared at her, with the blank, flat look of someone who has borne so much that she can bear no more.

"But it isn't true," she said dully. "I didn't do it."

Suddenly Justin stepped between his stepmother and Mrs. Drew.

"Are you seriously suggesting that Madeleine did this thing?"

"Certainly I am. I believe she did do it."

"And do you also suggest," pursued the boy grimly, "that she killed her husband?"

Mrs. Drew began to laugh—a terrible, strident laughter.

"My dear boy, don't pretend such innocence. You know very well they had a fearful quarrel the very day he died. You overheard it—or part of it—as I did."

She paused in the midst of a gasping silence, amid eyes that swung to Madeleine Huntington's frozen face and clung there. Brown, glancing at Justin, saw that the boy's face was as white as his stepmother's, and more terror-stricken. The lawyer suddenly took command of the situation.

"There is no occasion for you to answer any accusation offhand," he said to Mrs. Huntington.

He looked from one face to another but no one spoke.

"We're confronted with a horrible situation—all of us. No one of us is free of it. There is not one of us who could not have committed either or both of these crimes. With the exception of Miss Lane, Mrs. Stuart, and myself, any one of you could have killed Mr. Huntington." Again he paused, and again no one sought to interrupt. His swift, sidelong glance swept their faces. "The quickest and most reasonable way of getting at the truth is for each one of us to tell anything we know, or have observed, that could conceivably have any connection with the affair. Perhaps a very trifling thing would lead us to the truth. I have already in my hands a quantity of information, which needs, perhaps, only one little arrow to point the way to the true explanation of the whole matter. I will, very shortly, have more important information. If each one of you will tell candidly what you know—"

He paused again, but the faces turned to him were blank. When he went on his voice had a sterner ring.

"I don't know yet which one of you has done these horrible things, but whichever one of you it is, I warn you that you'll get no mercy from me. I'm not interested in bribes, and it would be futile to threaten me. I shall not rest until I am able to call the strangler fig by its human name." His lips curved in his characteristic wry smile. "An interesting problem in botany, you will admit."

Suddenly Lydia Vaughan came forward and put her hand on Brown's arm.

"My dear man," she said, and her sensible voice held an anxious note, "I'm a great admirer of heroics, and there's nothing I love so much as the dramatic touch, but if what you say is true, it strikes me that you're taking your life in your hands by making proclamations of that sort."

Brown laughed softly, and his eyes swept the circle of faces again with a swift, penetrating glance.

"My dear lady!" he retorted. "Does it strike you that way, too?"

Suddenly Adele was at his side, her hand clasping his arm.

"Don't!" she whispered. "Don't laugh so. Whatever it is you're doing—oh, don't do it! I'm afraid."

Dr. Simpson laughed suddenly, shrilly.

"I shouldn't worry, if I were you," he said. "I think—if Mr. Brown wanted to—he could tell us now who killed Mr. Grass, and who killed John Stuart—and probably who killed Mr. Huntington, too, for that matter."

Brown looked down at the girl beside him.

"It's perfectly true," he said gently, "that I'm as guilty as anyone else—in the eyes of a disinterested police sergeant."

The gray eyes looking up at him held something in their depths that he had never seen there before. For an instant the floor seemed to shift under his feet, and the color of the world changed. It was all over in a breath, for the lashes came down over the eyes, and hid that look. With a faint sigh, instantly suppressed, Brown turned to Mrs. Huntington.

"I should like to speak to you for a moment," he said courteously. "With your permission, I'll send for Myron and put him in charge of this room."

All trace of fight had gone out of her, apparently. She nodded silently and stepped back into her sitting room. The others waited until Myron appeared and watched in a sort of dazed silence while Brown locked the door of Grass's room and gave the key to the boatman with instructions to allow no one to enter. Then Brown crossed the hall to Mrs. Huntington's door. On the threshold he turned and looked at Jura.

"Perhaps you'll join us," he suggested. "And you, too, Justin."

They followed wordlessly, and he shut the door upon them.

Chapter XXI

The pleasant room was full of sunlight and sweet, cool air, and the sound of water breaking on the beach. Brown went to the window and stood for a moment looking down the island. It was still too early for the workmen to be about. The unbroken quiet and dewy freshness of sunrise lay over the scene. He turned back to the three who waited in the room behind him. Mrs. Huntington stood like a woman awaiting sentence, with a quiet desperation in her ravaged face. She held Solomon Jura by the hand. And behind them, almost against the door, Justin sat on the arm of a chair. Brown plunged into the matter at once.

"Of course, Mrs. Huntington, we'll have to notify the police at once —not the local sheriff, but headquarters in Patona. We have no longer any choice."

She opened her white lips to speak, but no sound came. Jura put his arm around her with a look of pity and devotion that was singularly moving.

"We have always known it would come some day," he said gently. "Now that the time is here we must thank God for the happy years and face what is to come."

She roused herself and nodded at Brown.

"You must do—what you think best," she said.

Brown turned to Justin.

"You must go to Summerville at once," he told the boy, "and call Patona on the wire. Get police headquarters and speak, if possible, to the chief of police. In any case, get hold of someone in authority and make it quite clear what has happened and that it will be necessary for them to send someone, as the local police are doing nothing about it. Then ask for instructions and come back as soon as you can."

"Right-o." The boy turned toward the door and then came back again. "I'd just like to say," he said hesitantly, "I'm afraid I've been rather a beast about all this. You were right all along, of course, and I made a complete ass of myself. I hope you won't bear a grudge?"

Brown smiled his odd, crooked smile.

"Do I look like that kind of an idiot?" he asked mildly. "Run along, young feller!"

When the boy had gone Brown turned to Mrs. Huntington.

"I wish," he said gently, "that you would not be quite so frightened. I don't know what the trouble is, but I'm increasingly sure that it's nothing that need alarm you so terribly. I thought at first that Mr. Jura must have some knowledge of the affair, and after witnessing the scene between you and Mr. Grass last night—"

"You—you heard *that?*" she breathed.

Brown nodded.

"It would be so easy to jump to the conclusion that you killed Grass because he threatened you," the lawyer said slowly. "But somehow I don't think you did. I distrusted you at first, I'll admit, because I couldn't make out what you were after. But I'm beginning to have some vague sort of premonition—" He broke off and then went on earnestly: "If you'll trust me, if you'll tell me what you fear and convince me that it has, in fact, nothing to do with this investigation, I give you my word that what you tell me shall go no farther and that I will do my best to help you."

She looked at him incredulously, a dawning hope in the back of her eyes.

"You mean—you mean that you'll help him? You'll let him get away before the police come?"

"If you can show me that he knows nothing of these murders—yes."

"But he doesn't!" she cried. "Of course he doesn't. Won't you believe it?"

"I think," broke in Jura mildly, "we must tell him the whole story. For some time I have felt that it would be best to do so, and now I think there is no longer time for delay. We will tell him everything and ask his advice."

For an instant she looked at Brown as though she sought to pierce with her eyes to the very source and inspiration of his motive in forcing her to this confession. What she saw seemed to reassure her somewhat. The strained lines of her face relaxed, and she managed a wan smile.

"You seem to have some magic, Mr. Brown," she said. "Sit down and I'll tell you the whole story."

She sat down herself in the deep chair beside the little table in the window, and looked about her as though wondering how to begin. Her eyes chanced on the paper-backed *Lettres de mon Moulin,* within easy reach of her hand. She picked it up and turned it over idly. Then she glanced across at Brown.

"You were surprised the other day when I betrayed the fact that I was disturbed by your noticing this book. I thought you had some special reason for noticing it. And I didn't want you to realize that I read French like a native—for the reason that, as a matter of fact, it is my native tongue. I haven't any accent, of course, but that's because I came to America when I was a very little child. But my parents were French, and we always spoke French at home."

Brown must have looked his bewilderment, for she smiled faintly.

"It's more relevant than you think," she said. "You see, Solomon never lost his accent, but then he was ten years older than I."

The purport flashed upon Brown's astonished intelligence with a vast illumination.

"Mr. Jura, I take it," he said wonderingly, "is your brother?"

"Yes."

"But I understood that—you are Hungarian, aren't you?" he asked, turning to Jura.

"French," said the older man quietly. "For reasons which you will understand later, I found it wise to change my nationality—as well as my name. My name was Champenois—Eugène Champenois."

Some dim sense of familiarity tugged at Brown's memory—a feeling that he had heard this name before in some forgotten connection.

"Go on," he said quietly. "I don't understand yet, of course."

"Eugène spent only a few years in this country," Madeleine went on, "and then he went home for his military service. And when that was over he served for a time with the French army in Algiers. At about this time—I was twenty—I met Waldo Bingham, the naturalist and explorer, and married him. He was planning a book about Africa at that time, and I was of an adventurous turn of mind and keen to go with him, so we went there on our honeymoon. We intended to stop off in Algiers on our way back, to see Eugène. But I did not see him for nine years.

"When we came out of central Africa, after having lost all contact with the world for eight months, I heard that Eugène had been indicted in the Romaine conspiracy, had been tried and convicted and condemned for life to Devil's Island."

Light broke upon Bolivar Brown.

"Of course," he murmured. "Of course. I began to recall as soon as I heard the name. I read a book about the Foreign Legion not long ago, and the affair was mentioned at some length in that."

"Then you know," cried Madeleine hotly, "that it was a purely political matter, and that the convictions were purely political. Yet my brother was convicted like any ordinary felon or murderer and sent to that horrible place for the rest of his life.

"Naturally I was prostrated. My mother had died before this, but my father was still alive and moved heaven and earth to get the sentence revoked. But without success. A man who has once gone to that place does not often find his way out again. It broke my father's heart, and he died not long afterward.

"For some time we heard nothing of Eugène. My husband and I traveled all over the face of the earth, and in the intervals he published his studies of the countries we visited. I don't know just when the idea of going to Devil's Island occurred to me. It must have been quite soon after Eugène was sent there. At first Waldo would not agree to it. It was, under any circumstances, a dangerous enterprise, and under the special circumstances, of course, it was particularly hazardous. But the idea undoubtedly appealed to him. He was always an adventurous soul, and the danger involved only made the notion more attractive. If it had not been for me I think he'd have come to it much sooner.

"But after a while I discovered that he was making covert inquiries about the possibilities and I renewed my urgings. This time he agreed, and we set about preparations in earnest.

"It was the year before the war. The French authorities at first refused us permission to visit the Devil's Island penal colony, but in roundabout ways, through channels we were not permitted to disclose, we finally got permission. Fortunately, as I had married out of France, they had no record of Madeleine Bingham as the sister of Eugène Champenois.

"Eugène, by some fortunate chance, was not at that time on Devil's Island itself, but in the prison of St. Laurent, which is on the mainland, some miles into the interior of French Guiana. When we went in we were warned of the danger not only of savage natives, but of escaping convicts. We learned that escape from the prison itself presented no insuperable difficulties. It seemed that prisoners escaped quite often, in their desperation, and got as far as the Dutch border before they were caught and sent back. Horrible notion, wasn't it?—playing with them as a cat plays with a mouse. For they were practically always turned back. Either the jungle or the frontier guards got them.

"However, as a matter of fact we had no trouble, except the natural difficulties of getting into the country, and those, after all, were no worse than we'd encountered in Africa and elsewhere. And we saw what we were allowed to see of the penal colony, and perhaps a bit more. Through some ingenious planning on the part of my husband we even saw Eugène."

Mrs. Huntington paused suddenly and looked at her brother. Pity and despair and terror were in that look, and love and steadiness and courage in the look he gave her in return. Brown averted his eyes. This was not for him to see. After a moment she went on with a sort of deadly quietness:

"We had, of course, no opportunity to speak privately together, but I knew that he had been trying to tell me something with his eyes, and I could guess what it was. When we went out again we traveled very slowly. Much more slowly than we had come in.

"The first night we encamped on the edge of the river beside our canoes, as our custom was. I will never forget that night. I sat in the door of our tent and watched. Everyone else was asleep. I could see the bearers sleeping in the light of the fires we always kindled to keep off wild animals. Now and then one of the men would rouse and put fresh wood on the fires. I couldn't sleep. It seemed to me that, if Eugène were coming at all, he would come that night. I was prepared for him. I had money and food and some clothes belonging to Waldo in my tent for him, if he came. And about midnight he did come. He came out into the light of the fires like a hunted animal, fearful of pursuit, moving like an animal, so lightly that he never roused the guards. I motioned to him, and he came to me, and I closed the flap of my tent on him.

"Waldo was dozing, but we waked him at once, and we set about what had to be done. There was not time for talking. We dressed him and fed him and gave him maps and a revolver and cartridges. He was so weak that we saw at once that he could not carry the knapsack I had prepared with blankets and food in it. Indeed, it became at once apparent that he would never get out at all if he had to tramp all the way. So we decided on a canoe down the river. An hour after he reached us he was off again, down the river in one of our smaller canoes."

Again she paused, twisting a handkerchief between nervous hands in her lap.

"For two months," she said, "I did not know whether he had succeeded in getting out. Then I had a cable from some place in Mexico. It said: 'Many thanks,' and it was signed 'Melanie,' which was the name of a doll I had had when I was a little girl. Then I heard nothing more until after the war—five years.

"Waldo Bingham died in the second year of the war, and I went to Washington and worked in the Walter Reed Hospital. The spring after the armistice I took a little house, intending to stay on in Washington. One evening my maid brought up a card to me. It read: 'Mr. Solomon Jura', and across the back was written: 'I have a message from Melanie.'

"I'll never forget that moment. My knees seemed to turn to water under me. I remember looking at the maid to see if she'd noticed anything amiss. And then I told her to ask the gentleman to wait and to say that I'd be right down."

For the first time she withdrew her eyes from far distances and looked directly at Brown.

"When I first saw my brother," she said, "but for the card, I should not have known him. He was as you see him now. Of course, except for the glimpse I had of him in prison camp and that night in our tent, in a very bad light, I had not really seen him since he was a young man. But even so, I do not think his intimates would have known him. He told me that he had been all over the world, in the outskirts, the wildernesses, making himself a new personality. He had always loved botany and natural history, and he had studied these things seriously in the countries he had visited. He had written articles for magazines that publish such things. He had made a personality for himself, so that anyone would say: 'Oh, yes, Solomon Jura: he's the naturalist.' He had stayed away from everyone who knew him until he felt confident that Eugène Champenois had ceased to exist, even in memory, and that his ghost would never rise to haunt either himself or me.

"The rest you can imagine. Even after all he had done, he was unwilling to take unnecessary risks. He loved the life he was living, and he continued to pursue it. He lived still in the wilds he loved, coming occasionally to see me. But of course his description and photograph had been issued to the police all over the world, and there was always the chance of recognition. And so he kept out of their way. This will explain to you, I think, why he disappeared from World's End while the police were investigating Mr. Huntington's disappearance, and again the other day when the sheriff was inquiring into Mr. Stuart's death."

Brown drew a long breath.

"Extraordinary!"

Madeleine nodded wearily.

"It's one of those things that don't happen, isn't it?" she assented. "But it's true—every word of it—nevertheless." She looked at Brown beseechingly. "There's no way of proving it, however, except by having someone—identify—Eugène Champenois."

The last words were barely audible. Brown turned his eyes from the anguish in her face.

"I think," he said gently, "that for the present we can assume that it is true."

She drew a long breath of relief—a relief that wiped ten years from her strained face.

"Then you'll let him go—now? Before the police come?"

Brown found it very difficult to make his lips form his answer.

"Did Mr. Huntington know of Jura's identity?"

"No," she answered quietly, but Brown saw by her eyes that she realized instantly what the question implied.

"Then don't you see," he said patiently, "that you've just given me the most convincing motive Mr. Jura could possibly have—for killing your husband?"

"No," she said again, with dry lips, "I don't see."

"Suppose—as the police would instantly suppose—Huntington had by some means found out about that secret and threatened exposure?"

"But he didn't," she whispered. "How could he find it out?"

"How did Mr. Grass find it out?"

There was a long, painful silence. At last she said:

"I don't know."

"I think," said Brown gently, "that Mr. Jura's only safety is the finding of the real criminal."

For a moment Madeleine stared at him, her face aging and hardening.

"You've tricked me," she cried hoarsely. "You've tricked me into telling you this. You've led me to confide in you, and now—"

"Madeleine!" cried Jura. She had risen to her feet, furiously. He grasped her wrists and held them. "Madeleine!" he repeated. Suddenly she swayed against his shoulder and burst into tears—tears the more moving and terrifying because of her habitual composure and reserve. Brown was tremendously upset.

"Look here!" he said. "Please don't act as if I were an ogre or something horrible. Believe me, I'm confident that every word you've told me is the truth, and I intend to act on that assumption. But don't you see that if Mr. Jura were to run away now it would immediately fasten the guilt of these murders on him? I would give a good deal if he had not made the attempt this morning."

Mrs. Huntington stopped crying. Now she said in a muffled voice:

"That was my fault. I lost my head. He would not have gone if I had not practically made him go."

"She thought," said Jura gently, "that if I could get out of sight until this was over and the real culprit discovered, that I would be safe. We acted hastily." There was infinite gentleness and comprehension in his voice and look. Brown, watching them, would have staked a great deal on the truth of their extraordinary tale, and yet—

"Mrs. Huntington," he said thoughtfully, "one more thing. About this quarrel which, according to Mrs. Drew, took place between you and Mr. Huntington on the day he disappeared. Is that true? Was there a quarrel?"

For a long moment she did not answer. She stared at the floor, troubled and deeply thoughtful. At last she looked at him.

"Once more I throw myself on your consideration," she said. "Since I have gone so far, I suppose I must go all the way, or you will leap to all kinds of unfounded suspicions. But I entreat your discretion." Again she paused, and then went on more composedly: "Yes, there was a quarrel, if you care to call it that. There was, at any rate, an understanding between us. I told Mr. Huntington that I intended to divorce him."

She had succeeded in surprising him, certainly. It was the last thing he expected her to say. "You intended to divorce him?" he repeated incredulously. "Was this a considered action, Mrs. Huntington, or the result of sudden impulse?"

"A carefully considered action," she said quietly.

"And upon what grounds?"

"I cannot see," she demurred, "that it can have any relation to—to anything that has happened since."

"On the contrary," urged Brown, "it may be of the utmost importance."

"Very well," she agreed, after a moment's consideration. "Mr. Huntington, several months before, had obtained from me a large sum of money, ostensibly for investment in a certain way. I had discovered that the money had not been so invested. I taxed him with it, and he admitted the fact but refused to tell me what he even had done with it. There were, of course, other things, but it was on that rock that we wrecked."

Brown felt himself suddenly out of his depth.

"But—I don't understand. You say Mr. Huntington obtained a large sum of money from *you*. I understood that he was a millionaire several times over."

Mrs. Huntington smiled faintly.

"He was certainly at one time very wealthy," she said, "but he lost practically everything in some speculative enterprise he went in for just before we went into the war—in 1916, I think it was. I believe it was not generally known. He'd worked under cover and managed to keep it fairly dark. But when I married him in 1919 he was heavily in debt—and was facing a campaign for reelection to the Senate. I didn't know all this," she added dryly, "until after we were married." She studied Brown's astonished face with faint amusement. "No doubt this amazes you," she said, with a certain edge to her voice. "I dare say you've been informed of my unnatural eagerness to have proof of Mr. Huntington's death so that his will might be probated. It's true that I've wanted proof of Mr. Huntington's death, but not on account of his will. His will means nothing to me—nor to anyone, I should say. It may interest you to know that I own World's End Island. I bought it just after we were married—before the whole situation was clear to me. It's my money—or, rather, the money Waldo Bingham left me—that has maintained it all these years."

Brown digested these facts for a moment in silence. Then he said:

"You said just now that you were anxious for proof of Mr. Huntington's death. Why was that? I mean, I gather you had some particular reason."

"I did," she said. "I have. When the technicalities are settled, I intend to marry Mr. Lane."

Again she had astounded him, upsetting all his theories.

"May I ask," he inquired, "if this intention antedates Mr. Huntington's disappearance? Had you it in mind when you threatened to divorce him?"

"Yes," she said quietly. "If I had been able to obtain my divorce at that time we would have been married then, but Mr. Huntington's disappearance presented all kinds of technical difficulties, and—we were obliged to wait."

Brown considered this statement in silence. At last he asked another question:

"Was Mr. Huntington aware of your intention?"

She smiled wryly.

"No, I thought it best not to inform him."

"One more question, Mrs. Huntington, and I have done, for the moment. Did Mr. Huntington take your decision quietly? Would he have permitted you to divorce him without a struggle?"

Her face darkened and hardened.

"He was very abusive about it—once he discovered that I meant what I said. He declared that he would fight any action I might take. It was that which decided me to tell him nothing—about Mr. Lane."

There was another question in Mr. Brown's mind, but he asked it only in silence, and of himself. Had Daniel Lane known of Huntington's determination to fight to the last his wife's action for divorce?

But he had no opportunity to pursue this consideration, for at this moment Justin broke into the room in great excitement.

"I say!" he exclaimed, "What are we to do? I can't get to Summerville. Every boat on the island has been put out of commission!"

Chapter XXII

When Brown went out into the hall again he found Myron still at his post. The young man had got himself a chair and was sitting in it at a perilous angle, the back propped against the door of Grass's room.

"All right," said Brown. "You go get yourself some breakfast and some sleep. I'll take charge now."

The young man grinned.

"Don't waste any sympathy on me, Mr. Brown," he said. "I'm having the time of my life. I'll get something to eat now, if you say so, but sleep—! Say, this is better than a dime novel. I'll be back."

He turned over the key and departed, kitchenward.

Brown let himself into the dead man's room, closed the door behind him, and locked it. Then he stood for a minute looking about him. It was a big corner room with two windows looking toward the mainland, and two on the northern side of the house, opening on the kitchen garden. The bathroom door was at the far corner, to the right. The room was shadowy, for no sunlight penetrated it at this time of day, and the dark shades had been drawn. The only light came from under a flapping shade drawn over an open window on the landward side.

Grass's body lay in a heavy, high-backed, upholstered chair near this open window. Beside the chair was a reading lamp, and a small table on which lay a novel, open, and turned upon its face to keep the place. A half-smoked cigar lay in an ashtray beside the book.

The bed had been turned down but had not been slept in. Grass's coat and vest lay across a chair, and his collar and tie had been tossed upon the bureau. There was no sign of disturbance of any kind. Except for the cord drawn tight about the neck one would have said that the man in the chair had sat down for an hour's reading before going to bed and had fallen asleep.

The lawyer strolled over and stared for a moment at that flapping shade over the open window. He wondered whose hand had pulled it down to cover what went on in that room inside. Then he jerked all the shades up, flooding the place with light, and turned to a more careful inspection.

The desk attracted his interest first, but it was a small affair, designed rather for ornament than use, and contained only a few unimportant papers and notes. Brown turned from it to the bureau. Here again he drew blank. Clothes; odds and ends of jewelry; nothing else.

He stood for a moment, hands hunched forward in his coat pockets, and looked about him. What he was looking for he could not have said. Some hint, some suggestive detail that would give him a start in the right direction.

The chair in which Grass sat was turned toward the door. Clearly, then, he had been aware of the entrance of his visitor—unless, of course, he had fallen asleep. But Brown examined the half-burned cigar beside the body and decided against that possibility. The butt had been carefully tamped out. Grass, then, had been awake and had known that there was someone in the room with him, unless—Brown considered the possibility swiftly—unless the murderer was already in the room when the politician came upstairs.

A brief inspection of the arrangement of the furniture, however, convinced the lawyer that this could hardly have been the case. The closet and the bathroom door were both in the opposite wall, and Grass must inevitably have seen, and been startled by, anyone who emerged from either place. And there was no place of concealment behind the chair.

Except the window? Brown crossed to it and looked out. A twenty-foot drop to the lawn below. Not the window. The door, then. Someone had entered by the door from the hall—someone whom Grass had expected to see—or, at any rate, had not been surprised to see. The politician had laid down his book, tamped out his cigar— Again the lawyer paused. Why had Grass tamped out his cigar? It was only half smoked. Brown's mind reverted suddenly to the drawn shade. A woman? What other possible excuse for drawing the shade— before the murder was committed? A woman, visiting Grass at that hour—

Brown shook himself. Best not jump to conclusions. Grass might, quite conceivably, have drawn the shade himself before his visitor arrived.

Well, this got him nowhere. It applied to any and every member of the household. What he needed was something more concrete than fine-spun theory. He crossed to the closet and flung open the door. There were several suits hanging from the clothes pole; an overcoat; hats on the shelf; shoes on the rack—nothing else. Not even a paper in any of the pockets. Brown shut the door again and turned back to the figure in the chair.

He had known all along that he would have to examine it but had shirked the necessity. There was something so unutterably repellent in that slouched figure. Now, however, he steeled himself to the task. The pockets first. He turned them out, one after the other. The dressing gown yielded only a rumpled handkerchief. The trousers' pockets contained a roll of bills, some change, and, in the hip pocket, a small, snub-nosed automatic. Brown turned it thoughtfully in his hand. Clearly Grass had anticipated no violence from his visitor or this would not have remained thrust in his hip pocket. The lawyer laid it on the table and proceeded to an examination of the vest and dinner jacket, which had been thrown down across a near-by chair. The outer pockets were empty, but in the inside pocket of the jacket he found a thick, very much worn notebook almost full of jottings.

An hour later Brown closed the notebook and sat for a long time staring blankly out of the window. Then he crossed the room, unlocked the door, and threw it open. He found Myron once more perched upon his tilted chair.

"I say," said Brown suddenly, "you don't know the precise date of Mr. Huntington's disappearance, do you?"

Myron straightened himself up and got to his feet.

"No, sir. Sometime in January 1922. That's all I know, sir."

Brown looked through him for a moment, apparently at the opposite wall.

"Yes," he said at last, bringing his gaze back to the boatman's face. "Well, that won't do. Would Franklin know, do you think? Yes, on the whole, I think Franklin's our best bet. Ask him to come up here, will you?"

"Yes, sir." And then in a burst of irrepressible curiosity: "Have you found anything, sir?"

But the lawyer, apparently, did not hear. He turned back into the room and shut the door. Then he sat down again at the little desk by the window, opened the notebook at a certain page, and read and reread a three-line entry at the top.

A discreet knock at the door roused him, a moment later, from his absorption, and in response to his invitation Franklin entered. The butler was clearly torn between his eagerness to be in, so to speak, at the kill, and his unwillingness to enter the room where Mr. Grass lay dead. He glanced uneasily at the slouched figure in the chair, and, more eagerly, at Brown.

"I understand, sir, that you want to see me?"

Brown closed the little book and turned to the butler.

"Sit down," he said. "I want to talk to you. Did you ever hear of a fellow named Micky Camp?"

Franklin, perched uneasily on the edge of a straight chair in the manner of one uncertain of the propriety of such a proceeding, wrinkled his high forehead in magisterial contemplation.

"Well, now, sir," he said slowly, "I can't be sure that I do. A tall, broad-shouldered fellow, was he—a tough-looking customer?"

"I don't know," said Brown impatiently. "I'm asking you."

Franklin nodded with dignity.

"Yes, sir," he said. "I'm aware of that, sir, and I'm giving the matter my most careful consideration, not wishing to make any mistake, sir. A tall, tough-looking fellow—that's what he was. I saw him two or three times, sir."

"You saw him?" demanded Brown. "Where?"

"Where? Why, here, sir, of course," Franklin informed him. "And once at Mr. Huntington's house in Washington. He used—" the butler coughed faintly with embarrassment—"he used to supply Mr. Huntington with wines and liquors, sir."

"A bootlegger, eh?" murmured Brown. "Where'd he pick him up?"

"Pick him up?" repeated Franklin, mystified. "I'm afraid I don't understand, sir."

"Who recommended him? How did Mr. Huntington come to employ him?"

"Well," said Franklin, "I did hear Mr. Huntington say that Mr. Grass had spoken highly of the fellow. In fact, I gathered, sir, that this Camp had been a detective on the dry squad but had decided he could do better for himself, and had retired, so to speak, and taken up bootlegging. And of course, sir, being in with everybody so to speak, you could depend on him to get good stuff. Mr. Huntington was always afraid of bad liquors, sir."

"Naturally," murmured Brown with extreme thoughtfulness. For a moment he turned the fat little book over and over in his hands. "Franklin, do you happen to know the date of Mr. Huntington's disappearance—the exact date, I mean?"

"Yes, sir, I know it," answered the butler instantly. "I know it very well, sir. It was the evening of January 26, 1922."

Brown shot out of his chair.

"Why didn't you tell me," he demanded, "that Micky Camp was here?"

Franklin looked at him as though he suspected him of having taken leave of his senses.

"Why didn't I—I don't understand you, sir."

"Why didn't you tell me that Camp was here when Huntington disappeared?"

The butler looked aggrieved.

"I didn't tell you so, sir, because it would not have been true," he said with dignity. "I believe—now that you mention it—that Camp was here at World's End that afternoon, but he had left before dinner."

"How had he left? I mean to say, how had he come? In one of the World's End boats?"

"No, sir. He came over from Summerville in a launch."

"Alone?"

"I believe so, sir. I really couldn't say for certain."

"And he left before dinner? You're sure of that?"

"Absolutely sure, sir. Mr. Huntington gave me a check to give him, to pay for the stuff he'd brought over, and I took it down to the boathouse and saw him go off."

"Then Mr. Huntington didn't see him while he was here?"

"Yes, sir; he saw him. They had quite a conversation about some champagne Mr. Huntington wanted."

"You were present?"

"Part of the time, sir. Then Mr. Huntington sent me up to the house to get his checkbook from his room, and when I came downstairs again he had come up and was waiting for me in the hallway. He went into the library to write the check, and gave it to me to take down to the boathouse and hand over to Camp."

"Do you know whether Camp saw anyone else while he was on the island?"

"Yes, sir; he did. He saw Mr. Grass. When I went back to the boathouse I found him talking to Mr. Grass. Mr. Grass was giving him an order, I should think. Or he may have been paying for something Camp had brought him. Anyway, as I came up he was giving him some money."

"Could you tell whether it was a large sum or not?"

"No, sir. I was too far away. I just saw him hand over some bills."

"And then what happened?"

"I gave Camp the check, and Mr. Grass and I stood on the wharf and watched him start back to Summerville."

For a long moment Brown said nothing. He stood with the notebook clasped between his hands, immobile, staring at Franklin with eyes that plainly looked through him to something beyond. Then he nodded briefly.

"Thanks very much," he said. "That's all."

When the butler had gone he opened the book and read over again the entry that had so excited him. It read:

Jan. 26, '22. Micky Camp reports S. H. up to the ears in Am. Shipyards. Stock held name of George A. Brush. Paid M. C. $1,000. This closes S. H. account.

Brown closed the book and put it, with the revolver, into his pocket. Then he went and stood before Grass, staring at him. Whatever secrets this man had held were closed now, and sealed from sight forever. One thing only remained to be done. But Brown could not face that distorted countenance. He went round to the back of the chair.

Clearly it would not have been a difficult matter to strangle even as powerful a man as Grass from that vantage point. The chair was large and heavy, and the back slightly higher than the head of the man sitting against it. A thin cord slipped around Grass's neck, and the end jerked tight over the high back, and the thing was done. Without touching it, Brown bent and carefully examined the dangling end of the cord.

It hung perhaps two feet below the top of the chair. Judging from the heavy dent in the cretonne upholstery, the murderer had drawn it sharply down, using the chair back as a lever. It was a thin, tightly twisted white cord, hardly bigger than a string, such as is sometimes used to tie heavy packages in a store; very strong. It would not, perhaps, have sufficed to support Grass's entire weight, but it was entirely adequate for the purpose for which it had been employed. Brown touched the end of it gingerly and was surprised to find how hard it was, and how stiff. Even now, after all these hours, it did not hang completely straight. It still preserved a hardly noticeable kink that—

Brown's heart leaped suddenly into his throat. Of course! What a blind booby! Nobody could exert pressure on a thin string like that. It would slip through the hands, unless—unless what? Why, unless it were twisted round the hand—twisted hard and tight and caught, doubled, in the palm.

Gingerly, carefully, moving out of the light, Brown picked up that dangling string and examined it inch by inch. When he had finished he took the leather collar box from the bureau, emptied it, and set it on the table. Then, with infinite care, he loosened the noose about Grass's neck, lifted the cord over his head, and laid it carefully in the box. Then, at last, he took a sheet from the bed and spread it over the chair and its grim occupant.

His mouth was set in a grim line, and his gray eyes were hard as steel. Unless he was sadly mistaken, the end of the chase was in sight.

Chapter XXIII

Fifteen minutes later Brown went downstairs in search of breakfast. He had been in the act of locking the collar box and the revolver in his Gladstone bag when he realized that he had had nothing to eat. His head was splitting. He slipped the notebook into an inner pocket for safekeeping, and went in search of food. On the way downstairs he encountered Lydia Vaughan. He smiled at her engagingly.

"What a comfort it is," he said, "to have to do with a woman who really knows how to dress." And he surveyed with admiration her white sport suit, which contrived to combine an artful sophistication with a rural simplicity. "Have you breakfasted yet?"

"My dear man!" The look she turned on him was full of mock horror. "You don't think I'd dream of appearing in public before breakfast!"

"Because," he went on imperturbably, "I was just about to ask you to come along to keep me in countenance. I know it's way past any decent breakfast hour, and I've hardly the nerve to beard Franklin all by myself. Besides," he added in a lower tone, "there's something I want to ask you."

She shot a swift glance at him.

"Come along," she said briskly. "I'm not afraid of Franklin."

They sat under the wide, striped awning in the gently somnolent heat of mid-morning. At their feet, below the terrace, the garden bloomed, a profusion of flowers. Franklin brought a steaming pot of coffee, and rolls delicately brown and crisp, curled leaves of butter.

"Here is richness!" cried Lydia. "I'll join you in a cup."

Brown watched her as she put sugar and cream in the cups and poured in the clear, brown, fragrant liquid. His head ached with little jabbing darts of pain. For a moment he put his hand up to his eyes, as though to shut out the glare of the sun beyond the awning. And when he took it down again Lydia Vaughan noticed that his face looked white and drawn.

"Poor man!" she said. "Try the coffee. It always picks me up."

He stirred it idly for an instant and took a hasty gulp before he answered her.

"I've had a shock," he said at last. "A pretty heavy jolt, as a matter of fact. There's something I want to ask you."

"You've found out something?" she asked eagerly.

"I think so. I don't know," he said cautiously. "I can't be sure—yet. Tell me: Stephen Huntington was the son of old T. H. Huntington, the millionaire, wasn't he?"

"Yes," she said wonderingly.

"He was very wealthy in his own right, wasn't he?"

A dawning comprehension appeared in Lydia's eyes.

"I see," she said, "that someone's been gossiping."

"Yes," he told her. "Now I want you to tell me not gossip, but the truth."

"Certainly he was a wealthy man," she assured him. "At least, let us say, as far as I have any knowledge. There was some talk just before we went into the war—just after the first Mrs. Huntington died, that is —about his losing heavily in some speculative enterprise. Well, I know for a fact that he did lose something through ill-advised investments, but nothing of any magnitude to a man of Stephen's resources."

"It's possible, however, that he may have lost more than you supposed?"

Lydia shrugged.

"Of course it is. Stephen certainly never made a confidante of me about his money matters. But, all the same, I knew him so well that I'm sure I should have known if anything very serious had gone wrong."

The lawyer stared down for a minute at his empty cup.

"Thanks," he said at last. "That's all I wanted to know. Give me another cup, there's a dear, and let's talk about the weather."

When Miss Vaughan had left him, and Franklin had cleared away his cup and plate, Brown took a letter out of his pocket and, spreading it out on the table in front of him, proceeded to make some notes upon the back. A sense of nightmare gripped him, a feeling of being overwhelmed by forces he could neither understand nor control, and he sought by this means to reduce to order the chaos of his mind.

Carefully, numbering them neatly, he jotted down the few items of his knowledge.

1. Huntington had, in 1916, lost his own money through speculation, and presumably had married Madeleine Bingham for her fortune. This marriage had taken place in 1919. (Lydia Vaughan declares this is not so, but she is strongly biased in H.'s favor, and was, moreover, in no position to be sure of the truth.)

2. Huntington speculated with a large sum of money, embezzled from his wife, using it presumably to buy stock in American Shipyards, Inc.

3. This company built rotten shipping, skimping their contract specifications and bribing government officials to overlook their practices.

4. Huntington was deeply involved, under the alias of George A. Brush, in the transactions of Am. Ship. Inc., at the same time that, as Senator, he was engaged in investigating the <u>Neptune</u> disaster.

5. *Grass knew this.*
6. *Lane suspected it.*
7. *Mrs. Huntington had told Huntington she intended to divorce him because, primarily, of his speculation.*
8. *Huntington had said he would fight suit.*
9. *Lane knew this.*
10. *Lane wanted to marry Madeleine.*

Brown looked discontentedly at his notes. The argument worked in a circle. Did Lane kill Huntington to get him out of the way and make his marriage with Madeleine possible? But why on earth should he, when they had a clear way to force Huntington's acquiescence in the divorce proceedings? There was no sense in it. He started again from a new angle.

This fellow Micky Camp had clearly been employed by Grass to determine Huntington's connection with American Shipyards, Inc. But why? Was Grass out to blackmail Huntington? Or was he simply protecting himself, being so deeply involved himself in the scandal? Or was it possible that he was acting on behalf of Lane? Was the connection between them, perhaps, closer than Brown had suspected? Or was Grass's motive to be found in his own designs on Mrs. Huntington?

Brown shrugged. Those questions were, for the moment, beyond his answering. Perhaps they were destined to remain forever unanswered. Or would it, perhaps, be possible to locate Micky Camp?

There was of course, always the possibility that all this had nothing to do with the question—at any rate, with the immediate question—of who had killed Grass. Improbable as it seemed, there was always the possibility that Stella Drew had carried out her threat. There was the suggestion of the tamped-out cigar and the drawn shade to indicate the presence of a woman in Grass's room at the time of the murder.

Furthermore, in spite of his very definite impression of their innocence, it was still possible that Mrs. Huntington or her brother had killed him to protect their threatened secret.

And there was Dr. Simpson, who had loathed and feared Grass.

But Brown could not abandon so easily the theory that all three murders were connected, that it was useless to consider Grass's death separately, for any explanation of Huntington's murder would, inevitably, explain them all.

And that brought him back—surely it brought him back!—to the *Neptune* scandal, to Simpson, or to Daniel Lane!

Simpson! His mind dwelt on the man. He alone of the household had been unaccounted for at the time of Huntington's exit. He had lied about his whereabouts when Stuart was killed. Why not Simpson?

Brown recalled suddenly something Adele had told him: that she and Justin had seen a man walking with their father down the island the night he disappeared.

Who was that man?

For a long time Brown sat quite still under the blue shade of the awning, his eyes fixed unseeingly upon the paper before him. He seemed to be making careful study of his notes, but he had forgotten them completely. His mind was full of the extraordinary suspicion that had come to him in Mr. Grass's room an hour before—a suspicion so wild and improbable as to seem appropriate only to a nightmare. He had been trying to push it from him, to hold it off by the thin wall of his logical erections. But logic, apparently, had nothing to do with it. It crept back and back, like a horrible miasma, twining itself around his speculations, strangling his initiative—

Strangling! The pencil jerked from his hand and fell with a little clatter on the tiling. He saw a vine, with leaves of a deep, luscious green, moving, according to some strange impulsion of its own, through a wood, killing, for its own obscure satisfaction, whatever impeded its progress or obstructed the consummation of its desires.

When a voice spoke softly at his elbow he turned toward it, eyes curiously drugged by this monstrous apparition.

On the terrace, in the full flood of sunlight, a tall Negro man in blue denim overalls was standing. He stood in awkward embarrassment, a straw hat clutched against his massive chest, his face shining with sweat. Brown recognized him as the man he had met on the beach on the afternoon when Huntington's skeleton was discovered.

"Boss, what are you going to do with this strangler fig?"

For a moment Brown, still dazed by his recent abstraction, did not understand.

"What are we going to do with it?" he repeated.

"Yes, sir. If this vine is dead, like you say, what are you going to do with the remains?"

"Oh!" Brown digested the query in silence. "I'm sure I don't know. I suppose the gardener will have it chopped up and burned."

"Burned—" the man's eyes glowed thoughtfully. "Yes! Burned it must be. Burned at midnight when the moon is full." He smiled suddenly, beguilingly. "To-night, Mr. Brown, the moon is full."

"Look here!" The lawyer swung round and faced the big man, smiling himself. "What's all this about? What are you driving at?"

The man grinned, but Brown noticed suddenly that there was a grayish tinge to his skin and around his wide mouth. The man turned slowly and pointed down the island toward the jungle, over which the shapes of two huge birds circled idly.

"See those buzzards?" he asked, "See those buzzards throwing their shadows on World's End? They're looking for their dinner. They haven't had enough. My father says that means death—death and destruction—unless the strangler fig is burned at midnight. Unless the devil is burned out of that vine!"

Brown felt an uneasy stirring of the spine.

"And do you think, if the strangler fig is burned, that will exorcise the evil spirit? Do you think the buzzards will fly away and the island will have no more wickedness?"

"Yes sir, sure enough! If the vine is burned those devil's birds will take up their shadows and go! And old Mister Death will go with them."

"Well," said Brown, "I'll arrange it with Platt. And you might tell that old woman to make her magic extra strong. I think," he added gravely, "that the situation demands it."

Chapter XXIV

None of the people who lived through that day on World's End Island are ever likely to forget it. The interminable hours that dragged themselves out, leaden minute after leaden minute; the intolerable mutual suspicion that made any genuine intercourse impossible; the still more intolerable suspense that drove them to herd together in spite of everything; the futile attempts to talk about the weather—politics—fashion—anything but the subject that occupied all their minds; the weary falling back to a rehearsal of the whole horrible situation, as a man will continually thrust his tongue against a sore tooth to see whether or not it will still ache.

As if by mutual consent they watched Brown continually, but he made no move of any kind that they could see. During that whole interminable day he did nothing but talk with those who approached him, or wander down to the boathouse and sit on the wharf, watching Myron fussing with the boats. On one of these expeditions Justin and Isabel accompanied him.

"Having a hard time of it, eh?" Brown asked the perspiring boatman. He and Justin were sitting in the launch that was used for bringing mail and provisions, and Myron was tinkering with the engine. Isabel was perched on a pier head. "Likely to get it in commission today?"

Myron sat back on his heels and wiped his streaming forehead with a handkerchief. Clearly he had previously used the handkerchief to wipe his hands, for it left black smears of oil on his forehead, giving him a look of desperation. He drew a long breath.

"I doubt it," he said gloomily. "Whoever did this made a good job of it. He not only smashed the more vital parts of the engine, but he stole all my spares. I'd never get the damned thing together except that I've been able to salvage some stuff from that engine over yonder and tack it onto this one. I reckon I'll be able to make it run somehow by tomorrow."

"Who on earth could have done it?" marveled Justin. "I suppose," he murmured tentatively, "it must have been Mr. Jura? He knows about boats. And there's this about it: whoever did it knew what he was doing. He smashed just the one essential thing every time."

"So you noticed that too?" murmured Brown.

"I'll say he did," agreed Myron fervently.

"Aren't you going to do anything to find out who did it?" asked the boy eagerly.

"I always thought detectives were awfully busy people," commented Isabel crisply, looking with scorn at Brown's lounging attitude.

"Well, you see," said the lawyer mildly, "I already know who did it." Isabel almost fell off her perch into the sea.

"You do?" she squealed.

"Well," Brown deprecated, "I can make a pretty good guess."

The two youngsters stared at him open mouthed, with respectful admiration.

"You know," said Justin awkwardly, "I feel pretty badly about the way I behaved at first. I thought you were being awfully nosey. You see, I didn't want to believe what you said, and so I didn't."

Brown nodded sympathetically.

"Only about ninety-nine out of every hundred people are like that," he murmured soothingly.

"That'll hold 'em, boys," gurgled the irrepressible Isabel.

"Anyway," pursued Justin, with an annoyed glance at his pretty sweetheart, "I just want to say that I'm doggoned grateful to you for being so decent to Madeleine."

The lawyer's face was suddenly somber.

"Better not thank me until it's all over," he said slowly. "God knows what's going to happen before we're out of this mess."

"My God!" whispered the boy, his face suddenly ashen. "You don't believe she did it?"

Isabel slipped from her perch and thrust her hand into Justin's. The boy turned his white face toward her for a moment and then looked back at Brown. The lawyer looked from one young face to the other, and his eyes softened.

"I want to talk to Justin," he said, smiling at the girl. "You won't think me rude if—"

"Oh, no!" There was no touch of frivolity in the grave little countenance she turned to him. "I'll go right away. I'll wait for you on the terrace," she told Justin, and was gone.

Brown climbed out of the boat and turned to Justin.

"Suppose we go down on the end of the wharf," he suggested.

But when they were settled, and his pipe was going to his satisfaction, Brown did not plunge at once into his subject. He sat for a moment arranging his thoughts. Then he said:

"Is it true, as Mrs. Drew suggested, that you overheard a quarrel between your father and your stepmother on the day he disappeared?"

Justin did not move, but the cheek nearest Brown grew suddenly white under the tan, and the muscles tensed.

"Tell me the whole truth," urged the lawyer earnestly. "It will hurt no one who does not deserve to be hurt, I promise you. And who knows what ghastly injustice may be committed if we do not discover —the truth?"

Justin looked suddenly, searchingly into Brown's face. What he saw there seemed to reassure him, for he suddenly blurted out:

"Yes, I did overhear it. They had a terrible row. Madeleine—" he hesitated, finding it unexpectedly difficult to go on—"Madeleine told my father she was gong to divorce him."

"Was that why," asked Brown gently, "you were so upset when I said something that suggested the possibility that your father had committed suicide?"

"Yes."

"Well, he didn't," said Brown wearily. "He didn't."

"Of course not," cried the boy instantly. "He wasn't that kind."

"Did you hear Mrs. Huntington say why she intended to divorce your father?"

"She said—" He broke off. "I'm not sure," he stammered. "I don't like to say. I only heard part of it."

"She said—what?"

Justin looked miserably down into the water at their feet.

"She said she wanted to marry again."

Brown digested this in silence. So Madeleine had lied when she said Huntington did not know of her intention in this respect. That was to protect Lane, of course.

"Did she say whom she intended to marry?"

"No!" cried the boy fiercely. "At least, not while I was listening. I went away almost at once. I couldn't eavesdrop on them. And I don't believe what she said was true. I don't believe she meant to divorce my father and marry someone else. Mad's not that kind. I think she got awfully angry about something and said more than she intended."

"But she did mean it," said Brown thoughtfully. "She meant it then and she means it now. She intends to marry Daniel Lane."

The boy turned a stricken face to him.

"Not Mr. Lane," he whispered. "Good God! You don't mean that he —" He broke off in sudden horror, and then added, as though it were a clinching argument: "But he's Isabel's uncle!"

For a long moment neither spoke. Then Brown asked:

"Did you know that Mrs. Drew overheard part of this quarrel?"

Justin nodded. He swallowed miserably before he answered.

"Yes. You see, it was in Madeleine's sitting room. The door was closed, but they were excited, and their voices were raised a little, so that you could hear quite distinctly just outside the door. That's how I happened to hear. I'd raised my hand to tap on the door when I heard their voices and waited an instant, wondering if I should go in or wait. Then I heard what they were saying, and I was so paralyzed with astonishment and horror that I didn't even think for a minute that I ought to go away. I stood there—oh, perhaps two minutes, and when I turned away there was Mrs. Drew beside me. I hadn't heard her come. She smiled horridly, so that I wanted to kill her. You know—sort of meaningfully. I guess I must have looked as mad as I felt, for she turned and walked away. And I took care that she didn't come back. I sat in my room with the door open and watched the hall until after my father went away and shut himself up in his study."

"Then she couldn't have heard much?"

"Hardly more than enough to know they were—quarreling, I should think," said the boy.

For a moment Brown stared thoughtfully at the distant coastline. Then he said:

"There's just one other thing I want to ask you. When Adele was telling me what she remembered of the night your father disappeared, she told me that you and she followed him down the path toward the jungle and saw him enter the jungle with another man. Do you recall that?"

"Of course I do."

"Adele says she was unable to recognize this other man. I suppose —" the lawyer was conscious of a sudden breathlessness—"I suppose you didn't recognize him, either?"

"No," said Justin thoughtfully. "I've thought of that a hundred times in the last day or two and tried to think of some way of identifying him, but it's no go. I just can't place him at all. And yet—" he broke off, and then added perplexedly—"and yet there was something familiar about him, too. If I could only think!"

"It couldn't have been Mr. Lane, because you saw him a moment later standing near you in the path," said Brown thoughtfully. "And it couldn't have been Jura, because you saw him hurrying along the beach. How about Simpson?"

"Not a chance," said Justin positively. "Simpson's a little fellow, and this man was as tall as my father. In fact, I couldn't tell which of the two was my father until I heard him laugh."

Brown nodded. He remembered now that Adele had said the same thing.

"Franklin?" he suggested.

Justin hesitated.

"Well, of course, it might have been. He was about Franklin's height and build. But why would father have been strolling along, talking and laughing with his valet?"

"I don't know," Brown admitted. "It doesn't seem reasonable. But none of it's reasonable." Again he lapsed into silence. Suddenly another thought struck him. "I say," he demanded suddenly, "do you know anything about a fellow—a bootlegger, I believe he was—named Micky Camp?"

And now Justin did a surprising thing. He turned on Brown with what amounted to a bellow of delight.

"By jingo!" he cried. "You've hit it. That's the man!"

The lawyer stared at him in amazement.

"What man? What are you talking about?"

"The man we saw walking with Father, of course. When Father laughed he turned toward him in a funny, stiff-necked way. I knew it was familiar, but I couldn't place it. But that's who it was, all right."

"But—but," stammered Brown, "it couldn't have been. He wasn't here."

"Oh, yes, he was," contradicted Justin rudely. "He came over about four o'clock in the afternoon. I saw him come up to the wharf in a dilapidated-looking launch."

"But he went away again," insisted Brown, "before dinner."

"I don't know anything about that," said the boy doggedly, "but if he did, he came back. Because, if that wasn't Camp, then I'm not I and you aren't you." For a moment Justin stared at the lawyer with growing excitement. "Gosh!" he cried with enthusiasm, "you're a wonder, sir. I don't know how on earth you found it out, but—that lets us all out, doesn't it? Madeleine and Mr. Lane and—all of us!"

The lawyer knocked the ashes out of his pipe. A red coal, still hot, sizzled as it plopped onto the water.

"Does it?" he said at last slowly. "Does it? I wonder."

Chapter XXV

When Justin had gone off to rejoin Isabel, Brown sauntered back along the wharf and stood looking down at Myron, still tinkering at the engine. After a minute he asked in a low voice:

"How soon could you get that thing into working order—if you really went at it?"

Myron glanced back into the shadowy depths of the slip.

"About ten minutes, sir," he said softly. "Just long enough to put back a couple of parts I took out this morning."

"All right," said the lawyer. "Get 'em and put 'em back."

He sat on a pier head and watched while the boatman crossed to a big wooden chest against the wall, unlocked the padlock, and took out two or three odd-shaped metal pieces.

"Funny," said Myron, closing the chest again and getting to work, "that these little things could make all the difference."

Brown smoked in silence for a minute. At last he said, in the tone of a man thinking aloud:

"Of course there just isn't any way of getting a message off the island—without using the boats."

"No, sir," agreed the boatman.

"No doubt," said Brown with a crooked smile, "no doubt you have heard the remark that hindsight is better than foresight. I don't know why it should be so annoying when one of those old adages is proved true." He looked with amusement at Myron's mystified face. "I suppose it's because it makes one feel such a fool."

"No doubt," said the young man, smiling, "you know what you are talking about, sir."

The lawyer chuckled, but his eyes were grim.

"I am lamenting the possession of a one-track mind," he said gently. "I was so convinced that the limits of these crimes might be fixed—geographically, at least—by the limits of World's End Island that it never even occurred to me that someone on the island might be interested in communicating with someone who was not on the island. And now," he finished morosely, "I suppose there's no possible way of checking the messages that have gone out since Mr. Huntington's skeleton was found."

Myron paused, wrench in hand. But after a moment he shook his head doubtfully.

"I'm afraid not, sir," he said. "That was Tuesday night, wasn't it? I was just going to say that I can practically take my oath none of the boats have been used—except this one, going for the mail, and Mr. Jura's launch for that little trip down to the point—since Tuesday night. I've got an eye for such things, and I looked the boats over when I collected them here yesterday afternoon. And I couldn't see any sign they'd been used. The gas was just about what I'd expect to find, and nothing amiss. I think you could safely bet that no one has taken one of the boats out. But of course that wouldn't clinch anything, because the mail has gone every day—until this morning."

Brown smoked thoughtfully for a moment.

"Every day," he repeated slowly. "That means you took the mail over Wednesday morning and yesterday morning."

Myron nodded.

"If a message went, sir, it went one of those two times—unless the sheriff carried it Tuesday night."

"I shouldn't think that was probable," the lawyer said thoughtfully. "Much safer just to drop a note into the mail bag than to entrust it to someone who might become suspicious."

Myron returned to his labors.

"No doubt you're right, sir."

"I suppose," suggested Brown hesitantly, "You don't look at the mail that goes out?"

He could see only the back of the young man's head, bent over the engine, but it did not escape him that the tips of the ears reddened.

"Well, of course—that is, one can't help noticing sometimes—"

"Oh, quite!" murmured the lawyer tactfully. "Look here, if you did notice anything, for heaven's sake, don't be delicate about it," he urged. "It's not a time, after all, for etiquette. Think, man! Anything— any little thing that seemed odd."

Myron threw down his wrench and, straightening up, thrust a long lock of dark hair out of his eyes.

"Well, honestly, I can't think of anything, sir," he said perplexedly. "The mail on Wednesday morning was just about as usual—the usual amount, I mean. I should think probably most of it had been put in the bag before Mr. Huntington was found—perhaps all of it. Anyway, I didn't pay much attention to it. It seemed just the usual run."

Brown nodded.

"How about yesterday?"

"Well, sir, yesterday was sort of funny, I'll admit. There were only half a dozen letters, and I was surprised, because usually there's quite a batch, so I looked to see what they were, and every one of them was addressed to some firm we get provisions from—the butcher, I mean, and the grocer in New York who sends out canned goods. That sort of thing."

"Who pays those bills?" Brown shot the question at him with sudden excitement.

"Why—why, Franklin, sir." They looked at each other with a sort of wild surmise. And then Myron added the thought that was in both their minds. "Franklin went over with me Tuesday night to take Mr. Justin's note to the sheriff."

"That," said Mr. Brown slowly, "is the most preposterous notion yet."

"I can't see any reason," said Myron stubbornly, "why a butler should value his own neck any less than—any other man."

Brown said nothing, for a moment. When he spoke it was to change the subject.

"I suppose," he said, "nobody goes ashore with you when you go for the mail—just for the ride, I mean—or for an errand, or something?"

"Well, naturally, sir. Someone goes almost every day—one of the guests, or one of the maids on an errand to the store, or somebody. It's a nice ride on a clear day."

"But nobody went with you on Wednesday—or yesterday?"

"Not Wednesday, certainly, sir. But someone went yesterday."

Brown felt a sudden throbbing in his temples.

"One of the maids?" he asked carelessly.

"No, sir. It was—"

At the name he mentioned Brown sat so still that Myron looked at him curiously. And he noticed an odd thing. After that first motionless instant the lawyer leaned forward and began to tap out, into the water, the fresh tobacco with which he had just filled his pipe.

A few moments later the brooding silence of the morning was broken by the strident roar of a speedboat gathering momentum. Myron was on his way to Summerville with a telegram in his pocket and, still ringing in his ears, instructions that caused his intelligent young face to wear a look of baffled speculation.

When Myron had gone Brown went in search of Solomon Jura. He found the older man on the beach, staring after the disappearing boat.

"I see," said Jura with a smile, "that the damage to the engine was not—irreparable."

"I want to talk to you," announced the lawyer without preamble. "I'm on the track of something, and I think you can help me."

The naturalist looked at him gravely.

"There is no longer," he said, "any question that you would ask me that I would not willingly answer—if I could."

He turned as though to stroll along the beach, and Brown fell into step beside him.

"Yesterday afternoon," the lawyer began presently, "you refused to tell me why you had gone down the island in such a hurry on the night Mr. Huntington disappeared. Why was that?"

"I don't think," said Jura slowly, "that I actually refused to tell you. I did not give my reason because I had no reason. I had been writing in my room—an article I was doing for a magazine. It didn't go very well, and the room was hot, and I became restless, and so I hurried out to walk it off. I meant to walk down to the point and back and then go to work again."

"And that was your only reason?"

Jura glanced at him with a half smile.

"You see," he said, "you do not really believe me. Yet why should the fact that on that particular evening a very terrible thing happened —why, I say, should that fact make it improbable that I should take a walk, for no particular reason, along the beach? I have done it dozens— hundreds of times, of an evening, before going to bed."

"You mistake me," said Brown. "I do not doubt your word. I am trying, simply, to be very sure of my facts as I go along."

"I beg your pardon," said Jura. "I had no other reason."

"Now," said the lawyer more briskly, "let me be very clear about what happened. You went down the back stairs, which are convenient to your rooms. You went around the back of the house to the beach."

"That is correct. I did not particularly wish to meet anyone who might offer to walk with me. I was full of a knotty problem in my article and wanted to think it over as I walked."

"Quite. Well, then, you went down to the beach and walked quickly along, seeing no one?"

"Seeing no one," assented Jura. "I was walking quickly, and I was buried in my thoughts."

"You followed the beach as far as the summerhouse, and then turned back, intending to come by the path through the jungle."

The naturalist nodded.

"Yes," he said.

"And you are perfectly certain that you saw no one during this time?"

"I am perfectly certain."

"Now, suppose you repeat to me what happened then."

"I walked perhaps halfway through the wood, more slowly, of course, for it was very dark, but still not very slowly, for I knew the path well and could guide myself by the break in the trees overhead. I was going along at a fair pace, then, when suddenly I—" His voice shook for a minute. He controlled himself and went on: "when suddenly I walked full into it—something inert yet yielding; something that struck me full in the chest and stopped me, and that yet, at the same time, gave before me.

"It is a curious thing that I should have known, instantly, what it was. I do not know why or how I did, except that there was nothing else in the world that could feel like that. Heaven knows I had no reason to expect to meet a dead body hanging in the path, yet I knew at once that that was what it was. Even so, I put up my hands and touched it before I could convince myself that it was so. And then I turned and ran.

"I do not try to excuse myself. It was the instant reaction of sheer blind terror—an animal instinct to fly from danger. And I suppose it was animal instinct, too, that led me to cover my tracks when I came out of the sand and to walk at the edge of the water, where the waves obliterated my footsteps."

"You went straight back to the house?"

"Yes. I went back the way I had come, in at the back door and up the back stairs. But I did not go to my room. Instead I went to Madeleine's sitting room. She had not come upstairs then, but I waited, walking up and down and wondering what I should do, for I realized quite clearly by that time the danger that hung over us.

"She came presently, and I told her what had happened. And here is another curious fact about that evening: she could not have known that it was Huntington, for I did not know it at the time, and I did not tell her so, yet she divined instantly that it was he. It was as though we were both informed by some curious prescience of what had happened.

"She declared that we must investigate at once and see what was wrong and whether, after all, I was not mistaken. So we waited until everybody had gone to their rooms and the house was still, and then we went out. I will never forget that next hour."

Brown, glancing at his companion's face, saw that it was set in a tragic mask in which the worn, candid eyes alone glowed and lived.

"We walked down through the garden," Jura went on. "I had put a flashlight in my pocket, but we did not use it then. There was no need. It was a clear, starlit night, and we could see distinctly until we got among the trees. When we were well within the cover of the jungle I turned on my flash, and we walked quickly to the place where I had— run against that thing in the dark. There was nothing there."

Again Jura paused. Even in the blinding sunlight Brown felt the horror of that dark, close-grown path, emptied of its grisly occupant.

"We looked and looked," the older man went on. "We searched the path from end to end and the underbrush on each side as well as we were able. We found nothing.

"Madeleine declared that I had been mistaken, but I had not been mistaken, and I think she knew it and was whistling to keep our courage up. After a while we went back to the house."

"And in all this time you saw no one?"

"No one. That is, until we went upstairs. Then several of the house party—Mr. Lane and Mr. Grass and Miss Vaughan and the others—came out and asked what was wrong. We told them that Mr. Huntington had not come in and that we had been to look for him but had not found him. The men volunteered to search the island. They went off, and I would have gone too, but Madeleine begged me to remain with her. In an hour's time they came back and said that Huntington could not be found. After daylight, however, we resumed the search, but, as you know, without success."

"And all the time," said Brown thoughtfully, "the thing you were seeking was hanging over your heads."

"That is so," said Jura in a low voice.

"The murderer," continued the lawyer, in the tone of a man thinking aloud, "must have cut the body down and strung it up again in the tree where it was found, during the time between your first two visits to the scene. No doubt he was standing in the wood near his victim the first time you appeared."

"So I think," agreed Jura quietly.

"Shrewd," murmured Brown. "Damnably, fiendishly shrewd; so extraordinarily simple and obvious. How much time, should you say, elapsed between your two visits?"

Jura reflected.

"Let us say it took me fifteen minutes to return to the house. I waited perhaps an hour in Madeleine's sitting room before she came upstairs, and we talked—oh, possibly twenty minutes or half an hour before we went out again. I should think it might have been two hours altogether between my first visit and my second."

"Plenty of time," said Brown, "for almost anything. Did you, at any time during the evening, hear or see a launch approach the island?"

"I think not," said Jura slowly. "I remember that the point was much discussed at the time, and no one could recall hearing the sound of an engine. Of course, one of the first things we did, as soon as it was light, was to look for any signs that a boat had landed at the island during the night. We found none."

"However, you wouldn't say it was impossible for a small launch to have come in—say at the summerhouse, yonder, without being noticed?"

They had turned the point of the island as they talked, and now Brown nodded at the little white structure standing on a ridge of low-lying reef before them. Jura considered it thoughtfully.

"It's possible, of course," he admitted. "If the boat had been moored on the far side I should not have noticed it, at night, and walking swiftly, buried in thought."

"But you cannot recall either seeing or hearing it?"

"I cannot recall either seeing or hearing it," repeated Jura positively.

Chapter XXVI

Brown, waiting in a fever of impatience for Myron's return, forced himself, nevertheless, to a superficial calmness and a more or less detached contemplation of the problem before him, for he realized clearly enough that even if the young man was entirely successful in his mission, his information would prove nothing. It would simply furnish a new approach to the question, and a new means of attack, in that it would make assurance doubly sure.

The lawyer, brooding over his problem, was like a chess player who has successfully passed the hazards of the "middle game" and is now confronted with the problem of his final moves. He smiled grimly as the parallel occurred to him. There was no doubt that he was threatening his opponent's queen, but whether he could force a checkmate he did not know. The game was being played with an amazing subtlety. He had so little to go on.

One weakness of his own attack had only recently occurred to him, and he berated himself for his stupidity. He did not, of his own knowledge, know what sort of man Huntington was. He could, therefore, make no accurate guess at what he would do, how he would behave in a given situation. He had received, to be sure, a very clear picture of his personality early in the game, but he had never checked that impression with the facts. And he realized now that the impression had come to him solely through people who were strong partisans—Huntington's children, and Miss Vaughan, who had known him almost from childhood, and who, by her own confession, was in love with him.

But, after all, he had received a hint that all was not, perhaps, as it seemed when Grass had suggested that Huntington was involved in the shipbuilding scandal. Even earlier than that, for that matter, when Lane had suggested that he had suspected Huntington of disappearing for his own private reasons. To be sure, at that time both Lane and Grass were open to suspicion of deliberately obscuring the issue, but still...

Brown went into the drawing room and stood for a long time staring up at Huntington's portrait.

He had not been trifling with the truth when he had said to Mrs. Huntington that it was a good portrait, or, at any rate, that it was a vivid portrait. The man's face stared out at one from the huge, formal frame like a living thing, mobile, revealing. Staring up at it now, the lawyer sought to penetrate the character behind the mask.

A handsome face, certainly, topping a pair of massive, impressive shoulders; a good forehead under the graying hair; gray eyes that were not unlike Adele's, and a handsome mouth. Indeed, one might have said that it was a beautiful face and not erred greatly on the side of exaggeration. And yet, as one looked, one was aware of something more and more amiss. Adele's eyes had a lovely look of clear candor; these eyes were oddly opaque, and wore a look at once bold and evasive. The mouth was too beautiful, curved, and feminine, and— weak.

The lawyer wondered if he were, perhaps, reading something into the picture that was not there, and yet, why should he read weakness into it? Boldness, perhaps, and evasiveness, but why weakness, unless the quality were there? He shrugged the thought away. This got him nowhere.

Certainly it was a face that would have impressed a woman. He wondered if Lydia Vaughan, shrewd as she was, had ever seen in it what he saw in it.

Thoughtfully he walked over to the wall and rang the bell.

When Franklin appeared he found Brown standing in front of one of the long windows, hands hunched forward in his jacket pockets, shoulders up about his ears, carefully rearranging the pattern of a rug with the toe of his shoe.

"You rang, sir?"

The lawyer started.

"Eh? Oh, yes. Franklin, do I remember that you once told me you were valet to Mr. Huntington before he disappeared?"

"Yes, sir. For several years, sir—since before the first Mrs. Huntington died, sir."

"Ah!" Franklin could not determine the significance of that long-drawn breath, and Brown's face was partly hidden from him in the shadow. "What sort of a man was Huntington?"

"Well, sir—" The butler hesitated uncertainly. The analysis of character was a little beyond him, perhaps, and he could not be quite sure just what points his questioner might consider of importance. "He was very liberal, sir," he offered hastily after a moment.

"Ah," nodded Mr. Brown, glancing at the portrait. "I should expect that."

"Yes, sir," agreed Franklin, "although you'd be surprised how many gentlemen are disappointing in that respect, sir."

"No doubt." The lawyer smoothed away a smile with a thoughtful hand. "I take it, however, that that is not a complete summary of his character—although no doubt revealing. I am interested, however, in his more private life—if, indeed," he added hastily, "a man can have any more private relations than his relations with his valet."

"Quite, sir," murmured Franklin helpfully. Light was beginning to dawn on him. "You mean his—er—affairs, sir—that is to say, his little affairs of a gallant nature."

"You take my meaning, Franklin."

The butler looked up at the face of his whilom master with a look of respectful admiration, and to Brown it seemed suddenly as though those cold eyes looked back with a warning.

"Ah, sir," murmured Franklin, "I could tell you a lot—there. He was a great man with the ladies. It was extraordinary how they fell for him. And the letters they used to write to him—you wouldn't believe it. But he was a strange man, sir. He didn't seem to care much about them. Used to tear them up and say what a nuisance they were."

"Oh!" murmured Brown. "He thought they were a nuisance, did he?"

"Well," said Franklin, and now, quite unmistakably, he winked with a ludicrous effect of coyness, "I won't say as how he was altogether unimpressionable, sir. Sometimes he would read a letter and say nothing about it and put it in his pocket. And sometimes he would be too busy to come home to dinner and would have me meet him somewhere with his dinner clothes."

Brown squirmed inwardly.

"That was before the death of the first Mrs. Huntington?"

"Yes, sir. That's when it was. Before her death. When she died, it stopped."

Brown looked at him curiously.

"What do you mean—it stopped?"

"I mean it all stopped, sir: these letters and dinner parties and what not."

Franklin looked over his shoulder and then came a step nearer Brown.

"Way I figure it, sir," he said, "about that time Mr. Huntington gave up spreading his attentions round, so to speak, and began to concentrate on one."

"Oh!" said Brown, enlightened. "You mean the present Mrs. Huntington."

"No, sir," contradicted Franklin surprisingly, "I do not. This was before he met the present Mrs. Huntington. I mean he met some other woman and fell for her like he'd never fallen for this letter-writing crowd. But if you was to ask me who she was, or where, or what, I'd have to say I don't know, sir. It was partly his being so careful about the whole business that gave away how serious it was. I tell you, sir, if ever a man was gone in his life, it was Mr. Huntington. He couldn't eat or sleep or talk sensible."

"Business worries?" suggested Brown.

"Business worries!" Franklin's tone was scorn itself. "Sir, you're a lawyer, and an educated man, which I am not, but I've been a gentleman's gentleman for more years than you'd believe, and if I can't tell the difference between business worries and a love affair, then you can't try a case in court, and that's all I can say about it. Why, sir, that's part of my business, as you might say. You see—" Franklin was off on his specialty, and he expanded helpfully—"you see, sir, it's these little things that's a matter of instinct, sir, a special talent, if you take me, sir, that is born in a man, and that makes the difference between a really first-class gentleman's gentleman and a—a valet, sir. You know, sir, in the matter of ties and socks, now. You might think it's a small thing, sir, but when a man's in love he likes to be humored in a matter like that. Why, sometimes I've known it to make all the difference in the little—er—bonuses at Christmas-time and the like. One gets to know."

"Of course, of course!" Brown looked at Franklin with a new respect. Clearly the man had definite pride in his profession, so to speak. "And you say that soon after the death of the first Mrs. Huntington, Mr. Huntington fell in love?"

"I do, sir. Head over ears. And I say more, sir. I say that the affair continued right up to the time he married again—and I'm not sure it stopped then. He didn't get on any too well with this Mrs. Huntington," confided Franklin, lowering his voice. "And it's my belief they hadn't been married very long before he was seeing this other lady again. He was awfully careful about it—more so than he'd ever been with me—but there were little things... In fact, I'd take my oath to it, sir."

Brown was silent for so long that Franklin contemplated a quiet departure, when suddenly the lawyer looked up under his brows.

"Do you know whether the present Mrs. Huntington shared your suspicions of this affair?" he asked softly.

Franklin hesitated.

"I don't know, I'm sure, sir. As I say, he was very careful, but women have a sort of instinct about such things. She may have known, sir."

"And you've no notion whatever about who this mysterious lady could have been?"

"No, sir."

Brown's hands came out of his pockets, and his shoulders straightened. The lethargy of the last few moments was thrown off like a garment no longer needed.

"Where's Platt?" he demanded. "I want to see him about

something."

"I'll send him to you, sir."

He turned away, but before he reached the door the lawyer stopped him with another question.

"Have you seen Miss Vaughan anywhere?"

"Yes, sir. I passed her in the hall as I came in. She had her bathing suit over her arm, sir. I imagine she was going down to the lagoon."

When Brown had seen the gardener and given instructions about the final disposition of the strangler fig he got his bathing suit out of his room and went down to the boathouse. There were dressing rooms there. When, a moment later, he emerged on the sand, he found Justin and Isabel disporting themselves in the lagoon with the grace and energy of a pair of lively porpoises, rolling and tumbling at their ease in the blue water. They shouted at him, and he shouted back, and strolled along the sand to join Miss Vaughan, who stood watching them, with a striped beach parasol over her white-capped head, and a smart beach coat over her bathing suit.

"How nice!" she greeted him, smiling. "I've just been wondering why on earth I ever got this coat—with not a soul to appreciate it. And it's really rather nice, you know."

"I might have known," said Brown scornfully, "that you'd do your bathing on the beach."

"Yes?" she looked at him quizzically. "My dear young man, don't leap to conclusions."

To his astonishment she suddenly threw down parasol and coat and appeared before him in an extremely serviceable white bathing suit, fashionably scant and extraordinarily becoming. With a withering glance at him, she strolled across the sand to a little pier upon which a diving board had been erected and ran lithely out upon it. For a moment she stood poised, her magnificent figure outlined against dazzling blue of sea and aching blue of the sky, and then she plunged, curving in a superb dive that cut the water as neatly as a knife cuts into cheese, with hardly a sound or a ripple. An instant later she reappeared and drew in to the beach with slow, lazy strokes of her white arms cleaving the water.

"Man," she said smiling, "I was brought up on salt water. Can you do that?"

He could not, as he demonstrated by miscalculating his distance and hitting the surface too flat, sending up a shower of spray. He came up to find her sitting on the beach, consumed with laughter.

"I always thought you a woman of tact," he mourned, clambering out beside her. "Must you rub it in that the age of man's superiority has passed?"

"I consider," she said, with an effort at gravity, "that laughter is good for my figger!"

But the eyes that met his held no laughter, but rather an anxious inquiry.

"Look here," he said. "I want to talk to you, and I think this is as good a time as any. Why have you been lying to me, Lydia Vaughan?"

"Lying to you?" she repeated. Idly she picked up a handful of white sand and idly watched it trickle through her fingers. "In what way—for what reason—have I been lying to you?"

"That is what I want to know," he said.

"If you're talking about Stephen's money," she said, looking up at him gravely.

"I am not talking about Stephen's money," he told her, "although I should be glad to know why you misled me in that respect. I am talking about Stephen Huntington's mistress." The tone in which he spoke was conversational and casual, but if it had been a revolver thrust against her side it could have had a no more marked effect. She started violently and turned toward him a face blanched and quivering. For the first and last time in his knowledge of her, he saw her completely unnerved.

"It's no go," he said at last gently. "It's quixotic of you and all that, but it's no go. You might as well tell me the truth. I saw, as well as you did, that mark on the back of her hand."

"Oh, my God!" whispered Lydia Vaughan, and she turned her white face away from him staring out to sea.

"What I can't understand," Brown went on, "one of the many things I can't understand, is why you shielded her. Have you known—all these years?"

Lydia nodded.

"How did you know?"

"I knew that she had found out—about Stephen's affair with Mrs. Burt."

"So that was the lady's name, eh?"

"That," said Lydia softly, "was her name."

"And you knew that Mrs. Huntington had found out about her? How did you know that?"

"Because Stephen told me. That night he disappeared—on the terrace—when we were talking. He told me. He was distracted. He said she had threatened to divorce him because of this affair—although it was a thing of the past, and he had never looked at another woman since he had known Madeleine."

"But," objected Brown, "Mrs. Huntington gave me to understand that she intended to divorce Huntington because of their—er—differences in financial matters, and that when she had gained her divorce she intended to marry Mr. Lane."

Miss Vaughan gave him a strange look.

"Naturally," she said, "if you had heard of the threatened divorce and pressed her about it, she had to give you some explanation."

"But you yourself assured me that she had never loved Mr. Huntington."

"I lied," said Lydia Vaughan. "I lied in my teeth. She was mad about him—and crazy jealous. He was a man who was very attractive to women, and they were always having rows about it. But, as I tell you, from the day he first met Madeleine he never looked at anyone else. The sun rose and set in her, as far as he was concerned. If she had only believed it! If she had only believed it!"

"And you think that Madeleine killed him—because of jealousy of this other woman?"

She nodded somberly.

"I have always—suspected it."

"That's what you meant when we first talked of it and you said: 'What if Madeleine had killed him and thrown him into the sea?'"

"That," she said softly, "was what I meant."

"Then why," he asked, "didn't you say so?"

She turned to him then, and her eyes were blazing.

"Because I didn't know. Good God, man! I didn't know. I thought perhaps Stephen had gone off of his own accord, broken-hearted. For seven years I thought that. And then, when he was found, I thought that perhaps he had killed himself. I couldn't believe she had done it. I'd known her and been fond of her. Was I to break down and confess to you that I thought my old friend was a murderess? I tell you I didn't know she'd done it—until I saw the mark of the cord on her hand this morning."

She broke off with a shiver, and for a moment neither spoke. The incredibly inconsequent sound of rippling water at their feet alone broke the vast, muffling silence. Justin and Isabel had gone in, and they were alone.

And then suddenly Brown, watching her, saw her stiffen to attention, and her eyes, no longer vacant and absorbed, turned intently to the far horizon.

"What's that?" she demanded in a low voice.

He listened, and it seemed that indeed she was right. Some other sound—faint and very far away—was making itself heard. He sprang to his feet and, shading his eyes with his hand, stared out across the water. The sun was dropping westward and dazzled his eyes, but as he listened the sound became more distinct and definite.

"It's Myron," he told her. "That's the speedboat motor we hear."

She too had risen and now stood beside him, her eyes straining into the glare.

"Why did he go to Summerville? Why did you send him? For heaven's sake, tell me, Bolivar Brown," she cried. "I've a reason for asking."

He turned toward her suddenly, faced her foursquare.

"I'll answer your question if you'll answer mine," he told her. "Why did you go with him yesterday morning when he went for the mail?"

Her lips were blue as she returned his look with a look just as searching. Suddenly she dropped her face on her hands.

"What have I done?" she whispered. "What have I done?"

He waited, giving her time. When she looked up at last she was quite composed.

"I went, primarily," she said, "to get away for an hour or so from the island. But I happened to mention to Madeleine that I was going, and she asked me if I would send a telegram for her. I reminded her that the wires were down, but she said to give it to the telegraph man, anyway, and ask him to send it as soon as he could. And to say nothing about it."

"And you did as she asked?"

"I did as she asked."

"To whom," asked Brown, "was the telegram to be sent?"

Miss Vaughan threw out her hands with a sudden, desperate gesture.

"How can I tell you?" she cried. "It's such a wretched, miserable thing to do."

"I'll ease your conscience," he told her gently. "It was to be sent to a man by the name of Micky Camp."

It seemed to him that she had suddenly stopped breathing. When at last she turned her face to him it was blank with astonishment.

"Micky Camp?" she repeated. "That's that bootlegger fellow Stephen used to get his liquor from. What's he got to do with it?"

"Unless I'm very much mistaken," said Brown grimly, "he's got a good deal to do with it."

"Well, it wasn't Camp," Miss Vaughan assured him. "It was a name I'd never heard before."

"An alias, then," said Brown.

"Possibly." She looked at him doubtfully. "You're so sure."

"I've reason to be sure," the lawyer assured her. "What was the name?"

"Must I tell you?" she entreated. "I promised her I wouldn't. And if Myron has found it out there's no need. Wait, at least, until he comes.

If he hasn't got it, I'll tell you then. I give you my word."

And with this perforce he had to be content.

When Myron drew into the slip a few minutes later Brown and Miss Vaughan were waiting for him. She had put on her gay jacket again, but she had not put back the gaiety of spirit she had lost on the beach. And her face, under the incongruous white cap, was worn.

"Well?" Brown demanded of the boatman. "What luck?"

The young man looked with some astonishment at Lydia.

"It's all right," the lawyer assured him. "You can speak frankly."

"Well, sir," said Myron with some embarrassment, "I inquired around a bit and got the address you wanted."

"He means," said Brown to Miss Vaughan, "that he got the address you sent that telegram to—and the telegram as well, no doubt."

Myron stared from one to the other and then gave in with a shrug.

"Yes, sir. The telegram was sent to Mr. Edmund C. Rogers, in Mobile, Ala. Here's a copy of it, with the address, sir."

Brown took the envelope and spread out the enclosure so that Miss Vaughan could read it, too.

Mr. Edmund C. Rogers, __Street, Mobile, Ala.
Stephen Huntington's skeleton has been found on World's End.
Murder suspected.

"It isn't signed," said Brown.

"She asked me not to sign it," said Lydia softly.

Brown put the telegram back in the envelope.

"Had any answer been received?" he asked.

"No, sir. I telegraphed the chief of police in Mobile, according to your instructions, sir, sending him this name and address. His answer didn't come till four o'clock, which is why I'm so late, sir."

"But you did get an answer?" cried Brown eagerly.

"I got an answer, all right, sir." And Myron handed up a second yellow envelope.

Brown glanced at the enclosure and swore softly.

Man answering description Camp lives at —Street house but has been missing since yesterday. Received telegram about noon and went out at once. Has not been seen since.

The lawyer stared at the telegram in disgust. Then he thrust it back into its envelope.

"Lydia Vaughan, Lydia Vaughan, you have messed things up," he cried.

She looked at him with eyes from which tragedy looked out. "How was I to know?" she asked. "How was I to know?"

Chapter XXVII

In the long, shadowy library Adele was standing, clutching a folded piece of paper in her tight little hand. Brown, standing in the doorway, forbore for a moment to enter, delighting in this stolen moment of watching her unobserved. Beyond her the long windows showed blue and translucent with early evening, and the room was full of soft light and warm, friendly shadows with which the soft gray of her dinner dress seemed strangely a part. How lovely she was, how infinitely touching with that look of pain and anxiety in her eyes!

But he had only an instant's glimpse of her, for she turned and saw him and came toward him eagerly down the long room.

"I want to speak to you, please." Her voice was hardly more than a whisper, but it reached him clearly in the stillness of the room.

"Yes. Yes, of course," said Brown. He took a step toward her and then stopped uncertainly. "I was dressing when your note was brought to me," he went on. "I came as quickly as I could."

She was trembling, but she was more composed than he.

"I had to see you at once," she said softly. "There was no time to lose."

And yet, when she had said that, she said, for the moment, nothing more. And so for an instant they stood, with half the room between them, and looked at each other.

"You know," she said at last, "what you said this morning was very true. I have had a nightmare, and it confused me so, and hurt me so, that I've been stupid with pain. It's been like a drug. Pain can be like that, can't it?"

"Of course it can, my dear."

"Yes," she said. "But once you are wide awake things become clear to you again. And after a little while the outlines of the nightmare begin to fade."

"Yes," he said. He could find nothing more to say. He could only gaze at her, seeing nothing else in the world.

Adele looked down at that paper in her hand and then looked up at him again.

"I have had something that has waked me," she said.

Now he crossed the distance between them with impatient strides.

"What is that?" he demanded. "What have you there?"

But she put her hand behind her.

"No!" she cried. "No! I have something to say to you, and you must listen to me—you must."

For a moment he looked as though he meant to take it from her by force, but he did not. He stood over her, looking down grimly into her defiant eyes.

"Yes?"

"This nightmare of mine," the girl went on earnestly, "has blinded me to what I was doing—to what I have been letting you do. You've been so good to me—you've spared me in every way possible. I begin to see how much—how deeply—you've spared me."

"I've done nothing—nothing!" he cried almost angrily. "Let me see that paper, Adele."

"What did they mean by saying this morning that you might be guilty of these murders? How dared they say it?"

"Because," said Bolivar Brown, "as far as the evidence goes, it might be true. I had as good an opportunity as any." And perhaps, he added to himself, as good a motive.

"It's a hideous lie," she cried. "This thing seems to have turned us all into beasts, ready to spring at each other's throats. Must you go any farther with it?"

"Ah!" murmured Brown, and the look in his eyes was the look of a man who suddenly understands the answer to a question that has baffled him. "So they've been threatening you. They've told you to call me off!"

Adele's eyes wavered and fell.

"No—that is, I—It is suddenly clear to me what risks you are running—what horrible risks! You haven't let me see—and in my selfish stupidity I haven't realized. But now—now you've got to stop. I'd never forgive myself if—"

Brown's eyes hardened suddenly. He thrust his hanging hands into his jacket pockets.

"No!" he said. "No!" Her face was stricken, but he would not look at her. "You haven't thought, or you couldn't ask such a thing. A series of cold-blooded, calculated murders— Good heavens, Adele! And I have the answer almost in my hand. You can see that I have. They are frightened. They know that, in another hour or so—another twist of the evidence, and the whole intrigue will be unraveled."

"But you!" she cried wretchedly. "What will happen to you?"

He looked at her then, and his eyes softened.

"Nothing will happen to me."

"But—but—" And now suddenly she held out to him that crumpled piece of paper and turned her head away, hiding her face from him.

He smoothed it out. It was again, as he had expected, a sheet of World's End notepaper, printed in staggering capitals.

CALL HIM OFF, ADELE HUNTINTON STUART. CALL HIM OFF. ON ANY PRETEXT YOU LIKE. BUT CALL HIM OFF NOW, IF YOU WANT HIM TO SEE ANOTHER DAY.

Brown laughed softly.

"It's curious, isn't it," he murmured, "how convenient banalities sometimes are?"

"You can laugh at it," cried the girl softly. "But I can't laugh at it. I could never forgive myself if—if—"

Brown looked at that sleek averted head. There was laughter still at the back of his eyes—the sort of look one might give a dearly beloved, foolish child.

"You must not blame yourself," he said gently. "Nothing will happen, but if anything does it will not be your fault. It will be my own stupid, bull-headed wish to know the truth that will be to blame."

She stood like a little statue. He could not see the look on her face, or he could not have said the thing he now said.

"There is just one thing—if anything should happen—it won't, but if it does—never believe that it was accidental or that I suddenly found life too much for me. No matter how it seems or what it looks like, never believe that."

She did not move or speak, and suddenly he took her shoulder and turned her round so that he could see her face. It was wet with tears.

"My dear!" he cried. "My dear!"

But she held him off.

"Let me alone!" she cried. "Let me alone! Tell me what we are to do! Surely there is something we must do!"

And now Bolivar Brown looked down at her with a look she could not meet.

"We must wait," he said softly. "My life, we must wait."

Into the silence that engulfed them a little sound broke—a sound so slight that Brown was hardly sure that he heard it, even while he knew that he had. He put his arm around Adele and drew her to him, bending his head against hers.

"Don't move," he whispered between lips that barely parted. "Someone is watching us. There's something I want you to find out for me, quietly, so that no one will suspect that you are asking for a reason."

Again that indescribably faint sound. He held her suddenly close and finished the sentence, against her cheek. He felt her stir faintly, in acquiescence, and watched her go, blindly, as a woman in a dream.

Then he crossed to the long wall opposite the hall door and stood against it. He took out his pipe and began to fill it, his eyes searching the room casually as he did so.

There was no place of concealment that he could observe. No screen. No curtains, except the flimsy curtains at the windows that could conceal nothing. The door into the servants' quarters was closed.

The windows, then! He scanned them furtively. They stood open to the ground along the terrace—three long blue oblongs beyond which could be seen the coiled stems of a bougainvillea vine that twined along the pergola outside. He had not noticed it before, but now he did, for the vine stirred and moved softly, with an indescribable effect —a writing motion as of a living thing. Nonsense, of course, but it startled him and sent a long cold shiver up his spine. Now the vine was still again, etched black against the warm blue night. Someone had touched it—leaned against it, perhaps....

Brown strode to the window and looked out. No one on the terrace; no one in the garden. Only a vast, deep stillness, broken by the voice of Madeleine Huntington behind him.

"You're down early, Mr. Brown."

He turned and looked at her. She was standing just inside the door into the hall, standing quite still, looking at him. He had never thought her beautiful before, but at this moment she seemed to him one of the most gorgeously lovely creatures he had ever beheld. She wore a trailing black lace gown, and above the lace her shoulders and her face seemed carved out of marble, majestically lovely. Yet, cold as they were, something glowed and burned behind her eyes, something that warmed and enlivened her whole person. He stared at her wordless, pondering.

Her lips curved suddenly in a perplexed smile.

"What is it?" she asked. "I am not a ghost."

"I beg your pardon," he murmured. "I—I was thinking of something else, and your voice startled me. I'm sorry."

But as he withdrew his eyes from her his glance lingered for an instant on her right hand that held and lifted the long flounce of her dress. Across the back of it was a thin red mark.

Chapter XXVIII

Nerves were on hair triggers at World's End that night. All through dinner conversation rattled and buzzed around the table as though no one of the people seated there dared to be silent. Brown had wondered if Stella Drew would put in an appearance. All day she had remained in the seclusion of her room, with drawn shades. But just before they went in to dinner she came down in a defiant orange-colored gown, which struck a strange harmony with her magnificent hair, her face ghastly under its heavy make-up. She had drunk three cocktails, one after the other, and talked all through dinner with a loud insistence.

Adele had come down only at the last moment, and had slipped a bit of folded paper into Brown's hand as she sank into her chair beside him. He found occasion to glance at it as he unfolded his napkin, and his heart stood still. Carefully, slowly, under cover of the chatter he tore it into many pieces and dropped them at last into the pocket of his dinner coat.

Until this moment he had not, perhaps, fully believed in the extraordinary tale he had been slowly unfolding. Bit by bit, as he uncovered it, he had believed himself to be on the right track. But the full villainy of the scheme, the diabolical ruthlessness of it, had not really struck him in full force until now.

He wondered, staring down at the admirably cooked fish before him, whether the moment had come for him to act. He had proof enough, heaven knew—conclusive proof. And yet, after all, it hinged upon very delicate points. A shrewd lawyer, he had little doubt, could play ducks and drakes with it.[7] The weakness of his own position, as he well knew, lay in the fact that there was one item of the story, one aspect of the situation that he could not explain, and without which his case was entirely and possibly disastrously incomplete.

He pondered the incident of that threatening note to Adele. Weak! Singularly weak for so astute an intelligence! Clearly the murderer's nerve was failing. Fear! A powerful string to play on. His mind raced after that possibility. Surely, if he could make it sufficiently clear that the end was in sight, the strangler fig could be made to strike again, and then— Mechanically Brown toyed with the fish on his plate, but he did not eat it. His mind was full of speculations and projects.

When dinner was over he went up to his room, took Jacob Grass's

---

7   Ducks and drakes: the pastime of skimming flat stones or shells along the surface of calm water.

revolver out of the locked bag in his closet, made sure that it was loaded and in good order, slipped it into his hip pocket, and went down again.

He found them in the drawing room over their coffee. His eyes went at once to Mrs. Huntington, sitting at the far end of the room behind a tall silver urn, filling delicate cups with the clear brown liquid, and he was struck again with the singular, warm impact of her beauty. Lane sat near her, his eyes on her, watching the slow, graceful movements of her hands, lifting his eyes gravely now and again to her face with a look that reflected hers.

Stella Drew sat sullenly on a sofa between the windows, talking now and then explosively to Dr. Simpson, who sat beside her. Brown would have said that she was half-drunk, no longer garrulous, approaching the point of tears. There was a dazed look in her blue eyes, and the flesh under her brows was flushed. Her prettiness had withered and coarsened. She looked haggard under the flaming gold of her hair, above the orange gold of her gown.

His eyes turned with relief to Justin and Isabel, sitting together in a corner, unashamedly holding each other's hands. The girl's pert, hard little face had softened in the last few hours. She looked white and anxious and very young, and the lawyer caught her looking at her uncle with a worried affection in her glance that contrasted oddly with her usual impertinent mockery.

Brown looked only once at Adele, sitting alone as she had sat that first night, pale and grave in her little gray gown. But to-night her eyes met his at once, eagerly, swiftly; full of questions he could not answer —yet.

Jura and Lydia Vaughan completed the party. They stood together, sipping their coffee and chatting. She was wearing another extraordinary gown, green velvet, cut to the waist in back and bespattered with rhinestones. Brown strolled over and joined them.

"You're an extraordinary woman," he said, smiling, his eyes on her gown. "The extravagance is bad enough, but the invention behind it is amazing. Something new, so to speak, every hour."

She laughed.

"I shall make a point," she told him, "of insisting that you be included in every house party I attend from now on. You've spoiled me for the ordinary, milder forms of adulation."

Franklin appeared at his elbow with a cup of coffee. Brown took it and watched idly for a moment while the butler moved about, refilling cups and passing cigarettes. Then he drank his coffee at a gulp and set the cup down on a table. He glanced once at Miss Vaughan and saw her eyes fixed on him with a look of apprehension that even her superb aplomb could not entirely disguise.

"What are you going to do?" she murmured. "Surely you're not going to—"

Franklin had gathered up the coffee things and was on his way to the door when Brown spoke. The lawyer's voice was very smooth and casual, but it stopped the butler like a tap on the shoulder; it stopped all conversation as if it had been a shout. Yet all he said was:

"Just set that tray down a minute, close the door, and wait, Franklin. There's something I want to say."

Franklin turned a paralyzed face toward him and stood immobile a moment, tray in hand. Then he obeyed. He placed the coffee tray on a table, closed the door into the hall, and stood before it, looking at Brown as if for further instructions.

The lawyer looked slowly round the ring of strained, expectant faces.

"I'm sorry," he said apologetically, "to be so dramatic about it, but the situation seems to resolve itself inevitably into drama. I'll be as simple and direct as I can." He took a slip of paper from his pocket and turned it over and over between his fingers as he went on. "The general outline of these murders is, I think I may safely say, tolerably clear to me, but there are one or two points that I can't clear up without your help. Only one of you can have, any longer, any possible reason for withholding that help. And so I—"

"Do you mean to say," cried Justin suddenly, his face blanched, "that you know who committed these murders?"

"I do," Brown told them quietly. "I know who committed them, and I know how they were committed, and I can guess—why they were committed."

Into the long silence that followed no sound intruded, hardly a drawn breath. And then Isabel's terrified, tremulous whisper:

"Do you really mean that one of us—is a murderer?"

"I do," said Bolivar Brown.

"Which one of us?"

So softly were the words spoken that Brown could not have said who had uttered them. Perhaps they were not really said. Perhaps it was the impact of their unspoken question that reached him—the question that stared at him from their straining eyes.

The lawyer looked down at a slip of paper in his hands.

"There are a few questions I want to ask before I tell you who it is," he said slowly. "Questions that you can answer more impartially and objectively, perhaps, if you are unprejudiced by any knowledge of the truth. But I promise you that before you leave this room you shall know. I think I may say at once that I was wrong in my first assumption that one person committed all three murders. But I was wrong, so to speak, only in fact, not in principle. In each case it was the same guiding will that directed the crime. The fact that the person who killed Mr. Stuart and Mr. Grass did not actually jerk the noose that killed Mr. Huntington is, surely, neither here nor there, except to indicate that there was an accessory to that first, and more important, crime."

He paused, but no one sought to interrupt him. After a moment he went on:

"I think I can make my story clearer by beginning at the wrong end, which is to say with the murder of Jacob Grass. I know who killed Jacob Grass. Clever as the intelligence is that conceived and executed these crimes, there was one little clue overlooked—a very small thing, but it pointed with a strong and undeviating finger at the truth. I have investigated and found that, incredible, unthinkable as it seemed at first—"

He broke of.

"I beg your pardon. What you want are plain facts, not rhetoric. Grass, then, was killed by some person whose name I will tell you presently. He was killed because he knew too much about Stuart's death. Perhaps he had seen the murderer enter or leave Stuart's room. Perhaps, in his search through Stuart's papers, he had found the same letter that Stuart had found, that had revealed to Stuart the secret of Huntington's murder. I do not know. Frankly I doubt whether we shall ever know. Only one of you can answer that question and that one can hardly be expected to speak. Whichever it was, however, because of the lapse of time between the two deaths, I should say that Grass delivered an ultimatum, probably in the nature of a blackmailing proposition, giving time for consideration. His murder was the answer to that ultimatum.

"Going back now to Stuart. Stuart was present with me when Huntington's skeleton was discovered, and he as much as told me that he knew something that would indicate that Mr. Huntington's death was not—accidental. He rushed back to the house in a state of great excitement. When I followed him a few minutes later he was already closeted in his room with someone. I could hear him distinctly talking to someone as I passed his door going upstairs. Half an hour later, which is to say at seven o'clock, or a few minutes before, he was murdered. I will not go closely into the argument now. It is sufficient to say that we can prove the fact of his murder, and the time of it, almost to the minute.

"Again I should like to ask the person most concerned what paper it was that Stuart found in Huntington's old desk. It was almost certainly a letter—a letter written by Huntington to someone but never sent; a letter that was caught in the sliding writing shelf and never found until Stuart used the desk seven years later. Clearly it was a letter that had no special significance as long as the possibility existed that Huntington was still alive, but that acquired an extremely sinister meaning the moment it was certain that Huntington was—dead."

Again he broke off. His eyes, turning from one white face to another, came to rest at last on the painted face in the portrait that looked down upon them all.

"We come, at last," he said softly, "to Mr. Huntington. But for him, this extraordinary train of events would never have started. If he had not been the sort of person he was—if he had been in any respect a different man, if he had not established with you the special and definite relationships which he did establish, he might, it is true, have walked out through those long windows on that evening seven years ago, but he would have come back again."

A gasping, sobbing breath broke the silence. It was Adele. She dropped her face in her hands and sat very still.

"During the last few hours," said Brown softly, "it has become more and more apparent to me that I was neglecting the most important item in the situation—Stephen Huntington himself. I was misled by the fact that he has been dead seven years. I forgot for the moment that there are things about a man that live on—the things he has done —the loves and hates he leaves behind him. I had almost forgotten that seven years ago, at just about this time in the evening, he walked out of one of those windows, and that one of you saw him go with hatred, with jealousy, with fear, with, at any rate, the cold determination that he should not reenter this house—alive."

They cried out against him then—a confused murmur of protest that mingled and drowned out momentarily another sound, a sound he had been listening to for some minutes without being able to place it —the drone of a distant motor. Could it be the boat from Summerville bringing Jones's promised telegram? But he knew vaguely that it could not be. There was a different ring to it—almost a musical note. Now he knew suddenly what it was—the drone of a seaplane. He glanced at their excited faces. Had they noticed it? He thought not—yet.

"In the garden," Brown went on quickly. "Huntington met a man by the name of Micky Camp. One of you knew that he would meet him. They walked down the path and into the jungle together. Camp had a boat waiting at the end of the island, moored close in behind the summerhouse. When Huntington was dead, Camp concealed the body by hanging it high against a tree heavily shrouded in underbrush.

Then he went away in his boat, towing the rowboat from the summerhouse pier after him so as to give color to the theory that Huntington had left the island by that means."

The roar of the approaching engine was more distinct now, but still they seemed not to hear it. What was it? Had it any bearing on this affair? Brown remembered suddenly the telegram Myron had brought that afternoon. "Man answering description Camp . . . missing since yesterday . . . noon. . . ." With an effort he brought his attention back to the quiet room before him.

"You will say at once," he went on, "as Justin said this morning, 'But that theory lets us all out. If Camp did it—came back secretly, committed the murder, and went away again, secretly—that exonerates the rest of us.' Unfortunately this argument does not hold. For this reason: that two subsequent murders have been committed on this island to cover that first crime."

"Just a moment, Mr. Brown." It was Daniel Lane who spoke, his pleasant, quiet voice sounding reassuringly reasonable and normal. "I admit that the theoretical structure you have built to connect these crimes is logical and convincing *if* it is true. But there are so many gaps in it—so much guesswork. You have given us no positive proof that you are right."

"I will give you that proof now," said Bolivar Brown. He stood for a minute as though in deep thought. Actually, however, he was listening to that teasing, distant hum. Why did it come no nearer? Was it perhaps a mail plane or a passenger plane skirting the coast? Or was it — He looked across at Daniel Lane. "Your criticism would have been entirely just—yesterday, Mr. Lane. But since yesterday morning several interesting things have happened. Yesterday morning a telegram was sent from Summerville to a man in Mobile, Alabama, who answers to the description of Micky Camp. And last night the person who telegraphed to the man who killed Huntington went into Jacob Grass's room and strangled him with a thin cord."

"Are you certain that the man in Mobile was—Micky Camp?"

"Morally certain. I shall be actually certain—before long. My partner is at present in New York, investigating certain details of the conspiracy."

Lane nodded.

"Go on."

Brown glanced down at the slip of paper in his hand.

"Dr. Simpson," he said suddenly, "why did you lie when I asked you where you were at seven o'clock on the night Stuart was killed?"

Simpson sprang to his feet and stood reeling. Brown looked at him curiously, uncertain whether it was drink or terror that had unnerved the fellow.

"Look here!" cried Simpson. "What're you getting at? You gotta—gotta stop it, y'know."

The man was half drunk, clearly, and correspondingly reckless. His usual timidity was replaced by a defiant swagger.

"Answer my question," said the lawyer crisply.

"The hell I will. I want to know what you're getting at, that's what I want," cried Simpson belligerently. "Are you trying to tie this thing on me?"

"I'm asking you a question," repeated Brown mildly. "I want you to tell me where you were at seven o'clock on the night Stuart was murdered."

It seemed as if, for the moment, Simpson had actually stopped breathing. When he spoke again all the bluster had gone from him.

"I was in my room."

"Oh, no, you weren't," said Brown coolly. "While I was dressing I lost my collar button and went to your room to borrow one—at five minutes to seven. You weren't there. You'd dressed and gone."

"I—well, I must have gone down a few minutes earlier than I thought."

"But yesterday you swore solemnly that you hadn't gone down until some time after seven and that you'd noticed the time particularly."

"I must have got confused, I tell you," cried Simpson wretchedly. "What are you trying to do—railroad me? It's getting on my nerves. I can't stick it much longer, I tell you. I've got to get out of it—"

"Where were you?" reiterated Brown.

Simpson collapsed.

"I'd gone downstairs a little early."

"Why?"

"No particular reason. It was hot in my room—and I was ready—so I went down."

"Well," said Brown surprisingly, "why didn't you say so?"

"Because I couldn't prove it, and I was afraid." The little man looked at him dazedly. "Do you mean to say you believe me?"

Brown shrugged impatiently.

"Certainly I believe you. But I had to check such an obvious discrepancy."

Simpson sat down dazedly.

"Since I first realized the importance of Huntington's personality—of the bearing it might have on the case, I have made certain interesting discoveries," the lawyer went on. "I have discovered that Stephen Huntington was very attractive to women." Brown knew the instant Adele lifted her stricken face, but he dared not look at her, steeling his heart against the pain he must give her. "I have discovered that, after the death of the first Mrs. Huntington, he had a mistress—in Washington. I believe—"

He was interrupted by a curious sound—a mirthless, rattling laugh. He looked at Stella Drew. She sat forward on the sofa, her hands on her knees, staring down at the floor, rocking back and forth and laughing.

"She's drunk," said Simpson scornfully. "Dead drunk."

As though feeling their eyes on her, she lifted her own and looked dazedly about her. Abruptly as she had begun, she stopped laughing and cowered back in the corner of the sofa, shivering.

"I believe," Brown went on, "that this woman in Washington is an important figure in the case. I believe that I have discovered her connection with these crimes." He turned suddenly to Madeleine Huntington. "Mrs. Huntington, did you know of this liaison of your husband's?"

She was leaning forward, stark white, her eyes on Brown.

"No," she said.

"You are sure you did not suspect? It seems almost incredible that you should not have suspected."

"I did not. I knew that Stephen Huntington was in many ways vile and despicable, but I didn't know—that."

Adele got to her feet with a choked cry.

"I can't—I won't listen—"

Brown put out his hand and caught hers, steadyingly.

"Please!"

She said nothing further, but crouched down in her chair again, her face turned away against the back. The steady thrum of the distant plane sounded in the little silence that ensued, but it got no louder. It seemed to be circling the island, far out.

"Mrs. Huntington," went on Brown gravely, "there is something more—that is—" He broke off and went on after a minute: "When Mr. Grass was killed, the cord that strangled him was thin and hard. In order to get any purchase on it, the murderer must have held it twisted fairly and tightly round the hand. And such a cord, so held, would have cut into the flesh. This cord, clearly, had done so, for it was very faintly marked along two inches of its length with a brownish stain—a blood stain."

The silence in the room had deepened to a positive presence, brooding, suffocating. No breath, no faintest stir of movement, so that it was as noticeable as the waving of a flag when Mrs. Huntington turned her right hand in her lap so that it lay palm upward. Brown crossed the room to her and, taking up that hand, turned it so that the red mark on the back was clearly visible to them all.

"Mrs. Huntington," he said softly, "will you tell us where you got that mark on the back of your hand?"

Nobody spoke. Only a soft, shivering breath. Daniel Lane got to his feet, but even he, after all, said nothing. Madeleine looked up at Brown quietly. After a while, she said:

"Yes, I will tell you. I knocked it against the edge of my closet door last night when I was getting ready for bed."

"Madeleine!" It was Justin's anguished voice.

Mrs. Huntington turned to him coolly.

"Be still, my dear boy," she said gently, "I must handle this thing in my own way. That is the truth, Mr. Brown, although whether you will believe it or not—I can't say."

"Was any one present when this occurred?"

Mrs. Huntington hesitated.

"My maid was going back and forth. She may have been present. I'm not sure."

Here Daniel Lane broke into the scene.

"Don't say anything more, Madeleine," he said abruptly. And then he turned to Brown. "If, as I take to be the case, you are accusing Mrs. Huntington, I must vigorously resent any further attempt to question her until she has the protection of legal advice. Your charge, of course, is perfectly ridiculous—"

Mrs. Huntington interrupted him crisply, her voice sharp and perfectly composed.

"I am not in need of legal advice, Dan," she said. "Nor am I in need of any sort of protection." Her lips curved scornfully. "I didn't kill Stephen Huntington."

Brown met her scorn with a sudden, undisguised admiration. What a gorgeous creature she was, handsome as a goddess in her angry disdain.

"Why should I kill him?" she demanded. "I was not interested in his death. I could have divorced him, and I was, in point of fact, at the point of doing so. But suppose, for the moment, that this interesting fable of yours were true, Mr. Brown, and that I had discovered the existence of my rival in Washington? Would I, do you think, have hired a fellow like Camp to do it? Would I have put myself in the power of a man like that and lived in terror the rest of my life? Would I have subsequently committed two other murders to cover a man like Camp? In all reasonableness, Mr. Brown, do you think that tale hangs together?"

"In all reasonableness, Mrs. Huntington," said Brown with a crooked smile, "I do not. I believe your story for two reasons: because it is entirely plausible—and because your maid did see you hurt your hand in the manner you describe. Adele questioned her for me—before dinner." His hand, thrust into his pocket, turned the fragments of the note Adele had given him at table.

This left her gasping a little. Mrs. Drew, in the corner of her sofa, began to laugh again.

"Before we go on with this point," said Brown, "there is something else—the result of a little investigation Mr. Jura performed for me this afternoon while I was swimming with Miss Vaughan." He took from his pocket an envelope, and from the envelope, two folded bits of paper, neatly labeled on the back. "When the cord was taken from Jacob Grass's neck," he went on, "it was found that something else adhered to it besides the mark of blood—something so small as to be hardly visible, so small that it could only be positively identified under a microscope. That something," said the lawyer softly, "is folded in this piece of paper." He looked gravely at the circle of attentive, absorbed faces. "Small as it was," he told them, "I thought I identified it—that I knew where it had come from. I obtained a similar minute piece from the garment in question"—he held up the other paper packet—"and asked Mr. Jura to examine them for me. He did so, this afternoon, as I have said, and his examination confirmed my first impression."

"For God's sake," whispered Simpson hoarsely, "what was it? How long are you going to drag this out?"

Brown paid no attention to him.

"There was, of course, one way in which Grass could have been strangled—with that cord—and no mark left on the hand: if the murderer had worn a glove, or had drawn down a sleeve to cover the hand. Then, afterward, a pricked finger would have supplied a drop of blood to stain the cord and throw suspicion on anyone whose hand chanced to be marked—across the back."

"My God!" muttered Daniel Lane.

"Did anyone see you after you hurt your hand last night, Mrs. Huntington?" asked Brown.

Madeleine Huntington did not move her eyes from his face.

"Yes," she said, and she said nothing more.

Brown looked down at his little paper packets.

"In this case," he said slowly, "the sleeve was used. A sleeve of some rough silk material such as might be used for a—dressing gown —possibly a brocaded dressing gown. And in color it was—a light lavender."

One could have heard a pin drop. Brown was suddenly aware that, in the interval, the throb of the distant motor had ceased. He could not have said just when. But it did not matter now.

"Mrs. Drew," said Bolivar Brown, "a few minutes ago, when I spoke of Stephen Huntington's mistress, you began to laugh. Why did you laugh?"

Stella Drew looked up at him sullenly, almost slyly.

"I'm drunk," she announced, in a dull voice. "*He* says so." And she nodded her head sideways at Simpson.

"I don't say so," said Brown quietly. "I know you are not. I know that you heard quite clearly what I said. Didn't you?"

"Yes." Mrs. Drew began to smile, an indescribably malicious look in her dull eyes. "I know you all despise me—everybody despises me—but a lot of people are afraid of me, too. You see, I know so much. I've known a lot of people in Washington—people on the inside of things—and they've told me a lot of things. Things that make me laugh. It's useful to know things like that, and so—I remember them."

She put her hand to her head and held to the arm of the sofa as if for support.

"Just which of these things," asked Brown encouragingly, "were you laughing about—just now?"

Stella Drew began to laugh again, and Brown was conscious of a sudden cold chill up his spine.

"I laughed when you spoke of the woman in Washington," she gasped. "It was so funny, you see, because, if you'd only known it, when you said that, you could have put out your hand and touched her. She isn't in Washington. She's right there!"

And staggering to her feet Stella Drew held out a shaking hand and pointed.

Chapter XXIX

Lydia Vaughan did not move or blanch before that accusing finger. For a moment she stared back at Mrs. Drew with a smiling disdain. Then she took her tortoiseshell cigarette case from her bag, extracted a cigarette, and lit it composedly. At long last she looked at Brown.

"Do you really mean to tell me," she drawled, "that you place any credence in the statement of a woman of that sort—and in that condition? One would know ahead of time that she would put that interpretation upon the most innocent of friendships."

"The lavender silk thread that clung to the cord that killed Grass," said Brown "was rubbed from the sleeve of your lavender silk dressing gown, Miss Vaughan."

She shrugged contemptuously.

"So he says," with an inclination of her head toward Jura. "How long do you think it would take a good lawyer to demolish that evidence in court, Mr. Brown?"

"And you think," asked Brown, "that your relationship with Mr. Huntington could not be proved?"

"I know," she said coolly, "that it could not be proved. For the very good reason that it did not exist. There have been times," she added calmly, "when I have almost wished that it did."

Brown looked at her with an unwilling admiration. It seemed to him that he had never seen such magnificent poise, such self-command. He turned to Mrs. Huntington.

"You said just now that someone had seen you after you hurt your hand last night. Was it Miss Vaughan?"

"It was. She came to my room a few minutes later, to borrow a book."

"Was she wearing her dressing gown?"

"No. She had just come upstairs. She said she was on her way to bed."

Miss Vaughan's smiling eyes mocked her. They said as plainly as if she had spoken: "You would say that, of course."

"It seems to me," she said to Brown, "—correct me if I am wrong— it seems to me that the same argument with which you brushed aside the indictment against Madeleine Huntington might easily hold good for me. Supposing, for the moment, that what you flatteringly assume was true, and that I was the 'other woman.' Why, in heaven's name, if Stephen was really my lover, should I wish to kill him—and at the very moment when his wife had declared her intention of divorcing him?

And why, supposing I did want to kill him, should I use as a tool such a man, put myself in his power, and afterwards kill, and kill again to protect him? Do you think that is credible, Mr. Bolivar Brown?"

"No," said Brown. "I do not."

"Ah!" murmured Lydia. "So this little excursion is another of your—preambles?"

"What I mean to say," said Brown, "is that I do not think you killed Stuart and Grass for the purpose of protecting Camp. It is perfectly clear that you would have been entirely ruthless about Camp—that you would have let him down without compunction—if you had not yourself been pretty heavily involved in the murder of Huntington. I do not think you actually killed him with your own hands, because, strong as you are, and athletic as you are, I do not think you had the strength for that. Huntington was too big a man, and the business of hauling him up into a tree would have been too much for you. But I believe you were present. I believe you took an active part in the murder."

"Really! Aren't you claiming a good deal for your powers of deduction to think you can prove a thing like that, after seven years, and with no definite knowledge of the time at which Stephen met his death? Or have you an eyewitness, dear Mr. Brown?"

"I have no eyewitness," said the lawyer grimly, "but I know, almost to the minute, the time at which Stephen Huntington was killed."

She looked at him shrewdly now, under her drooping lids.

"Yes? And when was that?"

Brown did not answer her question directly. For a moment he stared thoughtfully at the floor, pushing at it with his foot. Then he glanced sharply up under his brows at her.

"Miss Vaughan, as I understand it, the last time you saw Stephen Huntington—according to your statement—was when he left you sitting on the terrace outside the window there and went off for a stroll down the island?"

Lydia nodded.

"I never saw him after that."

Brown turned to Daniel Lane.

"How long should you say it was between the time that Huntington left you playing bridge and the time when you went out to look for him?"

"I can't tell you by the clock," said Lane, "but I do know that we played a rubber, quite leisurely."

"An hour, perhaps?"

"An hour certainly. I should say considerably more."

The lawyer glanced at Solomon Jura.

"Can you, by any chance, tell us exactly when it was you left your room to walk on the beach?"

"No," said Jura after a moment's thought; "not by the clock. But it was certainly not early. After dinner I sat on the terrace for a few minutes talking to Miss Vaughan while the others were settling to their game, but as soon as Huntington came out on the terrace I went upstairs to work on my paper. I had certainly been at it for an hour and a half or two hours before I went out."

Now at last Brown turned to Lydia.

"How long was Huntington with you before he went off for his—stroll?"

"I really can't say," said Miss Vaughan coolly. "Some time, I should think. He walked up and down smoking for some time before he joined me, and then we chatted for awhile. I should say he had been gone no more than ten minutes before Mr. Lane came out."

Her statement received confirmation from an unexpected source. Justin said suddenly:

"I guess that's about right, Mr. Brown. When Adele and I followed Father down the island that night and saw him disappear into the jungle with Camp, we stood around for a little while and waited for him to come back. When he didn't come we turned back toward the house, and we met Mr. Lane coming down the path, looking for Father."

"And you saw Mr. Jura coming along the beach?"

"Yes, sir."

"How long had you stood waiting for your father?"

"Well, it's hard to say. Time drags so when you're waiting like that. But it couldn't have been more than twenty minutes."

"And during that time you saw no one?"

"No one at all until we saw Mr. Lane."

The lawyer looked across at Daniel Lane.

"How long did you remain with Miss Vaughan on the terrace before you started down the path to look for Huntington?"

"A few minutes. Long enough to smoke a cigarette."

Lydia Vaughan broke into the cross-examination.

"Do you really think it possible, Mr. Brown, that I could have passed those two children, followed Stephen into the jungle, and got back again in time to be on the terrace when Mr. Lane came out—and all without being seen?"

"I do not know what you could have done, Miss Vaughan," retorted the lawyer coldly. "I know that I am going to check every statement you have made about that night as closely as I can, under the circumstances. I do know that it was during those few minutes, while

Justin and Adele waited in the path, while Lane strolled down the island looking for Huntington, and while Mr. Jura was hurrying along the beach, that Huntington was killed. There's a little gap in there—a matter of a few moments—the few moments that it took Mr. Jura to walk down to the end of the island and halfway along the path that comes back through the jungle. I want to know where you were—then."

Miss Vaughan picked up her cigarette case, took out another cigarette, and lit it. She looked at Brown quizzically over the blazing match.

"I congratulate you, Mr. Brown. I couldn't have done better myself. You've built me a perfectly airtight alibi. During those few moments you mention I was on the terrace talking to Mr. Lane."

"And afterward?"

"Afterward I went up to my room and went to bed."

"Afterward," said Daniel Lane softly, "you did nothing of the kind. You went down into the garden and walked back and forth along the path."

She stared at him, with knitted browns.

"I don't think so," she said at last. "If I did, it was only for a few minutes, and then I went upstairs. It was so long ago, I can't be sure."

"Why can't you be sure?" asked Lane, still with that intent look. "You are so sure about everything else."

"I am sure!" she blazed at him. "I did not go into the garden, even for a minute. You have confused it with another night."

"I have not confused it with another night," said Lane quietly. "I have been over and over every detail of that evening a thousand times. I confess I cannot see what the fact of your going into the garden or not going into the garden can have to do with this, but I know that you did so. I happened to look out of the window a few minutes after I left you, and I saw you there, walking up and down."

She turned to Brown with a gesture of supreme irritation.

"You must believe it or not, as you like," she said. "It is not true. Mr. Lane is—confused."

Brown looked curiously from one set face to the other. At last he said to Lane:

"You're certain that you could not be mistaken? After all, it is seven years."

"Seven years or yesterday—I tell you it makes no difference. I've been over the thing a thousand times. I could tell you almost every step I took that night and almost every word I said or that was said to me. When I came back to the terrace Miss Vaughan was still there, it is true. I remember exactly what she was doing; I can see it as clearly as a painted picture when I close my eyes. She had put on some sort of dark, filmy wrap, and she had risen and was leaning against the balustrade. She said something about being tired and going to bed, but she did not move, and we fell into conversation. Why, it's preposterous to say I've forgotten. I remember even the little gestures we made. I felt for my cigarette case, opened it, meaning to offer her one, and found it was empty. She laughed and said that, at the risk of wounding my natural masculine vanity, she would supply the deficiency. She had a sort of fancy bag on her arm, and she put her hand into it and took out—"

He broke off. His eyes, up to this point intent upon that little scene which he was conjuring up before his mental vision, suddenly widened and fixed as though he had seen a ghost. And his naturally ruddy face grew suddenly blue about the lips. He grasped the table before him as if for support.

"My God!" he whispered. "She took out Huntington's cigarette case and offered me a cigarette!"

Brown's hands jerked suddenly as though from a galvanic shock.

"Huntington's cigarette case?" he repeated blankly. "Why should she do that? I mean—"

"She said," explained Lane in a dead, level voice, "she said she'd run out of cigarettes, and Huntington had left the case with her. He never smoked cigarettes himself, you know, but he always carried them."

Brown felt himself lost in a fog of ideas that crowded too thick for understanding.

"But—but," he stammered, "which cigarette case? I don't understand."

"The gold case," said Lane, suddenly regaining control of himself. "The case that was found on Huntington's skeleton."

Now, at long last, Brown looked at Lydia Vaughan. Gone at last was her superb aplomb. She was breathing heavily, through blue lips. Only her eyes returned his look defiantly.

"How do you explain this?" he asked.

And she answered:

"I have nothing to say."

"But why—why, in heaven's name, did you put that case on Huntington's body?" gasped Brown.

"Because she'd forgotten that little incident," said Lane. "It was a small thing—a very casual thing. She didn't think of it."

Brown paid no attention to him. He never took his eyes from Miss Vaughan's face.

"But you—you wanted it to be believed that Huntington had left the island!"

There was blank astonishment in his look.

Lane interrupted again, impatiently.

"What's that got to do with it, Brown? That's a detail, surely. She's guilty—guilty as hell."

For a moment the lawyer appeared not to have heard him. He walked close to Lydia Vaughan and stared down into her stony face. She stared back, cold as stone, and as motionless, but in the back of her eyes he saw despair.

"So that is the explanation, is it?" he asked softly. "Good Lord, what an ass I've been! That's it. That's it, of course!"

And then suddenly he seemed to be aware of what Lane had just said. He turned to him with a look still dazed with sudden understanding.

"Of course, she's guilty," he said softly. "That's clear enough. The thing I have been uncertain about is—what is she guilty of?"

Beyond the windows, beyond the island with its white beaches, far out across the dim sea, picked out by the light of the rising moon, a dim shape lay on the quiet water. It lay just within Brown's line of vision. His eyes rested on it with a look full of startled speculation.

Chapter XXX

Lydia Vaughan's gaze followed Brown's, and suddenly she grasped his arm and, leaning close to him, whispered scarcely above her breath: "Don't say anything! Don't say anything—yet. I'll talk. I'll tell you the whole story—from the beginning. I promise you!"

The lawyer considered the bargain for a minute.

"Very well," he agreed. He glanced once at Franklin. "Ask Myron to come to me in the library," he directed. "Now, Miss Vaughan—"

At first she seemed too near collapse to move. She sagged against the table beside her, leaning heavily for support. Then suddenly she straightened. Her head went back, and she stared under drooping lids at the pallid faces about her. No one spoke. No one moved. They sat with averted eyes while Lydia Vaughan walked out of the room.

Brown followed her into the library and closed the door.

"Well?" he said.

She seemed to have recovered completely her self-possession.

"What a contrast," she murmured, "to our first—er—consultation in this room!" Her tone mocked him. She sank into a deep chair facing the long windows and felt for her cigarette case.

Brown grinned at her crookedly.

"I'm so sorry to disturb you," he told her apologetically, "but I don't like drafts—on my back. They tend to give one a crick in the neck." He chuckled. "That's pretty bad, isn't it? But will you sit here? Do you mind?" And he indicated a chair turned with its back to the long open windows.

She gave him a venomous look, but she got up without protest and sat down in the chair he placed for her. He took his place at the opposite side of the long library table and rummaged in the drawers for paper. When he had supplied himself he leaned back and looked across at her. She was sitting very still, listening, he fancied, the rhinestones on the bodice of her dress unmoved by any breath. Behind her the blue radiance of moonlight etched sharply the writhing stems of the bougainvillea vine. Heavy and coiled it hung upon its trellis, black against the moon, sinuous as a serpent coiled among the leaves; strong as a coil of hempen rope; sinister as its legendary sister, the strangler fig.

He looked at the woman before him and wondered that he had never seen before the ruthlessness of her poise, the cruelty in her cold intelligence. He realized with a start that one of the reasons he had not, for so long, suspected her, was that he was looking for another sort of character—a hot and passionate nature. The parallel with the tropical vine had misled him. And yet it should not have misled him. There was nothing undisciplined about the cold progress of the vine that seized and destroyed all that stood in its way. And as for the murders—he should have known that only the coolest and most poised intelligence could have executed those crimes without betraying itself.

What motive power had moved this singular, detached creature? Passion for Huntington? He doubted it. It did not seem credible that the impulse for any crime of passion could have sprung from the cold depths of her nature. Acquisitiveness? It seemed more probable, but he could not, at the moment, see how it fitted in with the facts of the case. Self-protection? That accounted undoubtedly for Stuart and Grass, but— He shelved the problem with a shrug.

"It's no good listening," he said, smiling crookedly at her. "That chug-chug is the boat from Summerville bringing my partner's telegraphed report of the manipulations of American Shipyards, Inc. I shall send back by it—"

A knock on the door interrupted him, the door opened, and Myron entered.

"You want me, sir?"

"Yes," said Brown. "I was going to ask you to send a telegram over to Summerville, but if that's the telegraph operator's boat he can take it back with him instead." The lawyer scrawled a few lines on a slip of paper.

"I think," said Lydia coolly, "you'd better let me see that."

"I intend to," said Brown. He tossed the paper across to her and turned back to Myron. "It is to inform the police at Patona," he said dryly, "that we are holding Miss Vaughan until they can make it convenient to send for her. Incidentally, Myron, get Platt and a couple of the men to help stand watch and watch in the boathouse to-night. Miss Vaughan is not to be permitted to leave the island."

Myron glanced once, curiously, at Lydia Vaughan.

"Yes, sir."

She held out the slip of paper to him.

"I have no objection to your sending that," she said.

"Thank you so much," said Brown. "That is all, Myron."

When the boatman had gone and the door had closed behind him the lawyer leaned toward Lydia Vaughan.

"Now," he said, "I have kept my part of the bargain. Suppose you keep yours."

Miss Vaughan smoothed the green velvet over her knee with a thoughtful hand.

"I was born," she began, with a wry smile, "of poor but respectable parents."

"Need we," inquired Brown, "go back quite that far?" And he glanced at the long window behind her.

"We will go back as far as I like, Bolivar Brown, and begin where I like," she said, "or we will not begin at all."

"I beg your pardon," said Brown. "I forgot, for the moment, that it is, after all, your story."

"As a matter of fact," she went on more equably, "both the poorness and the respectability have a very pertinent connection with the rest of the tale. I began at a very early age to loathe the one—and to find the other very useful. You will bear me out that I have always—been very respectable."

"Quite," agreed Brown dryly.

"What I told you about my early acquaintance with Stephen Huntington is quite true," she went on, "except that I did not go into it deeply enough. I married Stephen Huntington when I was sixteen and he was twenty."

"You—*what?*"

"Don't you believe it?" she asked coolly. "It's true. You'll find records of it, if you look. We were married by a civil ceremony in Portland, Maine. And the very next day his father died—practically bankrupt. Stephen was terribly in love with me, and he made a good many romantic protestations about his willingness to 'start at the bottom and begin again' with me as his inspiration. But I had begun at the bottom, and I did not choose to go back there. I hadn't any real faith that Stephen would ever get anywhere. Even at that age, I was a fairly shrewd judge of character, and he was always a windbag."

Brown stared at her incredulously, unable to believe his ears.

"So I made him hold his tongue about our marriage. I told him he'd get on better unhandicapped by a wife. We were able to conceal some of the facts regarding old Mr. Huntington's insolvency. Stephen borrowed some money, and we got along for a few years. One of his father's friends took him into his business, and Stephen talked largely about recouping the family fortunes, but I never believed in it. It was something very different that I had in mind.

"I'll tell you frankly, I meant, at first, to have our marriage annulled. I could have done it, of course. We were both under age. But I didn't have the social position that could stand a scandal of that sort and emerge with any hope of making a satisfactory marriage, and while I was thinking about it—I thought of something else.

"Stupid and helpless as he was in some ways, Stephen had one positive gift: he had a way with women that was extraordinary. Kipling says something somewhere to the effect that it takes a very clever woman to understand a fool—and there are so few clever women. So I wangled an introduction for Stephen to Miriam Van Slyke, daughter of the steel man—you know. And when everything was set I persuaded him to marry her."

"I take it," said Brown dryly, "that you did not first go through the formality of annulling your own marriage?"

Lydia Vaughan smiled at him, and he thought her smile the coldest thing he had ever seen.

"My dear man, what good—under those circumstances—would a wealthy marriage for Stephen have done *me?*" She knocked the ash from her cigarette into a little tray on the table and went on composedly: "You needn't look so virtuously shocked, Mr. Brown. I never bothered Stephen. It was a very good thing for him—really— although I believe he suffered a twinge of conscience now and then because of it. Which is something I've never understood. This marriage of his was an excellent thing for us both. It provided very well for me, and it gave Stephen everything he wanted. And, as I say, I didn't bother him. If Miriam Huntington had lived, that, my dear Mr. Brown, would have been the end of the story."

She paused, and Brown stared at her, aghast. Phrases she had used ran jumbled through his head: "Stephen was in love with me . . . he made romantic protestations . . . beginning again with me as his inspiration . . . twinges of conscience . . ." Over and behind her story its meaning ran: This boy with his generous impulses—weak, perhaps, but not, in the beginning, ignoble—and the thing she had brought him to. Brown's eyes strayed to the vine behind her. The parallel of the strangler fig was more accurate than he had dreamed. Soul and body! But she began again, and he tore his mind from this fantastic speculation to listen.

"But Miriam Huntington died. Stephen had just gone into politics and, against my urgent advice, had put a huge sum into the political campaign that elected him Senator. His success went to his head, and he took the bit between his teeth. Before I knew what he was doing he had thrown away the fortune Miriam had left him in a wild speculation, he was head over ears in debt, he'd acquired a mistress who cost him more money than he could afford—"

She had again succeeded in astonishing her hearer.

"Do you mean to say," exclaimed Brown, "that there actually was a Mrs. Burt?"

She smiled.

"You would persist in believing that it was me, wouldn't you? But I tell you I never bothered Stephen. We lived quite separately—after he married Miriam. It was much safer. We met occasionally, but only as old friends. What I said about Mrs. Drew's accusation was perfectly true. It was pure malice on her part—mixed with a little gossip and misinformation. She's that kind of a fool."

"I see," said Brown softly. "I see."

"Well," Miss Vaughan went on, "Madeleine was the solution to that problem. Waldo Bingham had left her immensely wealthy, and if Stephen had only kept his head and behaved himself everything would have been all right. But he'd got into bad company in those years between. And he'd got himself involved with that shipbuilding crowd. He got into a terrible jam and, to save himself, embezzled a very large sum of money from his wife, trusting to his talent for making it right with her if she discovered it. Unfortunately," said Lydia Vaughan, "Madeleine, unlike Miriam Van Slyke, is a very intelligent woman. She saw through him."

"This, I take it," said Brown, "was at the time of the *Neptune* disaster?"

"Even before that Madeleine had become suspicious. Stephen realized that the situation was beyond him, and, as always at such times, he came running to me. I advised him to draw out of it as much as he could. As a matter of fact, before the *Neptune* went down Stephen had sold out his holdings in American Shipyards and had salted the money away under another name in a bank in another city. So that that, at least, was saved.

"But, of course, if it came out that he'd been dealing in that stock or had any interest in that company, he'd have been ruined in every other way, even if he hadn't been open to criminal charges. It was, undoubtedly, a serious situation. And then Madeleine threatened him with a divorce suit on grounds of speculation and misuse of funds.

"They were down here at the time, and, as you know, Stephen was on the committee to investigate the *Neptune* sinking, which made it all the more serious. If Madeleine had pressed her charges at that time, the whole thing would have come out, and Stephen would probably have spent a considerable portion of the balance of his life in prison."

She smiled wryly.

"He lost his head. As I told you, Stephen Huntington was a fool. He began to write to me a letter about the situation, thought better of it, and wired me to come down and use my influence, as an old friend, with Madeleine. And he forgot to destroy the letter he had begun. He wrote it on the leaf of his desk, and when he was suddenly seized with the idea of sending the telegram, he thrust the leaf in with the letter still lying on it. I think what happened was that someone came into the room while he was writing, and he acted automatically to conceal what he was doing. And then he went off to telegraph and forgot the letter.

It remained there for seven years, and then John Stuart found it."

The hand lying loose in her lap clenched suddenly.

"But I haven't come to that yet, have I? At any rate, I received the wire from Stephen, and I came. And I suppose that not four hours after my arrival here Micky Camp came.

"I knew that night at dinner that something was ghastly wrong. Stephen drank far more than he usually did and acted as though he hardly knew what he was doing. That's putting it on too thick, perhaps. I dare say that most of the people here noticed nothing wrong, but I knew him so well. I thought he'd had another quarrel with Madeleine, but on the terrace after dinner I learned—that it wasn't that. I refused to play bridge and went out there, to give him an opportunity to speak to me, and, as you know, he availed himself of it. He told me that that little rat, Camp, had ferreted out his connection with the Shipyards and threatened him with exposure. He had made an appointment for Camp to return that night and meet him down at the end of the island at ten o'clock. And he wanted me to tell him what to do."

Lydia Vaughan looked up searchingly into Brown's face.

"You can guess the rest. I told him to buy Camp off—to get rid of him at any price—and that we would then decide what to do next. He went off to meet Camp. When he did not come back I became anxious, and, at the first opportunity, I went to find out what had happened. I came upon Camp concealing Stephen's body in the tree."

"And of course," said Brown quietly, "you decided that it would be pleasanter all round if there was no fuss about it, and so you let him get away."

Lydia gave him a long, penetrating look.

"Yes," she said.

"I think it was you, Lydia Vaughan, who lost your head that night," said the lawyer softly, "when you gave that cigarette case to Camp to put in Mr. Huntington's pocket."

For a long moment there was no sound in the library. Outside they could hear the launch draw in to the boathouse, and the sudden cessation of the noise of the engine, but in the room was stillness, absolute and complete.

"One more question," said Brown, "before we go on to—Stuart. In what name did Huntington salt down the proceeds of his shares in the Shipyards concern?"

"In my name," said Miss Vaughan surprisingly.

"That accounts, then, for the pleasant way in which you have been able to live since his—disappearance?"

Miss Vaughan nodded as she took out another cigarette and lit it.

"Naturally."

Brown noted, with some astonishment, that the hand that held the match was absolutely steady.

"So we come to Stuart," he said. "Stuart, I take it, found this half-written letter from Huntington to you?"

"Yes. It was a ghastly effusion, in Stephen's worst vein. But at the worst it would have betrayed only an indiscreet connection between us —if Stephen's body had not been found. But it put ideas in John Stuart's head, and he had the temerity to threaten me. So I— You know," she broke off, "it was extraordinarily interesting to see how close you got to the way in which it all happened. If you'd been an eyewitness you could hardly have done better." Her eyes mocked him.

"And so you killed him."

She nodded unconcernedly.

"Of course," she hastened to add, "I had no concern in Stephen's death, but it would have been very awkward—if the whole story had leaked out. I had quite a time finding the letter. I had to go back afterward, that night, and look. But I did find it, and I destroyed it."

"You know," Brown told her, "I fancied that Grass must have found it."

"No." Her eyes narrowed suddenly. "Mr. Grass had the misfortune to look out of his door just as I was coming out of Stuart's room. And next day he had the temerity to threaten me. I had no intention," she said quietly, "of living out my life under a threat of that nature."

"And so you killed him, too, and threw the blame on Mrs. Huntington."

"Murders," said Miss Vaughan softly, "were getting to be such a habit of this house that I thought it was time a really good suspect was provided. Otherwise, embarrassing questions might be asked the rest of us."

"Why did you send that telegram to Camp? Wasn't that an unnecessary risk?"

"I did not think so," she told him. The door from the servants' quarters opened behind him. Lydia's glance shifted to it and back to Brown's face. "There's your telegram from Mr. Jones, I imagine," she said. "No, I thought it highly necessary, as a matter of fact. You had called your partner on long distance, obviously to ask him to make certain inquiries for you. I knew if he inquired in certain directions, he might stumble on very inconvenient evidence—and so I wired—er— Mr. Camp to be on his guard. A warning which he evidently heeded. He ran away—only just in time—suspecting, what is now true, that you had discovered everything, and that—"

Brown looked at her curiously, wondering at her sudden

garrulousness, and then a sudden tightening in her look, an involuntary stiffening, warned him, too late. Even as he turned, something strong and soft was slipped round his throat, jerking him against the back of the chair. He reached back, catching at the hands that held and twisted that cruel band, but the wrists he found were strong as steel, and their hold was beyond him to break. As consciousness faded he was clearly aware of only one thing, and that was that the portrait on the drawing-room wall had come down from its frame and was bending over him.

Chapter XXXI

When Brown recovered consciousness a few minutes later he found Myron standing beside him with a revolver in his hand, while Franklin and Platt completed the operation of tying into the big chair Lydia Vaughan had occupied a tall, broad-shouldered man with iron gray hair. Brown stared at the man, his scattered wits not yet able to cope with the situation.

In spite of the fact that he was, to some extent, prepared for what he saw, he could not quite believe his eyes. In spite of the newly etched lines of age and dissipation, the face before him was the face that looked down from the portrait on the drawing-room wall. To be sure, the man in the portrait was a man in the prime of life, at the summit of success and security and self-satisfaction; and the man in the big chair showed in his evasive look and lax mouth a disintegration that was both moral and physical, and seven years of the sort of life this man must have led since that portrait was painted would account for the difference. There could be no doubt that Brown was at last face to face with Stephen Huntington.

His head was spinning. He put his hand to his aching throat and sat up.

"What has—" And then he discovered that he could not speak, but only croak hoarsely.

Franklin looked up from his completed job.

"Just a minute, sir." With the effect of a magician picking a rabbit out of a hat the butler produced a flask from his pocket and held it to Brown's lips. The lawyer choked and strangled and felt better.

"What's happened?" he asked again.

Myron answered him, while Huntington stared sullenly at the floor.

"I saw him come ashore from the seaplane, sir," he told Brown. "So I followed to see what he'd do. He came up and hung around these windows for a bit, listening, apparently, to what was going on. I was going to nab him then, and then I thought I'd just watch and find out what he was up to, so I trailed him. He went round to the back of the house like a man that knew his way around pretty well, and went in the back door. I slipped up on him then, and was right behind when he opened that door there and jumped you. Which was a lucky thing, sir. I was no more than on time, I tell you. If ever a man meant murder, he did."

The man in the big chair lifted his head and glared at Myron. Then his eyes shifted to Brown and shifted away again.

"What I can't make out," said Myron curiously, "is how he found his way around so well. He came through the servants' quarters and found the way to the library as well as if he'd always lived in the place."

The man raised his uncertain eyes to Myron's chin, but no higher.

"Why shouldn't I know the place, young man? I built it!" His eyes circled the library, dwelling on it with a look that was almost wistful.

"Built it?" repeated Myron dazedly.

"Don't you know who I am?" Again that look lifted as high as the chin and dropped again. "Franklin knows, don't you, Franklin? And the gentleman yonder knows, I should judge. I am the man who's been dead seven years—the poor devil who's been rotting down there in the jungle." The lax mouth curved suddenly in a wry smile. "I'm a ghost—a wraith—a phantom. As can easily be proved. For I understand that some fool discovered my skeleton."

"Stephen Huntington!" gasped the boatman, with a pallid face.

"You certainly caught me napping," said Brown, grinning crookedly. "And I was expecting you, too. Had been expecting you ever since I heard the plane and saw that it had come to rest over yonder."

"Expecting me?" repeated Huntington. "Expecting me?"

"Well," said Brown deprecatingly, "I had a wire saying that a man answering to the description of Micky Camp had disappeared from Mobile on receiving a telegram from—shall we guess from Miss Vaughan?—yesterday. And to-night someone arrives in a seaplane, circling far out from the island so as to approach as inconspicuously as possible. And then Miss Vaughan made a bargain with me to delay my ultimate revelation, and talked at great length to give you an opportunity to come ashore. By the way, you do answer pretty well to a verbal description of Micky Camp—as he was seven years ago."

"But you said you—" Huntington looked curiously at Brown. "You mean that you expected Camp."

Again that crooked grin and the swift upward glance under the lowered brows.

"I do not," said Bolivar Brown softly. "I mean that I expected you. From the moment I knew that Lydia Vaughan had had in her possession your cigarette case *after* the murder in the jungle was committed, I knew that Camp was dead, not you; that you had escaped in the launch, not Camp. That it was you, and not Camp, who was living in Mobile under an alias, and that it was you, and not Camp, who disappeared yesterday after receiving that warning telegram."

"But—but—"

"It was so very clear," murmured Bolivar Brown softly, "that the only possible reason for putting that cigarette case on the body—after the murder—was to make identification absolutely certain, even after the passage of time. But if it had really been you there would have been no point in that. It would not have mattered. Therefore it couldn't be you.

"It was so easy," he went on, "to guess what happened. Camp threatened you with his knowledge of your connection with American Shipyards, and you knew that this disclosure would ruin you—ruin your career and perhaps send you to prison. He may have held you up for more than you could pay, or you may have lost your head and acted without reflection. Miss Vaughan said that you had been drinking heavily. Anyway, you killed him—and ran and told her about it.

"You found her in the garden, where she was waiting for you to return and tell her the result of your interview with Camp. She went back with you to the jungle, and between you you hid Camp's body and arranged your disappearance.

"No doubt," said Brown, "you would simply have taken the body out and thrown it in the sea, if you had dared, but you could not be sure that someone had not seen you with Camp and that you might not be accused of murdering him. And you were in a blue funk. So when Miss Vaughan suggested changing clothes with Camp, disfiguring the body, and—"

"Oh, my God!" whispered Huntington, his face pallid again, contorted with horror of thought of that distant scene.

"You put your clothes on Camp, then, and your cigarette case in his pocket. Under Miss Vaughan's direction you passed a rope over a high branch of a tree several feet back in the underbrush, and you hauled the body up out of sight in the heavy foliage. You hoped that the question of murder would never be raised at all and that it would simply be assumed that you had disappeared. For this reason you took the little rowboat by the summerhouse and towed it behind you when you went off in Mickey Camp's launch. You did not consider, until you were irrevocably committed to this course, the life to which you were condemning yourself."

"What else could I have done?" muttered Huntington.

"You could have thrown Camp's body into the sea and remained at World's End."

"How could I know that Camp's disappearance would never be noticed, that no one knew he had come to World's End or would wonder if he did not return? How could I know that no one had seen us together? And besides, if I had stayed, Madeleine would have divorced me, and all the scandal would have come out. I was dead, anyway, as far as my old life was concerned."

"So that was it," said Brown thoughtfully. "I thought it must be that." He looked long at the broken man before him. "Why did you come to-night?" he asked at last.

Huntington lifted to him a strange, foggy, almost wistful look.

"I meant," he said slowly, "to kill you and to take her away with me. I could not bear to think of the risks she was running. She was always too brave—too reckless of her own safety. She would never consider herself. I was going to take her away."

And Brown realized with a shock of amazement that he was talking of Lydia Vaughan. And suddenly a new and surprising emotion fastened itself upon Bolivar's heartstrings. He found himself feeling uncomfortably sorry for Stephen Huntington. To cover this, he looked round at Myron.

"Where have you put Miss Vaughan?" he asked.

Myron shifted from one foot to the other uncomfortably.

"I don't know where she is, sir. She slipped out the window while I was grappling with Mr. Huntington, and—"

The lawyer was on his feet.

"You don't mean to tell me you've let her get away?"

"She can't have got very far, sir. I've men watching the boathouse and the seaplane and patrolling the beach. She can't have left the island. I'll get some of the fellows together and we'll have a look, sir."

When he had gone Brown turned to Platt and Franklin.

"I'll want you to stand guard on Mr. Huntington," he said, "until we hear from Patona." He thrust the revolver from his pocket into Franklin's hand. "Take it," he said. "I've something to see to. I shan't be long."

He went out, crossed the wide, deserted hallway, and went quickly upstairs to the door of Lydia Vaughan's room. He knocked, but no answer came from the silent interior. He thrust the door open and entered.

The room was dark, only the squares of the windows showing against the moonlight that flooded across the floor in long parallelograms of light. And so still that the silence could be felt, oppressively, like a wet towel across the face, stifling. The far side of the room was in heavy shadow, but some reflected radiance of moonlight caught and shivered there in tiny, winking specks of light— a great many tiny specks that glinted and flicked like fireflies against the wall, halfway between wall and ceiling. Brown's hand felt automatically for the wall switch, but before he touched it, flooding the room with light, he knew what he would see. For he knew that those specks of light were reflected from the rhinestones on Lydia Vaughan's dinner gown.

She was hanging, as Stuart had hung, against her open closet door, and under her feet was the overturned chair which she had kicked out when the rope was adjusted.

An hour later Brown sat in the library over the long telegram from Jones which the Summerville operator had brought. It threw no new light on the situation, but confirmed, as far as Jones had been able to do in the brief time at his disposal, the story of the manipulations of the American Shipyards, Inc.

Brown folded the sheets together and leaned his head wearily on his hands. He was tired—tired to the bone, and sore, mentally and physically. He would not soon forget that last hour—the heartbreaking meeting of Adele and her father, the pity and horror of the whole situation. He was beginning to feel the bitter reaction of these days of strain. He sat quite still, tasting the bitterness of his triumph, seeing only Adele's face.

The opening of the hall door made him turn. It was Adele. She came in quietly and shut the door behind her. He did not move, but only looked up at her, his ungainly form stooping wearily in the chair, his head sunk between his shoulders, glancing up at her under his brows.

She came forward to the corner of the long table and leaned against it, looking down at him. Her face was white, and her eyes were swollen with weeping, but she paid no attention to this, nor did he.

"Don't suffer on my account," she said. "I've courage enough for this."

"I know you have," he told her gravely.

"I can stand anything," she rushed on. "I don't want you to suffer because of me. I think you are the best and kindest man I have ever known."

"I'm not either good or kind," said Bolivar Brown. "I love you—and this is a devil of a mess."

"Don't be silly!" cried the girl almost angrily. "You talk like—like anybody, not like you. What's the mess got to do—with us?"

Before he could answer the room was invaded by a flickering red glare that danced along the dim walls.

"What's that?" Adele turned a frightened face to the open windows. Below them, on the beach, a huge pyre had sprung suddenly into flame, crackling and roaring to the sky. Around it dim figures moved, swaying. Above the crackle of the flames a dull, rhythmic, moaning song came to them, a cadence indescribably primitive, weighted with the fears and superstitions and terrors of the dawn of a race, the black hours before history was. "What is it?" repeated the girl.

Bolivar Brown came and stood beside her, and his hand grasped and held hers as they looked down together at the weird scene.

"They are burning the strangler fig," he said. "They are exorcising the devil of World's End."

Adele said nothing. Together, in a strange understanding, they stood and watched while the flames roared red in the moonlight and died.

THE END

Coming Soon

The next exciting mystery
by John Stephen Strange:

Murder on the Ten-Yard Line

Chapter 1

Across the windless breadth of Yorke College campus, Jim Gaynor of the New York *Sphere* lounged dejectedly, his portable typewriter clamped under his arm. A harassed sports editor, faced by the necessity of covering the seasonal outburst of football games, had borrowed him for the day.

"But, my God!" protested Gaynor aggrievedly, "you fellows give me a pain in the neck. You knew weeks ago that forty-seven bunches of little boys were going to kick footballs today. System—that's what you lack. You know gosh-darned well that football isn't my line."

"It's your line today," the sports editor had retorted grimly. "I didn't know weeks ago that Harrigan was going to be in the hospital under the knife for appendicitis, and Harry Van Zandt away, and—"

"Under the knife," groaned Gaynor with a grin. "You spout headlines like a front page. How do I get to the damn place?"

Which is how it happened that one o'clock found him in the little town of Hillsboro, crossing the campus of Yorke College, in a very bad humor.

It was not a scene to inspire the casual observer with a grouch. It was perfect football weather: windless, cloudless, mild for the time of year, with that heady November chill and sparkle in the air that sets the blood racing. The sun lay warm on the mellow red brick of the old quadrangle buildings and the worn stone porch of the little Poultney chapel that had survived from the founding of the college in 1793. It shone caressingly on the faded lawns and bare trees, from which the last leaves dropped reluctantly.

The crisscross paths were crowded with hurrying, laughing people: girls of a unanimous prettiness seen nowhere but at football games; young men scrubbed and garnished; parents motored up for the game, under the escort of self-conscious sons. The stream flowed unbroken toward the bowl, breaking here and there along the crest into the froth of excited laughter.

Jim Gaynor surveyed them with impartial disgust. Morons! Cases of arrested development. "Football," he reflected, turning phrases in his mind, "had no adult connotations." It sounded well, but it had a familiar ring. It lacked that flash and sparkle of originality that delighted him. He blue-penciled it and strove to think of something more biting.

But suddenly his line of thought was interrupted, never to be resumed. He stopped in his tracks with a soft whistle of surprised attention, his eyes on an approaching figure.

"By George!" he muttered. "I might have remembered."

There were elements of the ridiculous in the appearance of the boy who came headlong across the leafy grass, but it is a curious fact that Gaynor's risibilities, naturally sensitive, were not tickled. He felt, rather, a curious quickening of the pulse that preluded one of the famous Gaynor hunches. For the boy was Bill Adams, and Gaynor had had dealings with him before.

He was clad in a magnificent new tweed suit that, in spite of its mature tailoring, persisted in looking like its wearer's first long pants— a fact of which young Bill was happily unaware. His shoes shone, and his sandy hair glistened. The very freckles on his nose radiated a sense of serene importance. The only blot upon his dignity was the ignominious freshman cap worn by coercion on the very back of his head. For at least three minutes on this beautiful afternoon the cap had dulled his enjoyment of the fact that for the first time he was taking a girl to a football game, and a very pretty girl, a whole year older than he was, who had been to the Senior Prom the year before.

He came charging across the grass, head down. Only the proper realization of his dignity restrained him from breaking into a run. He almost barged into Gaynor before he saw him, and then he drew up with a jerk.

"Oh, it's you," he said with surprise. His hand went involuntarily to the objectionable cap, with the impulse to thrust it into his pocket, but instead he set it at a more rakish angle and held out his hand with marked condescension.

"I might have known you'd be here," he said with a grin. "I'm always falling over you."

Gaynor's eyes twinkled.

"Where's the fire?" he asked innocently. "And do you wear that thing to keep your hair from falling out?"

Bill blushed. His freckles swam suddenly upon a crimson tide. The skullcap scorched the back of his head. But he ignored the thrust with a lofty disdain.

"It's considered good form for all first-year men to wear this kind of cap," he informed Gaynor kindly. "You wouldn't know about it, of course, because you've never had a college education." His eyes traveled to Gaynor's typewriter. "Goodness!" he murmured with lively surprise. "Are they letting you report the game? Are you sure you know the difference between a field goal and a touchdown?"

Gaynor made a swipe for him, but Bill was already far on his way, running now. He called back over his shoulder:

"There's a friend of yours here—come up for the game. Mr.

Ormsberry is here."

Gaynor came suddenly and violently awake.

"Ormsberry? Here? Where?" he shouted.

But Bill pretended not to hear. He trotted on, chuckling to himself. That would hold him, he reflected.

The Yorke-Winslow game, played that afternoon before a crowd that packed the bowl to overflowing, played to its strange finish under the pale flood of November sunlight, was destined never to be forgotten by any one of the thousands of spectators who witnessed it. It seemed to Gaynor afterwards that he had been aware from the beginning of some sinister shade across the sunlight, some undercurrent of impending disaster in the prevailing holiday mood of the scene. That he had been in some curious way prepared for the sudden appearance of Bill Adams's sandy thatch at the back of the press box; that he had expected his low whistle and beckoning finger. Gaynor always insisted that this was one of his infallible hunches. Perhaps it was. Perhaps it was Bill's casual mention of Ormsberry's name, the newspaperman's consciousness that the great detective was somewhere present in that crowd of peering faces. Coincidence, no doubt; the sort of coincidence that is the gift of the gods to good newspapermen. If Harrigan had not had appendicitis—if Van Zandt had not been away—if Bill Adams had not chosen Yorke College for the honor of bestowing on him his education—if the great Van Dusen Ormsberry, Bill's friend and idol, had not run up for the Yorke-Winslow game—well, Gaynor would have missed the greatest story of his life.

He scarcely knew at the time, and certainly did not remember afterwards, what story he sent in of the first half of that never-to-be-forgotten game. Routine football stuff: crowds, color, line-up, play by play; Collins around end for a fifteen-yard gain; Winslow five-yard penalty. He was dimly aware of the rattle of typewriters around him, the continuous murmur of the fellow up behind broadcasting the game in the radio booth; the click of motion-picture cameras, the monotonous voice of the man calling the names of the players: "Collins to McNeil." "Atchison for Winslow."

From the crowd below and beside him scraps of conversation drifted up.

"This is football, I'm telling you! That Winslow crowd is good, and I don't mean maybe."

"Yeah? Well, they haven't scored yet."

"Sure, that's what I mean. This is *football*. That fellow Diederich is a miracle man."

"Uh-huh. Yorke hasn't played football—not what you could call football—in five years."

"When I think of what the Yorke team was like last year—"

A yell from the stands at a sudden play drowned out the rest. Gaynor reflected. In the next lull he leaned toward Leanard, of the *Press*.

"Who's Diederich?" he asked.

Leanard looked reproachful.

"And they send fellows like you to cover a good game like this! Diederich, my innocent young friend, is the coach of the Yorke team. It is no hyperbole to call it a team now. But when Diederich took hold of it in the summer it was a mess of little schoolboys playing ball. Diederich is a man who makes miracles."

Gaynor looked pained.

"You little guys think you know everything," he complained. "I've been to football games before. What I mean is, *who* is Diederich? Where'd he come from?"

Leanard squinted thoughtfully down the field.

"That's a funny thing. I asked a few people that question once, and each one gave me a different answer. So I tried to find out, just for fun. And the only thing I found out was that nobody knew."

"I heard he was from a small college in the Middle West—Illinois or somewhere."

"Nebraska," Leanard corrected. "But he was only there two years. Try and find out where he was before that. Just try it once. You'll—"

From the stands below them some old grad, becoming genial under the influence of a friendly flask, rose and, removing his hat with a flourish, bestowed on the interested spectators a few remarks.

"This feller Diederich," he said in a loud, serious voice, "my friend Diederich is an act of God. He is a direct answer to prayer."

From the Winslow supporters around him a gust of laughter went up. Leanard chuckled.

"That's about as close as you'll get," he said. "And not bad at that! 'An answer to prayer.'"

Bill Adams was having a good time. He had wangled seats in the middle of the home side, down front, right beside the cheering section, and almost directly behind the substitutes' benches. He glowed with satisfaction, basking in the admiring glances cast at his companion. She was a very pretty girl indeed, dark and lively, with merry brown eyes.

"Do you understand football?" asked the boy. "Because, if there's anything you don't know about, I'd be glad to tell you," he added obligingly.

The pretty girl had been to football games before.

"Oh, do tell me!" she urged prettily. "Of course, I've seen lots of games, but I always think people who play football must know so much more about it than people who just watch it, don't you? You play football, don't you?"

Bill had a beautiful time.

He expanded. He pointed out celebrities.

"That feller there—the big one—with his headguard off is Collins. He's captain of the team, you know, and, oh, boy, but he can play football. And that's Dave McNeil, who made the touchdown against Conover."

Below them, on the substitutes' benches, a tall man in a gray sack suit, with dark hair smoothly slicked back, was watching the play intently. Bill pointed to him.

"That's Coach Diederich—see? That man in the gray suit. He knows more about football than anybody else in the world."

As he spoke, Diederich turned and beckoned to a man warming up behind him. The girl exclaimed.

"My! Isn't he good-looking! And he looks like a gentleman."

"Huh!" grunted Bill ungallantly. "I suppose you think a gentleman can't coach football."

"No, but—" She broke off, but her puzzled eyes lingered on Diederich. They returned to him again and again with a sort of fascination. Between first and second quarters she watched him rise, walk across to the end of the row of benches where a young man—a very red-headed young man—was sitting on a blanket. Diederich dropped down beside him.

"Who's that?" she asked. "The red-headed one, I mean."

"That's Dyke," Bill told her. "Rusty Dyke. He's manager of the team."

"Is he really?" cried the girl, properly impressed. "You know everybody, don't you?"

Farther down, at the turn of the bowl, a tall man with a fine, thin face lounged easily, his hands clasped on the crook of his stick. His companion was a beautiful woman whose face, familiar to Broadway audiences both on stage and screen, had caused much craning of necks and turning of heads during their leisurely progress to their seats. Her name eddied about her in a whisper.

"Magda Fleming! Gosh, that's Magda Fleming."

"Must be. Couldn't be anyone else. Who's the fellow with her?"

"An actor? Looks like an actor to me."

"Never saw him before."

The tall man leaned to Miss Fleming with a faint smile.

"Your audience has found you out," he murmured.

She raised her beautiful sophisticated eyes to his face with a look well calculated to make any man a little dizzy.

"It is too bad," she said softly, with that faint, mocking smile that had been her fortune, "it is too bad they must miss an even greater thrill. Let us suppose that I could rise and say to them, 'My friends, this is the great Mr. Ormsberry.'"

Ormsberry's quizzical look matched her own.

"I am not going to bring you to any more football games," he stated. "You are a distracting influence. Don't you know that you must keep your eye on the ball?"

"That is why I never play golf," she murmured. "I have better use for my eyes. Listen!"

Time had been called for some minor injury. The water boys were running across the field, and a dark-haired man carrying a little bag. The doctor, evidently. The cheering sections had broken into song. The Yorke rooters were petitioning their team to "Fight, fight, fight!" but all that came to them was a hoarse, spasmodic murmur.

"Odd, isn't it?" she said softly. "They are almost beside us, and yet we can hardly hear them."

"It is not in the least odd," contradicted Ormsberry politely. "It is a matter of acoustics."

She looked up at him again.

"It is nevertheless odd," she insisted. "To call it a matter of acoustics does not remove the strangeness. It only gives it a name."

Ormsberry looked down for a moment into her eyes. Then he sighed briefly.

"Certainly," he said, "my decision was well taken. I will never bring you to another football game. It's sheer waste. You are—"

But he got no further, for the Winslow supporters across the field broke into song, and they could not hear themselves think.

The first half was drawing to a close with three more minutes to play and no score when Rusty Dyke, manager of the Yorke team, leaned toward Diederich and whispered in his ear.

"Coach, when you going to put Scrubby in?"

Diederich's cool, expressionless glance swept the field for a moment blankly. He was a handsome man, with dark eyes, a finely cut nose, and a narrow, close mouth. His clothes were good, and unobtrusive, and well cut. His hands were long and delicate. Only his wide, powerful shoulders indicated the athlete.

Dyke thought he had not heard.

"When you going to put Scrubby—"

Diederich turned and beckoned to a youngster who was running up and down the track behind him.

"I'm going to put him in now."

The boy trotted up. He had a round, good-humored face and surprised-looking hair, cut to resemble a shoe brush. He bent over Diederich, and for a moment they spoke earnestly together. Dyke looked on anxiously. There was so little time. He could not hear what was said, but once it seemed to him that Scrubby protested something the coach had said. He could not be sure. A moment later Akins nodded and raced off across the field, his short, strong legs flying. Dyke hugged his knees and waited.

To the longest day he lived he never forgot the few minutes that followed. The crisp sound of Collins's voice calling signals—Diederich preferred signals. He would not let them use the huddle. The numbers falling clear and sharp on the crisp air: "Forty-seven, thirty-nine, seventeen, twenty-five, fifty-three."

Dyke waited, scarcely breathing. It would be the lateral pass, or that tricky wide end run, Scrubby with the ball tucked under his arm, his short legs pumping like piston rods, over the line for a touchdown. And then suddenly Dyke was up on his knees, rigid with horrified astonishment, for the line surged forward, broke on the stone wall of Winslow's defense, and Scrubby, carried on the crest of the wave, was beaten back and held for no gain.

"But—but—" stammered Dyke in a dazed voice to no one in particular—"but Whitlock had come in!" He meant that Whitlock, star Winslow center, who had been playing a roving game during the last few minutes of defense, had come back into the line, stopping the center hole with his hundred and eighty pounds of brawn and muscle. Dyke blinked his eyes rapidly, as though to clear his vision, and looked again. He had not been seeing things—or, rather, the things he had been seeing were really there and not the figment of a nightmare imagination. Had the whole team lost their minds? What had happened to the carefully planned strategy that had been laid down before they went on the field?

Again the signals, crisp and clean cut. Dyke waited, hoping against hope for a return of sanity. Surely, surely, the lateral pass. He waited on his knees in a not inappropriate attitude of prayer.

This time the Yorke line opened out, winglike, giving Scrubby room. Dyke groaned, for the little halfback bucked the line again, squirmed his way for a short gain, and went down before the giant Winslow center. Dyke watched dolefully. It couldn't be true. Third down and nine yards to go.

The ball was on Winslow's eleven-yard line now—and the half was nearly over. Surely Collins must do something about it. It was sheer madness, bucking the line now—now, within easy scoring distance, and no time to lose. Surely he'd open up and let Scrubby do his stuff. The kid wasn't built for line play. He was too light and too small. Speed was his meat—speed, and an open field, and the goal line winging nearer and nearer to his flying feet. Why put him in at all for this sort of racket —save him, if you weren't going to use him—

He held his breath. Again the line bucked and broke. Scrubby, wiggling like an eel, digging in his toes, grabbed out another yard. That was all. From somewhere, shivering down his spine with a sickening shrillness, Dyke was aware of a whistle blowing. Still on his knees, he became conscious of the crowd, the Yorke bleachers behind him, a howling mob, shrieking and gesticulating; the Winslow stands opposite a pandemonium of excitement. And then suddenly the Yorke bleachers had grown silent, and Dyke realized with a sickening sense of surprise that the half had ended, and the touchdown was still unmade.

He turned frantically to Diederich.

"He didn't have time. My God, coach, if you'd only put the boy in sooner!"

Diederich did not answer. He was lying on his side, his knees drawn up under his chin, as though he had fallen sidewise where he sat. Dyke shook his shoulder. He couldn't have fainted. He wasn't that sort. Sick, maybe.

Dyke leaned over him and spoke again.

For a moment the boy was as still as the man. Then Dyke reached out a long arm, picked up a sweater that was lying near by and wrapped it round Diederich's shoulders. Then he looked up. Nobody was paying any attention. They were watching the teams trotting off the field. Dyke got to his feet and grabbed the arm of a substitute.

"Here, Dooley. Lend a hand. Coach is sick. Appendicitis, I guess—or something. He's fainted. Let's get him off without a fuss."

They drew Diederich's arms across their shoulders, holding his limp body between them, and hurried out through the tunnel that led to the dressing rooms.

Chapter 2

Diederich did not appear at the beginning of the second half. Ransom, the assistant coach, took his place. Something was wrong. Some subtle influence was at work on the morale of the Yorke team. They held ground manfully, stubbornly, but they could not score. Even Scrubby Akins, running, tackling, fighting like a madman, was powerless to punch through his plays. Winslow made one touchdown in the third quarter and another in the fourth, kicking both goals.

In the middle of the third period Gaynor heard a whistle behind him and, turning, spotted Bill Adams at the entrance to the press box. The boy's freckles stood out startlingly against his white face, and his eyes were black with excitement. A premonitory tingle found its way up Gaynor's spine. He had noticed Diederich's absence, and, as has been said, he had had dealings with Bill before. He slipped out of the box and followed Bill into the mouth of the tunnel.

"What's up, skipper?"

"Plenty!" The youngster's breath came short and panting. He caught his friend's arm and, leaning forward, spoke in his ear. "Diederich's been shot. They smuggled him into the dressing room and gave out that he'd been taken with appendicitis—on account of the game, you know. Appendicitis, my eye! I saw Diederich lying on his side and saw how limp he was when they carried him out. So I came out, too. And they said it was appendicitis. But I had a hunch it wasn't. So I asked Rusty Dyke. And he almost killed me. So then I knew he was lying. So when Doc Saunders came I hung around the window outside, and I heard him say Diederich had been shot."

"Has he regained consciousness?"

"No."

"My God!" murmured Gaynor piously. For a brief instant he reflected. Then he burst into rapid action. "Anybody know about this?"

"Nobody but Doc Saunders, Rusty Dyke, and Dooley, who helped carry Diederich into the dressing room. They're keeping it dark till after the game."

"Haven't they notified the police?"

"They were arguing about it when I left. Rusty wanted to stall awhile, but the doc said he wouldn't take the responsibility. I guess they'll notify them all right and try to get them to keep it quiet till the game's over."

"Know where Ormsberry is?"

"No, but I'll find him."

"Then let's go. I'll meet you in the dressing rooms in twenty minutes." Yet before he started his hand fell for a moment on Bill's shoulder. "Oh, boy, what a story! I'll never forget this, kid, as long as I live."

Bill grinned crookedly over his shoulder as he turned away.

"What about the game?"

"Damn the game!" said the neophyte sports writer heartily.

Not long afterwards a bored-looking messenger boy strolled up to Gaynor, who was talking to Dooley at the door of the dressing rooms.

"You Mr. Gaynor? Somebody said you was."

"Yeah," grunted Gaynor. "What do you want?"

The boy held out a yellow envelope, and Gaynor tore it open impatiently. It was from Grimes, the editor, and it wasted no time in polite circumlocutions.

WHAT THE BLANK BLANK! HAVE THEY FORGOTTEN TO PLAY THE SECOND HALF OR HAVE YOU GONE OUT TO TEA?

Gaynor snorted. He turned the missive over and scrawled across the back:

YALE BEAT HARVARD. WHAT THE BLANK BLANK, MY DEAR EDITOR. HOLD FULL FRONT PAGE COLUMN. I WILL TELL YOU ALL IN TEN MINUTES.

He signed it and thrust it into the boy's hand. And then a sudden idea occurred to him. He took out a five-dollar bill and looked at it thoughtfully.

"Want to earn five bucks?" he asked.

A faint quiver of interest crossed the bored vacuum of the boy's face.

"Bet your life."

"Then go up to that drugstore at the corner—you know; just opposite the main gate."

"Sure. I know. Smith's."

"Get hold of the telephone in the booth there, call this number—" he scribbled a number on the bottom of the blank—"ask for Mr. Grimes and tell him I said to put Harrison on the wire. If Harrison isn't there, tell him you want the best man he's got. Then you sit on the telephone till I get there, understand? Don't you let anybody get it. Swallow it, if you have to. Get me?"

The boy grinned slowly from ear to ear.

"Gee!" he murmured happily. "I get you all right. Leave it to me, mister."

Bill's method of procedure was simplicity itself. There were six entrances to the bowl. He went to the back of the cheering section, spotted six skullcaps, and removed their wearers to the runway outside. Here he made known his desires, assigning each boy to one of the entrances.

"Ask round till you find someone that's seen Magda Fleming," he instructed them importantly. "Then tell the guy that's with her—a tall, thin man—that I say he is to come right away to the dressing rooms and ask for me. You can show him where he—"

"But, I say, Bill," gasped one of them incredulously.

"Don't stop to argue," retorted Bill loftily. "He'll come all right. He's a great friend of mine. His name's Ormsberry—Van Dusen Ormsberry."

They considered that Bill was spoofing them, but it had all the earmarks of a lark, and they scattered joyfully, scuttling like leaves before the wind.

A few minutes later, in the lull in the game, Ormsberry was conscious of hearing his name spoken. He looked round into the face of a boy standing in the aisle beside him. It was a somewhat embarrassed young face, with bright black eyes. The detective smiled involuntarily.

"I say, sir," began the boy awkwardly, "Bill Adams told me to find you. I don't suppose you even know him—" He broke off hopefully.

Ormsberry's smile broadened.

"I know him all right," he said. "How in the world did you find me?"

The black eyes swung eagerly to Magda Fleming's face, lingered a moment, and were regretfully withdrawn.

"That was easy, sir."

Ormsberry laughed.

"That sounds like Bill's idea. What does he want?"

"He wanted you to come right away to the team's dressing rooms. I'm to show you the way. He says it's important."

For a moment the detective did not speak. His lips still smiled, but the laughter had gone out of his eyes. Then he turned regretfully to Miss Fleming.

"It's the Admiral, you know—Bill Adams. I don't like to leave you, but—the boy isn't given to exaggeration. Perhaps I'd better just see what's wrong. I'll be back in ten minutes."

But he did not come back at all. Instead he sent an apologetic note by the black-eyed boy—a note which caused the pretty lady some moments of rueful regret.

The team's dressing rooms were in a long, low building just outside the bowl and connected with it by means of the central entrance tunnel through which the team made its way onto the field. This building was divided into three big rooms, whitewashed and garish. In one of these rooms were ranged round the wall the lockers of the team; in the next, the substitutes' lockers. The third room was seldom used. It was at the extreme end of the building, away from the field, and was the smallest of the three. Between it and the other rooms were rows of showers, and a very small office for the use of the coach.

It was into this third room that Diederich had been carried. There was a long table in the middle, such as is used for rubbing down the players, and on this they had laid Diederich, propping his head with sweaters rolled together to make a pillow, and covering him with a blanket. His heavy breathing was the only thing heard in the high, bare room, in which the blue shadows of the early autumn twilight were already gathering.

Dr. Saunders stood beside him, one finger on the wavering pulse. He was a well set-up man of middle age, with thick, dark hair and a sunburned, square face. He was the official college physician, and a very good doctor, capable and conscientious.

On the other side of the table stood Roscoe Sutherland, dean of the college. He was a stout man, past middle age, with gray hair, a florid, clean-shaven face, and shrewd, intelligent eyes. He glanced uneasily from Diederich's face to Dr. Saunders and back again, and sucked at his cheeks nervously with a little anxious, clucking sound. He had been summoned from his study a few moments before and had himself notified the police of what had happened. Now he appealed to Saunders anxiously.

"Do you think there's a chance?

Saunders shook his head and laid down the limp hand.

"No," he said. "It's a matter of minutes. I've done all that can be done. Perhaps, however, you'd like to call Larkin."

"No need of that," said Sutherland decidedly. "Will he regain consciousness, do you think?"

"Can't say. He might—or he may go out suddenly, any minute."

"You'll stay with him, of course?"

Saunders nodded.

"Of course."

At this moment Rusty Dyke opened the door and looked in.

"Sergeant Robbins is here with two policemen," he said to Sutherland. "He wants to speak to you."

Sutherland looked across at Saunders.

"I'll be right outside if you need me," he said. "Dyke, you stay within call."

Dyke looked anxiously at the figure on the table.

"Will he get well?" he asked the doctor. "Is there any chance?"

"I'm afraid there's no chance."

The young man turned his face away suddenly.

"Gosh," he whispered. "That's tough."

When the dean had gone Dyke looked back at Saunders.

"I'll be right outside the door," he said. "You've only to raise your voice."

In the coach's little office Sutherland found Sergeant Robbins talking to a tall, thin man in tweeds who carried a walking stick. The stranger looked up as the dean entered and addressed him courteously.

"My name is Ormsberry," he said. "I'm from headquarters. I happened to be up here watching the game, and one of your students whom I know, a freshman named Adams, got word to me what had happened. Is it—murder?"

Sutherland looked at the card Ormsberry gave him and nodded.

"It will be—in a few minutes," he said grimly. "Diederich's at the point of death."

"Has he made any statement?"

"He hasn't regained consciousness. Dr. Saunders says he may not. Do you want to see him?"

"If you please. And I'd like to see the men who brought him out."

The dean looked out into the passageway. Finding Bill Adams hovering round the door, he sent him in search of Dooley. Then he led the way to the room in which Diederich lay. At the door he laid his hand on Rusty Dyke's arm and looked at Ormsberry.

"As far as I know," he said, "this is the only man who actually witnessed the shooting."

The detective looked at the young man's white, stricken face and nodded kindly.

"I'll want to talk to you in a few minutes," he said, "if you'll be kind enough to wait." Then he followed Sutherland into the room, and the door closed behind them.

Rusty Dyke, leaning against the wall, was gripped by a paralyzing sense of unreality. This couldn't have happened. Why, only a little while ago Diederich had stood in that room yonder, giving his final instructions to the team. He had been vigorous and full of life, full of a superabundant energy which he had instilled into the players, so that their eyes had kindled as though he had blown the flames of his own enthusiasm into them. And now—

His lips trembled as the picture rose before his mind of that pallid face in the next room, the labored, uncertain breathing, destined so soon to cease. For he loved the coach. He pressed his handkerchief to his lips to steady them and thrust his clenched fists into his pockets.

Dimly he was aware of a whistle blowing, a sudden crescendo of noise that fell apart in the low murmur of a dispersing crowd. He heard doors opening and banging and the scattered sound of many feet approaching. Looking along the corridor into the dressing rooms he saw the team come in. The game was over. He stared at them uncomprehendingly.

Collins saw him and came down the corridor.

"What's up?" he said. "What's the matter with the coach?"

Dyke looked at him blankly.

"He's been shot," he heard himself saying. "He's dying."

"No!"

The word passed from one to the other, and they came crowding into the passageway.

"Dying! My God!"

"Who shot him! Tell us who shot him!"

"I don't know," said Dyke with stiff lips. "He was shot on the field. From the stands, I suppose."

"Where is he?" asked Collins.

Dyke jerked his head toward the closed door.

"Can I see him?"

"I don't think they'll let you go in. The doctor—"

The door opened, suddenly flooding the dim corridor with a garish light that fell strangely on their white, bewildered faces. Ormsberry stood in the doorway. Seeing them, he answered their unspoken question.

"Mr. Diederich," he told them, "is dead. He died just now, without regaining consciousness." He turned to Rusty Dyke. "Will you come into the office for a moment?" he said. "There are a few questions I want to ask you."

Dyke followed without a word. The door closed behind them. A moment later it opened again. One of the policemen came out and took up his stand at the door of the room where Diederich lay.

Twenty minutes later Ormsberry was conferring with Dr. Saunders and Dean Sutherland in the big white room at the end of the corridor. The single uncovered bulb in the ceiling flooded the room with garish light, shone down on the figure on the table. It was still now, and the blanket had been drawn up over the face.

They were waiting for the ambulance.

"There'll have to be an autopsy," Ormsberry was explaining to the dean. "After that the funeral can be arranged whenever you think best."

"I know nothing of his relatives," said the dean uneasily, rubbing his hand through his gray hair. "However, someone's sure to know."

For a moment Ormsberry stared down at the covered figure. Then he glanced at Saunders.

"You've no doubt that he was shot from the front?" he asked.

"None whatever," said Saunders. "There can be no doubt. The bullet is lodged in the wound."

Ormsberry nodded and turned to the little collection of objects that lay on a chair near by. They had been taken from Diederich's pockets, and he turned them over curiously, studying them with care. There was a plain gold watch with neither fob nor chain; a fountain pen; a wallet containing a rather surprising amount of money—something over six hundred dollars in bills. Ormsberry laid it down with a shudder. His hands were wet. He wiped them hastily on his handkerchief and thrust the handkerchief out of sight in his pocket. There were two small bills from local tradesmen, an unstamped note from the registrar's office on some college matter, two clean, unmonogrammed handkerchiefs, a handful of small change—and that was all. Nothing much to go on except the possible suggestion contained in that plump wallet.

But Ormsberry got no further in his speculations. He was interrupted by the voice of the policeman on guard raised outside the door.

"I'm sorry, sir, but you can't go in. I was told not to let anyone—"

And then another voice—an older voice, vibrant with some unexplained emotion.

"But I've got to see him. Is it true he's been hurt?"

"Why—er—yes, sir, he's been hurt. Now you can't go in—"

But the door swung open, over and round his protest, so to speak, and a man stood on the threshold. He was rather small, with slender hands and slight shoulders upon which was supported a massive head. The face was beautifully molded, nose and chin finely cut, and an exquisitely sensitive mouth. The eyes were full of intelligence, and the brow stamped with a benevolent dignity that could not fail to inspire even a stranger with respect. He was almost bald, although he could not have been more than forty years of age. He wore a rather shabby brown overcoat and a brown knitted scarf that dangled loosely round his neck. He blinked a little, coming suddenly into the brilliantly lighted room, and addressed Ormsberry, as the first one upon whom his eyes rested.

"I understand," he said in a mild, cultivated voice, "that Mr. Diederich has been hurt."

"Yes," said Ormsberry gently. "He has been seriously hurt."

"I hope," continued the unknown, "that I may be allowed to see him for a moment? It is vitally important. You are the doctor, I suppose?"

Ormsberry stood in the doorway, between the stranger and the figure on the table.

"I'm sorry," he said. "You'll forgive me if I ask your name."

"Of course, of course. I am Professor Julian Hallett. There is a question I must ask Mr. Diederich. I give you my word I shall only be a minute, but I must see him."

Ormsberry noticed how white the stiff lips were and with what difficulty they formed the words.

"I'm sorry," he said. "Mr. Diederich cannot answer any questions."

"But I shall only be a moment," pleaded Professor Hallett.

The detective saw the blank despair in the eyes, heard the sudden crack in the timbre of the quiet voice.

"I am truly sorry to tell you," he said kindly, "that Mr. Diederich is dead."

For a minute Hallett did not move or breathe. His eyes remained fixed on Ormsberry's face. Then he fumbled his hat suddenly and bit his dry lips two or three times.

"I see," he said quietly in a voice that jumped uncontrollably up and down the scale. "I see. I am too late."

He turned away, knocking against the frame of the door like a man who does not see where he is going.

"My God, Hallett!" cried the dean suddenly. "Watch where you're going. Are you sick? Do you want someone to go with you?"

Hallett turned back. He looked past Ormsberry, who had stepped aside, and saw for the first time the others in the room and the covered thing on the table.

"I'm sorry, Sutherland," he said quietly. "I didn't see you." His grave glance traveled from one to the other, lingered for a moment on the table, and was quickly withdrawn. "I'm extremely sorry to hear about Mr. Diederich. There was something— However, no doubt he would not have answered." He looked up at Ormsberry. "I'm sorry to have disturbed you," he said. "Goodnight." And he turned and walked away.

Dyke and Bill Adams, waiting in the corridor, held open the door for him and watched the bent figure move slowly away across the campus. Then Dyke's glance swept the bowl, already empty. The last of the chattering, laughing crowd were already moving away up the street.

"The crowd's about gone," he said.

His words, simple enough, produced an electrifying effect.

"Great guns!" cried Bill suddenly, and grasped his hair like a man distraught. "I've forgotten my girl!" And he dashed out with the violence of one pursued by the furies. His steps echoed in the deserted entrance tunnel, dark with twilight; clattered out into the surprising silence of the bowl. What he expected to find he could not have said: a pathetic little figure waiting patiently in the cold dusk, shedding tears, perhaps; an irate goddess with lightning in her glance—

He found nothing. The bowl when he entered it was empty. Not a soul in the vast, empty tiers of seats; not a sound but the clattering of his own feet. The great stadium, so lately full of sunlight and shouting, was filled to the brim with silence and shadow, and upon it the cold foreboding twilight of the autumn evening settled swiftly down.